# ALSO BY RANDALL SILVIS

# WHEN ALL LIGHT FAILS

## A Ryan DeMarco Mystery

## RANDALL SILVIS

Poisoned Pen
PRESS

Published by Poisoned Pen Press, an imprint of Sourcebooks
P.O. Box 4410, Naperville, Illinois 60567-4410
(630) 961-3900
sourcebooks.com

Library of Congress Cataloging-in-Publication Data

Names: Silvis, Randall, author.
Title: When all light fails / Randall Silvis.
Description: Naperville, Illinois : Poisoned Pen Press, [2021] | Series:
    Ryan DeMarco mystery ; 5
Identifiers: LCCN 2020058165 (print) | LCCN 2020058166 (ebook) |
    (trade paperback) | (epub)
Subjects: GSAFD: Mystery fiction.
Classification: LCC PS3569.I47235 W48 2021  (print) | LCC PS3569.I47235
    (ebook) | DDC 813/.54--dc23
LC record available at https://lccn.loc.gov/2020058165
LC ebook record available at https://lccn.loc.gov/2020058166

Printed and bound in Canada.
MBP 10 9 8 7 6 5 4 3 2 1

*For my sons, Bret & Nathan,*
*heart of my soul,*
*soul of my heart*

THE QUOTES THAT INTRODUCE EACH OF THE SIX
SECTIONS OF THE NOVEL ARE ALL FROM *THE TIBETAN
BOOK OF LIVING AND DYING* BY SOGYAL RINPOCHE.

# PROLOGUE

APPEARANCES CAN BE DECEIVING

D eMarco was feeling very good about the future when he unlocked the back door that morning and came into the kitchen. But then he saw the white envelope lying in the center of the little table. He had seen an envelope exactly like it on the floor of his foyer the previous summer. The sight of this one weakened and dizzied him, and for a few moments he could not believe what he was seeing. Then a wave of chilling fear washed over him and he dropped Hero's leash and tossed the sacks of coffee and breakfast sandwiches toward the counter and raced up the stairs.

Jayme was sleeping, just as he had left her, and the wave of relief that swept over him nearly drove him to his knees.

Still unsteady, pulse throbbing, he made his way back down the stairs. In the kitchen the coffee had spilled inside the sack and was dripping off the counter and onto the floor. But his fear was morphing into outrage now, a blind fury that Daksh Khatri or one of his loony disciples had violated the sanctity of his home. And how was that possible? Because DeMarco had not reactivated the security system after bringing Hero in from his first pee of the morning.

Nearly as angry with himself as he was with Khatri, both hands shaking, DeMarco used a paper towel to hold the envelope in place

while he lifted the unsealed flap with a clean fork and carefully drew
the single sheet of paper out onto the table.

*Dear Sergeant Detective*, he read,

> *Imagine what I might have done to her in your absence.*
> *Imagine what I will do to her if you refuse my invitation.*
> *You will meet me at the old mill on Slippery Rock Creek.*
> *I will wait until 6:30 a.m. There are eyes on you wherever*
> *you go, whatever you do, even now. If you do not come alone,*
> *or if you are late, consider my invitation withdrawn.*
> *No future invitation will be extended.*
>
> *I am Magus*

The clock on the stove read 6:19 a.m. From a drawer under the
counter he grabbed the 9mm and then spun in the opposite direction to yank his car keys off the hook on his way out the back door.

Only when he was in his car and moving in reverse with the tires
spinning the wet grass into a gel did he remember his cell phone
still on the kitchen counter where he had left it. Then he slammed
the gearshift into Drive and prayed no one would get in his way.

The time was now 6:21 a.m. Nine minutes for six and a half miles.
He would stop for nothing. The seat belt warning kept beeping but
he would not take his hands from the steering wheel or look away
from the road except for a quick glance at the 9mm sliding back
and forth on the passenger seat with every squealing turn.

Twenty yards past a yellow diamond-shaped sign that read *Hidden
Drive*, DeMarco made a hard right onto a long gravel lane and
glanced at the clock: 6:28. He took a deep breath and tapped the
brakes to slow. Three more deep breaths and then he came to a stop
halfway across the old blacktop parking lot where brown weeds now

stood up through the cracks and frost heaves. He put the gearshift in Park but left the engine running, then, keeping his movements slow and, he hoped, undetectable from the building a hundred feet away, he covered the 9mm with his right hand, slid it across the seat, leaned forward and slipped the barrel and the trigger housing into the waistband below the small of his back.

He had already decided that Khatri would not walk away this time, not even if he was accompanied by two goons carrying assault rifles. If that happened DeMarco would slip the gearshift into Drive, aim the car directly at Khatri, hit the gas and flatten himself across both seats. The bullets would have to rip through a lot of metal to reach him, but steel-jacketed rounds from an L115A3 would pass through a radiator like gamma rays through cardboard. Still, he would take the chance if one were offered.

The old mill had stood empty for most of eighty years, useless and in decay, surrounded by cracked and broken pavement where nothing grew but the toughest of weeds. The sun had only now reached the bottom of the steeply slanting roof and threw a bright red aura all around that side of the building. He counted four rows of six tall windows each, set deeply into the sandstone blocks, most of the glass broken out, with sheets of weathered plywood on the inside of every window. Only the single window below the peaked roof was not boarded shut. Six glass panels in that attic window, all intact except for the one in the bottom right corner.

The rage still seethed in DeMarco but the tension was slowly slipping out of his body. He had beat Khatri's deadline. And now he was prepared to die to keep her safe. If it happened this morning, so be it.

He glanced out the passenger window, then out of his own. Nobody on either side. Trees and weeds and scrub grass. The morning haze had lifted and now the sky was a perfect, unbroken blue. His gaze slid along the flat front of the building then to each of the corners and then to the uppermost window. Nothing. The sun peeked above the bottom corner of the roof and stabbed a sharp light into the windshield. He put a hand to his eyes and tried to cut the glare.

His hands were still shaking a little and he told himself it was because the air was cold, though he also recognized then that he had acted impulsively, no doubt just as Khatri hoped he would. But DeMarco was not built to hide from danger. Was not wired for it. And there had been no time to think. So he was here now whether he should be or not. Waiting. Hands shaking. Alone with the soft rumble of the engine.

He glanced at the clock: 6:34. And when he squinted through the windshield this time he saw a figure, backlit by the sun, coming around the side of the building. Tall and slender, all legs and arms. Khatri. He was taking his steps gingerly over the uneven ground, even put his hand out against a skinny tree to steady himself. Something about the prissiness of his movements made DeMarco smile.

Khatri angled toward the center of the building as he moved forward. Held his hands up, palms out and even with his shoulders. He was wearing cream-colored linen trousers baggy around his legs, a blue nylon windbreaker, the hood pulled over his head.

DeMarco placed his left hand on the door handle. *Wisely and slow*, he told himself. *They stumble that run fast.*

Khatri came to a stop maybe fifteen yards from the front of DeMarco's car. He called out something, but DeMarco heard only a muffled wave of noise. He briefly considered driving forward, staying inside the car, though he would not run down a lone unarmed man, not even Khatri. Foolish was one thing but cowardice was another. He would rather be considered a fool than a coward.

He opened the car door. Glanced to the unboarded window at the top of the building, saw no shadow, no movement. Then fixed his eyes on Khatri again. And reminded himself, *This is the man who stabbed her. This is the man who killed your baby.* He welcomed the rage as it flowed back into him, filled him with strength and resolve.

He put his feet outside the car door, felt the chill in the air and smelled the dirty scent of broken asphalt and the fumes from his vehicle's exhaust. He stood behind the door, head cocked, waiting.

Khatri pushed back his hood. "I said I am glad you came!" he called.

"I didn't come here to make you happy." He was shivering now and heard the tightness in his voice.

"And yet I *am* happy. I have traveled all this way to see you again."

DeMarco said nothing. Calculated the distance. A skinny man running would not be an easy target. Beneath the car's window, he let his hand slip along his thigh and toward his back.

Khatri said, his voice oddly musical in the stillness of the morning, lilting, "Do you not wish to know, good sir, why I have invited you here?"

DeMarco offered no reply. He could not stop shivering and knew the tightness of his muscles would do him no good, would slow down every movement but he could not make the quivering stop.

Grinning, Khatri lowered his right hand to his side. Then lowered his left. And in that moment DeMarco knew his mistake. Even as he moved to duck back inside the car, all of his movements in slow motion now, seconds becoming minutes, he looked up at the highest window in the building and saw the flash like a tiny star exploding.

He saw the car window shattering and was knocked backward off his feet a second before the loud crack reached him. He landed on his left side, still reaching for the gun at his back. Sucked in a breath and heard the whistling in his throat. Tasted blood in his mouth. Heard pigeons burst explosively off the rooftop, wings thrumming. Only then did he recognize the blow to his chest and the searing pain. His first thought was, *Please not now, I have too much to do.*

"*That* is why I invited you here!" Khatri called.

DeMarco scraped his head across the cracked asphalt. Tried to find Khatri in the pool of water that had filled his eyes. He fumbled for the gun and finally found it, struggled to free it and fired blindly. With each of the four shots his arm rose and the aim went higher, so that the barrel was pointed at the sky with the final shot. Two more shots from the building struck the pavement near his head and sprayed his face with slivers of asphalt and dirt. His arm dropped and the gun in his hand clattered away.

He heard footsteps running, quickly fading. *Khatri*, he told himself. Then a muted thumping echoing inside the hollow building, footsteps banging down wooden stairs. *The shooter.*

He blinked, felt a piece of grit in his eye. Both eyes watering, vision blurring. He slid his right hand along his body toward the center of the pain, covered the bullet hole with his palm, pressed down with as much pressure as he could muster. His left arm, stretched out at his side, jerked back and forth, fingers scratching at the rough blacktop. His breath was sticking in his throat now, each inhalation a sloppy, rasping gasp.

He thought of Jayme sleeping. Wished he had had a chance to thank her for finding him and loving him and bringing him back to life. Felt that pain, too, suffuse him. That sweet, sorrowful pain. He closed his eyes and waited.

Now that the adrenaline was seeping out of his brain, he knew what he should have done. He should have called out the horse cavalry to surround the old mill with men and armaments three layers deep. A simple 911 call would have done it. He should have locked the doors and sat tight and enjoyed a nice cup of coffee in the quiet of the morning. But Khatri had played DeMarco's ego like a fiddle. The kid had perfect timing. Don't let DeMarco think. Don't give him two seconds to take a deep breath. A simple phone call, three simple digits, would have changed everything.

*Yep*, DeMarco thought. *He played you like a cheap violin.*

Sometime later, how soon or long he could not say, a sound emerged from the stillness, a softly treading sound of someone approaching in no hurry, rubber heels scuffing the ground. *The shooter*, he thought. DeMarco opened his eyes and moved his head, tucked his chin and blinked to clear his vision. Scratched a quivering hand across the pavement, feeling for the gun.

But no, the man coming toward him was a shadow against the sky, arms low at his sides, both hands empty. A silhouette of a man taking long, easy strides. The sun rising above the roof of the building surrounded the man with a brilliant nimbus of golden light so that bit by bit his features came into view, the clean-shaven smiling face and the neatly combed blond hair, the clean firm lines of his face and limbs and the easy, rhythmic gait of his stride. He was a tall man, slender but not thin, dressed in a pair of faded blue jeans, a crisp white shirt untucked, a pair of white Chuck Taylor high-tops. The sudden clarity and keenness of his vision surprised DeMarco. And although he had never before looked at a man and considered him beautiful, he did so now, the most beautiful man he had ever seen.

And that was when DeMarco recognized the man and realized that he had been waiting for him a long time, had been searching for him as a boy escaping into the safety of the woods, and in every grain of Iraqi sand and in the flames and screams in Panama. And here he was now, unbidden. Not some comic book character. Not some actor in costume and makeup. He was the real thing. The bona fide. *Imagine that*, DeMarco thought.

The man strode up to him, stopped just short of DeMarco's feet, and smiled down.

Only seconds earlier DeMarco had thought his last breath gone, but he found himself breathing easier now, the air warmer, his body relaxing in the stillness of the new day. To the man smiling down at him, DeMarco said, "You don't look the way I expected."

"I am sorry to disappoint you."

"No apology necessary," DeMarco said, and found that he could now push himself up on one elbow and return the man's smile.

The man held his smile as he turned slowly to the side and lifted his gaze to the whitening blue of the sky. "It's a beautiful day, isn't it, Ryan?"

"Every day is beautiful," DeMarco said, and knew that as the truest sentence he had ever spoken.

The man nodded. Then he looked down at DeMarco once more, the beautiful smile widening as he extended his hand. "And now, my friend," the man told him as their hands came together palm to palm, "I have many things to show you."

# I

PERHAPS THE DEEPEST REASON WHY
WE ARE AFRAID OF DEATH
IS BECAUSE WE DO NOT KNOW WHO WE ARE.

# ONE

At about the same time DeMarco was speeding toward the old mill, frantic to beat Khatri's deadline, Daniella Flores had been dreaming about a dirty old woman, small and brown and wrinkled, barefooted and mean-looking, with red and brown mud streaked over her cheeks and caked in her graying, braided hair, more mud dried on her feet and legs and hands. The woman stood there beside Flores's bed, staring hard, arms crossed over her chest. Flores in her bed in the apartment above the hardware store was surrounded by darkness but every detail of the woman was plainly visible though Flores could identify no source of light. She studied the woman from several feet away, Flores just lying there in her dream in the middle of a deep, soft darkness and waiting to see what the strange woman would do. Then her cell phone rang with its Space Funk ringtone. Flores looked away from the woman and into the darkness from which the ringing emanated.

"Don't get that," the old woman told her. Flores looked at her again but the ringing was growing more adamant and spidery white cracks were forming in the blackness all around her, so Flores turned toward the phone again and the woman said sharply, "I said don't get that!"

But Flores was coming awake now and shook herself out of her dream, rolled onto her side and made a grab for her cell phone on the bed table and read the name on the screen as she was bringing the phone to her mouth.

"Captain Bowen," she said, still seeing a fading image of the old woman, Flores's heart hammering because the room was barely gray with morning light and her heart seemed to know something ominous that her mind did not.

"Get out to the old mill right now!" Bowen told her, speaking too loud and a mile a minute, so fast that she could comprehend his words only after a moment or two of groggy recollection, as if the words were reeling past her on a ticker tape and her recognition was racing along several words behind Bowen's voice. "DeMarco might be in trouble. Boyd and I are on our way too but you're a lot closer."

She was on her feet then and though feeling drunk or hungover stepped to the doorway and smacked her hand against the light switch as she said, "What's the situation?"

Bowen's words were a blur, a jumble, a shifting cloud of words in her ear but she picked out *Khatri* and *feels like an ambush* and then she stopped listening and lowered the phone as she plunged her right foot and then left onto a pair of yellow flip-flops, and with one flimsy shoe turned sideways on her foot she yanked open the top drawer of her dresser and grabbed the service pistol in her right hand and the car keys in the phone hand. Four strides later she used two knuckles to twist the dead bolt on her door and then burst out into the dark corridor with no hand free to yank the door shut behind her.

She was on the road in less than a minute, in only her flip-flops and a short pair of rayon shorts the color of red wine with black leaves and closed white petals, a black T-shirt and no bra, driving left-handed as she pulled away from the curb and yanked and clicked her seat belt into place. With headlights blazing and four-ways flashing she overtook and passed a slow-moving pickup truck just outside of town. She knew she would be the first on the scene if she and Bowen and Boyd had all left within a minute or two of each other, but she had no idea what she would find there and kept up a low muttering prayer to *keep him safe, keep him safe*, while glancing at her dashboard clock again and again and feeling the blue minutes slipping past like flies—one blue flickering fly after another too quick for her to grab and shake in her fist. *DeMarco in trouble* kept pounding in her ear while *keep him safe, keep him safe* echoed in a little girl's voice in the pitch-black prayer nook of her mind.

The old mill was patrolled every Friday and Saturday night and she had rousted more than one drunken kid from there, had tapped her flashlight against more than one tinted window while the couple inside scurried to pull on their clothes, so she knew the way and only wanted more speed. But the sun was rising off to her right and throwing a harsh hot glare into her right eye. She drove leaning over the steering wheel as if that would make her way clearer, the seat belt harness pulling against her shoulder and biting into her waist. She could have slapped down the visor or grabbed her sunglasses out of the console but her fingers were too tight around the steering wheel to let go for even a moment.

Then finally there was the turnoff up ahead, the opening in the brush, the yellow diamond-shaped *Hidden Drive* sign. She slowed only a little as she made the hard right turn and felt her rear wheels sliding in the gravel. In the direct glare it was hard to see anything at all except for the upper half of the old sandstone building itself like a black backlit wall some fifty yards ahead. But then out of the brush on her left a vehicle came diving onto the narrow lane and turned toward her, a black compact sedan with the dark shapes of two figures in the front seat. She tapped the brakes and edged her vehicle to the right and heard the brush whipping and scratching against the side of her car as she ducked and bobbed her head for a clearer view into the oncoming car.

Later she would say that something happened to her vision at that moment, that it suddenly went telescopic as if she were looking at Khatri in the passenger seat from only a few feet away, his thin lips grimly set and his dark eyes wide. She saw him place both thin brown hands against the edge of the dashboard and lean toward her and in that same instant she knew that if the vehicle blew past she would lose him. They would lose him again. DeMarco would not allow that to happen and neither would she. So she slammed on the brakes and spun the wheel to the left and turned broadside in front of the other vehicle.

Later she would remember the shock and explosion of impact and the sound of the airbag popping and the chalky smell as it smacked into her face. There was a brief sensation of rolling in slow motion followed by a crunching, cracking sound. Then there was the pain that bit like a rattlesnake into her leg and sent its hot poison coursing up into her skull.

# TWO

## THREE MEN, TWO WOMEN, SAME NIGHTMARE

Captain Bowen had raced out of the house leaving the back door open. He knew before even peeling out of the driveway that his wife would be lashing her robe tight around her waist as she followed his path to the door, already praying just under her breath as she locked the door and yanked the knob to be sure. Then she would go to each of the children's rooms and reassure herself they were all right.

He had made an instantaneous decision to skip the 911 dispatcher and save precious seconds by calling Flores instead. She lived on Route 19 and had the straightest shot to interdiction. Now, demolishing the posted speed limit through his subdivision, he called Trooper Boyd and informed him in as few words as possible of the situation. "DeMarco at old mill…confronting Khatri…Flores en route…make the calls."

Boyd was awake and fully dressed when he received the call. Joe Boxer lounge pants, gray Dickie socks and a gray T-shirt. He was halfway through his twenty-minute qigong exercises, warming and stretching for the free weights to follow, when his screen lit up, the phone vibrated, and the "Wasted" intro ringtone jarred him out of his meditative "embrace the tiger, return to the mountain" movements. He said only three words throughout the entire conversation. "Captain?" and "Roger that." He was out the door in under forty seconds, and, six minutes later, caught up with Bowen's Ford Edge just beyond the I-80 overpass. He glanced down at the speedometer: 93 miles per hour. *Thank God there's no traffic.*

Boyd backed off an extra car length when the Ford's right taillight started blinking. Six seconds later, on the road to the mill, he spotted the wrecked vehicles ahead. Flores's red Crosstrek on its hood, a black sedan upright but with a body sprawled across the buckled hood. Then Captain Bowen's arm coming out the window, his vehicle swerving past the Crosstrek, left hand gesturing for Boyd to stop there while he, Bowen, steered around the black coupe slantwise in the road, Khatri a bloody mess halfway out the smashed windshield, his driver motionless behind the wheel with the steering column rammed into his chest, no sign of airbags. Then Bowen sped up again to reach DeMarco's vehicle and the body lying faceup on the cracked blacktop.

Tires screeching, his car bucked to a stop. He grabbed his phone and leapt out. *Good God no,* a sucking chest wound. Bowen slapped a hand over the hole, slippery with blood. Scanned the area. Nobody in sight, truck engine growling somewhere off to the left. Sirens in the distance. "Keep breathing, you son of a gun!" Too much blood. Hypoxia? Nonresponsive.

On his knees, using his left hand to try to roll DeMarco onto his side. Had to let go with his right hand momentarily, heaved with all of his might. Slapped a hand over the wound again. Sirens louder, closer. "Hurry up, damn it! Hurry the hell up!"

In the meantime, Boyd's Jeep slid to a halt beside the Subaru. He was out the door the instant the vehicle stopped moving. Down on his knees, his face close to the ground. Flores lay pressed against the broken window, her shoulder to the pavement, face twisted in pain, eyes wild with fear. His first thought, after seeing Flores's face and torso intact, was *God bless airbags*. But then he'd winced to behold the condition of her left leg, imprisoned as it was below the dashboard but conspicuously oozing blood. He crawled headfirst in through the broken driver's window but couldn't get a close look at the damage from that angle, so he scraped back out and then in through the passenger window. He touched her face, felt warmth, angled her head so that her mouth was not pressed against the still bloated airbag, then felt his way down to her leg and found it hot with blood and crushed hard against twisted metal just below the knee. "Aw, fuck," he'd said, only his second ever use of that expletive, and fought the urge to weep. He crawled out long enough to summon ambulances while also glancing up ahead to where Captain Bowen was bent over DeMarco's motionless body.

DeMarco was barely breathing. Bowen probed the blood-soaked sweatshirt and found the entrance wound just below the left nipple, heard the faint sucking sound it made and immediately flattened his left hand atop it. The fingertips of his right hand scraped up and down DeMarco's back, searching for an exit wound, and found none. *Thank God for little favors*, he thought, just one of several people that morning who would thank God in earnest or sardonically. DeMarco's pulse was weak and irregular, his breath feathery.

With his left hand Bowen fished his wallet from his pocket, flipped it open and dug into the little leather pocket in which a teenage boy might keep a condom. Bowen, like many troopers and other cops, kept a rectangle of folded duct tape in his. He laid the tape within reach, yanked up DeMarco's sweatshirt and quickly used a dry patch of the hem to clean the bullet wound as best he could, then immediately slapped his right hand down atop the wound again. Using his teeth and left hand he exposed a sufficient length of tape, tore it off, leaned close to listen to DeMarco's breath until he heard an exhalation, then flattened the piece of tape atop the wound and felt the next inhalation draw the tape tight.

And just like that a terrible silence engulfed Bowen. But it was more than silence, was a synesthetic knowledge that his friend and mentor was gone. No breath, no heartbeat, no sensation of life beneath his hands.

Bowen broke the silence with a shrill moan, and immediately thrust himself forward over DeMarco and began CPR. A siren whined in the distance, and Bowen went to work on the man he loved like an older brother and who, until recently, had always intimidated him.

Twenty minutes earlier that morning, Jayme had been awakened by Hero's chilly nose against her cheek, saw the leash still dangling from his collar, and felt her body go cold. She raced downstairs to find the kitchen empty, DeMarco's phone on the counter, Khatri's letter on the floor, Hero now looking up at her with wide, wondering eyes. She ran throughout the house from basement to upstairs calling *Ryan! Ryan! Baby, are you here?* while also calling Captain Bowen on DeMarco's phone. She arrived on the scene moments after Bowen and Boyd—soon enough to spell Bowen with the CPR until an ambulance pulled close and a pair of EMTs rushed the scene. Then she staggered, collapsed onto her hands and knees. Lowered her forehead to the dirty asphalt and howled with pain. Bowen knelt beside her, an arm around her waist. Soon he too lost the strength to hold himself steady, laid his forehead against her shoulder and wept his own violent tears, their bodies bucking against each other like lovers in a last embrace.

The next twelve hours were hellish for everyone who knew DeMarco. Sympathies and concern extended to Flores too, though she was not known as well, and her injuries were less critical. People came and went, several staying to huddle together in the waiting rooms as they held their collective breath in anticipation of the doctors' verdicts. Prayer chains were alerted, vigils held, routine duties neglected.

In the meantime, Flores swam through one morphine dream after another, some of them pleasantly unfamiliar, some horrifically sketched from her youth, the best involving a hundred shaggy brown bison that came lumbering down a hillside to nuzzle and warm her with their earthy scent and breath.

# THREE

## OF WAVES THROUGH A VACUUM AT THE SPEED OF LIGHT

S ix hours after the shooting. Jayme dozing uneasily in the chair
beside DeMarco's bed, him still comatose. She had dragged
her chair close so that she could hold his hand without straining
her arm. In sleep her hand would slip from his so she took it again
each time she woke because just to hold it was reassuring, just
to feel it still warm, his pulse discernible against her palm. She
had learned to disbelieve in the veracity of machines and therefore
never looked at the heart monitor but relied on his touch instead,
relied on the sibilance issuing from between his lips, relied on the
rise and fall of the thin blanket atop his chest.

He held such power over her. He could simply lie there with
eyes closed yet shorten her own breath, grip her lungs and squeeze
her heart so that every beat resounded with an ache of fear. It had
always been that way with them, ever since the beginning, his very
presence reaching out to seize and command her attention. Other
people's electromagnetic fields extended only a few feet from their
bodies but his had rushed out to envelop her from some fifteen feet
away that first time, and it had never once relented, never loosened
its grip on her but instead had ensconced and merged with her
own so that she no longer knew where hers ended and his began,

or which was the magnetism and which the electricity, which the electron and which the grappling force of gravity.

She had been fresh from the academy when they first met, green but cocky, feeling damn good about herself, easy around the rest of the men, enjoying their appraising glances, their aggressive self-introductions. Then he had entered the building. Truth is, he didn't look all that sharp. A bit haggard around the eyes. He had walked straight to the coffeepot, not a word or glance to anybody. Poured a cup black, stood there greedily drinking it while staring at the wall behind the pot. She couldn't take her eyes off him, her heart racing just a little, her mouth going dry, his energy seizing her in its force field, doing all manner of rippling, agitating things with its radiation even from fifteen feet away.

She had watched him that morning, spellbound, as he finished the first cup and poured another. Took a couple of sips. Then he turned finally and surveyed the room. Caught her eyes and looked away. Stood there for a moment as if wrestling with a decision. Then turned abruptly and strode up to her and stuck out his hand. "DeMarco," he said.

She took his hand. A staggering jolt of electricity widened her eyes. She did her best to suppress the tremble. "So I've heard."

He looked away. Nodded. Then withdrew his hand, glanced at her once more, almost furtively, said, "Welcome," and turned and walked away. And ever since then she had been trapped in his field, unable to break free even if she wanted to, and she had never wanted to. Never would. She had never stopped holding his hand, not since that first awkward meeting.

And now he lay there helpless and still, but his hand remained warm in hers, his breath still slipped like a whisper between his lips, his chest still rose and fell.

She pushed forward in her chair, leaned over the mattress to kiss his cheek, which was feverish and scruffy. Placed her mouth to his ear, felt the plastic tubing cold against her neck. "Where are you, babe?" she whispered. "It's time to come back to me now. You need to come back to me, Ryan. I know you hear me, baby. Please don't leave me. Please, baby, you can't. You just can't."

# FOUR

## THE SCENT OF SOMETHING ROTTEN

Trooper Boyd stood just outside the hospital gazing up into the Clorox sky, breathing in through his mouth then pushing the air out through his nostrils in hopes of clearing the stink out, that antiseptic, soiled laundry, ammonia, hydrogen peroxide, sick people smell. He stood all but motionless with his hands clasped at parade rest behind his back and washed his eyes out too on the bleached hue of the sky, still cloudless in its October morning chill, empty but for a single buzzard cutting circles over the woods to the east. The bird should have migrated by now, should be cruising to Venezuela or some other sunny oasis with the rest of its ilk. This one must have a broken compass or be a real misanthrope, and now had gotten a whiff of something rotten, a body in decay, a tasty bit of carrion out there in that copse of mostly denuded trees.

Boyd had paid little attention to buzzards before that moment but now he wondered what became of the roadkill and other abandoned dead through the late falls and winters when the buzzards were on vacation. During the sopping wet springs and unpredictable summers, he couldn't drive a quarter mile without passing something dead along the road, everything from black snakes to squirrels to dogs and cats and whitetails, possums and raccoons and rabbits and a virtually infinite supply of chipmunks, nearly all of their smashed corpses attended by crows and sometimes buzzards squatting nearby. Twice in his life he had come across black bears that had been struck by speeding trucks, one small bear dead, splayed out across the gravel shoulder like a fly-infested rug, the other a full-grown animal dragging its guts toward the adjacent field. He had put that one out of its misery, and then, as he had done with the smaller one too, phoned the Game Commission to come and haul the carcass away. But now he wondered how many buzzards would be required to clean the landscape of such a large animal. And what became of the dead when the buzzards were sunning themselves in the tropics?

*Well, for one thing,* he told himself, *crows don't migrate, do they? Or rodents either. Microbes and other scavengers.* No matter the season, the dead always got chewed up bloody chunk by maggoty chunk and dragged away bone by splintered bone. Death never went out of style, a new feast every day. Enough, certainly, to keep this last buzzard hanging around, this straggler.

The month of October was nearly dead itself, breathing its last. *So leave,* he beamed to the buzzard, which was now merely a short black line gliding across the sky, a frown. *Go ahead and go. We don't need you here.* He had struck one once with his vehicle, had expected it to fly or waddle away from the squashed rabbit in the southbound lane but it only turned to look up at him a moment before he heard the *thunk* against his grill. Dumb, ugly, vomit-spewing bird. Served it right.

*Go on, scram,* he thought now, but the single procrastinator in the distance ignored him, wheeled round and round in wide, lazy, offensive frowning circles like it had all the time in the world, like it could feast on Pennsylvania dead forever, no hurry, no rush, just hang out and wait for the nearly dead to drop. He wished he could shoot it right out of the sky.

The cell phone vibrating in his pocket startled him. He jerked it out and looked at the screen. Dani. He tapped the phone icon and said, "Hey."

"What are you doing right now?" she asked. Her voice was small and hoarse, the voice of a little girl.

He turned to face the hospital. Counted the windows up to the fifth floor. "Shooting a bird with my imaginary gun," he answered.

"Anybody I know?"

"You doing okay?"

"I'm really scared."

He was already taking long strides toward the hospital. "I'll be right up."

# FIVE

## A STRANGE PLACE THIS

For DeMarco, there had been absolute blackness for a while, not long, but he wasn't afraid because he knew the man was still with him, could feel his presence in the darkness, the handsome man who had come for him as he lay bleeding on the dirty asphalt, a hole in his chest.

Then the feeling of being watched disappeared and he knew he was alone, abandoned without a word. Just as panic began to rise in him, the blackness flicked out, and though a light returned it was smoky and uneven and he found himself looking down on the remains of an obliterated city. Far, far below, the city spread out in all directions in a bleak and blackened devastation, whether from war or fire or some other carnage, he could not tell. He was standing high up on a parapet of some kind, splintered beams and shattered windows, crags of broken concrete walls, gaping holes and eviscerated buildings everywhere he looked. Not a single light burning anywhere. Odd-looking plants with thick, oily, muscular tendrils weaving in and out of the broken buildings. And the stench in his nostrils was sickening, ashes and smoke, the decay of all things.

Something moved through the wreckage below but he could not identify it, something dark and sluglike, not a thing he had ever seen before or had a name for, as big as a manatee, apparently headless but with a long serpentine tail dragging behind it. "What the hell?" he muttered. And there, a few blocks over, another of the creatures. And another farther out, each laying down a narrow shimmer beneath their ponderous hulks, some kind of slime, he thought. Almost pretty as it glinted in the meager light, yet disgusting.

Otherwise there was no movement to be seen, only the things below and himself. Even the sky felt foreign to him, gray and soundless and dead. He asked aloud, "What is this place? Where am I?"

*This is you*, he heard in a male voice that sounded familiar but unattached to any name.

"Bullshit," DeMarco said. "*I* am me."

*The I you call you is the tiniest part of you. All below is the greater part.*

"Not true!" DeMarco said, and then cried it again, though with all resolve fading. And then he dropped to his knees, too weak to stand, and he screamed into the bleakness, expelled his griefs and guilts and terrors in a bellowing plea for insentience.

A loud cracking sound brought his gaze down. The floor split open and fell away beneath him. The sudden drop was startling, a submersion into something fluid but thick enough to slow his drop, something even darker than the sky and city had been but streaked with milky swirls. He could see no bottom, no end to his slow-motion fall.

There was no telling how long he drifted down, but, strangely, it did not matter to him, it was what it was. Even the sensation of falling ceased to exist. Maybe he was holding still and the fluid was moving upward over him. No difference. He recognized his mother, his father, his uncle Nip and grandparents, each of them one of the swirls of milky movement. He passed through them or they through him, it made no difference which.

When he passed through or was passed through by the swirl

that was his father, he sensed without seeing the bloom of red on the man's chest, the rosy stain blooming, a stain not much different from the one that had blossomed on his own chest when he had lain on the asphalt however long ago that had been. His mother passed through him too and he sensed the oddly satisfying feeling as her wrists spilled red ribbons into the darkness, her red smile smiling, eyes full of love and regret. He was not only seeing all of this but experiencing it too, his and everybody else's feelings all at the same time yet each one distinct from the others, not as mere images but as sensations experienced throughout his entire being. Fondness. Love. Remorse. A melancholy longing. Soldiers he had known and not known drifted through him. Skulls half blown away. Skin charred, blackened bubbles. Horrific images seen without seeing but he could not flinch because he had no eyes, could not avoid them because he was a milky swirl too, just like the rest of them, absorbing it all. They were all separate and distinct from him at the same time that they *were* him and he was them. He was everything and knew everything and there was nothing he did not know and nothing he was not…

## SIX

## Choose your disguise

And then DeMarco was out of the milky water that was not water but was everything. Standing in the body of DeMarco again in a soft whiteness that was total and all-enveloping but did not limit his vision in any way, standing there perfectly dry as the knowledge of everything trickled and dripped away from him.

Out of the whiteness, a smudge appeared. As it grew closer and larger, it separated into two figures not one. One taller, one half as large. A man and a boy. DeMarco raised his hand to wave. The boy returned the wave. DeMarco strode toward them.

He knew them before their faces came into view. Knew them without recognizing either. So familiar, so different. *My son!* he said without speaking. *And Thomas!* And the distance between them disappeared. They stood an arm's length apart. The man said, *Hello, my friend.*

The boy at five. Ache, ache, a hard white brilliant ache of love.

DeMarco went to his knees. Staggered by love and gratitude, he reached for the boy. But after only a moment of embrace, a moment of warmth and solidity, the boy became fog, dissolved and floated away. The pain that seized DeMarco then! The cold. The fear. He wheeled toward Thomas Huston to ask why, what had happened, but his old friend was fog now too, a last wisp of smile twisting into the air.

DeMarco cried out, the pain too much to bear.

And then there was another man a couple of yards away, slender, brown-skinned, completely naked, shivering with cold. He was startled to see DeMarco there, was frightened, confused, and took a step back. *What happened? What are we doing here?*

DeMarco rose to his feet. Smiled. *So what do you know? You too?*

Khatri's eyes were bright with panic, his thin body wracked by shivers.

*Truce, brother*, DeMarco said.

And with the next blink he was standing alone in a field of tall grass, DeMarco alone, warm bright sunlight but no sun to be seen, unblemished blue sky, tall green grass as high as his knees, yellow buds of goldenrod dabbing and dusting his trousers, the fulsome scent of spring, growth, a rampant fecundity. The field went on forever in all directions. And in the air…music.

What was that music? A single sustained note from an organ, then a piano joining in, a sweet slow melody, a guitar echoing, then a clear male voice singing. And with the voice, DeMarco recognized the singer and the song, Mark Knopfler, "Our Shangri-La." And DeMarco chuckled, said out loud, "Ha ha. Very funny." But where was the music coming from? What was the meaning of all this?

The male voice again, the one he had heard in the blackened city. *You have a choice to make.*

"What choice?" he asked. "A choice of what?"

*Scegli il tuo travestimento. It is for you to decide. Either way is fine.*

For only a moment he did not understand the Italian, did not speak it, only a few random phrases not including the one he had heard. *Scegli il tuo travestimento.* But then yes he did know it, yet the meaning was not clear. *Choose my disguise? What disguise?* And a word flowed through his mind like a banner hauled across the sky behind a silent invisible jet. *Jayme*. And oh, oh yes. Oh yes! Oh my god yes! Now he remembered.

# SEVEN

## Blue morphos tumbling to the rain forest floor

I n all likelihood, the orthosis will be required permanently."

"The what?" Flores asked. She squinted to read his name badge. Dr. Kevin Webb, DO, Orthopedics. Had she spoken with him before? His face had a vagueness to it, the room too, the words on his name badge, her brain slowed by morphine, every breath of the hospital-scented air like swallowing a scream.

He held the leg brace up above the side of her bed. "Do you want me to show you again how it works?"

No, she remembered it now. It had slipped away for only a few seconds. Maybe a few days, what difference did it make? Black pads with black Velcro straps that would fit around the thigh, above the knee, around the calf, above the ankle, black hinges, metal buckles and flattened rods. Despicable. Humiliating. Shattering.

"Hyperextension," the doctor said. He used too many words, she caught only a few of them, a rush of clumsy blue butterflies of words fluttering from his mouth, tumbling away. "Stabilization… extensive nerve damage…moderation of pain."

She felt sick to her stomach, wanted to vomit. "Pan," she said.

"Excuse me?"

"Bedpa—" she said, then lurched forward leaning to the opposite side and sprayed the floor with her vomit, would have fallen off the bed and into the mess had the doctor not seized her by an arm, held her awkwardly in place as she vomited again and he called toward the door, holding his breath against the stink, "Nurse! Nurse! We need assistance in here!"

Flores remained hovering over the side of the bed, could feel his hand around her bicep gripping tight, could feel his weight pressing down on the bed, her body twisted and shivering as her stomach heaved again but her face blazing hot, throat burning, her body scalding hot in every laceration and wound, every splintered bone. Yet a violent shiver raked up and down her spine and there was nothing in her mind but a swarm of curses and muffled screams as she gazed down at the vomit, the puddle and smears of ugliest color, no butterflies here, no fucking butterflies here.

# EIGHT

NOT ALL IS UNREMEMBERED

In another room on another floor DeMarco coughed softly, but he had coughed before, so Jayme was not startled. But then he sniffed, and then his nose wrinkled, and a long, low moan issued from him as he tried to sit up, tried to work his eyes open. She was out of her chair in an instant, thrust upward by the leaping of her heart, leaning over him. "Baby, baby, lie still. I'm here. I'm here with you."

He settled back into the pillow. Pushed his eyelids halfway open and squinted, drew back from the light. "It's awful," he muttered, his voice weak and raspy, and coughed again, harder this time, then sucked air in through his mouth.

She had to keep herself from falling onto him, crushing the tubes against him. "What is, baby? The light? Do you want me to turn off the light?"

"That stink," he said. "What is it? It's awful."

"You're in a hospital," she told him, laughing and crying as she spoke. "There's an oxygen tube under your nose. You're in a hospital bed."

He blinked. Squinted. Breathed warily through his nose. Jerked a little from the mechanical scent of the air. "How long?" he asked.

"This is the fifth day. You've been out since they brought you in." She pressed a hand to his cheek. Leaned closer to kiss his forehead, his nose.

"I smell you," he said.

"I'm sorry, baby, I haven't been back home much—"

"Good," he told her. "You smell good."

And she broke down sobbing then, her cheek bucking against his, her face in the pillow that smelled like his hair.

And for a while she did not speak, nor did he try to. He tried only to lie still, to hold the pain in one place like a brick of pain shifting atop his chest with every breath. No, more like a cinder block with one corner dug in deep. A cinder block of throbbing, stabbing pain.

Then he said, and moved his head slowly away from hers, tried to turn his head without pain to look at her, his voice soft with surprise, with finality, "He's dead."

She drew back a few inches, uncertain. "Who is, baby?"

"How did they get him?"

She drew back a little farther. "How could you know that?" she asked. "How could you even know that?"

# NINE

Prior to that morning at the old mill with Flores and DeMarco, Boyd had never before been so close to a life-threatening injury to a brother or sister in uniform. Thirteen years of service, thirty-three years old, and no fallen comrades in Troop D. The morning lived in his memory now like some kind of fever dream or searing hallucination. For a while he could think of little else, only of how close to death his friends had come, and how close, by proximity, he was throughout the course of every day and night on duty. And for what—$65K a year? The lowest paid NFL quarterback hauled in nearly three times as much for every single game. The highest paid, two million every game. Two million dollars per game! That broke down to $500,000 per hour, and at least half of that time was spent standing on the sidelines. Compared to that, Boyd earned peanuts plus change for every day on duty, for every day he risked his life, while grown men made a fortune for playing a game that was essentially about knocking each other down.

He was thinking these thoughts while sucking on a mocha shake in Arby's. That night's dinner, a King's Hawaiian roast beef with onion rings, had gone down without making a strong impression on his taste buds and now lay in his stomach like a clod of wet earth.

Seated in the booths and tables around his two-chair high-top were five senior citizens, six teenagers crowded into one booth, and a family of four at a table, both children under three. *They all have lives,* he told himself, and not without some bitterness. He was the only person seated alone. The only person in uniform. *There is probably some correlation in those two facts. Probably some cause-effect relationship.*

He had an older sister in Front Royal, Virginia, but they had never been close. She was a heavy drinker and chain-smoker and he got angry every time she blew smoke in his nephew's face. How old was little Harley now? Just shy of five when they had come back for Grandma's funeral. Must be in third or fourth grade by now. All those years inhaling his mother's poison.

He thought about his father then, an hour away in assisted living. Assisted living and not yet seventy—how sad was that? All of those pesticides and farm chemicals. All of those back-breaking years. It was probably time to check in on the old fella again. If only it weren't so awkward to sit in that little room with him and stare at the TV together. Neither one of them had ever developed a talent for conversation. *How you been? Been all right. Yourself?* That was about the extent of it.

Boyd crumpled up his wrapper and napkins and picked up his plastic tray. Dumped the garbage in the container near the door, walked outside without meeting anybody's gaze. The sky was graying, still a while before dark, the air chilly. He stood there beside his car wondering where to go now, what to do next. In a world so vast he seemed to have very few choices, and not one of them was appealing.

# TEN

## A LOT OF GOOD, AN EXTRAORDINARY AMOUNT OF DAMAGE

K hatri's sniper turned out to be a seventeen-year-old homeless man last known to be living on the streets of Markham,
Ontario. The rifle he used to shoot DeMarco from the top-floor
window of the old mill was a scoped .30–30 deer rifle tied to a
Buffalo, New York, home break-in. The soft-point bullet struck
DeMarco at a downward slant, ripped through his left lung and
lodged in his latissimus dorsi between the fifth and sixth ribs. "It
was amateur hour from the word go," Bowen later told DeMarco.
"And thank God for that." A higher caliber rifle, a true sniper rifle
like a .50 BMG, or even a .338 Magnum loaded with cop-killer
Teflon-coated ammo and capable of taking down moose and bear,
would have torn a huge hole out of DeMarco's back, and he would
have bled out before anybody could reach him.

DeMarco only smiled and said, "Khatri never was much of a
gun expert. Just a crazy, angry, messed-up kid."

"Geez, Ryan," Bowen said. "He was a lunatic. Don't go easy
on him. He killed three people and almost took both you and
Jayme out."

DeMarco held his smile. He, too, was surprised by his lack of
anger, his lack of righteous indignation.

Jayme, of course, was DeMarco's most frequent visitor. She was with him around the clock until assured by the doctor that DeMarco was on the road to recovery, and only then did she begin to spend a few hours at home every night. On occasion she was given permission to bring Hero into the room, and, after the head nurse saw how docile and affectionate he was, she allowed Jayme to lead him from room to room so that any patient who wished could soak up some of his furry warmth.

Jayme also visited Daniella Flores in her room two floors above DeMarco's, then reported back to him. "She tries to put a good face on it," Jayme reported, "but she's devastated. Who wouldn't be?"

"They're sure she won't walk again?" he asked with tears in his eyes.

"Not without the brace or crutches. She has no feeling from her thigh to her ankle."

"Because of me," he said.

"Stop it. That's the only thing she has to be happy about. That she stopped Khatri. For you, she told me. 'At least I stopped him for Ryan.'"

"She said that?"

"Exact words. What she did was just so brave, so…"

"Selfless. But…"

"Don't say it, baby. She knows already. She doesn't need to hear it from anybody else, and especially not from you. She had one split second for a decision, and she did what she thought she had to do."

He hoped the investigation board would feel the same way, but they probably wouldn't. Flores might be let go, not even allowed desk duty. And that would destroy her. Although desk duty probably would too.

"We're going to have to fight for her," he said.

"You better believe we will."

A week earlier he would have blamed himself for her decision and her injury. Would have saddled himself with another bag of grief and guilt. But things had changed for him in the milky whiteness. The knowledge that had raced through him was difficult to call up at will, but sometimes a trickle or two appeared spontaneously, as it did now.

*We write our own stories,* he told himself. *Truth #12.* And all it had taken to discover that simple truth was a visit from Mr. Death. What a handsome, friendly guy he'd turned out to be. Not the kind to hang around long, though. Takes you where you need to be and poof, he's gone. Not even enough time for a quick orientation.

"Dani needs to believe that she did a very good thing," Jayme told him. "And she did. Probably a lot more good than any of us can imagine."

*Good and evil,* he thought. *Positive and negative. The eternal struggle. Yet all of it good somehow. All of it positive.* It was a difficult concept to grasp.

He told Jayme as much about the experience as he could remember, about never losing consciousness, not even when he was thought to be dead and, later, in a coma. But he was still trying to process it all, still trying to fill the gaping holes in his memory.

On an evening at the end of his first wakeful week in the hospital, Jayme helped him climb into a wheelchair, then pushed him to Flores's room. Dani would have been sent home days earlier were it not for her deep depression, her near-catatonic detachment from life. In her room DeMarco struggled to stand so that he could embrace her. In his arms, her face wet with his tears, Flores's fortress of solitude collapsed, and she sobbed uncontrollably until able to pull herself away from him.

Jayme helped him to sit again, then urged him to share his near-death experience with Flores. He did so. When he finished, Flores sat quietly for a few moments, then asked, "What do you mean by *everything*?"

"Just that," he told her. "Everything there was to know. I knew every little bit of it. How everything was made, why it was made, who made it, and what all of us had to do with it. And I understood it all. It made perfect sense to me."

"But now you can't remember any of that?"

"All I remember is that it was like a beautiful spiderweb glistening with drops of dew. But an infinitely huge spiderweb. And multidimensional. All layered and interwoven. All of it singing. And that was just the framework. Like I was looking at it through a microscope, even though I was a part of it. It's hard to explain. Impossible to explain."

"What do you mean, it was singing?"

"Honestly, I don't know. It was alive and singing, that's the only way I can explain it. Except that the description doesn't begin to touch how grand it really was."

"And that was God?" she asked.

He shrugged. "God is just a word. And no word can touch what it was. What it is."

That silenced all three for a while. Exhausted, DeMarco said, "We should probably go for now and let you rest."

"You'll come back, right?" Flores asked.

"Of course we will. We love you."

And that set Flores to crying again. Jayme sat on the bed and hugged her until she quieted. DeMarco squeezed her hand.

Minutes later, in the elevator, after the door had closed, Jayme told him, "Hey. That was very sweet what you said to Dani."

He looked up at her from his wheelchair. "I feel a lot of love now."

"I think you always have."

He leaned his head back against her belly. "Just don't let me get sappy about it."

She laid a hand on the top of his head. "Old trees like you don't have a lot of sap."

God, he loved her. He loved everybody. He wondered how long it would last.

That night, alone in his room, he could not sleep. There was a strangeness to the realization that he was becoming a different person. Was already different. The change had happened to him without his collusion, was intact the moment he awoke from the coma. Not that he disapproved of it. The fires of guilt and anger that had fueled him for so long were cooler now, the flames not always roaring. Despite his frequent doubts, the heat no longer threatened to consume him. It was interesting to watch, as if he were a spectator. And to wonder what the end result might be.

What it all boiled down to was a different understanding of death. Living had been all about trying to avoid death, to not think about death, to stay out of death's way. To fear death. All of society was built around that fear, promulgated upon that fear. And how strange to no longer feel that fear, but, in its place, only longing.

Out of that longing, a memory returned to him. Something about making a choice. About choosing a…a what? A mask? A path?

*Choosing a path*, he told himself. *That sounds right.*

Gingerly he rolled onto his side, opened the bedside table, and was glad to see a pen and notepad there. He wrote with difficulty, haltingly, lying down with the notepad upright a few inches above his chest. It took more than an hour to finish what he had to say. He then copied it over, printing as neatly as possible. Read it again. It wasn't perfect but it didn't need to be. He buzzed for a nurse.

# ELEVEN

## BLOW THE BUBBLE, POP IT GOES

Flores had her eyes closed but wasn't sleeping when the nurse came into the room. But Flores didn't feel like talking, didn't feel like interacting in any way. It never took long for her anger to come flooding back, the self-pity and fiery rage. Within minutes after Jayme and DeMarco left her room, she hated everyone again, hated nurses and doctors and everybody else too, hated life with a searing fury for the way it always screwed you over, always kept you down no matter how much good you tried to do. So when the nurse appeared, Flores kept her eyes closed and her breath soft and regular. After just a moment beside the bed, the nurse exited again, her rubber soles going *shh shh shh* out the door.

Flores opened her eyes. What was the nurse doing in her room? If she had brought meds, she would have awakened Flores.

On the wooden tray that could be swung over the bed was a slip of folded paper, standing there like a tiny pup tent. Flores picked it up and opened it but the light was too dim. She pushed herself into a half-sitting position, reached behind the low headboard and switched on the light. And read this:

# THE PATH

*for Dani, with love and gratitude from Ryan*

To begin, all you need to know is
where to place the first step.

Look to the right, the left,
to the front, behind.
Test the ground.
Take a step.
Choose your path.

The ground can shift at any time.
A fallen tree, a raging stream,
a death. A bog to
suck you under.
It will happen, yes.
Look to the right, the left,
to the front, behind.
Choose your path.

There will be the hungry, the sick
along the way. The poor, displaced
and dying. Assist those you can but
do not your quest defer—
unless it is your path to stay.
But first look to the right, the left,
the front, behind.
Consult your heart and
choose your path.

Do this every day, every morning.
Reaffirm your decision or
change it and seek another way.
Every step you take
is a soap bubble.
Love and laugh with both
the shimmer and the pop.

Know this and do this
joyful every day and
then a morning will come
when you rise slowly from your bed,
when you linger at the open door.
*I like it here*, you will think,
surprised. *I will stay.*

You will look long down that twisted trail
your years carved through the weeds of doubt.
All of those half stops, turns,
they will stand out clearly now,
all of those gnarls of will and wanting,
all of those thwarts and urgings you carried
and tossed along the way.

That is the path you laid.
It was always there,
always waiting for you
to take the first step.
Look to the right, the left,
to the front, behind.

Consult your heart.

Test the ground.

And choose your path.

# TWELVE

## A COOLING RIVER BETWEEN TWO UNQUENCHABLE FIRES

The movement awakened him. He watched her coming into the room in the dim light and midnight hush, watched her swinging the crutches forward one after the other, one leg bent and held above the floor, that foot naked, still swollen and dark. She came lurching forward without looking at him and moved around the foot of the bed and sidled up close. She hoisted herself up onto the right side of his bed, one hip and then the other, then let go of the metal crutches so that they fell softly clanking atop the adjacent chair. Her dark eyes were wet, her face wet from tears, so he said nothing, but only reached for her. She curled against him, her face to his chest, her breath hot through the thin fabric of his hospital gown, and she pressed herself into him as if into the coolness of an enveloping cave, and he held her close, unspeaking, his heart weeping its silent invisible tears for the love that swelled it, this tragedy-strewn life, this broken child in his arms.

## II

WHAT YOU ARE IS WHAT YOU HAVE BEEN,
AND WHAT YOU WILL BE IS WHAT YOU DO NOW.

# THIRTEEN

ON THE BUMPY ROAD TO RECOVERY

After the thoracoscopic surgery, after the chest tube had been removed, after the danger of pneumonia and other complications had passed, DeMarco had been sent home with the warning to remain vigilant for any indications of atelectasis, a dangerous scarring of his lung. Any chest pain, wheezing, fever, chills, night sweats, breathlessness, a dry cough, or high blood pressure should be reported to his doctor immediately. The long list of symptoms made him chuckle to himself. How many days of his life had he not suffered from at least one of those symptoms? He was given a device called an incentive spirometer that worked like a Breathalyzer in reverse, so that he had to suck in great lungfuls of air and then blow them out again—payback, he decided, for all of the breath tests he had administered over the years, all of the DUIs he had handed out. He was told to sleep with the good lung to the mattress and not the other way around, which made it necessary for him and Jayme to switch their sides of the bed. And he was cautioned to remain observant for a tendency for his fingertips to curl toward his palms, another curious symptom that made him smile while he tried to look solemn and grateful for the medical education.

It wasn't that he did not believe in the possibility of dire complications but that he now understood that even unpleasant circumstances would be for his own good. There was almost something playful to it. And there was also the recognition that every instant he lived after being scraped up off the asphalt was a gift. When he considered the anguish he had suffered in ignorance for nearly a half century, the only tenable response now was to shake his head and smile. The world is indeed a stage, and all men and women players. Amateur theater.

For her part, Jayme passed those next few months in a kind of breathless suspension. Always watching DeMarco while trying not to be caught watching him, always wanting to do things for him but knowing he would resist. Little things he did made her want to shriek with worry. Climbing the stairs without holding to the banister, for example. And even worse, galloping down the stairs like a kid. Sometimes in bed she would watch his chest rise and fall, just to make sure he was still breathing. She bought a blood pressure monitor and insisted that he use it every day, which, of course, he did not. She bought a Fitbit to monitor his heart rate, but he laughed when she asked him to wear it. She dumped all of the sugar in the house into the garbage and bought pure stevia extract, filled a refrigerator bin with supplements he had never heard of, things like spirulina and boswellia and chlorella and fenugreek. He would indulge her for a few days, mixing chia seeds and bee pollen into his oatmeal, but then he would smile and pour on the maple syrup and tell her not to worry, he was fine, all was right with the world.

But he was different somehow. Even quieter than he had been before. Yet it was more than that, more than simply being laconic. He was *different*. They were just little things maybe, but really… He would whisper to the dog, for example. And would sometimes mutter in his sleep. He had never done that before either. He could stare up at the moon for fifteen, twenty minutes at a time. Could sit all but motionless for an hour or more, a faraway look in his eyes. And he had taken to standing in the yard in his bare feet. In the snow, for God's sake! What was *that* all about? And when was this crazy behavior going to end? When would he snap out of it? It was driving her mad.

# FOURTEEN

## A NEW LEASH ON LIFE

The next to last day of March. DeMarco was up and walking around looking as normal as dirt, yet not pleased to have only one fully functioning lung, not pleased at all. Quiescence was wearing thin. According to his doctor, DeMarco was doing just fine, coming along nicely, but *nicely* didn't cut it for DeMarco. A man can read and watch and otherwise spectate for only so long before he has to *do* something. Anything. It was okay if there would be no Ironman competitions for him, no marathon races, especially since he had never participated in one nor had ever wanted to. Still, to be sidelined like this was starting to get irksome, and he resented it. Left lung wheezing in a way that only he could hear, a way that didn't even register through the doctor's stethoscope, there was something embarrassing about that. And the left one had been his favorite lung too. He hadn't known it was his favorite until it got perforated, but he knew it for sure now. You only miss something when you lose it, truth #68. True on Earth and all through the universe and its multitude of dimensions. Longing as a life lesson. He'd had his fill of that lesson. Let's move on to something else now, can we?

He and Hero, both out of work, a couple of early retirees shuffling and sniffing around the still dewy yard. The ides of March behind them, no *et tu Brutes*, no thrusting of knives. Khatri dead and buried, the misguided shooter too. The judge in Connor McBride's case hadn't gone easy on him, had levied an upward departure judgment and sent him away for three lifetimes, plus twenty years extra for his part in the conspiracy that wounded DeMarco and Jayme and took away their baby.

DeMarco felt more than a twinge of sympathy for the kid. Raised by a prostitute mom, a junkie, surrounded by the worst society has to offer. Yes, McBride had assisted in the deaths of three innocent people, so justice had to be done, but still. What if the judge and jurors all had near-death experiences and learned what DeMarco learned? Would the sentencing have been so severe and absolute? It had probably been a tough call to make. But this side wasn't the other side, and both sides had their own set of rules.

And that case up in Otter Creek, what a clusterfuck that had been for a while. He smiled to remember how ambitious Chase Miller had been, how reckless he was willing to be to prove himself. He and Georgina, the Lost City girl, had played significant roles in putting Luthor Reddick behind bars, and now, thank goodness, both were flourishing. Miller's story detailing Reddick's crimes and the path that led to his arrest had been picked up by both the Youngstown *Vindicator* and the *Pittsburgh Post-Gazette*, and he used them to win a position as an assistant researcher with the Drudge Report, where, he boasted in his last email to DeMarco, he was "striking an occasional blow for truth" by combing through online stories the mainstream media ignored. He had his eyes set on a position with Project Veritas and promised to keep DeMarco posted as to his progress.

Georgina, on the other hand, had chosen a quieter path. In January she had started classes at WVU. Reconciliation with her parents was not total, but, as she told Jayme by phone, "We're working on it. They still sometimes act like the same clueless assholes they used to be, but they're trying, I guess." Her goal was to be an elementary school teacher. In the meantime, she was dipping into her trust fund now and then to make sure the residents of Lost City stayed warm and well fed and aware of their options.

Jayme and DeMarco both enjoyed receiving such reports and took a bittersweet satisfaction from watching their former charges quickly grow away from them. The cases that had brought them all together for a while were history now, written by the survivors, already forgotten by all but a few.

The spring equinox was history too. It had come in like a lamb and, but for a few windy nights and sodden days, was retaining a lamblike temperament. Such was the way of all things, DeMarco told himself, to come and to go. Except for that one time with Flores, he had spoken of his NDE to only Jayme and the dog. People did not like to hear that death is a good thing. It invalidated their grief to be told such a thing, and they did not want to give up their grief, it was the chunk of wood they clung too when the waters rose all around them, and even when the waters lapped only against their ankles. DeMarco knew that need. He had waded around in his own pool of stagnant water for how long? Too many years. Too many years of feeding on self-pity. What if somebody had come to him back then and said, "Hey, bud, let it go, okay? So what if your car got T-boned by a drunken driver? So what if your baby boy's neck got snapped? Death is great, man! Death is when all the good shit happens!" He would have punched that person in the face. Because, in a strange way, embracing death as superior to life would have invalidated Baby Ryan's short time on the earth and all of the revivifying joy those few days had brought to DeMarco.

So he had to be careful and not show too much enthusiasm for death. People need their bugaboos. Life is too directionless without them, like a dim highway with no road signs.

Most people cannot understand something until they are ready to understand it. Jayme was ready and even desirous of understanding, yet the details of his NDE were not easy to communicate let alone remember. They returned to him spontaneously sometimes, usually when he was alone, and seldom lingered. Plus, Jayme had a tendency to ask questions, which only frustrated both of them because of the inadequacy of his answers. Hero, on the other hand, was an ideal audience. His large, open eyes and ears took everything in without question. His was a soothing presence, and he had been a boon companion all throughout DeMarco's convalescence.

And now, out in the yard on an early Monday morning, the next to last day of March, Hero pranced and raced about, watering every bush in the yard while DeMarco, still in his nightclothes of red basketball shorts and V-neck T-shirt, scuffed along behind him. *Showing off*, DeMarco thought as he watched the dog, but with not a hint of resentment or malice in his heart. He did indeed love that hairy beast. Loved Jayme too, though she was mostly hairless. Loved this second chance he had been given with them. *A new leash on life*, he sometimes joked.

But he was a different man now and he knew it. The change was difficult to explain. Impervious to analysis. It showed in little things, his new tenderness, for example. His patience. The enigmatic smile that might rise unbidden to his lips. And in what might be viewed as peculiar behaviors, such as a fondness for walking barefoot through the yard. He'd started it the first morning home from the hospital. Holy moly, the frozen ground had been cold at times! Even now he felt the chill in his toes, but that was good too—a kinder March chill, a bit of friendly discomfort was all it amounted to. There was just something so energizing about feeling the ground beneath him. Taking the temp of Mother Earth, so to speak. Sucking up her goodness and strength, Antaeus-style. Yes, there was something intimate and enlivening about it, no matter the season. Any touch is better than none.

In many ways his NDE had turned him into an odd duck, even in his own eyes. He heard how foolish he sounded when he tried to tell Jayme about it. And for that reason he resented it. He wasn't going to be one of those people who makes a YouTube video about his experience, or goes on the lecture circuit. What would he have to say about it? *It was weird. Scary even. I really don't understand much of it.* Maybe the debunkers were right. Maybe all that happened during his coma was that his brain went into a spasm and started squirting out a lot of chemicals, a Timothy Leary cocktail of bug juices and toad slime and who knows what else. The thing is, it had all felt so *real*. So honest. Everything brighter and deeper and more meaningful than anything he had come back to. This grass, this sky, this dog with its goofy grin—it was all great, very pleasant, but somehow only skin-deep in comparison. At times this life felt more like a reflection on a flat screen, a quivering mirage, a trick of the light—

"Hey, babe?" Jayme called from the porch. He turned. Blinked. Saw himself as she was seeing him, a grown man with wet toes, goose bumps up and down his naked legs, and he smiled sheepishly, embarrassed for himself and for her.

She held up her phone. "Just got a strange text. You guys almost done out there?"

He gave a short whistle, then slapped his thigh twice, and Hero came running, followed him to the porch. Jayme asked, "Are your feet okay? Too cold?"

"Tickety-boo," he said. "Who's the text from?"

"Do you know a judge named Morrison?"

"Jack Morrison?"

She read the text. "'Good morning. District court judge J. D. Morrison here. Emeritus.'"

"That's Jack. I think he does a little teaching now. Why is he texting you at barely sunup?"

"Actually it came in just before two this morning. And it's a long one."

*Okay, so he's an insomniac. Or a late-night drinker.* "And?" He sat on the edge of the porch with his feet on the concrete steps. The concrete was colder than the ground. No life in it. *Or is there?* he wondered. *Rocks have life. Why not concrete too?* He rubbed one foot and then the other as Jayme read the rest of the text.

"'I am writing to inquire of Sergeant DeMarco's health,'" she read. "'Rumor has it that he is fully recovered from the unfortunate incident last fall. It brought me great happiness to receive that news, and I pray that it is true. Though I know him well enough to suspect that he would answer the call to duty even if bedridden, and I hesitate to offer him that possibility, which is why my first contact is with you. If he is not yet truly recovered, please say nothing to him of this message. But if he is, I would like to offer you and the sergeant a temporary employment. It is nothing extravagant, and certainly nothing along the lines of those cases that have brought you both such well-deserved attention. It is a minor investigation, actually, but one that demands the utmost discretion. I would appreciate hearing from you, one way or the other, as to whether or not this might be of some interest. At your earliest convenience, of course.'"

"I'll be darned," DeMarco said.

"Not an answer, babe."

He turned his head, looked up at her and grinned. "Let's hear him out."

"I vote no."

"Of course you do. So that's one yea and one no. Hero! C'mere, boy."

"Oh no you don't," she said.

"We need a tiebreaker. Who better to cast that vote? He's impartial to a fault."

She reached down to grab a handful of his hair. Gave his head a gentle shake. "Grrrrrrr," she said.

"You don't trust the judgment of your own adopted son?"

"Forget it," she said, and turned back to the door. "You're hopeless. I'll set up a meeting. How do you think he got hold of my cell number?"

DeMarco shrugged. "Contacts," he said.

"It kind of ticks me off. You know?"

"Nothing is private, my love."

"Ain't that the truth?" she said before going back inside, leaving him there to smile at her words, she meaning one thing, he something else, that all things are known, all things are always.

# FIFTEEN

## SWEETNESS AND LIGHT BUT LACKING NUTRITIONAL VALUE

When he first told her about his NDE, still in the hospital, she had sensed that he was indeed doing his best to explain what he had experienced, yet the elucidation factor seemed absent from his explanation. He'd said that he could still feel everything that had happened but could not articulate it, said the necessary words were like glistening bubbles in his mind, but they popped the moment he reached for them.

"Then tell me how it *felt* to know everything," she suggested. "Tell me how perfection feels."

"Nothing is ever perfect. Nothing is ever still."

"How can that be?"

"I guess that what I mean is, it is perfect because it's exactly what it should be at that exact moment. But it's also supposed to change from moment to moment. Which means that it is perfect and yet it isn't. Or something like that."

"Darn you, DeMarco. You can't remember even a little of it? Nothing specific?"

"It comes and goes. But it's more like it is remembering me than I am remembering it. It runs past just to say hello, here I am, see you later!"

She couldn't conceive of anything more frustrating, yet he remained annoyingly imperturbable. Imperturbable and impregnable. Before the shooting he had finally been opening up to her, sharing his feelings and even his fears, but now he was a closed door again. And when she told him that, he had said, "Not on purpose, baby, I promise. But it's all sort of like a…like a…"

"Like a what?"

"Let's say I've eaten something unimaginably delicious. Something you've never tasted but always craved."

"A champagne and chocolate macaron?"

"Okay, that. And I've just eaten one, even though it sounds disgusting to me. Ask me to describe it for you."

"Describe it for me."

"I can't. Because it was literally too delicious for words. No word can touch how good it was. Sweet? Sure, but more than that. Scrumptious? Yep, but so much more than that too. The thing is, I can still taste it on my tongue, but I can never share that taste with you. Any words I use will be limiting and insufficient. I can't even describe it to myself."

"What if I lick your tongue?" she asked.

He shook his head. "You'd taste my mouth and a tiny bit of macaron, but the full experience of macaron would remain as insubstantial to you as a shadow. Because that's what we are here, sweetheart. We're shadows of who we really are."

*Okay,* she conceded, *okay, he really is trying. He isn't hiding it from me on purpose.* Yet it stung nonetheless. Almost as if he'd had a lover, confessed to it but couldn't remember her name, couldn't recall how the woman looked or why he had done it. He'd had a life-altering experience and was discernibly changed by it but it had happened without Jayme, without the love of his life, and she couldn't help but to resent him a little for it. He had gone away and come back to her a different man.

# SIXTEEN

*TOMAR. COMER. ESTE ES MI CUERPO*

Morrison was a big man with bad knees and swollen ankles and seven decades of plenitude piled atop his groaning bones. He came into the Mexican restaurant with a subtly shuffling gait while carrying his upper body stiffly erect as if to hold in abeyance a pain that was waiting for an opportunity to surge through his joints and render him immobile. He was wearing a loose gray suit, a navy-blue knit shirt with the top two buttons open, and a pair of white high-top sneakers.

DeMarco watched him pause in the lobby to speak to the hostess, and said to Jayme, seated beside him in the booth, "He's aged twenty years since I've seen him." The hostess, a middle-aged woman with streaks of gray in her black hair, had already brought their water, a basket of tortilla chips and two small bowls of salsa. DeMarco played with a chip, absently turning it over and over between finger and thumb.

"How long since you've seen him?" Jayme asked with her water glass raised.

"Four years or so. It's rheumatoid arthritis. Hit him fast, apparently. He used to stand six-five."

"How old is he?"

"Early seventies."

Morrison looked their way then, and DeMarco raised a hand.

What little was left of Morrison's hair was snow white, his face round and fleshy, his cheeks red and mouth smiling. Grinning, he made his way to their booth and, just as DeMarco stood, stuck out his hand. "You're looking fairly good for a man who catches bullets with his chest."

"Bullet. Singular," DeMarco told him. "Low velocity. You're looking pretty fine yourself, Judge."

"I look the way I feel, which is like yesterday's roadkill." He leaned across DeMarco, hand extended. "And this Irish beauty must be Trooper Matson."

"Scottish," she said, and gave him her hand.

"Scottish, then. Happy April Fools' Day."

"And to you," she said.

Morrison nodded toward DeMarco but kept his eyes on Jayme. "Did this joker play any pranks on you today?"

"She woke up and I was still there," DeMarco answered.

"Worst joke ever," Jayme added.

The judge grinned and gripped the edge of the table and lowered himself onto the empty bench seat. Then he looked up at the brightly colored mural on the wall to his immediate left. It ran from well beyond Jayme to a couple of feet past his shoulder and depicted a rendition of da Vinci's *Last Supper* with Jesus and the disciples all wearing sarapes mexicanos and sporting Pancho Villa mustaches. All around the large room were other Christian-themed murals with similar Hispanic characters. "I love surrounding myself with all these saints," he said. "You been here before?"

"Many times," DeMarco told him. "I'm surprised we never ran into you here."

The hostess came bustling over with a third glass of water, which she set in front of the judge. "*¿Tendrás lo de siempre?*" she asked.

"*Sí, gracias, Estella. Burritos Aztecas y uno Dos Equis. Y para mis amigos, lo que quieran. En mi cheque, por favor. Y prepara mi cena para llevar.*"

"*Sí, ¡por supuesto!*" She turned to DeMarco. "And for you, *señor?*"

DeMarco ordered the enchiladas supremas and chili rellenos, Jayme the chori pollo.

"Nothing to drink?" the judge asked.

"We're water people," DeMarco told him. Estella nodded and strode away.

"You mean like dolphins?" the judge said with a grin as he reached for a tortilla chip. "Which bowl is mild?"

"The one on your right," Jayme answered.

He dipped a corner of his chip and told her, "I'm glad to see you're keeping him in line."

"Down the straight and narrow and loving it," DeMarco said.

Judge Morrison continued to smile. He put the chip in his mouth, chewed while wiping his fingertips on a napkin, then said, "First things first. Tell me about last fall. Every story I hear is more grandiose. So I want it straight from the horse's mouth. How did it all go down out there?"

DeMarco looked to Jayme. She smiled but said nothing. He faced the judge again. "We'd just wrapped up the thing in Otter Creek Township."

"The triple homicide," Morrison said.

DeMarco nodded. "Next morning the dog and I walked up to Sheetz for some coffee. I came back to find a letter from Khatri on the floor. You know about Khatri?"

"Yes, sir, I did my research. Called himself Magus. Thought he could reform society by sowing chaos?"

"Something like that."

"The letter basically said meet me at the old mill or else, correct?"

"Correct. So, like an idiot, I did. Even left my phone behind by accident. I got there, he showed himself, we had a momentary chat, and then his shooter in the mill put one in my left lung. And down I went."

"Jesus," the judge said. "And that young trooper...that, uh..."

"Flores," DeMarco said.

"How did she know to go out there after you?"

DeMarco nodded his head at Jayme, which caused Morrison to turn his eyes on her.

"I came downstairs," she told him. "No sign of Ryan, though the dog was there, but still wearing his leash. Ryan's phone was on the counter, and the kitchen drawer where he kept a handgun was open, but the gun was gone. And the letter was faceup on the floor. I read it, then called the station house while I was pulling on some clothes. Captain Bowen did the rest."

The judge nodded, looking somber. "You went out there too, though?"

"The second I could." She had been paralyzed for a few moments after telephoning Bowen, had stumbled around the bedroom yanking open the closet door, the bathroom door, the dresser drawer, so completely overcome by terror that her brain had stopped working, her body stiff and shivering violently, her vision reduced to a pinpoint. "I got there maybe thirty seconds before the ambulance."

DeMarco put a hand on her knee. "Soon enough to blow the life back into me."

Morrison said, "I thought we didn't do that anymore. Just the chest compressions."

"Actually Captain Bowen was giving him CPR," Jayme said. "What I did was more of a kiss, I guess. I couldn't help myself."

Now the judge was shaking his head back and forth. He looked from her to DeMarco. "It's a miracle you survived."

"So I'm told," DeMarco said. "I slept through most of the excitement."

"Ha," Morrison said with a little laugh. "I saw the photo of the girl, Trooper Flores, in the paper. Getting the commendation. How's she doing?"

"On the mend," DeMarco answered after a pause. She wasn't doing well. Depressed. Disheartened. Her pretty face always dark with despair. On those occasions once every two or three weeks when she and Boyd and sometimes Bowen joined DeMarco and Jayme for lunch, she always drank too much and eventually lapsed into a brooding silence. She was seeing a therapist but DeMarco could discern no leavening of Flores's misery. For a while back around Christmas he'd thought that she and Boyd were secretly a couple, and maybe they had been, but there were no later indications that the relationship was continuing. And he was reluctant to question Boyd about it. It was their business, not his, he told himself, and told Jayme, who was equally concerned. But neither knew what to do for her.

Now, in the restaurant, Morrison said, "Glad to hear it. The good guys win again." He slipped a hand into his breast pocket. "Listen, the orders come fast here. Do you mind if we get down to business?"

"Please do," DeMarco said.

The judge produced a single sheet of white printer paper, folded twice. He unfolded it and pressed it flat, then centered it on the table between Jayme and DeMarco. "I received this a few days ago," he said. He held the corner of the paper down with the index finger of his left hand, and with his other hand reached for his water glass. It was not yet to his mouth when a young male server appeared with his bottle of Dos Equis and an empty glass. "Gracias," Morrison said as he placed the water glass on the table and picked up the bottle.

On the paper was a photocopy of what appeared to be a letter composed on a sheet torn from a child's school tablet. The printing was childlike but neat, the letters made carefully along the printed lines but sometimes slanting to one side or the other. Jayme and DeMarco leaned together over the paper and silently read:

Dear Sir,

My name is Emmaline Christina Barrie but most people call me Emma. A couple of the teachers call me Emmy but I like Emma better. I am nine years seven months old. My mother thinks that you might be my father. She is sick and said it would be okay if I write to you. Her name is Jennifer Barrie and most people call her Jen or Jennie. I would like very much to know if you are my father and I hope that you would like to know that too. We live at 271 Walker Road in a green and white mobile home. It is in Branch Township in Mason county in Michigan USA 49402. Our telephone number is 906-743-3901. My mother has a cell phone too but she wants you to use the other number because it has a recording machine attached and sometimes our cell service is bad. She said to tell you that she met you one night when you were up here fishing. You can call us if you want to. If you don't want to call you can send an email to mom at jbarrie@yahoo.com. She said to tell you that she is 5 feet 5 inches tall and has dark brown hair and that she met you at the Bear Paw grille which isn't far from where we live. She said you liked to call her Jen-Jen and maybe you will remember that. Okay

that is all I know but she will tell you the rest if you want
to meet us and I hope you do.

Sincerely yours,

Emma Barrie, daughter of Jennifer
Barrie who you called Jen-Jen

P.S. Everybody says I look just like her. I hope that's true
because I think she is beautiful though we are both a little
too skinny especially me.

Jayme was the first to finish reading and look up at the judge,
her eyes sad. He said nothing, gave her a crooked smile, then tipped
up his beer bottle again. It was nearly empty.

When DeMarco looked up from the letter, the judge laid his
hand atop the sheet of paper and slid it back across the table, then
picked it up and folded it and slipped it into his breast pocket again.
"Doesn't that just break your heart?" he asked.

Jayme said, "Is she right?"

"That's what I would like for you two to find out. Discreetly."

"Were you there?" DeMarco asked. "That would be…"

"Ten years, four months ago," Morrison said. "Yes, I was there.
Me and three buddies. We rented a cabin and spent a week there
fishing for walleye and bass. Had them for breakfast, lunch, and dinner, we did. Fried them, baked them, poached them, even toasted
them on a stick. It was one heck of a week."

Jayme asked, "Do you remember Jennifer Barrie?"

"Very well. She spent a good bit of time with us."

"With *us*?" DeMarco asked.

The judge nodded. He leaned into the table and lowered his
voice by a few decibels. "So you can understand my concern. If
the girl is my daughter, I want to do something for her. For both

of them. Good God, I would have done something long ago if I'd had any idea. But I need to be certain, of course."

"Has she also contacted the other men?" Jayme asked.

"Yes and no. The same letter was sent to three of us. One of my friends has passed. I inquired of his widow if she had received a handwritten letter addressed to him from Michigan, and, thank God, she had not. Apparently the elder Ms. Barrie did her research before contacting us."

Jayme asked, "Can we assume that the other two men wish to remain anonymous?"

He nodded. "For the time being. Both are married and want to stay that way. Which is why I am sitting here and they aren't. My wife passed a couple of years ago."

"Sorry to hear that, Judge," DeMarco said.

Morrison leaned back against the booth cushion. "It's why I retired, actually. To be with her at the end. She'd been ill for quite some time."

"I didn't know that," DeMarco said.

"She didn't want anybody to know. A very proud woman. She often said that only the weak enjoy pity."

Jayme held her silence for a few seconds, then said, "I'm not sure why you need us for this job. All you need is a paternity test."

He held her gaze for a moment, looked away, then to DeMarco. "Sergeant, in your honest opinion—and please don't sugarcoat anything on my account—would you say that I have earned a fairly solid reputation after all my years on the bench?"

"I can't think of anyone who doesn't hold you in high esteem."

"Thank you. I would like very much to retain that reputation, and to go out of this world with it intact. The same holds true for my friends. We all rely on a certain public persona, you might say."

Jayme said, "Nobody is going to fault a man for taking care of his child and her mother."

"Of course not. It's the…originating situation, I suppose, that is more than a little indelicate."

"The gangbang," Jayme said, which caused Morrison to flinch.

DeMarco noticed both Morrison's flinch and Jayme's subsequent whisper of a smile. He said, "Just so we're clear on all of this, Judge. Was this little party previously arranged, say through an escort service or—"

"No, no," said Morrison, shaking his head. "It was wholly impromptu. After last call. Jennifer was the barmaid. We were all a little tipsy, dancing, laughing… One of my friends invited her and another female, one of the servers, back to our cabin. The server demurred. Jennifer didn't."

"In other words," Jayme asked, "she didn't go with you expecting payment?"

Morrison shrugged. "Underlying intent is impossible to gauge. She never asked for payment. Yet she never declined our generosity."

DeMarco could feel an uncomfortable heat radiating off Jayme. Morrison was being too careful to whitewash his participation in the affair while subtly demeaning Jennifer. If the conversation continued its present course, Jayme was likely to give the judge a salsa shampoo.

DeMarco asked, "Do you have any idea how sick Jennifer is now?"

"I'm guessing it's serious. Otherwise why contact us after all these years? What you need to know is that my own health is not the best. I've had a couple of 'incidents,' the doctor calls them. Myocardial infarctions. Not uncommon with rheumatoid arthritis."

They waited for him to say more, but when he didn't, Jayme asked, "Okay. But why us? You need one person to follow the little girl around and pick up something she drank from, held, whatever.

You don't need two people who together will cost $400 per day plus expenses. And if I'm not mistaken, DNA testing of a minor child requires the mother's consent."

"Which we will obtain, through the courts if necessary, if this preliminary test comes back positive for one of us. It's not a matter of cost, it's about getting at the truth without exposing ourselves. We worry that if Jennifer is asked for consent to test the girl, she will say no and threaten us with exposure. At this point, being completely in the dark as we are, it would be a terrible mistake to give her an opportunity to take advantage of us in that way."

Jayme chewed on her lower lip for a moment. Looked at DeMarco. He tilted his head. She said, "You're asking us to do something illegal."

"I don't think so. The legality or lack thereof is a gray area here. If I thought for a moment that it would ever become an issue, we would never ask for your assistance. But we need somebody we can trust. And consider the little girl in this. Consider Emma. She wants the truth of who she can call daddy. I believe that her appeal is genuine and without guile. I also believe that she deserves to know the truth, whether she is my daughter or somebody else's."

Again Jayme looked to DeMarco. His face told her nothing, a slight smile, soft eyes, that annoying placidity of expression.

"You have to believe me," Morrison told her. "If that little girl is my daughter, I will make damn certain that she and her mother are well taken care of for a long, long time to come. I have two kids of my own already, and three grandchildren, but there is plenty of money to go around. Plenty of room for another child in my will. My friends feel exactly the same way."

"If the test is positive for one of you," Jayme asked, "will that person then go public as her father?"

"I can't speak for the other two," he said, "but I, without question, will own up to my responsibility. But I have to be honest with you. I don't have a lot of time left to play the doting father. It is a hard but irrevocable truth. The next infarction could well be my last."

Another silence befell their booth, which only made the ambient noise seem louder and more intrusive. Morrison again leaned forward, his belly against the table. "All we are asking is for someone reliable and unimpeachably honest to acquire, very discreetly, a sample of the girl's DNA, and to certify that Jennifer's illness is not just a ploy."

"A ploy?" Jayme asked. "Are you insinuating that Jennifer is blackmailing you now? Ten years after the fact?"

Again Morrison winced. "I'm sorry," he said. "I'm sure that's not the case. It's just that this is highly embarrassing for me. Behaving the way we did, having to remember all of that now…" He shook his head. Then addressed DeMarco. "I have the least to lose. My friends are still working, still married. For them, I ask that you indulge our request for the utmost discretion. No mention of my name, no reference to me whatsoever, no implication that you are working on behalf of all of us. You bring the information and test sample to me, and my friends and I will have it tested. If it's a positive match for one of us, then and only then will that man come out of the shadows, so to speak. And then the child and her mother will want for nothing. Trust me. I would *love* to provide that dear little girl with the future she deserves. Every time I read this letter of hers, I weep. My heart aches for her. But why risk blemishing a sterling reputation, or three of them, until we know the truth? If the truth is that I do have a daughter, then, by God, I will embrace that truth. And to be completely honest about it, a part of me longs to be Emma's father. I loved every second of raising my boys. And

I have had plenty of time to regret that my job kept me away from them so much. To be given another chance to do a better job? To feel a child's love again?"

He stared down at the table for a moment. Then he raised his eyes to Jayme. "I am deeply embarrassed to recognize the lack of dignity with which my friends and I comported ourselves on that fishing trip. Utterly and completely embarrassed. But our activities were wholly consensual, I want you to know that. Jennifer was fully aware of what she was doing. Still, in this current era of…"

Again he averted his eyes for a few moments and looked out upon the assembled diners. Then his gaze trailed slowly around the room to fall upon the mural of the Hispanic *Last Supper*. "Shakespeare said it best, didn't he? 'No legacy is so rich as honesty.'"

DeMarco and Jayme watched his face as he continued to consider the mural. His mouth seemed to be trying but failing to hold a smile, the lips going crooked as his eyes narrowed and forehead pinched, which caused their faces, in sympathetic response, to mirror his. He was either on the verge of tears or suffering from acid reflux.

"Judge," DeMarco said, only to be interrupted by the arrival of their dinners.

The young male server placed the heavy plates in front of Jayme and DeMarco, muttered "*Cuidado, muy caliente,*" then slid away. Estella set a large foam take-out box in a plastic bag atop the judge's place mat, which caused him to turn.

"Ah gracias, gracias," he said, and started pushing himself to the edge of the seat. Estella answered with a nod and a smile and moved away.

The judge stood and picked up his take-out dinner. "You two make a drive up to Michigan," he said to Jayme and DeMarco, "or fly, if you'd rather. Take as much time as you need. Spend a couple of extra nights on Mackinac Island if you feel like it, put it all on my tab." With his free hand he reached into his side pocket and fished out a yellow Post-it Note and handed it to DeMarco. "The Barries' address. I appreciate you meeting with me, I really do. Enjoy your supper. It's on me."

# SEVENTEEN

## THE PHOTONS WALTZ, THE ILLUSION SHIMMERS

Shortly after the judge's departure from the Mexican restaurant, DeMarco started eating. Jayme sat still a while longer, sorting out her feelings. She didn't like the judge and was uncertain whether to trust him or not. But that sentiment hadn't arisen until he brought up the fishing trip. Four men and one woman.

On the other hand, was she being too presumptive? Even sexist? If four men can have sex with one woman, why blame the woman for that? Why is she the one who gets dragged through the dirt?

If it even happened in Jennifer Barrie's case. Maybe it did, she told herself, and maybe it didn't. But let's say that it did, and that Jennifer accepted the men's money for it. Did that make her a prostitute? No more than it would make a wife a prostitute when she uses sex to get what she wants from her husband.

And when you get right down to it, Jayme argued with herself, why shouldn't a woman have the right to use her body however she wished? If a woman is forced to choose between earning $12,000 a year by selling beers and greasy hamburgers, for example, or making $100,000 a year by selling her body, why shouldn't she be not only permitted but encouraged to better her life? Why shouldn't she be encouraged to lift herself and her children out of poverty and despair in any way she can?

But now Jayme also had to ask herself: Was it unfair for her to resent the judge and his friends for taking part in those activities?

She cut a chunk from her chicken and sausage dish and forked it into her mouth and chewed. Swallowed it and tasted nothing. After her second bite, she sat with the fork standing in her hand. "I think we should go to Michigan," she said.

"Okay," DeMarco answered.

"What? Just okay? Just like that?"

"I've always wanted to visit that state. Hemingway spent summers in the Upper Peninsula as a boy. Most of his Nick Adams stories are set there. And we have an RV parked in the backyard. If we're never going to use it, we should sell it."

"That's why you want to go? To hang out with the ghost of Hemingway?"

"It's not the reason why. More like a second reason why not to not go."

"And what's the first reason?"

"The girl, of course. Emma."

"Okay," Jayme said. "You want to talk about Morrison's actions, his motivations, any of that?"

"I don't *need* to. But we can if you want to." He sliced his beef enchilada in half, lifted up one half with his knife and fork and laid it on Jayme's plate.

"None of that matters to you?"

"None of it makes me feel any less compassion for the girl. Or for her mother, for that matter. The woman is reaching out. In desperation, I think."

"What makes you think that?"

He shrugged. "Just a feeling."

Okay, she could buy into that. Knowing that you know without knowing how you know. It happened to her all the time. Yet when it came from somebody else, she craved more information. More words.

She tasted the enchilada. "This is good. You want to try mine?"

He reached across to her plate, used his fork to cut off a piece of chicken, speared it and stuck it in his mouth. "I prefer the spicy version," he said.

"You think she's so sick that she's searching for a father for her child before she dies?"

"She's fearful of something. Why didn't *she* write the letter? Why didn't she call the judge and the other men and speak to them personally? Why didn't she send an email? Why encourage a child to send a personal note in a child's words and a child's handwriting?"

"You think she's being manipulative?"

He smiled. "Everything a person does is manipulative, isn't it? Every kiss, every handshake, every kind or harsh word. It's what we do, who we are. Some of us are better at it or more obvious or more deceitful than others. But we all do it."

"Is that supposed to be an answer, Ryan? Do you expect me to read your mind? Are you just playing with me here or what?"

"Yes. No. Maybe," he said, and gave her a shove with his shoulder.

"Babe, please. Let's figure this out. A smiling Buddha just isn't going to do it tonight, no matter how sexy you look when your eyes crinkle up like that."

"That was the name of India's first successful nuclear test. Operation Smiling Buddha."

"You're going to make *me* go nuclear if you keep this up."

"Love you madly," he said.

"Arrrgh!" She took a drink of water. Dragged a chip through

the salsa and popped it into her mouth. Chewed and swallowed. "Okay, practical issue," she said. "The car will get us to Michigan a lot faster than the RV, and a lot cheaper. Flying will get us there even quicker."

"RV, baby," he said.

"That's a whole day of driving. Aren't you supposed to avoid opportunities to get a pulmonary embolism?"

"I'll do laps in the aisle while you drive. We'll be fine."

"What about Hero?"

"He'll love it. Our first vacation together. I wonder if dogs are allowed on Mackinac Island. I know cars aren't."

"Ryan," she said, "Morrison and his friends want us to spy on a little girl and her mother. What are we supposed to do—steal a lock of Emma's hair while she's sleeping?"

"Hair is unreliable."

"You know what I mean. You're okay with all of this discretion, as he calls it?"

Again he shrugged. "Things happen when they're supposed to happen."

"And what is that supposed to mean?"

"Isn't an investigation by its nature discreet?"

"What is *that* supposed to mean?"

"It means what it means, darlin'. Everything means what it means."

She still hadn't gotten used to his *all's right with the world* attitude. His docility. His Zen-like koans and cosmic truths. She believed that he believed that he had had an authentic near-death visit to the astral plane, but so much of it had been troubling to her, even frightening. Pain is still pain, loss is still loss, death is still death. She wished she could experience his equanimity for a while, just to see how it felt. But what if it was all a delusion? What if something had been damaged in his brain, and he never recovered from it?

He chuckled.

"What?" she said.

"Your tension is like a feather tickling my nose."

"My what is what?"

"Relax, baby. You have a nice plate of free food in front of you. We have an offer of a free vacation with very little effort involved. And we have each other. All's right with—"

"Don't you say it," she interrupted.

Again he chuckled. "*Sei bellissima*," he said, and kissed her cheek. "Everything happens for a reason."

That was precisely what Lathea, the psychic she had visited prior to her miscarriage, had said. But DeMarco hadn't heard that conversation, hadn't been in the room at the time, and Jayme had never repeated it to him. She had been skeptical when Lathea said it, was even more skeptical now. This man beside her—who was he? Where was her DeMarco?

"Hold on a minute," she told him. "If everything happens for a reason, and everything is as it's supposed to be, why should we do anything at all? Why should we even worry about Emma and her mom if everything is as it should be?"

And for a moment, then, his eyebrows knitted together, his lips pursed, and he looked troubled. But soon his forehead smoothed and a little smile relaxed his mouth. "Everything is as it's supposed to be *at that moment*. But change is the rule, the guiding principle. All is flux. All is refinement, correction, rectification. And that, my love, is the reason for everything. Change. And its potential for improvement."

She almost groaned out loud. Another cosmic truth. She needed to start writing these things down. They could publish a little book of them, the kind of book full of sappy sentiments that got sold in the Hallmark stores. She regarded him with her head cocked, her mouth a thin line of bemusement.

God, how she wanted to throttle him. But she also wanted to believe him. Life as a beautifully choreographed dance, but one whose steps we write as we make them? She didn't know whether he had awakened from his coma as a gentle lunatic or a shaman.

He smiled as if he knew what she was thinking. Shrugged. Said, "We're all just photons anyway. All clinging together in an illusion of matter. But that doesn't make us any less real. These chili rellenos are really good. You want a bite?"

She shook her head. Pondered the possibilities as he finished his meal. Then something moved to her immediate right and she caught it out of the corner of her eye. But there was a wall to her immediate right, the garishly painted mural static and unchanging. She studied the Hispanic Jesus's face. That crooked smile, one eyebrow raised—why hadn't she noticed that oddly taunting expression before?

# EIGHTEEN

G randma Loey had showed Emma how to make the filling for graham cracker cookies by stirring canned condensed milk into a quarter cup of powdered sugar, then adding a few drops of artificial vanilla flavoring from the little brown bottle in the cupboard. After you spread the paste over one graham cracker and pressed another one atop it, you had to put the whole plate full of cookies into the refrigerator until the paste hardened a little. That way the paste didn't drip out between the crackers when you dipped the cookie in milk.

"We could have used chocolate syrup instead of vanilla if you had any," Grandma Loey said. "I like chocolate better but this will have to do."

Grandma Loey lived somewhere back through the Manistee where Emma had never been, but now she was staying in the trailer with Emma, making sure she got a bowl of cereal in the morning and got on the bus on time, though these were all things Emma did by herself and always had. But it was Saturday now and Grandma was watching *Divorce Court* on TV while the paste on the crackers hardened and Emma as usual had one of her library books spread open on her lap. Grandma Loey never wanted to play Tenzi or do a puzzle or anything interesting. Sometimes she would give Emma a nickel and let her do a couple of the scratch-off tickets but Emma never asked to do that anymore because her grandmother seemed to blame her when the ticket wasn't a winner and they never were.

"I don't know how anybody can live without cable," Grandma said. "Even I get cable. What kind of house don't have cable in this day and age?"

Emma sat there on the vinyl-covered banquette and smiled and said nothing and tried to keep reading, but in her mind she could hear her mother answering Grandma Loey's complaint with, "We can't afford cable, and besides TV will rot your brain." It was what her mother always said, especially the *we can't afford it* part. It used to make Emma mad to hear it all of the time but now when she thought of her mother she just wanted to cry, and she thought about her nearly all of the time, except for those moments when she could lose herself in one of the books from the school library. She had read all of the Goosebumps and Nightmares! and Holes books plus *A Wrinkle in Time* and the Narnia books and the first four Harry Potter books and everything else on the fifth-grade reading lists and half of the sixth's. She was finishing fourth grade this year and planned to start on the seventh-grade reading list by summer. But first she planned to read *Little Women* again because it was her favorite book ever and one she never had to return to the library. Mrs. Wilkerson had given it to Emma to keep because "nobody but you has checked it out since 1992," she'd said.

Emma liked Beth best of the four March sisters and thought it would be nice to have a kitten and a piano someday. She always cried a little when Beth died, and after that part the rest of the novel wasn't as interesting. She kept the book on her headboard and read several pages every night that the Gray Man came and stood in the corner of her room. She wasn't afraid of him anymore because he never did anything but stand there and look at her, and by the time she was six she had learned that she could make him disappear just by turning on her ballerina light, which her mom had bought for her for $3 at a yard sale once. Whenever she wanted the Gray Man to go away she would turn on the light and read from *Little Women* for a while. Sometimes she could feel him there even after he disappeared but she didn't care. He reminded her a little of James Laurence from the *Little Women* book, the kind old man who gave Beth March a piano. Emma imagined he would be nice to her too if he could but of course there isn't much you can do when you are a spirit, her mother had said. There were some who could push things off a table or make a shiny penny appear at your feet, and there was one time, Emma's mother had said, when the spirit of her grandfather had stepped in front of her as solid as a wall to keep her from getting hit by a car, but in most cases the spirits were limited to hanging around and moving light things like pennies and feathers and maybe now and then a fork. Her mother's grandfather was one of the rare ones who could control matter, her mother had explained. Because it's all about the power of intention and how much you really want something. Just like prayer, her mother had said. You have to want something very badly or prayer won't work.

Emma had been doing a lot of praying this past week, all of it asking for her mother to get better and come home. It didn't seem to be working, though, which Emma couldn't understand since there was nothing more in the whole world that she wanted as badly as she wanted that.

Today Emma was trying to not think about her mother being sick by reading *Eragon* but she wasn't able to concentrate on the book because Grandma kept the TV too loud. "Are we going to go see Mom today?" she asked. She liked sitting on her mother's high hospital bed and being held close and sharing the dreams they had

had since the last visit. Grandma would go down to the cafeteria for coffee or would probably go outside to smoke because Emma could always smell it on her afterward. And that was why she didn't really care that Grandma Loey had "never been very big on hugging," as she often said.

In answer to Emma's question about going to the hospital that day, Grandma didn't even look away from the TV, not even for a quick little glance. "I am so tired of that place. It wears me down just being there."

It wore Emma down too. Always made her feel heavy and sleepy and sad to see her mother getting tired and weak just from lying there talking. Emma was never allowed to stay in the room very long and sometimes she had to wait a long time before a nurse would let her go into the room at all. Sometimes she could hear her mother screaming at the nurse and sometimes her mother would start talking funny or laughing at nothing at all. Still, Emma had never been away from her mother like this before, the two of them sleeping in different places. And Grandma Loey didn't like sharing the bed the way Emma's mom used to. Her mom never said, "Go on back to your own bed. You take up too much room, and I need to get some sleep." Mom always just made room and tucked Emma in close to her. It made the days lonesome without her and the nights even lonesomer.

Grandma Loey had come in her own little car eight days ago but she said she couldn't afford the gas to drive to the hospital every day even though it wasn't all that far. It was only nineteen miles away. Emma knew because she had watched the odometer during their first trip to the hospital. And at the end of that day, when they returned to the trailer, Emma had said, "Thirty-eight miles, Grandma. That's how far it is to the hospital and back."

"Good lord," Grandma Loey had said. "That's two whole gallons of gas every trip we make. We need to cut down on going there too often."

Since then they had visited the hospital only twice, the last time four days ago for just a few minutes after school. Emma wished she hadn't watched the darned odometer at all, hadn't said a single word about it. She missed her mom so much. She had never before understood what a terrible ache it is to miss somebody. The whole body hurts like it's coming down with the flu or something, but even worse. All Grandma Loey ever wanted to do was watch TV and complain about not having cable and not having anything decent in the house to eat. "I oughta start going to school with you and getting those free lunches every day," Grandma said. "You don't know how lucky you are to get a nice hot meal every day." One day though when Emma got off the bus and came back home, the trailer smelled like hamburgers and French fries, and when Grandma was in the bathroom Emma looked in the trash can and found the Burger King bag all crumpled up with ketchup stains on it. Another day she smelled something sweet and found the little bag and paper tray the Taco Bell Cinnabon Delights came in. At Emma's first visit to the hospital, where her mother had been for two days then, Emma's mom had pulled her close and hugged her and asked Loey, "Is my baby getting enough to eat? Are you feeding her good, Mom?" And Grandma Loey said something like, "I'm doing what I can with what little you give me. You got another twenty in that purse of yours?"

Emma liked to lie in the hospital bed with her mother while her mother kissed Emma's head and stroked her hair. "When are you coming home, Mommy? I miss having you there."

"I miss you too, baby girl. Mommy's trying to get better. I really am."

But on Emma's second visit, her mother didn't look any better.

She looked even sicker than Emma remembered her. She was getting thin and her face was gray and on that visit she didn't like it when Emma leaned against her too hard. "My skin's just sore right now, baby," she said. "It's just sensitive is all."

"Why aren't the doctors making you better?" Emma asked.

"They're trying, honey. There's just not a lot they can do right now."

"Then you should come home with me and I'll take care of you."

"I will, baby girl, I promise. I'll be doing that pretty soon, I think. You just keep praying and try to be patient for me, okay? I need for you to be patient."

There was another woman in a bed in the same room with Emma's mom, and Emma didn't like being around sick people she did not know. Maybe the other woman was who was making Emma's mom sick and keeping her from getting better. If Emma's mom came home Emma would open a can of chicken noodle soup and heat it in the microwave. She knew how to make grilled cheese sandwiches too in the little black skillet.

To her grandmother now, Emma said, "Can we take some of the graham cracker cookies to Mom today?"

"I told you I'm spending too much money on gas for that. I'm not made of money, you know. Your mother only gives me so much. I can't make it out of thin air."

Emma was doing her best to pray really hard and to be patient. But being patient wasn't easy. Doing anything without Mommy in the house wasn't easy. If she had a piano it might be easier, but where would they put a piano in a mobile home? If she had a kitten she would have somebody to hug anytime she felt like it. But now, on a day when she wasn't in school, all she had was her grandmother, who didn't like to hug and sometimes smelled of cigarettes, and who kept reminding her that she wasn't too big for a good spanking, or that Loey had "took a switch to your mother more than once and I'm not too old to do the same to you." Emma didn't know what a switch was, so she'd asked her phone and finally found a definition that fit: "A switch is a thin branch cut from a tree, used for striking, often as corporal punishment." There were a lot of trees around the trailer. It made Emma tremble just to look out the window and see all of those thin branches just waiting to be pulled down.

One night when her grandmother seemed especially angry, Emma lay on her bed and prayed to the Gray Man to not let Loey go outside and grab a switch. Later that night the Gray Man showed up, just standing there watching her as he always did. But his face looked especially sad that night, and Emma understood that he was telling her with that face that he was just a spirit and couldn't do much of anything about anything. She cried then but with her own face pressed to the pillow, because Grandma didn't like the sound of her crying either.

# NINETEEN

M arcescence," DeMarco mumbled.

The drive that Friday to Michigan's Mason County, near the center of the west coast of the Lower Peninsula, had taken 136 times longer than Jayme and DeMarco's discussion and ensuing decision to accept Morrison's job offer. Both he and Jayme were road weary and hungry when they arrived at the used car lot west of their destination, where Jayme had arranged to pick up their rental car, a black Jetta. She found the keys under the gas cap, just where the manager had promised they would be, then followed the RV to a campground in Scottville, where she found a place to walk Hero while DeMarco got the RV hooked up. Then in the thickening darkness they left Hero in the RV with his favorite squeaky toy while she and DeMarco took the Jetta to Walker Road for a bit of preliminary surveillance.

She parked as close to the drainage ditch as possible, fifteen yards back from the dirty white mailbox with *Barrie* hand-painted across the side, and hoped no large truck came by to knock the little car into the ditch. Then, as the sun slowly buried itself behind the trees, leaving only a dusky gray glow, she slid her seat back and opened up the laptop while DeMarco studied the mobile home and its surroundings. They had been sitting there in weary silence for twenty minutes when he muttered, "Marcescence."

Jayme looked up from her laptop, which was braced with one edge against her belly, the upraised lid leaning against the steering wheel. "What, babe?" she asked.

"Sorry. Just thinking out loud." He brought his gaze back around to the green-and-white single-wide parked in a cleared pocket of scraggly yard surrounded by a half circle of second growth timber. To the immediate left of the car were tall pines full of dark needles, but the oaks and other hardwood trees just beyond the other end of the trailer were still bare of spring's first red buds, with some branches holding on to the dead brown leaves of the previous fall, the other limbs naked and skeletal and looking black against a glaucous sky. A single light glowed dimly through the curtain over the trailer's biggest window. The nose of an avocado-green compact car was visible parked behind the trailer.

"What were you thinking out loud about?" she asked.

"Marcescence. I like the sound of it."

"What does that word mean?"

"Nothing as pretty as the way it sounds. It's when dead plant material doesn't fall away from the living plant. Like those brown leaves still hanging on for dear life."

She looked through the windshield, said, "How can they hang on for dear life if they're dead?"

He smiled. Thought, *Because dead isn't dead.* Told her, "Sitting here like this stopped being productive ten minutes before it started. I'm starving and you must be too. I could go for a big salad right now. With grilled salmon maybe. Something easy on the stomach."

"You want to leave?"

He shrugged. "Any luck with social media?"

"There's an old MySpace page, mostly pics of her and her friends partying. More recently, though not all that recent, over four years old, looks like she was trying to promote herself on Pinterest as a Reiki master. She was working on her level 2 certification, but that was…over four years ago. Nothing on Pinterest since then. Facebook…lots of photos of sunsets and autumn trees, deer, squirrels, birds, but mostly of Emma. She's a cutie." She swung the laptop around so that he could peruse the photos, which he did without comment.

"Tell you what," he finally said. "Back up another twenty yards. If I go in through the pines, I can come out around the back of the trailer and get the plate number on that vehicle. I'll sneak up close to the trailer too and see if I can hear anything."

"See if you can hear?" she said, smiling, and passed the laptop over to him. "Don't you have to *listen* to hear?"

"I have to listen to see if I can hear."

She chuckled and slipped the gearshift into Reverse. "We're both road punchy, aren't we?"

He smiled, nodded. "*Marcescence*," he said again. "It's too lovely a word to mean what it means. It should mean something else. *Il mare* means the sea in Italian. So maybe marcescence could mean the essence of the sea."

"Sounds fishy to me," she answered, and they both chuckled again.

≫————————≪

The woods were damp and fragrant and redolent of DeMarco's boyhood. It felt good to be moving again, on legs instead of wheels, stretching the kinks out of his muscles, sucking up the clean air. He picked his way between the pines, enjoying the scent and whispery silence of the needles and branches, occasionally laying a hand on the rough bark or pushing a branch out of the way. As he closed in on the trailer an oscillating mumble of voices and a canned laugh track filtered toward him, and he felt a sudden frisson of déjà vu, knew he had done all this before, not just once but numerous times. How many drug dealers and weed farmers and meth cooks had he sneaked up on in venues similar to this? How many deadbeat dads and pea-brained drunks who thought they could escape their crimes behind a hollow metal door? But this time he was sneaking up on a little girl. Why? It wasn't even necessary. But he wanted to. Felt a need to put a living face to the name, to the letter that had broken his heart. Wanted to make sure she was okay. And her mother too. Was Jennifer really sick or running a con, just a manipulative woman and maybe in cahoots with some pea-brained man, thinking they could shake down a district judge over a ten-year-old gangbang?

He came out of the pines and approached the green compact from the rear, a battered Corolla. Used his cell phone to snap a quick shot of the license plate, then texted it to Jayme. Then he crossed to the trailer and stood with a shoulder against the metal panel near the rear corner, stood very still and heard only the television set. No living voices. The surrounding area was all woods, with farmland across the blacktop road. A distant crow, its caw full of lament. *What a lonesome place this must be for a little girl*, he thought. If he were scoring this scene for a movie, he would put it to Pink Floyd's mournful "Marooned."

He moved farther along, creeping toward the first yellow light as it shone through a side window near the back. Then stood at the bottom corner of the window, pushed himself up on his toes till his calves shrieked, steadied himself with one hand flat against the metal, fingers splayed, and peeked inside through an opening in the flowered curtain. A girl. Flat on her back on the bed. "Emma," he whispered to himself.

She was wearing jeans and a yellow sweatshirt and pink socks, lay there thin and motionless with eyes open and staring at the ceiling, a book open against her chest. Yep, that would be her. Nine years old. Emmaline Barrie. Brown-haired innocent and fatherless child.

He brought himself down onto flat feet again. *Damn*, he thought. He'd been hoping she wasn't real. Hoping no child had to live that way. Though he knew that millions did, and in circumstances far worse than hers.

He was always wrestling with pain these days, it seemed. Weltschmerz, it was called in German. World pain. The pain seemed permanently locked in an arm wrestling match with a sense that all was copacetic, the universe in eternal tickety-boo. He knew how ridiculous he must sound to Jayme sometimes with his cosmic truths and other remembered bits; he sounded ridiculous to himself, to the old DeMarco, the one without a stitched-up hole in his chest.

*Okay, enough of this*, he told himself. *Emma Barrie, check. Now for the mama bear.* He hunkered down low and crept along close to the building in case she might be looking out a window. Moved toward the sound coming from the television. And heard it growing louder step-by-step.

The wide rectangular window a third of the way back from the front end. Living room probably. Again he raised himself up on his toes, saw a woman crossing toward him from the kitchen, coffee cup in hand, and immediately dropped into a low hunker again, hands flat against the cool grass. But the glimpse had been enough. The woman was too old to be Emma's mother. Skinny, haggard, lank gray hair.

Okay, time to skedaddle. Still in his hunker, he turned. And saw for just a moment a man all in gray staring at him from the rear of the trailer. DeMarco sucked in an involuntary breath and faltered sideways. Caught and righted himself. But now no one was there.

He held himself still, blinked, waited and stared and listened. Only the TV. What the heck?

He raised himself a little and quickly monkey-walked to the rear of the trailer, stood and looked around. Nobody. Not a soul in sight. He slipped back into the trees, alert for an ambush. None came.

He emerged from the pines and onto the road and brushed off what felt like cobwebs covering his face. Climbed back into the passenger seat and eased the door shut. "Did you see a man over there?" he asked.

"Now?" Jayme asked. She had the laptop in front of her again, but closed it and passed it to DeMarco.

"I thought I saw a man watching me behind the trailer. He was there but then he wasn't."

"You definitely are road punchy, babe. I didn't see anybody."

"Okay. I guess so. What about the license plate?"

"The vehicle is registered to one Lois Irena Barrie. Sixty-four years old. Resident of Haslett, which is a few miles east of Lansing."

"And Lansing is how far from here?"

"Two to three hours, I'd guess."

"Sixty-four, huh? Yeah, I guess so. But hard years. Jennifer's mother probably."

"You saw her?"

"The girl too. No sign of Jennifer."

"Could be out partying."

"A couple of hours is a long way to come to babysit. If Jennifer is really sick, she might be in the hospital."

"What was Emma doing when you saw her?"

"Lying on her back on the bed."

"Was she sleeping?"

"Staring up at the ceiling. She had a book open atop her chest."

"Did she look sad?"

"I don't really know," he told her, though that was not the whole truth. Better to change the subject. "Any luck finding a place to eat?"

"There's no Applebee's in Scottville. Ludington, yes, but that's another nine miles. There is a burger joint in Scottville, plus pizza, Asian, and an Old Country Buffet."

"Anybody deliver?"

"I bet the pizza place does. You want to dine in tonight?"

"Let's, okay? It will make Hero happy. And give us time to check with the local hospitals. I've had enough excitement for the day."

"If you really want a big salad with grilled salmon…"

"Pizza and a basic salad is fine. Manna from heaven."

"What about your stomach? Pizza isn't a soothing food."

"We have milk, right? It will balance things out."

She shook her head. Then told him, "Buckle up," and started the engine.

He reached for the strap, juggling the laptop while clicking the belt into place. "Who did you speak with back home?"

"Carmichael tracked the plate down. But then Boyd came on for a minute, just to say hello."

"He must be doing p.m. shift tonight. Or back-to-back. Everybody okay?"

"Boyd said he would like to talk with us about Dani when we get home."

"Uh-oh. What about her?"

"He wouldn't say. Said it could wait until we get back. Nothing serious. Just talk, he said. You know Boyd."

"I know he wouldn't have said anything at all if he wasn't concerned about something."

"He's concerned about her being depressed all the time, that's my guess. Stuck behind a desk. I'd be depressed too."

*Because of me*, he thought, but said nothing more. There he was fluctuating again. Old DeMarco, new DeMarco, old DeMarco. He was doing more flipping lately than a line cook at IHOP.

He watched out the side window all the way to the campground. He was sure he hadn't merely imagined a man standing near the trailer. He was 90 percent certain of it. Or 75 percent anyway. A man in a gray suit. His shirt had been gray too, hadn't it? And his face too, now that he thought about it. Wait; did the man even have a face? DeMarco couldn't remember one. No face and no feet.

*No feet?* he asked himself. *You're just now remembering that? You really are punchy, aren't you?*

# TWENTY

## No pain like the present

Flores trudged into her apartment, closed and locked the door and immediately started stripping off and kicking away her uniform even as she shuffled to the refrigerator, took out a fresh bottle of chardonnay, unscrewed the cap and took a swig. Then she poured half of the bottle into a water glass and, now wearing only panties and a bra and her leg brace, dropped onto the sofa, picked up the remote and clicked the TV on. Connected to the internet and pulled up the YouTube mix she had watched the previous night. Skipped a Liberty Mutual ad and waited for the first song to start. Bonnie Raitt and Jackson Browne singing "My Opening Farewell."

God, he looked so young back then. They both did. The video was at least ten years old. And she, Flores, had been what at the time? Twelve or thirteen. Still playing with white Barbie dolls and Tonka trucks. Dreaming of being a badass Barbie with a killer body and a gun.

Stupid. Stupid things we think about when we're young.

Raitt and Browne sitting side by side onstage, both dressed in black, the light dim, her red hair a cascading halo against the blue-black backdrop, his hair as dark as his hooded eyes. Their blond-faced guitars. Raitt singing melody, Browne harmonizing.

Dani drank from the glass and leaned back against the sofa and turned up the volume and let the music flow over her. Felt it entering in slowly at first, cool like the wine in her mouth, warm in her stomach. A little of the rigidity began seeping out of her shoulders, out of her neck. Those lethargic guitar licks washed against her cheeks, brushed away the stiffness in her jaw. Raitt's voice like a nameless longing, Browne's an ancient sadness.

This song did things to her, no denying it. The melody stroked her like a mother's weary hand. And Browne had written it when he was not much older than she was now. Too young to write a song that old, pain that deep. A man searching for something hopeful to say but knowing how futile, how stupid to hope.

God, if only she had his talent. Or Raitt's. She had a little talent and a whole bunch of pain and not a second of training. No pretty words, no poetry. A fatal combination if ever she'd seen one. Like wine and Elavil. Gonna do her in sooner or later. The sooner the better.

She looked to the side wall where the Yamaha keyboard stood, the one DeMarco and Jayme had given her for Christmas. She loved it but just wasn't up to it tonight. Would feel like a clumsy child sitting down at a grand piano to play chopsticks. She thought about going to the bedroom for her little keyboard, maybe try to pick out the chords by watching Raitt's and Browne's hands on the strings. Maybe with time she could learn to play and sing like that. Write songs like that to slip their gentle needles into the skin, like kind and loving needles to shoot their magic into people's veins, help them forget all the shit of their lives, help her to leave all the shit of her own life behind.

Yeah, right. Like she could ever do that. A gimp with a toy piano. Voice like a saw blade, her father had said. Yeah, well, he didn't know everything, did he? Didn't know anything, as a matter of fact. Still...

Like she had a shot at anything now. Public communications officer, that was her life. PCO. Get used to it, *chica*. From cop to charity case. This is your prison now, like it or not. Purgatory *para siempre*. Forever and ever, big fucking amen.

# TWENTY-ONE

## The frayed, the frail, the unforgiven

I hate the smell of hospitals in the morning," DeMarco whispered to her in the elevator. Jayme gave his ribs a little elbow-jab.

At the nurses' station on the third floor, DeMarco stood a few feet back from the desk while Jayme approached the male nurse in blue scrubs seated behind it. He was a young man slightly over-weight, round-shouldered, and with a black, neatly clipped goatee.

"Hi," Jayme said. "I called last night about my sister, Jennifer Barrie? I was told I could speak with her doctor today about her condition?"

Something like a momentary panic flashed in the man's eyes. "I'm sorry. She was transferred out early this morning."

"Transferred where?"

He looked at her, blinked. Then turned away, leaned over a file already open on the desk, and read for a few seconds. To Jayme he said, "Okay, she did list a sister as next of kin. What is your name?"

"Jayme Barrie Matson. The nurse last night told me that I could—"

"Sorry, but that's not the name she provided."

"Look, we've been…estranged, okay? We haven't spoken to each other in years. Mom called me just the other night, and I got here as soon as I could. I love my sister, I do. We just had a falling-out, is all. But I need to know what's wrong with her. Where has she been transferred, and why?"

He kept his eyes steady on hers, blew out a long breath. "She was taken to Great Heart Hospice this morning."

Jayme hadn't expected that; her look of shock was genuine. "Hospice care? For God's sake, *why*? Please, you need to tell me what is wrong with my sister."

A few moments passed, then he leaned into the desk. Jayme leaned toward him. "Officially," he said, "there has been no agreement on the diagnosis. But it looks a lot like Creutzfeldt-Jakob disease. She's in a coma now. It's the final stage. I've been trying to get in touch with her mother all morning but it keeps going to voicemail."

Jayme fought a rush of dizziness, didn't want to think about what this development forebode for Emma. "I don't know anything about that disease."

"The symptoms are like Alzheimer's and Huntington's, but it can come on fast, as it did in your sister's case. According to the file, she had her first symptoms about seven weeks ago, but she didn't see a doctor until ten days ago, when she started hallucinating."

"It's neurological?"

He nodded. "A degenerative brain disorder. But don't worry, it's not hereditary. Unfortunately, there's no real treatment for it. Most people suffer for a year or so after the initial symptoms. Your sister is one of the lucky ones. Her coma was induced for her own safety. She won't come out of it."

Jayme stared helplessly at him for a few moments, nauseated and weak. "When will she...?"

"It could happen anytime. I give her a week at the most."

Her left knee buckled, but she pulled straight and locked it in place.

DeMarco touched her shoulder; she turned and drew away from the desk.

"I'm sorry," the young man said. "I've been trying to call her mother."

"Keep trying, please." Then she walked with DeMarco back to the elevator. Stood waiting for the door to open. Walked in and went to the corner and leaned against the wall.

DeMarco stepped in and hit the Lobby button, went to her as the doors closed with a hiss and slipped both arms around her. She leaned into him, her face pressed into the side of his neck, hands clutching at his waist, fingers pinching and squeezing his flesh, and sobbed for a woman she did not know, sobbed for a mother and her soon-to-be motherless child.

# TWENTY-TWO

IF THE CAT DEVOURS THE MOUSE,
DOES THE MOUSE BECOME THE CAT?

t was supposed to be spring but DeMarco stood with both hands atop the damp roof of the rental car in the hospital's parking lot, his body against the closed door, and inhaled two long breaths of November. He didn't like the taste of it. Jayme sat in the passenger seat with her hands on her lap, staring through the windshield. The sky was gunmetal gray, the sun occluded behind an irregular wall of dirty clouds.

After a minute or so Jayme turned to look out the driver's side window but could see only DeMarco's waist and chest, the gray fleece pullover he had chosen for the day. She leaned across the console and knocked on the glass.

He opened the door and climbed in frowning. Closed the door and said, "I don't like this at all."

She nodded, her eyes still wet. "Tell me again how she looked last night," she said.

He cocked his head.

"Emma. When you saw her through the trailer window."

He called the image back, watched it forming. "Like a little girl," he told her. "Kind of skinny, I guess. She was wearing jeans and socks and some kind of sweatshirt. Pink socks, I think. Yeah, they were pink."

"What color was her sweatshirt?"

"Yellow. But like a washed-out yellow, you know?"

"Sort of butter yellow?"

"You could say that, yeah."

"What color was her hair?"

"Baby," he told her, and laid a hand atop hers. "You're just hurting yourself now."

"I want to see her too. Same as you did."

"You saw the photos on Facebook."

"It's not the same. I want to see her the way you did. Describe her hair for me."

"She has brown hair. A little darker than medium brown. And cut fairly short, I think. Though she was lying down, so... She had a little earring, it would be her left ear I saw. A little blue stud. It sparkled from the light overhead."

"And what was she doing? You said her eyes were open?"

He nodded. "Staring at the ceiling, thinking, dreaming, it's impossible to say. But there was a book open on her chest. And she had her hands crossed over her belly."

"What was the book?"

"Baby, I don't know. It was just a quick glance."

"She was probably lying there thinking about her mom," Jayme said. "Missing her and worrying about her."

"Probably." He didn't want this to go too far, didn't want her to start sobbing again. He knew what it was like to feel every child's pain. Knew how it drained the body and withered the soul. Especially when you do not understand that you *are* every child, that every child is you, and that all pain is your pain, all love your love, every moment a moment in the life that is life.

"I don't like what we're doing here," he told her. "This sneaking around. We're treating a little girl like she's a criminal of some kind."

Jayme nodded in agreement. Then handed his own words back to him. "But isn't it the nature of an investigation to be discreet?"

"So we quit," he suggested. "I'll call him up and tell him we're out."

"And then what?"

"Then we go to work for her. For Emma. Pro bono."

"Doing what?"

"Same thing. Find out who her father is. But do it in the open, with her cooperation."

"We'll have to get the grandmother's agreement first."

"Of course."

"And then the judge's too. Are we going to do that in the open, with his cooperation?"

"Why wouldn't he agree? It's what he wants, or so he claimed. He won't like that we switched sides on him, but he'll be getting the same deal for no money."

"I don't know," Jayme said.

"I've never been comfortable with this anonymity he claims to need. She sent the letter *to him*. She knows who he is. Her mother knows who he is. Her grandmother probably knows who he is. For all we know, the whole town of Scottville might know who he is."

"He's worried about his reputation back home. Even if he's not her father, word could get out that he took part in the whole... you know."

"Why are you defending him?" DeMarco asked. "I got the feeling you didn't much care for him."

"I'm playing the devil's advocate is all. Same as you always do with me. Truth is, I love your plan."

DeMarco grunted. Then asked, "In that case, may I express myself freely?"

"Always, babe."

"Then fuck his reputation. This is a little girl's life we're talking about here."

She smiled. Turned her hand in his and squeezed his fingers. "This is why I love you," she said.

# TWENTY-THREE

THE PAST LAYS THE EGG, THE PRESENT CRACKS IT
OPEN, AND THE FUTURE COMES CLIMBING OUT

After his son's death, DeMarco went to war against the world. He had the legal authority to do so. A Pennsylvania State Trooper uniform, a badge, a 9mm handgun. And, he told himself, he had the moral authority to do so. In truth he had no such authority, and his war against the world was really a war against God. DeMarco's nine-month-old son had died while sitting in his car seat, watching his mommy up front or the back of his daddy's head or maybe just watching full of wonder as the lights of night twinkled through the windows. Until a red pickup truck ran the traffic light and T-boned DeMarco's car. The drunk at the wheel of that truck served some time but not enough, and DeMarco's wife, Laraine, blamed him for the loss and stopped talking to him and eventually left him and started picking up strangers in bars as a way to either punish DeMarco or to expiate a bit of her own anguish. So yes, DeMarco had been angry. He had been furious. And for a dozen years his fury and guilt could find no relief.

For all of those years and more he had been mired in the sewage of the world, his daily life a series of confrontations with lawbreakers of every ilk and of interviews with their frightened, grieving, despairing victims. Every time he investigated a crime, he waded neck-deep into the muck again. He had never wanted to be there but was compelled by a powerful need to be useful, to justify his existence, and he knew no other way to do it. He would rather sit in the woods and listen to the breeze through the leaves but that wouldn't pay the bills nor would it satisfy his deeper need to understand the true nature of reality.

A part of him, even as a boy, had wanted to just start walking. To drop everything, every concern, every burden, every obligation, and to just walk and keep walking, no destination in mind. Only with the intention of never setting foot on pavement, never again walking a sidewalk or a city street. Never sleeping inside a building with walls thicker than 68-denier polyester. He wondered if it were possible. How many years did he have left? Maybe thirty, if he were lucky. How many states could he cover? How many continents? He knew a lot of people who were afraid to be out of doors, afraid of solitude and silence and darkness and nature, people who hid from those conditions, ran from them, trembled at the mere thought of being trapped inside one of them. But not him. He preferred them, singly or, better yet, all at once. God, how he would cherish that freedom!

And now here he was again, wrestling with the demon, his own mirror image. Fight or flight. There was no question, really. No doubt of which option he would choose. Maybe he just needed to believe that there *was* an option. It always came down to that, didn't it? An option was hope, a way out. His own big two-hearted river. How long had Nick Adams stayed in the woods? He couldn't remember. A couple of days at least. But DeMarco didn't have a couple of days. A couple of minutes would have to do. And he had already used them up by staring out the gnat-speckled windshield.

He made the call right there in the hospital parking lot, with

Jayme at his side, the phone on speaker. The judge's hello sounded as if he had a mouthful of food, so DeMarco got straight to the point and was secretly hoping the judge would choke on his breakfast. "We're terminating our agreement with you, Judge. We don't like the sneaking around part of it. So we're just going to go ahead on our own dime and get the sample from the girl and pass the results on to her and her grandmother. We trust that you will cooperate."

He heard the judge swallow, then clear his throat. "You are reneging on our agreement?"

"We've reconsidered your terms and we don't like them. As I said, this is at our own expense. We're all square as far as I'm concerned."

"Not a good move, Sergeant. Backing out on a handshake. Very unprofessional."

"C'est la vie, Judge. Can we assume that you *will* donate a sample of your own DNA? And see that your friends do the same?"

After a few moments of silence, the judge said, "On one condition. You provide me with the DNA breakdown of the girl so that we can have our own tests run."

"Sure. Why not?" DeMarco said.

"And I owe you nothing?"

"Nada y nada."

"What was that about a grandmother? Where's the mother in this?"

"Dying," DeMarco said. "In hospice."

And the next thing he heard, five seconds later, was a click.

Jayme said, "I think you ruined his breakfast."

"I hope he likes his eggs scrambled," DeMarco answered. "Because we just scrambled them for him."

# TWENTY-FOUR

## OF ROOTS AND RINGS AND BUDS AND THINGS

DeMarco at the grave of Daksh Khatri. This was in the previous November, back when the trees had retreated into a dormancy, a drowsy abscission—back when every breath DeMarco took still hurt, when Jayme was still reluctant to grant him leave of the house alone, as if only her vehement and adamantine love could keep him safe, sequester him from another error in judgment, another impetuous act. But he needed to see this place in the ground where the body that had once housed a deranged man had been laid without benefit of prayer or any semblance of ritual. Khatri's own parents had refused his body, said he had shamed the family through both avenues of time forward and back. And so he had been laid to rest courtesy of Mahoning County, Ohio, where he had first wreaked his havoc.

The feds were still watching the plot for the appearance of any lingering confederates, any demented groupies or wannabes. But all they would see this morning was Khatri's lone male survivor, DeMarco, shivering inside his too-thin jacket, the dead leaves blowing about his legs like brittle, papery demons sucked dry of all power, impuissant and doomed to crumble.

It was strange what DeMarco felt for Khatri now, strangest of all to himself, though any who saw him standing there above the still-mounded earth might wonder why he had come and what he was thinking. To gloat, no doubt. To exult in his enemy's death, his own triumphant recovery. But that wasn't what DeMarco was thinking or feeling. Instead, no bitterness, no self-satisfaction, but something like a kinship. Something like amusement that needed to be shared, and which only the dead could understand.

*So now you know, brother. Now you know it all, same as I did. Now you see the trick of it all. The many, many ways we get it wrong.*

And DeMarco wanted to thank Khatri for that knowledge before it was all lost to him again, before DeMarco forgot every crumb of the everything he had known. That was why he had come to the grave that morning. Why he shivered and smiled and mumbled aloud, knowing he would be heard. "Thank you, Daksh," he said. "Man, you had me going. Good luck on your journey, brother. And thank you for helping me with mine."

And then the days and weeks passed and his body grew stronger while his memories retreated. But the memory of his visit to Khatri's grave remained, as he knew it would, and it preserved for him, as he had hoped it might, his memory of why he had made that November visit—because memory is both a gift and a curse, just as life itself is, depending upon one's perspective at the time, depending on the condition one's condition is in.

Remembering this now, months later, midmorning Saturday in early spring, as he silently drove from the hospital and back toward the Barries' green-and-white trailer in its pocket of woods, with Jayme watching out the side window and pondering who knew what, pondering mankind's cruelty and lust and basest urges and desires probably, he thought he understood again the necessity for forgetting, the imperative to don the mask and become the character and to forget that the play is just a play. Understanding was itself but a glimmer, a flitting firefly of light. But without Khatri he would never have come to know that. His gratitude, for the moment at least, was too huge to keep quiet.

"Thank you, brother," he whispered again.

"Hmm?" Jayme said, and looked his way. "What did you say, babe?"

He took a quick glance. Saw her pretty, troubled face lit by a slanting golden light, a ray of sun breaking through the clouds. That tiny sprinkling of pale freckles that always made him smile, made his heart feel hollow yet full. "Did I say something?" he asked.

"I thought you did."

He tried to bring it back, but found nothing there. Only Jayme, only now, only the Michigan woods and the stark, naked beauty of the still-leafless trees. Only the emptiness of another pending death, a woman he did not know except through a purloined glance at her daughter. "I have no idea," he said.

# TWENTY-FIVE

OH THE CONSTELLATIONS OF MISERY
AND SORROW SHE WORE

I t was the girl who answered Jayme's knock, the girl still in pajamas though the morning was waning, a navy-blue T-shirt and
leggings covered with white and purple stars of all sizes, the collar
and cuffs of the shirt and leggings a faded pink, all of the colors
faded from a hundred or more washings, the cuffs of the leggings
barely reaching her naked ankles, her feet in faded blue crew
socks with white cat prints across her toes. Emma Barrie looked
out through the aluminum storm door with its full panel of dirty
glass and saw Jayme's puzzling smile, the mouth turning upward
in forced happiness but the eyes frowning, the big man standing
behind her with his own sad face, and she felt a chill go through
her as if straight through the glass, a gray chill slicing into her like
the enemy of light itself, so that her own face scrunched up and
her belly tightened and she shivered and began to cry.

"Oh, baby," Jayme said, and reached for the handle and found
the door unlocked, pulled the door open and moved onto the first
metal step. She would have continued except that Emma backed
away and then turned and ran toward the rear of the trailer. So
Jayme stepped down onto the grass again and let the door close.

She turned to DeMarco. "I think she knows. I think she knew just by looking at me."

DeMarco swung an arm around her but said nothing. They waited. And soon a smallish woman in her sixties came trundling from the back, quick footsteps thudding onto the floor, and appeared behind the glass, her eyes still sleepy but suspicious, thin graying hair brittle and mussed. She tightened the belt of a dirty white fleece robe and yanked the door open eight or so inches and spoke through the opening. "What's going on here?" she said.

"I'm sorry," Jayme answered. "The hospital has been trying to reach you. Have you heard from them yet?"

"I put the phone off when I'm sleeping. What's the matter? Is it Jennie?"

"I'm afraid it is," Jayme said. "She's been transferred to hospice care."

"Oh for Christ's sake," the woman said in a long, sighing breath. "Son of a bitch."

"I'm so sorry," Jayme said.

The woman continued to look at her, saying nothing. Then she asked, angry, "Did you tell Emma that? Is that what set her off? You have no right telling her something like that without me knowing about it."

"I didn't even speak to her," Jayme said. "She just looked at me and started crying."

Again the woman was silent for a moment. Then she turned her gaze to DeMarco. "She does that sometimes. Like she knows stuff we don't. She's probably got the same thing my Jennie's got. Poor little thing."

DeMarco could think of no appropriate reply.

"Well, shoot," the woman said. She pushed the door open a

little farther. "You might as well come in and tell me where they took her," she said. "I suppose we're gonna have to go there. Who are you people anyway?"

# TWENTY-SIX

JUST SIGN YOUR NAME ON THE SULLIED LINE

Grandma Loey stood with one hand clutching the robe closed at her throat as DeMarco explained that he and Jayme had stopped at the hospital to speak with Jennifer but were informed that she had been transferred to another facility, that the desk nurse had been trying all morning to reach the trailer by phone. Emma stood watching from the far end of the hallway, hands flat and crossed at the base of her neck.

Loey asked, "What did you want to see her about? Are you two from that collection agency that's always calling here? None of her bills are my responsibility. I told you people that time and again."

"No, ma'am," DeMarco said, and cut a quick look down the hall at Emma, and wondered only briefly if he should speak in front of her. "It was about a different matter."

Jayme listened to the conversation from a half step behind and to the side of DeMarco, who spoke softly and deliberately, careful to avoid the judge's name and other distinguishing words. She also took in the interior of the trailer and the measure of Grandma Loey looking hungover and prematurely aged. The woman was small but unyielding, unafraid, *a tough little bird*, Jayme thought. And Emma standing there some twenty feet away watching and listening outside an open doorway, which must have opened onto her bedroom, her sanctuary. On the opposite side the hallway opened onto another small room, probably the bathroom, with the master bedroom taking up the rear of the trailer. The trailer was longer than their RV but barely as wide, its worn furnishings and décor from the previous century. It even smelled and sounded old, the scent of old fried food and decades of poverty and a leaky roof and dirty carpets and the dry air blowing from the rumbling oil burner and the too-loud humming from the ancient Frigidaire and the vaguely musty scent common to homes surrounded by trees.

But it was Emma who commanded most of Jayme's attention. The girl stood with one foot pressed atop the other, shoulders hunched and body tensed though shivering perceptibly as she sniffed back her tears.

"What kind of different matter?" Loey asked.

And Emma said, "Is it about the letter I sent?"

DeMarco didn't reply. He turned briefly to Jayme.

"Hunh," Loey said. "I suppose he's trying to deny it ever happened."

"Doesn't he want to know about me?" Emma asked.

The girl's voice so innocent and small, it gripped the heart. Jayme stepped forward. "Ryan, we can drive these good people to the other facility, right? Then hang around until they're ready to come back?"

"Sure," he said. "We can all grab some breakfast while we're at it."

Loey said, "I don't have no money to pay for any of that."

"Our treat," Jayme told her. She squeezed past DeMarco and Loey and started down the hall. "How about if I help you pick out something nice to wear, Emma, while Ryan and your grandma talk? I would love to see how you've decorated your bedroom."

"Is my mom going to be okay?" Emma asked.

Jayme said nothing until close enough to swing an arm around the girl's thin shoulders and sweep her into the bedroom. "Everybody's working real hard on that," she said, and eased the door shut behind them.

Loey squinted at DeMarco. "I'm not in the business of trusting people offering something for nothing."

"Nor should you be," he told her. "We have been asked to collect a sample of DNA from Emma. To prove paternity."

"Hunh. I told Jennie he'd never admit to it without a fight. Here today, gone tomorrow."

"He is more than willing to take responsibility. With proof of paternity. And, ma'am, the man does have the right to know for certain, one way or the other."

She thought for a few moments. "What do they have to do to get that sample? Take some blood from her?"

"No, nothing like that. I run a little swab around in her mouth. That's all there is to it."

"And then what? Once he finds out it's him to blame?"

"Then he mans up and does what's right. And I promise you, right here and now, that I will make certain he does."

"Why? What's any of this to you?"

He wondered what to tell her. Not some platitude, some useless cliché. No, nothing but the truth would suffice. "I had a baby boy once," he told her. "He was my whole world. And then I lost him. But I will love him forever." He paused, choked down the lump rising in his throat. "We need to take better care of our children, ma'am. That's all Jayme and I are here to do."

She inhaled through her nose. Nodded. And then her face became pinched. "Is my Jennie going to die today?"

What to say? Probably? Soon? Today or tomorrow? Then a

phrase came into his head. He smiled and repeated it. "Death cannot kill what never dies."

"Hmpf," she said. "I figured you for one of them Bible thumpers."

He almost laughed out loud.

"You're not going to charge me for driving us around?"

"I just need the mouth swab, that's all. Then we're square. I have the kit in my car."

"Don't I need to sign something? I don't particularly like putting my name to paper."

"It's a very simple form. You sign it, I get a mouth swab, Jayme and I are your chauffeurs for the rest of the morning. Free of charge."

Her gaze lingered on his face a few moments longer. "You said something about getting some breakfast too. That little girl hasn't ate nothing yet."

"We'll take care of that."

"Yeah? Well…if you wasn't a man, I might believe you."

His smile cracked open. "Ask Jayme. She's the boss here."

"Famous last words," the old woman said, and turned away.

# TWENTY-SEVEN

## FROM PLAYLAND TO THE LONGHOUSE OF LOSS

Is he a nice man?" Emma asked. "Do you think he would like me?"

"You're kind of likable," DeMarco answered, and gave her a wink that made her blush.

They were seated at a small round table in the enclosed Playland at McDonald's, Emma's choice, with Highway 10 at DeMarco's back, Emma directly across from him and flanked by her grandmother and Jayme, each with a cardboard tray loaded with scrambled eggs, a sausage patty, hash browns, hotcakes and a biscuit. Emma had a cup of hot chocolate beside her tray, coffee for the adults. The only other customers in the area were a two-year-old boy and his mother. The boy ran from one piece of equipment to the next, slapping each with his little hand as he ran. His mother followed wearily, alternately sipping from a caramel latte and telling the boy, to no avail, to "slow down, bubby. Slow down before you fall down."

To Emma, Jayme said, "Ryan tends to underestimate everything. Everybody knows you're adorable."

She and Emma had bonded quickly that morning. In the trailer, while Emma had washed her face and brushed her teeth with the bathroom door open, Jayme had sat at the foot of the bed, speaking across the hallway, and explained what was happening. "So your mom is being transferred to another place where she will be more comfortable. We're going to take you and your grandma there to spend some time with her, okay? We'll either stay there too, or, if there's a taxi service available, or Lyft or Uber or something like that, we'll make arrangements for that. Either way we'll make sure you get back home safe and sound."

"How long do we get to stay?" the girl asked.

"As long as you want."

"Grandma doesn't like to stay very long. Never long enough for me anyway."

"I know. You love your mom a lot, don't you?"

Emma nodded, looked as if she might cry. "I love you big as the sky, she always says. As big as the sky and twice as wide."

"That's pretty darn big," Jayme said.

When Emma returned to her bedroom, she laid out her clothes atop her bed for inspection. The skinny jeans that Emma now wore rolled above her ankles were pronounced "perfect," the pink Old Navy long-sleeved T-shirt with a logo that read *We Are the Future* elicited an "I *love* that!" from Jayme, and the pink mesh sneakers from Walmart brought a "You really know how to dress, girl! I bet you have all the boys gaga, don't you?" that made Emma giggle and hide her face behind both hands.

Then Emma had snatched up the jeans and shirt, run back into the bathroom and closed the door, and returned two minutes later fully dressed. "A vision to behold," Jayme had said. She held up the girl's hairbrush. "May I?"

Emma nodded and sat on the bed while Jayme, standing beside her, smoothed out the girl's hair. "So what we need to do," Jayme told her, "is to get a sample of your DNA. Do you know what that is?"

"Like on *CSI.* Where you put a Q-tip in my mouth."

"Exactly. What I will be doing is collecting some saliva from the inside of your cheek. Do you know why?"

"To find out if one of them is my father or not."

"Righto."

"Were they happy to know about me? Or were they mad?"

"Happy," Jayme told her after a beat. "Surprised, but mostly happy." She leaned back, looked at Emma's hair, patted down a couple of staticky hairs that had followed the brush as it moved away, and said, "Perfection, my dear. Absolute perfection." She returned the brush to its place on the dresser and said, "Okay if I get the DNA kit from the car and we take care of it now?"

"Okay," Emma said.

And now they were finishing their breakfasts, only minutes from the Great Heart Hospice. Nobody had mentioned the word *hospice* in front of Emma, and neither DeMarco nor Jayme had any idea if Emma understood the severity of her mother's condition. It wasn't their place to mention it. They were strangers, interlopers—despite the tenderness and concern both felt for the girl.

Eventually they stood at their table in McDonald's, ready to leave. DeMarco gathered up the trays and empty cups and carried them to a waste bin. Then they drove in relative silence to a long one-story building a block from Lake Michigan, the wood siding painted a pale yellow with blue trim, the building designed with a slightly rounded roof peak to simulate an Ottawa longhouse.

They emerged from the parked car and gazed down the intersecting street to the gray expanse of water beneath a brightening sky. Jayme took Emma's hand. "Big, isn't it?" Jayme said.

"I'm glad we're so close to the beach," Emma told her. "Mommy loves the beach." She looked up at Jayme. "Maybe we can go down there today?"

So, she didn't know. Didn't know that her mother was in an induced coma. That her life would now be measured in hours rather than days. Jayme felt all the breath go from her lungs, felt her breakfast rising in her stomach.

"We'll see," Jayme said, and turned the girl away and led her inside.

Emma's grandmother stopped at the front desk and flashed a scowl at the smiling young blond woman in dark-blue scrubs seated there. "Jennie Barrie's my daughter," Loey said. "Where you people keeping her?"

The young woman turned her soft brown eyes to Emma, then back to the grandmother. Slid the visitor's register, an attractive journal bound in maroon leather, to Loey and said, "We'll need your names and addresses. Thank you. I'll fill in the time."

As Loey scrawled the information, the young woman said, "She's in suite 119. I'll let Dr. Bissett know you're here. She will be in to speak with you soon."

Grandma Loey turned to Emma and said, "Let's go if we're going," then proceeded down the hall on her own. Jayme and Emma, still holding hands, followed, with DeMarco speaking to the front desk nurse for a moment before trailing behind.

At the door to Jennifer Barrie's room, Jayme drew the girl aside, knelt and took her other hand too. "Sweetie," she said, "your mommy is sleeping now. The doctors gave her something to make her sleep so that she's more comfortable. Okay?"

"Can I wake her up?" Emma asked.

"Mmm, it's probably best if you don't. She's in a lot of pain when she's awake. But I bet she will still hear you if you talk to her."

"She'll hear me in her sleep?"

"I bet she will."

"She told me last time that she sometimes visits me when I'm sleeping. In her dreams, I mean."

"You see?" said Jayme. "So you go ahead and talk to her all you want. She'll hear you."

"Are you coming in?"

"Visiting hours are just for family. If Ryan and I aren't still here when you and your grandma are ready to leave, I want you to stop at the desk and pick up my phone number and email address. I'm going to leave it there for you, okay?"

"Okay," Emma said, and cut a glance toward her mother's door.

"I want you to call me or text me if you have any questions about anything. Or if you just need a friend to talk to sometime. Don't forget to pick up my number, okay?"

"Can't you come in just to say hello?"

"Not right now, sweetie. Maybe later if we're still here. But I want you to have my number so that you can call me anytime you want. For any reason whatever. Okay?"

Emma nodded. She looked at DeMarco standing against the opposite wall. "Thank you for breakfast," she said. "And for letting me pick the place."

He smiled. "Any time, sunshine."

Jayme said, "Can I get a hug?"

Emma stepped into her arms, stayed for a long squeeze, then was released, turned and went into her mother's room.

Jayme remained on her knees, unable to rise. DeMarco stepped close and slipped a hand under her arm, lifted her up, and held her when she fell against him. "I'm going to lose it, baby," she said.

He said, "No you're not," and walked with her back up the hallway.

At the front desk she pulled away and spoke to the nurse. "I told Emma that I would leave my contact information with you. Would you make sure that she gets it when she leaves?"

"Of course," the young woman said. She slid a pad of white Post-it Notes and a pen toward Jayme, who wrote on the top sheet, tore it off and handed it to the nurse. Then she started crying and turned away and headed quickly for the door.

DeMarco lingered behind. He wanted to rush after Jayme, but some business remained. To the desk nurse he said, "Do you have any kind of taxi service up here?"

She smiled. Used to dealing with angry, fearful, grieving people. "We do, yes. Would you like me to contact one for you?"

He reached for his wallet, pulled it out and opened it. "For the Barries," he said. "Jennifer's mother and daughter. Whenever they're ready to go home. Do you mind?"

"Not in the least."

He took out a twenty, asked, "Will this be enough?"

She looked at the address Loey had scrawled. "Hmm, maybe not quite. That's what, about twenty miles away?"

He took out another twenty and laid both bills on the counter. "Thank you so much." He turned and headed for the door, then stopped midway, turned and asked, "Would you happen to know of a grocery store out that way? Cell service is a bit sporadic out there."

"Sure. That would be Jensen's Market. On Highway 10."

"Great, thanks. I probably passed it on the way here."

"No problem. Have a blessed day, sir."

A blessed day, how nice. And the way she smiled, so serene. He walked away wondering if she knew things or only believed them. Belief was good, of course, a grand substitute, but knowing was so much better. Knowing was not as susceptible to erosion, to chipping and cracking and growing brittle with age. Someday he would know it all again, 98 percent of everything there was to know. The last 2 percent would remain beyond the ken of anybody anywhere, even beyond the source of the other 98 percent. And he found that knowledge pleasing, that there would always be a mystery, always a tantalizing something that could never be known.

He was smiling as he approached the rental car, then saw Jayme doubled over inside, weeping, and his smile faded. She had so much compassion in her heart, so much empathy. Too much for a pleasant passage through this unpredictable journey. He needed to remain mindful of the fact that she didn't know what he knew, and that her grief was real. That even in a three-dimensional illusion, every second of the pain experienced by the players within that illusion is all too real.

# TWENTY-EIGHT

## A THEORY OF THE GENERAL AND
## SPECIAL RELATIVITY OF STUPID

Boyd asked himself, *Why is it that you always look forward to your days off, but when they come around you never do anything with them?*

He wasn't a man who rested easily. A restless man. Here it was April already and how many of his days off had he put to good use? Question was, what would be good use? Going to a movie? Taking a hike? Cleaning the house? Those were the things he typically did, but none appealed to him this time. He sat in his Jeep in the driveway with the engine off and tried to think of somewhere interesting to go. All of the interesting stuff was hours away, and he had already been to all of them. Cleveland Zoo. Pittsburgh Zoo. The Strip District. The Rock & Roll Hall of Fame. Nothing was new anymore. He always drove home tired, wishing he hadn't wasted the gas.

He thought of Flores then because she had the day off too. For some reason he had noticed that on the schedule. A rare day off at the same time. Not that it mattered. Why would it?

He had tried to be a good friend to her, spent time with her after work, watched Netflix with her, was her designated driver a couple of times, sometimes stopped by her desk with a cup of coffee and a doughnut. Once—it happened when they were watching *Better Call Saul*, when Jimmy was rattling on about something while making a cup of tea for Chuck—she had leaned up against him, her head on his shoulder. And when he'd turned to look down at her, she had lifted her mouth to his, and he'd pulled away. He hadn't done it on purpose, it had just happened. He still didn't know why. She had stiffened and sat there until the episode ended, her eyes locked on the screen, then had shut off the TV and told him she was tired. That was the last time he had spent any time with her. Oh, he'd stopped by her desk at work from time to time, never failed to say hello when their paths crossed, but nothing had been the same after that. She hadn't been the same. He couldn't blame her, really. She felt insulted, rejected. He'd been thinking of her as a little sister, and had tried to explain that to her. But what had she said in return? She'd said, "You're too white to be my brother." He had no idea what she'd meant by that.

And now, twelve minutes after remembering all this, he was on the little balcony at the top of the stairs on the second floor of the hardware store. He stood with his right hand's knuckles resting mute against the wood of Flores's door. Then he told himself to leave her alone, just go, she probably wanted company no more than he did.

He lowered his hand.

Then he thought again about her Subaru turned onto its roof, the tight grimace on her face when he had lain down on the pavement and looked in at her. She was suffering then, had to be suffering mightily, but what were her first words to him? Had she cried out? Begged him for help? No. She had asked, in a voice nearly strangled by her pain, "Did I get him? Just tell me I got him."

He raised his hand to her door again and knocked—four firm raps.

No sounds from inside, no movement. Just as he was about to knock a second time, the peephole darkened. He flashed her a smile.

When she opened the door he was struck by how small she looked. Out of uniform, she was a whole different person. He had thought the same thing when he visited her in the hospital. She was barefoot now, wearing baggy black nylon shorts and a white tank top. No makeup, hair loose and frizzy. Left leg with a long puckered incision from ankle to knee. She stood listing to one side, all of her weight shifted to her right foot. For some reason her vulnerability and femininity made his chest ache.

He said the first thing to come to mind. "You ready?"

Her forehead wrinkled. "Ready for what?"

"I signed us up for a 10K. It starts in five minutes."

She squinted her eyes at him for a few seconds, then snorted a little and shook her head. "Asshole," she said, and walked away, leaning on furniture for support.

But, he noticed, she hadn't slammed the door in his face. Had, in fact, left it standing open. He stepped inside and softly closed the door and followed her path to the little gray sofa facing the front window. She had taken a seat against the farthest armrest. The small Yamaha keyboard lay in the middle of the sofa.

He stood against the opposite armrest and nodded toward the instrument. "You been playing?" he asked.

"No. I use it as a footrest."

He nodded toward the larger keyboard across the room. "How come you don't play that one?"

She shrugged. "This one is more my speed."

"Don't you ever play it? The big one?"

"Don't you ever mind your own business?"

Okay, so it was going to be like this, was it? Her little smile of amusement…she was challenging him. Trying to make him flustered. "So play something for me," he said.

"I don't know anything you'd like."

"How do you know what I'd like?"

"I'll put it another way. I don't play anything you know."

"Then play one of your own songs."

"If you can call them that," she said.

"What else would you call them?"

Her only answer was a shrug.

"Seriously," he said, "I'd love to hear one of them."

"Which one?"

Again he smiled. "How about the latest one? Your newest composition."

"Composition, ha," she said.

"So you're saying it stinks?"

"Something like that."

"Then for God's sake don't play it. Last thing I need to hear is another song that stinks."

"It's just that I'm not a professional is all," she said.

"The stinkiest song I know is 'Achy Breaky Heart.' Does yours stink as much as that one?"

"No song stinks as much as 'Achy Breaky Heart.'"

"So you're saying yours is better than 'Achy Breaky Heart'?"

"A series of farts is better than that song. Are you going to sit down or just stand there all day?"

He crossed to the front of the sofa and sat crookedly, wedged into the corner against the armrest. "Is that what your song is then? A series of farts?"

She pulled up her legs, the left one with help from her hands, and crossed her ankles. "More or less. The chorus is all belches, though."

He shrugged. "Sounds original anyway."

"So you still want to hear it?"

"Naw. I've never really been drawn to farts and belches. Just the opposite, really."

She lowered her gaze. Smiled. Asked, "What kind of music do you like?"

"Stuff that's musical. Has a nice melody, good lyrics."

She looked up again. "Give me a couple of examples."

"I don't know. I like Bob Dylan's 'Sara.' Better yet his 'Forever Young.'"

"Is that the same one Jay-Z did a few years back? I didn't know Dylan wrote that."

"Yeah, it's been covered a ton of times. Dylan first wrote it for his son Jesse in 1966. He recorded it in two versions, one fast, one slow. I like the slow one best. Rod Stewart did a decent cover of it too but none of them can touch the original."

"You seem to know a lot about music. I never would have guessed."

He shrugged.

"What else do you like?"

"Lots. I was really into the old stuff for a while. Stuff my mother used to listen to. The Bee Gees are probably my favorite from that era. Not their disco crap but earlier. Especially 'How Can You Mend a Broken Heart.' That was 1971, I think. Michael Bublé does a nice cover that I like too."

She cocked her head and studied him for a moment. "How come I've never known this about you?"

He shrugged. "You never asked."

"Huh," she said. "'How Do You Mend a Broken Heart.' Really?"

"It's a good song. Do you know it?"

"I've heard it," she said. "Why do you like it so much? Do you have a broken heart?"

That one threw him for a second, but he tried not to show it. "Me? Nah. Not unless you can be born with one and not know about it. I passed my academy physical with no problem."

"Sometimes you look like a man with a broken heart," she said.

Geez, she was digging right in, wasn't she? "What does a man with a broken heart look like?" he asked.

"Sad. Aloof. Doesn't talk much. Keeps to himself. Never mentions how much he knows about music."

"Then I guess that would make you a man with a broken heart," he said.

She tapped her left knee. "Broken dreams is more like it."

He nodded, lips pursed. "You don't have to wear the brace all the time?"

"I'm supposed to. Not supposed to put any weight on my leg."

"Then why don't you have it on now?"

"You want to try wearing it for a while?" she asked.

Yeah, she was right. What right did he have to give her advice? "You know what?" he told her, and picked up the keyboard by one end, laid it across her thighs. "I think I do want to hear that stinky song of yours."

"Maybe I don't want to play it now."

"You're a free woman," he told her. "I was just asking is all."

"You're not very good at asking, are you?"

"Ha," he said, a little laugh of recognition. "I would love to hear the song you wrote, Ms. Flores. Would you play it for me, please?"

She moved the keyboard to a more stable position across her legs. Hit the Power button. "It's called 'I Wash My Face.'"

"You wrote a song about washing your face? You *are* an original, aren't you?"

"Maybe you should just shut up and listen."

"Maybe I should."

Her voice was soft, with a shyness he hadn't recognized in her before. She watched her fingers on the keys as she sang, her voice supplying the melody, her hands the chords. And the song wasn't about washing her face at all. That became clear with the second line: *I wash my hands of you.* The rest of that verse provided all of the speaker's motivation, her bitterness and anger and resolve. *The lies that were so sweet / until the truth broke through. / The warmth of your embrace. / The way I cared for you. / I wash my hands of you. / I wash my face.*

Then came another verse, a chorus, a verse, and the chorus again, with the phrase *I wash my face* repeating five times, scrubbing the tears away, scrubbing some son of a bitch out of her skin.

Boyd was impressed. The song was a lot better than he had expected it would be. "Geez," he said.

She hit the power button to turn the keyboard off. "Geez that really stinks?"

"Geez that's pretty good. Who was this guy you were singing about?"

"Who says it was anybody? Maybe it's every guy I ever dated."

"So you, what? Switched sides now?"

She chuckled. "If you have to know, it's about my father. He was a real asshole. Still is probably."

"Yeah," he said. "Parents can be a bitch sometimes."

She looked up at him again and held his gaze this time. His stomach fluttered.

He looked away, scanned the room. "So this is how you spend your time off?"

She was silent for a few ticks. Then, "What brought you here this morning, Mace? You been feeling sorry for me?"

He shrugged. "What would be wrong about that?"

"I don't want your pity. Not yours or anybody else's."

He nodded. Watched the gray morning out the window. Put his hands on his knees as if to stand, but didn't. "I was thinking earlier about what you did."

"What I did when?" she asked.

"Back at the end of October."

"What did I do?"

He looked at her now. "You know what I'm talking about."

"Yeah?"

"That might be the bravest thing I've ever seen."

"Don't you mean the stupidest thing?"

"Ha. Yeah, well, sometimes bravery isn't the smartest choice, is it? But I'm sure you knew that before you did it."

She laid her right hand atop her left thigh and lightly, absently, massaged her knee. Her skin was brown and smooth—*flawless*, he thought. The red line stitched along the inside of her calf, he wanted to put his hand on it. Wanted to caress it. It was going to make a dandy scar, a badge of honor she would wear forever.

He looked up then and found her studying him, her eyes soft. "Sorry," he said.

"For what?"

Again he shrugged.

She said, "I think I want to do something now. I'm not sure if it's brave or stupid or both."

"What?" he asked.

She blinked twice more before speaking. "I'm going to go into the bathroom and brush my teeth. Then I'm going to take off my clothes and climb into bed."

"There's nothing stupid about that," he told her, and scooted forward a little, getting ready to stand. "Sorry if I interrupted—"

Her hand on his knee silenced him. "The stupid part," she said as she leaned toward him and pushed her feet to the floor, "is that I plan to leave the bedroom door open." She stood, pressing hard against his knee for balance, then drew away and crossed behind the sofa and let her hand trail across the back of his head.

"Maybe we should think about this," he told her.

"No problem," she said as she headed for the bedroom. "You go ahead and think about it. One door is closed, one door is open. Your choice."

He sat there on the sofa and listened to the water splashing into the bathroom sink. Her shuffling footsteps as she returned to the bed. The creak of the floorboards. The *shhshh* as her clothes dropped to the floor. The higher-pitched squeak of the bedsprings.

Through it all he shook his head no, no, and no again. Then he rose and crossed as softly as he could to the bedroom threshold, stood there looking in at her. She lay with two pillows under her neck and shoulders, had pulled a corner of the sheet across her waist, leaving the rest exposed. Her eyes were open, brown and dark and wet, hands composed and motionless atop her belly, the tiniest of quivers on the corner of her mouth.

"Stupid or not stupid?" she asked.

"Stupid for sure," he answered. Then he came forward, bent over, and pried off a shoe. "But I'm doing it anyway."

# TWENTY-NINE

## MAKING A DOWN PAYMENT ON WHAT MONEY CAN'T BUY

When he saw the words JENSEN'S MARKET printed above the door of the large white building ahead, DeMarco understood why he hadn't noticed it on earlier drives past the store. There were no other markings anywhere else on the building. In structure it looked more like a small barn than a general store, with only an attic window on one end, no other glass in any of the walls. He slowed and put on the turn signal. As he pulled into the gravel lot, Jayme twisted away from the side window and asked, "We're stopping for something?"

"I thought maybe some road food for the ride home." He parked facing the building and shut off the engine.

"Can't we get that after we return the car?"

"At twice the price," he said. "This place is priced for locals. Plus I would rather not stop after we switch to the RV. If we drive straight through we can be home by ten." He reached for the door handle. "You want to come in and pick out some things?"

She turned the rearview mirror her way, looked in it and winced. Eyes red and puffy, mascara smeared. "Ugh," she said. "I'll wait here."

"Anything special you would like?"

"Something other than beef jerky and PowerBars, please. We do have a working oven and microwave in the RV, you know."

"Roger that," he said with a smile. "Back soon."

The only reason he hadn't told her his true motivation for stopping was because she would have joined him inside and then would have wept every step of the way. He would tell her after the fact. She would cry then too, and hug him and make a fuss over him, which was okay in private but not in front of strangers.

He moved quickly through the aisles of the little grocery store, grabbed only one bag of beef jerky, two Marie Callender's chicken and mushroom pot pies for the microwave, two individually packaged Caesar salads, a large bottle of Starbucks Cold Brew for him, black and unsweetened, a can of mixed nuts for snacking, and a six-pack of off-brand vanilla Frappuccinos for Jayme.

After paying for his supplies, still holding his wallet, he asked the cashier if the market made deliveries. She was a middle-aged woman with sad, weary eyes. He had chosen that register, rather than the one manned by a chubby twentysomething male with a scruffy hipster beard, because of the woman's eyes and her age. He hoped he had chosen correctly. She answered, "Not usually, no."

"It would be for the Barrie family out on Walker Road," he told her.

"You mean Jennie Barrie?"

"For her daughter and mother, yes. While Jennifer is in the hospital."

"Hell's bells, I'll take them out there myself for Jennie. Are you friends with her somehow? How is she doing?"

"About the same," he told her.

"It's a damn shame, isn't it, her with that sweet little girl and all. Loey was in here a couple days ago picking up some beer. How are those two doing?"

"Holding steady," he said. He thumbed through the bills, pulled out two fifties and held them out to her. "Could you maybe pick out some things for them? They're at the hospital now, will probably be there a while. So maybe it could be delivered later this evening some time?"

She took the bills, folded them together and shoved them into her shirt pocket. "Perfect," she said. "I don't get off till four thirty. It'll be five before I can get out there. What kind of stuff you thinking of?"

"I don't know, healthy food mostly, I guess. Maybe some ground beef, chicken, canned tuna. But not a lot of food that will spoil fast. There's only the two of them out there."

"I hear you. Maybe a few bananas, apples, bag of frozen pine-apple chunks. Some lunch meat and bread, a gallon of milk, cereal and oatmeal?"

"Excellent. And maybe some ice cream treats for the girl?"

"Absolutely, I'll take care of it. Don't you worry. What's your name again?"

"Ryan," he said.

She smiled. Held out her hand. "It's nice to meet such a kind gentleman. I'm Darla. Named after the girl in *The Little Rascals*, if you can believe that."

He took her hand, but only briefly. "Nice to meet you." Then said, "What else do little girls her age like these days?"

"Emma? Well...are you talking toys or music or what?"

"I'm thinking something to, you know, help her deal with... not being with her mother and all. They seem very close to me."

"Close? Those two are attached at the hip. Peas in a pod."

"Do you think maybe a doll, or a stuffed animal? She likes to read, I think."

"Hmm...hey, you know what I would get her?"

"What's that?"

"Some colored pencils and a new sketch pad. She loves to draw, that girl. Not bad, either, for a kid her age."

"Do you sell those here?"

"No, but I can get them, no problem."

"That will be great. I really appreciate your help. Is a hundred dollars enough for all that?"

"Oh yeah. If not I'll make it enough. Hey, you want me to send you a photo of Emma when I give her the sketch pad?"

"Oh man, that would be excellent."

She reached for a small pad and pen on the cash register and handed them to him. "Give me a phone number and I'll text some photos to you later tonight."

He wrote down Jayme's number and returned the pad and pen to her. She looked at it and said, "She's going to want to know who the stuff is from, Ryan. She knows you, right?"

"Just tell her it's from Jayme," he said.

"Funny, you don't look much like a Jayme."

He smiled. "Jayme will be relieved to hear that." He reached for his bag of road food. "Thank you for taking care of all this."

"Hey, it's not a problem. We watch out for each other around here."

He smiled again, turned away, went out the door and to the car. Placed the grocery bags in the back seat, then climbed in behind the wheel. Jayme had been crying again, her face still wet with tears. "I feel so damn helpless," she told him.

He took her hand. "I know, baby. I know."

# THIRTY

WHEN THE THING YOU FEAR THE MOST
IS THE THING YOU NEED THE MOST

It was late afternoon when Boyd left Flores's apartment, the sun a soft yellow orb behind dirty white clouds layered across the horizon. To Boyd it looked as if the sun had simply pulled over for a rest, needed to catch its breath before starting another day on the other side of the world. Boyd needed to catch his breath too, needed to curtail the feathery sensation in his stomach. He needed to walk a while and think about what had happened back there above the hardware store. He needed to sort out his feelings, needed to label and categorize them appropriately. Brandy Springs Park was the closest place for serious walking and cogitation, just three blocks south, so he picked up a sixteen-ounce French roast at Sheetz and, sipping as he walked, entered the park at the lower end, near the doggie runs. The goose pond looked dirty and thick with mud, but the geese didn't seem to mind. The park was quiet, only two people and their dogs so far, and their voices faded behind him inside the chain-link kennels while he moved on.

The first thing Dani had said after he'd climbed into bed beside her was, "If it feels good and doesn't hurt anybody, why not? Right?"

"Right," he'd said, but he had lain there stiffly on his back, staring at the ceiling. Then she'd rolled toward him, laid a hand on his chest. It moved slowly down over his stomach, then stopped.

"You plan on taking your shorts off?" she'd asked, and he'd said, "Eventually."

"Why not now?" she said, so he had, and she touched him, and soon he stopped wondering about the wisdom of his actions. He liked that she seemed almost coldly objective in her approach, that she skipped all but a few of the kisses most women demand before getting down to business. He liked kissing too, liked it a lot, but in this case he considered it dangerous. To him kissing was one of the most intimate things two people could do. You did it only with people you cared about deeply. He cared about Flores but a relationship was just out of the question, could turn his entire life into an unpredictable mess. He didn't need the drama, the complications of such a troubled young woman. Not to mention the looks and remarks he would get from the guys at the barracks if they found out. The warnings he would get from Captain Bowen. But the main worry was Flores herself. She was so, what was the word? Unpredictable.

Even before Flores's injury he had sensed an undercurrent of anger in her. Previously it had shown itself only in an occasional sarcastic remark, but now it radiated off her like a hot breeze. Even the sex had seemed angry. She took control right from the start, and her heedless actions had emboldened him. But then, just as her orgasm began, he'd felt dampness against his shoulder and realized that she was crying, that she was weeping and clinging to him more tightly than he had ever before been held.

Not that he hadn't enjoyed the sex, it was great. But the way she held him afterward—that frightened him. And the knowledge that it frightened him only exacerbated his suspicion that it had all been a big mistake.

Now as he played it all over in his head, he didn't even realize that he had picked up his pace significantly and was striding along like a man trying to put some distance between himself and something following. His hand was wet with coffee that had splashed out of the little hole in the plastic cap. What caught his attention was a sound off to his left, a high-pitched "Unh!" soon followed by another. "Unh!"

The sound was coming from a small playground. A little boy trying and failing to leap high enough to grasp the bar suspended from a zip line strung between two poles fifteen feet apart. At its highest point the line was maybe seven feet off the ground. The boy looked to be only four or five, and the bar was well out of reach for him. His mother, a young woman in her early twenties, was seated atop a picnic table several yards away, fixated on her cell phone. Boyd watched the boy leap again and again, each time with a grunt of frustration to which his mother failed to react.

Boyd turned and crossed to the zip line, approached the boy, then asked, "You need a little help there, pardner?"

"I can't weach it," the boy said.

Boyd looked toward the mother, who had not yet raised her eyes to them. "Excuse me, miss?"

She looked up. Was surprised to see him there.

"Is it okay if I give your little boy a boost here?"

"Oh," she said. "Okay, sure. Be my guest. He's too heavy for me to lift."

Boyd set his coffee cup out of the way and spent the next twenty minutes hoisting the boy up to the bar, then hurrying along beside him, hands poised to catch him if he lost his grip. The boy might have continued longer but his mother finally tucked the cell phone into her jeans pocket and came to take her son by his hand. "That's enough for today. We need to get home."

The boy hurried to keep up with her. But after three steps he twisted around to call out, "Thank you, mister!"

Boyd gave him a two-finger salute. Retrieved his coffee, cold now, and continued his walk, but at a more leisurely pace. He made four full laps of the park's loop before turning back up the sidewalk and toward his car. His legs were pleasantly tired, his body pleasantly warm, and his mind was pleasantly if intriguingly calm.

# THIRTY-ONE

LIKE A FLAILING SPECK IN AN ANGRY SEA

D eMarco driving with the dying sun at his back, Jayme with her face relaxed finally, eyes closed and head lying back in her captain's chair, earbuds in as her cell phone ran through her playlist, Hero asleep on the vibrating floor between them. It had been a long day and was not yet over. Before pulling out of the campground five hours earlier they had let Hero run until he wore himself out, and since then they had stopped twice to let him pee. Would stop one more time before pulling into the backyard, ETA 10:30 p.m., nothing but four hours of flat Ohio ahead.

During the first hours of the drive Jayme kept looking at her cell phone. Then she would look out the windshield and gaze into the distance and say, "I wonder if she knows yet." Or, "The doctor would tell her, I'm sure." Or, "I wonder how she's taking it." Or, "She must be scared to death right now." Or, "I wish we were there with her. I wish we had stayed."

He had responded to only the last statement. "We're still little more than strangers to them, sweetheart."

To which she had answered, almost angrily, "I don't feel like a stranger to her. Or her to me. We should have stayed with her."

Around five thirty her cell phone had beeped, a text from an unknown number, and she had opened the text to find three photos: one of the Barrie's kitchen counter covered with groceries, one of Emma's wide-eyed surprise as she pulled a new sketch pad out of a grocery bag, and one of Emma standing with a page from that sketch pad pressed to her chest, the words *Thank you!* in bold blue script in her hand, a big red heart underneath.

Jayme had been surprised and a little confused at first, but DeMarco's smile gave the secret away. He told her then about the groceries, and she nearly sent them into a ditch with a strangling hug around his neck.

Only recently had she stopped fidgeting in her seat, staring to the side, then forward, then glancing backward into the RV as if she heard something there. Earlier in the trip she would get up and make her way past the kitchen area and into the bedroom. Twice she had stood at the threshold to the bedroom, her hands on the doorframe as her body swayed in response to the RV's movements. He wished she would climb onto the bed and find some peace in sleep, but she always returned to sit beside him again. Only thirty minutes ago had she finally grown still, her breath regular, one hand, even in sleep, holding her cell phone close.

Now, with Jayme and Hero both blessedly drowsing, DeMarco kept both hands on the wheel except when he reached for his coffee in the cup holder. The RV shuddered each time an eighteen-wheeler blew past. He wondered what the old ship pilots had sipped when sailing the seven seas. Grog, maybe. In a heavy metal mug. But wouldn't that be a soporific, the very opposite of what they needed? Tea, then. A dark, bitter, unsweetened tea, brewed in an iron pot swaying over a fire in the ship's galley.

It felt good to be at his land yacht's wheel. Maybe he had been one of those seamen in a previous life. One of those lonely men who never felt at home on land but could think of nothing but the land while sailing to some foreign port, the ship a mere speck out there on the endlessly churning sea.

He glanced in the rearview mirror, saw his tired eyes. *You're not lonely anymore, are you, matey?*

Or was he? The irony of having an NDE, or of any encounter with the supernatural, was that even as it connected you with a larger reality, it further separated you from everyone else in the current reality. The encounter was always a personal one, unshared and, in the end, unshareable. Each time he thought about his experience, he entered into an utterly private place. No one else could join him there, not even, he supposed, if they had had their own similar experience.

Jayme was inside her own experience too. As was Hero. Whether dreaming or awake, everybody was in his or her own experience. Their experiences could overlap with others', of course, but it was a temporary union and merely a glancing blow compared to the intensity of what he had experienced when outside of his body. As a consequence, he now had knowledge he could not articulate. Experience he could not transfer or adequately share with anybody else.

And what of God? What of the Source? It could divide itself into a trillion trillion consciousnesses yet always be only itself. Only a trillion trillion tiny specks bobbing and flailing about in a sea of lonely self.

Yes, no question, no doubt. DeMarco was sailing his own ship across a vast sea. No other sailors aboard. No land in sight. His body, and Jayme's, and Hero's were their own personal schooners, their own personal anchors. He wished he could merge with them, pass through and experience them as he had when he passed through his mother and father and everyone else he had known when they were all just milky clouds of being in an infinite sea of black. Someday he would. Someday.

He looked down at Hero, who had awakened now and was watching him curiously, head cocked. "Someday," DeMarco whispered. Then he whispered the same to Jayme, her eyes still closed, chest rising and falling evenly, her eyelashes fluttering a little as she dreamed. So close and yet so distant. He barely knew her. He knew death better than he knew her, was more intimate with the infinite than he would ever be with her. At least in this life.

Oh, yes, he was lonely. And how he longed for an end to it.

# THIRTY-TWO

HELLO, MY FRIEND

During his first hour back home in his own bed, DeMarco felt the RV still rocking beneath him. Then he slept, but restlessly, dreaming of somebody chasing him, their footsteps echoing so loudly through the great hollow space that his eardrums ached. And when he was awakened at 7:20 the next morning by Hero's cold wet nose against his cheek, and tried to roll silently out of bed, he stifled a groan. His shoulders were stiff and sore, ribs sore, his spine a brittle, gnarled twig.

But it was good to be home again. His bedroom smelled like sunlight. Like more or less fresh linen on the bed. And Jayme lying there on her side, the rise of her hip, one leg uncovered from midthigh down… When was the last time they had made love? Four full days ago. Too long. He stood there gazing at her, his genitals growing heavy. Then Hero rubbed against his leg, and DeMarco reacted with a start like a schoolboy caught stealing a look at pornography.

"Shh!" he told the dog, even though it hadn't made a sound. Then a last, nostalgic glance at Jayme before he turned and tiptoed to the door.

Back to routine, the same old same old.

A gray, chilly morning. "Good morning, morning," he said

softly. He stood on the edge of the porch for a few moments, coffee cup in hand, the rising heat from the cup warming his face while Hero loped around the yard doing a security check of each of his pee posts and reestablishing his pheromonal claim to them. Then DeMarco, clothed only in red-and-black basketball shorts and a gray T-shirt, stepped down into the dew-wet grass. His breath caught at the startling cold. "Whew!" he said, but he did not move. A little shock was a good thing in the morning. Gets the eyes opened up. Gets the juices flowing. A jolt of cold stabbing at his toes was a benign kind of pain, and he wanted to experience it.

He sipped his hot coffee and felt his toes tingling and looked up at the sky, and for some reason he thought of Seneca then, the Roman sage and philosopher of the first century AD. In one of his epistles, Seneca had quoted Hecato of Rhodes, "I have begun to be a friend to myself." DeMarco had never read Hecato but maybe he would someday. For now, he was pleased to recognize that he, too, had finally entered into that stage of evolution. He no longer despised himself. It changed everything.

During his last years as a teenager and after his father was gone he had liked to rise early, washing and dressing in darkness. He had taught himself as a boy how to move quietly, like an Indian in moccasins in the old Westerns on TV, and he had taken pleasure from the independence he felt from having a few dollars in his pocket from seasonal construction work, liked how strong and light on his feet he had felt. Most of the people in the trailer court were on welfare or social security and there were few lights shining inside the metal boxes as he passed silently between them on his way to the street. He liked going into the convenience store and getting a large black coffee in a cardboard cup and walking with it warming his hand in the cool, clean morning, then taking the long way back home with the first long streaks of sunlight painting the ground, the old leaves brown and looking softened by the dew like old leather, the grass new and sparkling green in the yellow light. His mother would still be sleeping when he returned home, and he would scramble some eggs and fry a slice or two of ham, would eat half of the food straight from the skillet and cover the rest with aluminum foil for his mother to warm up later. Then he would set out again to either school or work and begin the necessary business of the day feeling like his own man for a change, not the fearful boy always wondering if the next day would bring his father into his life again like an explosion of foul air.

Those had been mostly good days for him, between his father's death and the rotten business in Panama during the invasion, all of that unnecessary carnage and the deceit behind it. After Panama he had seldom felt like his own man again, and seldom since then felt light on his feet or as stealthy as an Indian. But now he did. All it had taken was a bullet in the chest. *You should have thought of that sooner*, he told himself with a smile.

The sky was the color of a dirty nickel that had passed through a thousand hands yet had spent most of its life in the blackness of a pocket, bouncing against its mates of lesser and greater value. *A nickel*, DeMarco told himself, *isn't much good on its own*. No coin is. Generally they get doled out in the company of others. Between enlistment and Ryan Jr., there had seldom been a time when he had not felt like a dirty nickel apart from all the others, no matter how much he liked them. Apart by then from even his mother, apart from his fellow soldiers, apart from Laraine and the women he had lain with before meeting her. Then Ryan Jr. came and he'd felt suddenly complete and unalone, a sum total. Then that was torn from him too and back he went into aloneness, more abjectly alone than ever. Because *alone* is not always the same, not just one condition and always that condition. There are numerous gradations of *alone*.

He had spent time in all of them. In *solitary*, which is sometimes the best variation of *alone*, potentially benign and often courted, prized and hoarded. The other depths were less enjoyable. Take *desolate*, for example. *Forlorn. Bereft. Inconsolable.* He possessed an intimate knowledge of all of them and more. All classifiable under the single heading of *wretched and alone*.

*But now I have Jayme*, he told the gray sky. *And she makes gray not nearly as gray as gray used to be.* And he had Hero too. It was funny how four legs and a wagging tail and big brown eyes could provide such good company. *Plus I have a different way of looking at gray*, he thought. *And a different way of looking at the sky. And at me.*

But cold feet, he realized, are still cold feet. Numb is numb. Back up onto the porch he went, the cold boards a few degrees warmer than the grass. "Speed it up," he told Hero, and had to chuckle when the dog froze in place and cocked his head at him.

Yes, life after death was pretty damn okay. All of that past misery, all of that anger…

*Let it go*, he told himself. Life after death was more alive than ever. More alive than he had ever believed he could be. So alive that he felt like screaming out in joy. But that would wake Jayme. Would startle old Mrs. Nellis next door, have her tumbling out of bed to grab a seventy-year-old rifle from the closet. So instead of screaming he whispered an enthusiastic, "Ya-hoo!" Wiggled his toes and felt the warmth of life flowing back into them. And had to smile again as he watched Hero come loping toward him, grinning his silly grin that seemed to say, "All drained for now, boss. What's for breakfast?"

# THIRTY-THREE

## BOY, WE'RE GONNA CARRY THAT WEIGHT A LONG TIME

Not until nearly ten did Jayme come downstairs, fresh from the shower, dressed in jeans and a black T-shirt with a cartoon picture of Lucy and Ricky Ricardo on the front, only one cup of coffee short of being ready to take on the world. She found him still in his boxers and T-shirt, lying on the sofa with Hero sprawled awkwardly atop him.

"I would ask how long you've been up," she said, "but it doesn't appear that you are."

He stroked Hero's head and side. "I called the judge. He'll be over at noon with his and the other guys' swabs."

"So we're going to run the tests?"

"We're doing one set, he and his friends are doing another. If there is any disagreement in the results, all parties will be tested at an accredited lab."

"He agreed to that? They all did?"

"There's really no choice in the matter. I made it clear that we're working for Emma now."

"I bet he loved hearing that."

"He didn't seem to mind. He did use the word *quisling* once or twice, but I'm sure he wasn't referring to me."

She scowled. "Did he even ask about Emma and her mother?"

"Actually, he did."

"And when you told him about Jennifer?"

"Silence. But who knows what that means? He might have been shedding a tear, might have been jumping for joy."

She said, "Your opinion of the good judge seems to have cooled since we met him at the restaurant."

He gave Hero an easy shove, and the dog jumped down to the floor, then crossed to Jayme for a scratch between the ears. DeMarco sat up and said, "I don't want to use the word *coward*, but he could have reacted to the letter in a more respectable fashion."

"You know that if he's the father, he's not going to want to adopt Emma after her mother dies. All he'll do is to throw money at the problem and hope it will go away."

"I suspect that's true. Of him and the others too."

"Did he ask about who was with Emma? Who's taking care of her now? Did he want to know anything about the grandmother?"

"Let's say his curiosity was underwhelming."

She shook her head, her mouth hard.

"Give him a little time," DeMarco said. "Let the dust settle a little and he'll maybe—"

"Oh screw that," she told him, and turned sharply toward the kitchen. "Men are such assholes."

She moved so abruptly that Hero was left standing motionless, watching as she disappeared into the next room. He turned and looked at DeMarco.

DeMarco told him, "And that, my boy, is the cross we bear."

# THIRTY-FOUR

## THICKER THAN WATER, BUT NEVER THICKER THAN TEARS

The exchange of the duplicate sets of swabs was made quickly, with Judge Morrison standing just inside DeMarco's front door, which was left open behind him. Jayme remained upstairs but could be heard twice during the brief conversation below, each time banging a drawer or door shut. Hero, as he often did when Jayme and DeMarco were on separate floors, lay on the landing at the top of the stairs.

"How you doing, Judge? It's nice to see you again. It's good of you to make the trip over."

"Eight miles is hardly a trip, Sergeant. Here you go."

"Thank you. Here's yours. But, uh, you gave me two, not three."

"I thought you'd probably prefer to take mine yourself."

DeMarco nodded. Morrison wanted to be seen as a straight-up guy, nothing up his sleeve, all of his cards on the table. "Sure thing," DeMarco said. "Fortunately, I have a couple left over from Michigan. Have a seat, if you want. I'll be right back."

Morrison smiled but did not move. DeMarco went upstairs to get one of the unused kits still in his suitcase. He found Jayme standing on the bedroom threshold. "He wants us to take his," he told her.

"Be my guest."

*Good thing,* he told himself as he went to the closet. *She'd probably try to choke him with the swab.*

Downstairs again, Morrison was still standing in the foyer. DeMarco laid the kit on the little table in the corner of the foyer, donned the collection gloves, then vigorously brushed four buccal swabs against the inside of the judge's mouth, two on the right cheek and two on the left. "All done," he said. "Sorry, but I need to get these labeled and packaged…"

"No problem. I was just wondering if you encountered any resistance up there, any—?"

"Why would we? Both Emma and her grandmother are eager for the results."

"Of course. Of course. As am I and my friends."

"I bet you are," DeMarco said. "So…three to five days, I guess. I'll text you when ours come in, you text me when yours come in."

"Agreed. I, uh…I don't recall discussing this in our earlier conversation, but you did say that Jennifer was in a coma when you arrived there."

"That's right."

"So you had no chance whatsoever to speak with her?"

"None. I already told you that."

"And, of course, as per our agreement, no names were mentioned? To the girl or her grandmother?"

"Not that I remember. But why would you assume that you and your friends' names aren't already known to them?"

"All the letters were identical. Photocopies, in fact. Each with the salutation of Dear Sir. The envelopes in which they were sent, however, were addressed by a more mature hand. Jennifer's, I'm sure. Which leads me to believe that neither the girl nor her grandmother were informed of the…circumstances under which Emma was conceived. It seems more likely that only one man in our group was implicated by Jennifer. And I see no reason why the girl should ever think otherwise. I am suggesting only that you allow her idealistic image of her mother to remain unsullied."

"Of course. But for her sake, Judge, not yours or your friends'. My agreement with you, and any commitment to put your interests before Emma's, ceased the minute I called you from Michigan to terminate it."

"Understood, understood. But as a point of honor…"

Before DeMarco could reply, quick footsteps were heard on the floor above, and then Jayme was descending the stairs, her tread heavier than usual. Hero followed her down. Both men turned and watched as she appeared and then paused on the bottom step, one hand on the curved wooden rail of the stairway, her mouth hard, eyes wet, a smear of mascara beneath the left one, Hero with his front paws on the step behind her, rear paws on the next highest step. In her right hand she held her cell phone.

"Jennifer Barrie passed away this morning," she told them, her laser gaze aimed directly at the judge. "At 2:47, to be exact."

DeMarco asked, "Did Emma call you?"

"I called the hospice," she answered, her gaze still locked on the judge. "So now what are you going to do?"

Judge Morrison moved his right foot back a half step, as if he had taken a blow. "Well…it now seems more imperative than ever that we find out who the father is. And that is exactly what we are doing, is it not?"

Jayme did not flinch. "What is imperative is that that little girl is not left hanging. She needs a home, and she needs it now."

DeMarco caught the judge's eye and nodded toward the door. "We'll talk soon, Judge. Thanks for coming over."

Morrison paused on the threshold, looked back at Jayme. "She *will* be taken care of. I give you my word."

Jayme said, "I'll make sure you keep it."

The judge nodded once, then said to DeMarco, "Have a good day, sir."

"And you," DeMarco said. He waited until the judge was out on the sidewalk before softly closing the door with his foot.

Then, smiling a little, he turned to the stairway, still with the four swabs standing up in his hands. He saw the rigidity of Jayme's body, sensed the anger in her heart. "Sweetness," he said, "I understand exactly how you feel. But I think maybe you're jumping the gun just a little bit, aren't you?"

"This has come to us for a reason," she said.

"Uh...exactly what has come to us?"

"Emma. And her situation."

"We have become involved, yes."

"Aren't you the one who said there are no accidents? That everything happens for a reason? Isn't that one of your precious truths? Number 10 or 14 or 612 or something?"

He crossed to her and leaned forward to kiss her cheek, but she flinched and drew away. He said, "I need to get these swabs—"

"Then do it," she said.

He was bent over the foyer table when Jayme said, "You saw that woman. That so-called grandmother of hers."

He turned and looked at her.

"She hadn't even fed her yesterday morning!"

"If you're thinking that she's going to abandon Emma now..."

"And what if she does? What if it comes down to us?"

"Sweetheart, we're—"

"It's going to come down to us, Ryan!"

He smiled. "And how do you know that?"

She leaned toward him, her eyes streaming tears now, a quiver in her voice. "I know it in my fucking bones, that's how!"

He nodded, and wanted to comfort her, but he needed to get the swabs in the bag. "Okay, baby. I believe you. I believe every word you say."

# THIRTY-FIVE

A FOUNTAIN OF SORROW SPRAYING
UP FROM AN OCEAN OF LOVE

According to the hospice administrator, Jennifer Barrie had an older brother, Jerome, who lived in Ottawa, and a younger sister, Judith, who lived near Detroit. Both had been notified of their sister's passing. Other than that, the administrator was reluctant to divulge personal information to anyone but immediate family. "I've probably told you more than I should already," the woman said. "I'm sure that you can track down the siblings without my help. You say you're working for the girl's biological father?"

"No, ma'am," Jayme explained. She had the phone on speaker so that she could jot down any information she received on a yellow legal pad. The kitchen was warm with sunlight, her bare feet warm tucked under Hero lying on the floor. "My partner and I are working on Emma's behalf to try to identify her biological father. We're awaiting the results of a paternity test. Can you tell me if Emma and her grandmother are still there in your facility?"

"They were notified by phone. Jennifer's body was removed immediately upon her death. She was an organ donor."

"With Creutzfeldt-Jakob disease?"

"The disease will be confirmed by autopsy, and then the brain and other organs will be donated for scientific study. Those were her wishes."

"I understand. Thank you for your time. You've been very helpful, and I do appreciate it."

Jayme's finger moved toward the phone to end the call, but stopped when the administrator said, "Have you, uh… I'm assuming that you have spoken with the grandmother already?"

There was something about the woman's tone, some insinuation of a proffering of confidential information. "We spoke two days ago when she gave permission for Emma's DNA swab." How to get at that information? "Frankly, I wasn't impressed with the grandmother. That's the real reason I called you. I'm concerned about leaving Emma in her care."

"Oh, thank goodness," the woman said. Her voice grew softer and less clear, as if her lips were nearly against the mouthpiece. "Do you know what she asked when I informed her of her daughter's bequest of her body for scientific study? She said, 'And then they'll do something with it, right? Like cremation or something? So that I don't have to deal with it?'"

Jayme's groan emanated in a loud huff, and her body tensed so suddenly, her feet sliding forward against the floor, that Hero jerked away and stood beneath the table. "Thank you for that," Jayme told her. "I'm going to take care of this. Thank you for confiding in me."

"I don't want to see that child go into the foster care system," the woman said.

"I'm not going to let that happen."

"I didn't know Jennifer," the woman continued. "I never once spoke to her or saw her when she was conscious. But any woman who can raise a sweet little girl like that…"

"I agree," Jayme said. "I agree one thousand percent."

She ended the call trembling, her skin cold with anger but

something fevered and deep inside giving rise to the tears again. Why was she such a fountain of sorrow these days? Ryan was recovering well, they had put McBride and Khatri behind them, they had the space and time to live again without a heavy black sky hovering overhead. Yet she had cried more times in the past few days than she had since the miscarriage. Why now? Emma had reawakened some need in her, had, in fact, amplified it. Why did she see herself in that little waif even though there was no resemblance whatsoever? Was she going to be like this every time she looked at a child in need? Was this the consequence of having carried life in her womb?

She opened her cell phone's address list, found the number for the landline in the Barrie mobile home, and pressed the Call icon. She wasn't surprised when the answering machine took the call. After the beep, Jayme said, "Hi, Emma. This is Jayme. Ryan and I heard the news about your mommy, sweetheart, and we just wanted to reach out and tell you how sorry we are for your loss. And to say that if you need anything, anything at all, you should call me, even if it's just to talk. I want you to know that I'm here for you, honey, whatever you need. You can call me anytime at all, okay? And I hope you will, because I would really love to talk with you again." She left her number and a few more words of consolation, then ended the call and sat silent and trembling with the phone against her chest. Hero pushed his snout between her knees and she laid one hand atop his head and kept the other hand pressing the phone against the blue-black grief pulsing like a drumbeat from her heart.

# THIRTY-SIX

*Au revoir, mirepoix; adios, serenidad*

N ow we wait," DeMarco said after he returned home from overnighting the four DNA swabs to the lab. He stood in the open doorway between the kitchen and dining room, hands shoved deep in his pockets as he listened to the sizzling coming from the stove.

"And in the meantime?" Jayme asked. She was using a wooden spatula to push something around in DeMarco's old cast iron soup pot. The air smelled of frying onions, mushrooms, garlic, and olive oil.

He stepped closer and peered inside. Saw everything he had smelled plus diced celery, carrots, and chunks of yellow and green peppers, a kind of mirepoix she had already cooked too long and too hot; the onions and mushrooms were caramelized and some of the bits of garlic were burnt. In answer to her question, he said, "The lab will send an email when they receive the kits, we pay the lab fee online, and they send us a link to get the results when they're ready."

She didn't smile; stirred and stared into the heavy black pot. "Ain't technology swell," she said.

*Uh-oh*, he thought, and looked around the kitchen. "Where's Hero?"

"Upstairs on the bed, I think."

"Really? I thought he never leaves your side."

Now she turned to look at him, her mouth pouting. "I yelled at him."

"You? Yelled?"

"He kept sticking his cold nose between my legs. And I was trying to…do this."

He nodded toward the pot. "And what is this going to be?"

"I don't know yet. I haven't gotten that far."

"Um-hmm. Tell you what," he said, and reached in front of her to turn the flame off on the burner. "What say we move it off the heat until you decide? It's, uh…"

"Burned," she said, and tossed the spatula into the sink.

He used a pot holder to move the pot to a cold burner. Turned to her and smiled. "So what's the haps here, James? You still worrying about Emma?"

"Still worrying? Why would I not be worrying?" Her mouth went into another pout, and she looked as if she might cry again. "I'm sorry."

He laid a hand against the small of her back. "It's okay."

"I called the hospice. The director there doesn't have any more faith in the grandmother than I do. In fact I have even *less* faith now after talking to her."

He nodded, cocked an eyebrow, pursed his lips. Said, "Why don't you give Emma a call?"

"I did already. Got the answering machine. I told her to call me back if she felt like talking."

"That's about all you can do for now, isn't it?"

"In other words, nothing," she said.

He didn't know what to say. When two people commit to loving each other and to living together in a loving relationship, they are committing not only to sharing their daily rewards and joys but also to working toward ensuring the other's joys and rewards; to not only sharing their daily sorrows and pains and travails but to working to ameliorate the other's; and to not only sharing their dreams and their necessary struggles but to struggling hand in hand to help the other's dreams come true. It was a commitment to doubling one's own problems in exchange for increasing one's happiness. Was that a commitment DeMarco was ready to make? And at an age when most men were slowing down and striving for a simpler, less complicated and frenetic life?

Hadn't he already made that commitment? Wasn't he already in the thick of it? So his choice was not whether or not to start but whether or not to stop. And now, seeing her standing there sloop-shouldered and sad, grieving not for herself but for a little girl, he had no intention of stopping. No intention of ever going back to the man he used to be. He had never been busier or more worried or more reflective or more prone to request celestial guidance, but he had never been happier either. He had never before been a tenth as happy as he was at that very sorrowful moment.

"Let's go see a movie," he said.

"You hate movie theaters. All those people munching popcorn and laughing and stuff."

"You're right. People are disgusting. How about kayaking?"

"And fall in and freeze to death."

"Baby," he said after a pause, "what would *you* like to do today? We need to do something."

She thought for a few moments. Then looked down at the still sizzling pot. "Can any of that be saved?"

He moved closer to her and tapped his finger to Lucy's nose. Then said in his attempt at a Cuban accent, "Ju want me to sing a little 'Babalú' to cheer you up?"

"Thank you, no," she said with a short laugh. "I think I'll just get another shower. I smell like burnt garlic." She kissed his cheek, turned and left the room.

He went to the stove and peered into the pot. A sticky, blackened mess. He recovered the spatula from the sink and started scraping up the vegetables. "Babalú, aye Babalú!" he sang softly, Ricky's plea for good luck, the love of his unpredictable woman, and protection for all.

# THIRTY-SEVEN

SADNESS SEEKING AN EAR AT THE SPEED OF LIGHT

That night at 11:52 Jayme was awakened by her phone vibrating on the bed table. As she pulled it toward her she read the familiar number, and below it, *Michigan*. She swiped the Answer icon and said softly, hoping to not waken DeMarco, "Hello?"

"Hi," came Emma's small, hoarse voice. Jayme knew in an instant that the girl had been crying all day. She slid her legs out from under the sheet and sat up on the edge of the bed, her bare feet to the floor.

"Hi, baby," Jayme whispered. "How are you doing, sweetheart?"

"I'm okay," Emma said.

"I'm so, so sorry about your mama. You know she's in a better place now, right? She's not sick anymore."

"I know," Emma said.

"It just wasn't a very good day at all today, was it?"

"It wasn't," Emma said.

Jayme sniffed, leaned forward, rested her elbows on her knees. "Did you call about anything in particular, honey? Or just to talk?"

"Just to talk, I guess."

"Okay, that's great."

"The people from the bar where Mom worked are going to have a party for her there on Saturday night."

"Are they? How nice! I bet they all loved your mommy very much."

"They're going to close the bar up for her and invite everybody from town who wants to come."

"That's pretty special, honey."

"They're going to do a pig in the smoker out back and set up lights and stuff."

"That all sounds wonderful. I wish Ryan and I could be there."

"My uncle Jerry isn't going to come but Aunt Judy said she'll try."

"Oh, that's nice! Do you get to see your aunt Judy often?"

"Not really. I think I was six the last time I saw her. She's pretty busy."

"Mm-hmm, yeah. People are pretty busy these days."

"Grandma told her that she needs to let me live with her. But she said she doesn't have room for me. She has three kids already."

"Oh. Well…I'm sure things will get straightened out soon, Emma. It's nothing for you to worry about, okay?"

"Aunt Judy said she'll need to check with the welfare to see how much they'll give her to keep me. But it probably won't be enough."

Jayme shook her head, held her tongue, was afraid of what she might say. But when the girl said nothing either, was probably hoping for a lifeline from Jayme, Jayme said, "You know what, sweetie? Maybe after the memorial for your mom you can come spend some time with me and Ryan. I would really love that. Would you?"

"How would I get there?" Emma asked. "It's a long way, isn't it?"

"Well, how about if Ryan and I get you a ticket to fly here? You can fly to Cleveland and from there to Franklin and we'll be there waiting to pick you up. Would you be interested in doing that? Just for a couple of days or…however long you want."

"I've never been on an airplane before."

"I think you will like it," Jayme told her. "Ryan doesn't like to fly, but he's a big man and has to squeeze into his seat. Plus he doesn't like talking to most people. None of that bothers me, though. And I bet it won't bother you either."

"Isn't it scary to be up so high?"

"We'll get you a window seat. That way you can look out and see how beautiful the clouds are all spread out below you. I really think you will love it, Emma."

"What's it like where you live?"

"Well, we live on the edge of a fairly small town. It's not as big as Ludington, but a little bigger than Scottville. With lots of farms all around it."

"What would I do if I came there? About school, I mean?"

"Well, I could talk to your teachers, if you want me to. We'll get your homework assignments, and you and I can work on them here every day. And we can go walking in the woods together, or in the park. Ryan and I like to do that a lot. We have a dog we take with us. He loves to go running through the woods. His name is Hero, and he is very, very affectionate."

"What kind of dog is he?"

"He's sort of a German shepherd and sort of a husky maybe. His fur is a little longer than a shepherd's but not as long as a husky's."

"Can you send me a picture of him?"

"Absolutely I can. The minute we stop talking, I will send a couple. He loves to have his picture taken."

Emma giggled a little. Then said, her voice softer now, "I don't know if Grandma will let me come, though. We don't know you very well."

"That's true," Jayme said. "We haven't known each other very long. But we're good people, sweetie. I think you know that. We used to work for the state police. Your grandma can call our former boss if she'd like. I'll be happy to give her the number."

"Okay," Emma said. "But she'd have to drive me to the airport if I come, and she doesn't like using up her gas."

"You tell her that I will send her all the gas money she needs. It won't cost her a cent."

"Oh. Okay." A pause. "But she might not want to do it anyway. She doesn't like driving me places."

"Well, you don't need to worry about getting to the airport, honey. Ryan and I will take care of all that for you. You can tell your grandma that too, okay?"

"Okay," Emma said.

Jayme felt herself choking up with emotion again, and she didn't want Emma to hear it. She wanted Emma to hear nothing but the love in her voice. "I hope you will come, I really do. I am so looking forward to seeing you again. Maybe you and me and Ryan and Hero will go camping in our RV, would you like doing that?"

There was a pause before Emma spoke. "I think I'd rather be in a house," she said, and immediately Jayme thought, *Of course you would! Duh!*

Emma asked, "How big is your house? Is there room enough for me there?"

"There is plenty of room for you! There are three bedrooms on the second floor. One is for Ryan and me, but you can have your choice of the other two. Or choose both of them if you want. You can go back and forth from bed to bed until you find the one you like best! Just like Goldilocks."

Again Emma giggled softly, and the sound of it deepened the ache in Jayme's chest. She said, "Well, it's getting late, sweetie, and you should probably be in bed now, right?"

"I am in bed. I'm just not sleepy yet."

"Yeah, me too. What are you and your grandma planning on doing tomorrow?"

"I don't know. I'd like to go see my mom again but I don't know where they took her or what they're doing to her."

"Oh, baby," Jayme said. "Didn't the doctor or somebody at the hospice explain that to you?"

"She said Mommy gave her body to science. But I don't know what that means."

Jayme swallowed hard. "It means that other doctors will look at her body and try to figure out how to cure her disease. So that other people won't have to die because of it. It's a really good, really generous, wonderful thing she did, Emma. You should be very proud of your mommy for doing that. I am."

"I am too," Emma said. "I just miss her is all. I'm not ever going to see her again."

Jayme squeezed her eyes shut. Swallowed again. "You know," she said, then opened her eyes and blinked, "my daddy died a while ago, and I thought I would never see him again. But I still do. You know how?"

"How?" Emma asked.

"Every night when I go to bed, right before I fall asleep, I close my eyes and remember him when he wasn't sick. When he was happy and smiling. Can you remember a time when your mommy was like that?"

"Just a couple of weeks ago," Emma said. "We were running along the beach together and she was holding my hand and laughing."

"Oh, that's a beautiful memory to have. You think of it every night, okay? Think of it every night and you will always have it forever. Your mommy will always be with you."

"Okay," Emma said. "I will."

Jayme could tell that the girl was crying now, could hear the congestion in her voice, could hear her muffled staccato breaths, so like her own. "Okay, sweetheart," she said. "I'll let you go now so that you can think about her. And in the morning, you think about whether you'd like to come stay with us for a few days, okay? And talk to your grandma about it too. And then you can call me and we'll start making plans."

"Does Hero ever bite people?" Emma asked.

"Oh, Hero is a big old softy. He might lick you to death if you let him, but he would never ever bite you. Except maybe a little tiny nibble just to see how you taste."

Another tired giggle. "Okay," Emma said.

Jayme squeezed her eyes shut. Used a thumb and the tip of a finger to pull the dampness from the corners of her eyes. Her chest ached with a soreness so full that little space remained for her breath. "Okay, baby girl," Jayme said. "We'll talk again soon. So I'll say good night now, all right?"

"Good night," Emma said.

Jayme remained sitting bent forward on the side of the bed, sniffing and blinking. Soon the screen on her phone went black. Thirty more seconds passed. She laid the phone softly on the bed table, then turned and pulled her feet up onto the bed and slowly eased out her legs and laid her head on the pillow. Only then did she turn her head to look at DeMarco, who hadn't made a sound or a movement throughout the entire conversation. To her surprise, his eyes were open and looking her way. She could not read his face in the dimness, and a fear shot through her that he might be angry or upset.

"I'm sorry," she said. "I should have discussed it with you first. I just felt like...I just..."

"You were wrong," he told her.

She nodded. "I know. I know..."

"Wrong about two things. First, you were wrong about Hero," he said, and reached for her hand. "He would never lick anybody to death, let alone a motherless little girl. And two: you promised her some photos. And you haven't delivered them yet."

"Oh, baby," she said, and rolled into his arms.

# THIRTY-EIGHT

SUNFLOWERS BLOOM, SUNFLOWERS WITHER

Throughout the ensuing week, Jayme and Emma talked frequently by phone. With each conversation, both grew more excited about the upcoming visit. The principal of Emma's school agreed, pending the grandmother's approval, to excuse Emma for a full week, in addition to the typical three days of absence following the death of a family member, and to instruct her teachers to email Jayme a summary of all essential homework. Jayme also had one conversation with Grandma Loey, in which the older woman readily agreed to the trip—"God knows I can use a few days to myself"—and even insinuated that a longer stay would not be out of the question. "I've had my fill of this here trailer, and I know full well she ain't going to take to my little place back in the senior high-rise. We'll just be tripping over each other there."

After inquiring of Emma's favorite color—pink and yellow—Jayme bought a new set of pink sheets and pillowcases for Emma's bed, and a comforter decorated with huge yellow sunflowers, plus matching towels and washcloths for the guest bath. DeMarco trudged along dutifully through Kohl's as Jayme piled his arms full, and kept his mouth shut about the startling color combinations and the mounting bill. He hadn't seen her this lively, this excited, since…

WHEN ALL LIGHT FAILS    173

well, since never. She did not mention the word *adoption* but he suspected that she was thinking it, especially when he walked past her one afternoon and saw her perusing full sets of bedroom furniture online, all white and girly and curving and elegant, and that was when he knew that he alone would never be enough for her, that he alone could never fill the emptiness she had only recently realized existed.

He had to admit that he was a little excited too. And worried. What could he possibly find to say to a nine-year-old girl day after day? He was only now coming to understand Jayme's moods, and most of that was guesswork, usually wrong. But a nine-year-old? Would she like his cooking? Would he have to stop walking around in just his boxers and a T-shirt? Would he have to stop using the guest bathroom when Jayme was using the other one? And when did a girl start menstruating? Good lord, what if she went into puberty while she was staying with them?

*It's only for a week*, he told himself, although he knew that maybe it wasn't. Maybe it was a whole new change of life, all of a sudden, in one fell swoop. Was he okay with that? Could he learn to be okay with that?

A little voice inside his head reminded him that all things are temporary. Change is all. Some truths, though, are inviolate. Such as, change is all. *Let it go, let it be.* Thus spake somebody or other, he could not remember who.

≫———————≪

Early Friday afternoon, the DNA test results came in. DeMarco called Jayme over to his laptop before he opened the link. She leaned forward over his shoulder, one hand gripping the edge of the dining room table, the other hand braced atop his shoulder.

No matches. Negative three times in a row.

"What does that mean?" Jayme asked, even though she knew exactly what it meant. Her question, he assumed, was really asking, *What does it mean for Emma?*

"One of two things," he said, just to hear the answer out loud. "It means that either the judge's deceased friend is the father, or somebody else is. Somebody unknown."

Jayme leaned away from him, stood erect, and slid her right hand onto his left shoulder. "Now she'll probably never know," Jayme said. "Ryan. Now she'll never know who her father is."

Deep in his gut he felt the implication of that pronouncement. He felt it in the way Jayme's hand squeezed his shoulder. And in the way his heart had begun to thump.

"Do we call the grandmother?" he asked.

"Not yet," Jayme said.

"Right. We need to wait for the judge's results. They might not agree with these."

"But they probably will. And I want us to tell Emma first. Not her grandmother. We'll tell her after she gets here and settles in."

"I'm not sure that news like that should come from us."

"From who then, Ryan? Tell me who is better suited to give her that news?"

He said nothing.

"Thank God she has us, Ryan," Jayme said.

He heard finality in that statement. In her heart, she had already appropriated the girl. Had already claimed her. He hoped she wasn't setting herself up for a catastrophic fall.

# THIRTY-NINE

## OF MOBSTERS AND WORMS AND
## OTHER TRICKS OF THE LIGHT

That same evening, DeMarco was trying to concentrate on a History Channel biopic about the mobster John Gotti, but he could think only of Jayme out in the kitchen baking chocolate chip cookies, and Emma in Michigan packing and repacking a bag for her flight on Monday morning. Deep in his heart he knew that he was not responsible for their happiness, was but a secondary player in their own individual stories, but as a human being he did have a responsibility to be the best friend and companion he could. He thought of Flores too and of how she was still struggling to adjust to her physical limitations, and how negligent he had been. He needed to spend more time with her. Could be doing so right now instead of staring at a TV screen. He used to be fascinated by men like Gotti, wanted to understand every nuance of their twisted psyches, but now the entire world with all of its mayhem and guile and subterfuge and yes with all of its altruism and beauty too seemed a kind of Kinetoscope show to DeMarco, with him peering down through a slit to watch painted images in simulated action, and with him too a painted image inside another painted world, an ignis fatuus, a trick of the light.

The beep and vibration from his cell phone, faceup atop the coffee table, startled him like a mild electric shock. He leaned forward to read the screen. A text from Judge Morrison. Are you home?

DeMarco picked up the phone and sent a reply. Been waiting to hear from you. Where do you want to meet?

I'm out front. Heading to your door.

DeMarco stood and went to the kitchen threshold and told Jayme, who was easing a hot sheet of cookies from the oven, "The judge is here." He turned and went into the foyer and opened the door. Morrison had his hand raised to knock, but now lowered it. "Come on in, Judge," DeMarco said.

Jayme joined them in the dining room to compare printouts of the DNA test results, two sheets of printer paper laid side by side atop the table. The results matched.

"I have to admit to a disappointment on my part," Morrison told them. "A part of me was hoping to discover that I was a father again."

Jayme ignored his remark. "So your deceased friend," she said. "Does he have any children we can test?"

"There are two adult children, yes," Morrison answered. "Not that it will do any good. I know for a fact that he had a vasectomy back in the '80s."

"Still," Jayme said.

He gave her a long look, a lopsided smile.

"What?" she said.

"I did a little investigation myself," he told her. "Just a feeling I had."

"What kind of feeling?"

"While I was waiting for the results to come in," he told them, "I spent a lot of time thinking about and remembering Jennifer.

Remembering how eager she was. It was she who approached us that night at the bar. I mean yes, there was some flirting going on, but we didn't go there looking to get involved with a woman. She came on to us."

"What are you saying?" Jayme asked.

"I had Emma's birth record pulled. She was born February 3. Our fishing trip ran from May 12 to 17 of the previous year. So unless Emma was born a bit premature, Jennifer was already pregnant when we met her."

Jayme cocked her head, her eyes in a squint. "Are you saying that Jennifer screwed you and your friends so that she could blame one of you for her pregnancy?"

At the word *screwed*, DeMarco laid his hand in the small of her back. Her body felt hot.

"Not at all," Morrison said. "Or else she would have gotten in touch with us years earlier. No, I think she did it for the money. We were all very generous with her. She was pregnant and she needed money."

"Such *gentlemen!*" Jayme said. She pivoted away from DeMarco's hand then, strode back into the kitchen. Stood up against the little table there, both hands on the surface as she leaned over the cookies laid out on a cooling rack.

Morrison gazed out at her, then turned to DeMarco and nodded toward the kitchen. "May I?" he asked.

"It's your head, Judge."

Sheepishly, Morrison approached her. As he did so, he removed a brown letter envelope from inside his coat and laid it on the table near Jayme's right hand. "I know this doesn't excuse our behavior," he told her. "And honestly, that isn't what it's for. It's for Emma. For her future care, her college, whatever her guardian might deem appropriate."

She gazed down at the envelope as if it were stuffed with a rotting fish. "What is it?" she asked.

"A cashier's check. In the sum of $20,000. From the three of us. I was hoping that you would be so kind as to—"

"Judge," she interrupted, her voice hoarse and strained, and lifted her head to look him in the eye. "I would appreciate it if you would get the hell out of my kitchen now."

He nodded. Turned away. And paused for a moment beside DeMarco in the dining room.

"Sergeant," he said sotto voce, "all we ask is that no names are mentioned when you give the girl the money. No good can come from destroying other families over this."

DeMarco kept his eyes on Jayme. "Good evening, Judge," he said.

>>————————————<<

They went to bed early that night, neither able to read or watch TV or otherwise distract their thoughts from the day's proceedings and the imminent future.

"My concern is in turning the money over to her grandmother," Jayme said. She had called Hero up onto the bed that night, in disregard of her own prohibition, and now stroked his head and back as he lay between her and DeMarco. Hero's head was turned toward DeMarco, and his long mouth seemed to be smiling, smug in his usurpation of Jayme's bedtime affection.

DeMarco lay with his hands clasped atop his chest. "I share that concern."

"So, legally speaking, Morrison gave it to us to do as we see fit. Am I right?"

"It would be nice if we had that on paper."

"You can talk to him if you want," she said, "but I'm finished with him."

"Understood," he said.

"If we put it in a college fund, it could grow significantly over the next ten years."

"The question is, do we tell Emma about it. Because if we do…"

"We'd have to swear her to secrecy. And we can't do that."

"No, we can't," he said.

"What if you were to call Morrison and ask him to stipulate that the money goes into a college fund?"

"He won't put his name to paper, though. That much is clear."

"He's a worm, you know."

"There does seem to be a bit more slime in his genetic makeup than I expected."

She scratched between Hero's ears, which made the dog's grin widen and his eyes go glassy. "What do you think about his suggestion that Jennifer was already pregnant?"

"Fifty-fifty," he said. "Maybe even sixty-forty. Though I don't see how it really matters now. Not where Emma's future is concerned."

"To find out that she will probably never know who her biological father is? I think it matters a lot."

Now he too needed some comforting; he spread an open hand atop Hero's warm belly. Could feel the breath going in and out. Could feel the doggie heart laboring away inside the ribs.

"All we can do," he told her, "is to see how it goes."

"Baby," Jayme told him, "you know how it's going to go. She's grieving, she's frightened, she's probably desperate for affection. What you mean is we'll have to see how it goes with *us*. Isn't that what you're really saying?"

Sometimes she was too intuitive for her own good. *Or for my own good*, he thought. *Isn't that what you really mean, DeMarco?*

# FORTY

The weekend dragged on. Jayme had hoped that Emma would call on Saturday, or at least on Sunday to tell her about the memorial at the Bear Claw, and about how much she was looking forward to flying to Pennsylvania, but no call came. Jayme understood why. The memorial would have exhausted the child, all of those stories about her mother, all of those tears and hugs and emotion. Every laugh would have stung like a slap, while every tear would have squeezed at her heart. Still, Jayme looked at her cell phone frequently that Sunday, even picked it up and wanted desperately to make a call. But Emma would call if she wanted to speak. Their bond was already strong. And tomorrow they would be together.

>>————————————«

At 9:40 the next morning, following a winding two-lane road as it twisted through several villages and past thousands of acres of fields still brown with last year's corn stubble, they drove to the small Venango Regional Airport in Franklin, just over twenty-five miles away, and waited at the chain-link fence along the edge of the parking lot for the 10:23 flight to arrive. The air was cool and still pleasantly aromatic with the scent of a fog that had lifted well before their arrival. The parking lot held only nine other cars, the runway was empty, and the orange wind sock fluttered lethargically in the occasional breeze. The only other person visible was a man in a white coat carrying a stack of heavy white packages from the meat locker beside the side door of the airport's restaurant.

Hero, on a leash with its other end wrapped around DeMarco's hand, stood with his snout pressed into an opening in the fence. Jayme stood nearly as close to the fence as Hero did, the fingers of her right hand extending through the cold links.

At 10:26 they heard the air taxi's engine and looked to the west. The plane was coming down through a layer of wispy gray clouds, its wings tilting just a bit from side to side, buffeted by a gust of air. Jayme gripped the fence and said, breathily, "Here she comes."

DeMarco said nothing. Something about the little Beechcraft troubled him, but he was not sure what. It touched down at the far end of the runway and came speeding toward them, ailerons down, engine throttling back, brakes screeching. Then it was past, moving slowly now, and turned toward the gate. Jayme's body turned with it. "Let's go," she said.

"You go," DeMarco told her. "Hero and I will wait out here."

Without argument she hurried away toward the terminal's entrance.

Twenty minutes later, after fifteen or so people had exited the building, only ten of them carrying luggage, and had all crossed to cars in the lot and drove away, DeMarco and Hero were still walking back and forth in front of the glass doors. Finally DeMarco paused and sent a text: Everything okay?

Three minutes passed without a reply. Then Jayme came out,

moving toward them with short, shuffling steps, shaking her head and looking confused. "She wasn't on board," she said.

He asked, "Did you try calling her?"

"Of course I did. Both the landline and the cell phone, twice each. They all went to voicemail. I checked at the desk and she was on the manifest but never showed up."

"That's odd," he said. The premonition he had felt at first sight of the plane now darkened. "Let's go sit in the car and figure this out."

In the vehicle Jayme stared at the empty field and runway behind the fence. "So maybe they got the flight time wrong," Jayme said. "Maybe she left the house without Jennifer's cell phone and they're still driving or whatever."

"Did you try the taxi service you scheduled for her?" DeMarco asked. "See if the dispatcher can get in touch with the driver?"

Jayme yanked the cell phone from the pocket of her denim jacket. "I didn't think of that. I've been so confused," she said. She pulled up the service's number and called. Spoke briefly to the person on the other end, listened, asked, "Can't you call the driver and find out?" then listened for a few moments longer before saying a curt "Thank you," and hanging up.

She turned to DeMarco, her forehead pinched. "The log says that the driver arrived at 7:00 a.m. as scheduled, but then the pickup was cancelled. No reason was given for the cancellation. And the driver is apparently off duty and unreachable."

Nausea bubbled in DeMarco's stomach. "Jitneys," he said, as if that explained everything. "Hey, what was the name of that market where I bought the groceries for them? Was it Johnson's?"

She thought for a moment. "Jensen's," she said. Then, before DeMarco could respond, she tapped her phone and said, "Siri. Phone number for Jensen's Market in Scottville, Michigan."

"Here it is," Siri said. "Would you like me to dial the number for you?"

"Yes!" Jayme said.

After four rings the call was answered by a female voice.

"Yes, hi," Jayme said, and turned questioning eyes to DeMarco. "I was hoping to speak to one of your cashiers?"

"Darla," DeMarco whispered.

"Her name is Darla," Jayme said into the phone. "Is she working today, by any chance?"

Jayme frowned at the response.

"I hope so," Jayme said. "I am trying to get in touch with Jennifer Barrie's daughter, Emma. She was scheduled to fly to Pennsylvania to stay with us a while—"

She listened for a few seconds, then said, "What?"

As she listened, her mouth scrunched up but her eyes grew wide and filled with tears. "*What?*"

She listened a few moments longer, her breath coming in short gasps now, her head going back and forth, eyes glassy with disbelief.

"What happened?" DeMarco asked.

She kept shaking her head, had moved the cell phone from her mouth and was now squeezing the phone in her fist, her entire body quivering.

DeMarco seized her hand in his and leaned across the console. "Baby, what happened? Tell me what happened!"

She could barely choke out the words, her voice glutinous and thick. "They found the bodies...on Sunday sometime."

"What? What bodies?"

"Carbon monoxide poisoning," she said. "Emma and Loey. Died in their sleep."

He slipped both arms around her. Pulled her head close to his. Felt her body racked by violent convulsions of grief, his own body draining, emptying out and going weak. Because he knew, he knew. It was all too convenient somehow. Carbon monoxide poisoning? Too, too much of a coincidence. Especially when there is no such thing as coincidence.

III

THE NATURE OF EVERYTHING IS
ILLUSORY AND EPHEMERAL.
THOSE WITH DUALISTIC PERCEPTION REGARD
SUFFERING AS HAPPINESS,
LIKE THEY WHO LICK THE HONEY
FROM A RAZOR'S EDGE.

# FORTY-ONE

DECIDUOUS. RHYMES WITH UNAMBIGUOUS

At the station house DeMarco nodded to two of the troopers who looked up at his entrance, but without speaking he left Jayme to greet them while he marched into the station commander's office, closed the door behind him, then crossed to one of the two padded armchairs facing the captain's desk, sat, leaned forward with elbows on knees, and said, "I have a favor to ask."

Initially Bowen had smiled upon seeing DeMarco at his door, but the smile quickly dissolved. He had never seen DeMarco looking so somber, so pale. Bowen said, "What's going on?"

"I'd like for you to call the police chief in a little place called Scottville up in Michigan. Ask about the deaths at the Barrie place. Carbon monoxide poisoning. Grandmother and a little girl, asleep in a mobile home. Ask if he is absolutely certain it happened the way they've reported it."

"And how have they reported it?" Bowen asked.

"Clogged vent."

"Why don't you call him?"

"I'm a civilian. I'll get the public story."

"And you're not buying that story?"

"I'm not."

"And why is that?"

DeMarco said nothing. Sat there with his lips closed while thinking how much to tell. Bowen knew Judge Morrison, of course. Probably better than DeMarco did. Socialized with him. Rubbed elbows. DeMarco wasn't yet ready to get any of those elbows skinned.

"You know it's not an uncommon thing," Bowen told him. "Trailers and carbon monoxide poisoning."

"I am aware," DeMarco said.

"Especially in older trailers. Was this an older trailer?"

"It was."

"So then?" Bowen said.

Again DeMarco remained silent, trying and failing to think clearly, objectively.

Bowen said, "As a civilian, what is your interest in this case? You need to tell me that much, at least. As a friend, if nothing else."

DeMarco shook his head, not in negation but still in disbelief of what had happened. "The girl," he said. "Nine years old. We were trying to help her identify her biological father."

"You were working for a nine-year-old girl?"

"Now more than ever."

"You and Jayme?"

DeMarco nodded.

"And did you? Identify the father?"

DeMarco waggled his head. *I think we have, maybe we haven't, I can't say for sure.* He said, "Her mother passed away of some crazy brain disease. And then, on Sunday—just yesterday, Kyle—both the grandmother and the girl died in their sleep of carbon monoxide poisoning."

Bowen leaned back in his chair. "That's all you have? The unlikely juxtaposition of those three deaths?"

"I have more," DeMarco answered.

"Which you're not going to tell me."

How do you explain intuition? How do you explain a heavy black cloud that has gripped your heart in a smothering fist? "I would if I could."

Bowen blew out a breath. Kept studying DeMarco's face. "Why don't you make the call yourself? Tell the chief what you told me. He'll respect that."

"It might be prudent right now to retain my anonymity. Plus, you come with the imprimatur of power."

"Imprimatur, huh?"

"Seal of approval. In case you have to throw your weight around."

"Hmm. Would I be correct in assuming that the biological father does not wish to be identified?"

"That would be my guess."

The two men kept looking at each other. Bowen asked, "How in the world did you get involved in a paternity case in Michigan? And how was she paying you? In bubble gum?"

Something happened to DeMarco's face then, a softening, a collapse of the muscles, an unexpected dampness in his eyes. He could feel it happening, so he knew Bowen could see it, but DeMarco didn't really give a damn. "How old are your girls now, Kyle?" he asked.

Bowen cocked his head momentarily. Let out another breath. Then he gave DeMarco a little nod, and reached for the phone. He punched a button, then asked Trooper Carmichael to track down a number for the Scottville chief of police, call him and put him through ASAP.

"He'll do his stuff," Bowen told DeMarco. "Shouldn't take long."

DeMarco nodded. "So how's every little thing?"

"How's every little thing? Two people dead, and, you suspect, not by accident, and you ask me how's every little thing?"

"We're killing time, boss. Humor me."

"Every little thing is every little thing."

"How is Dani adjusting?"

Bowen shrugged. "That's a tough diagnosis to make. She's seeing a therapist, but…"

"But? You want to get more specific?"

"Her attitude is in the process of adjustment."

"She's still depressed?"

"That's what's underneath it all, I suppose. On the surface, I've had a few complaints that she's short-tempered and sometimes downright nasty. I've talked to her about it but, you know, I can't bring myself to be too hard on her. After everything she's been through."

DeMarco chewed on the inside of his cheek. He couldn't shake the feeling that he was somehow responsible for her injury and her transfer to a desk job. On a theoretical level he knew that he was not responsible, but theory did little to ease his conscience.

Then a button flashed on Bowen's phone. He punched it, picked up the receiver and said hello just as Jayme eased open the door and peeked into the room. Bowen nodded her inside. She came in and took the other chair and reached for DeMarco's hand.

Then Bowen was introducing himself to the Scottville chief and outlining the reason for the call.

"Speaker," DeMarco whispered.

"You mind if I put you on speaker, sir?" Bowen asked. "I have a couple of investigators here with me who are working a relevant case."

Only Bowen heard the chief's response.

"I'm sorry, but that's not something they can divulge just yet," Bowen told him.

He listened for a moment, then said, "We appreciate it. Thank you," and he pressed the speaker button.

"Okay, we're all here," Bowen said. "So then. About the inspection at the scene. I understand that the culprit was a clogged vent?"

"Correct," a male voice said. "We sent our fire inspector out to have a look. The roof jack extending from the roof was filled with leaves. Not surprising considering that the place is all but boxed in by trees."

DeMarco leaned toward the speaker box. "Ryan DeMarco here, sir. Isn't there usually a protective cap over the roof jack? To keep the rain and debris out?"

"I didn't see it myself, but I was told that this one was so old and rusted out it was useless. In fact it wasn't even covering the pipe. We can get some pretty fierce winds up here. From the looks of things, the whole crown assembly was as old as the trailer."

"Dang," DeMarco said. "Did your man happen to mention what kind of leaves he pulled out of the pipe?"

"What kind? No, no mention of that. Said he put a wire down and pulled out a wad of leaves. Leaves, dirt, all decomposing in there for a good long time, I'd say."

*Right*, DeMarco thought. In small towns and rural areas, the local fire inspector could be as little as eighteen years old with a GED and only perfunctory training. Might even have a full-time job in a maybe related field. DeMarco took a shot in the dark. "Is it typical for a fire inspector to handle an inspection like this? I mean one that doesn't involve a fire?"

"It's sort of hard to say what typical is around here. The coroner's the one who called me. He's not in any kind of shape to be climbing up on a trailer roof. Wouldn't be safe for him or the roof, if you know what I mean."

"I get the picture," DeMarco said. "What's your inspector's main line of work?"

"HVAC," the man said. "So he's been in a lot less pleasant places than the roof of a mobile home. He was up in my attic last summer, a hundred and ten degree heat, knee-deep in insulation. Try two or three days of that, and a few minutes on top of a trailer feels like a vacation."

"Roger that," DeMarco said. "The thing is, if I remember correctly, the trees closest to the trailer, at the back and to the rear, those are mostly pines, am I right?"

"I guess I would have to go out and take a look for myself to be sure, but...I'm going to assume you know what you're talking about. You've been up here already?"

"I have," DeMarco said. "But here's the thing. Your guy said the cap on the crown assembly wasn't in place?"

"He said it was hanging to the side. Barely hanging."

"Hmm. You know, I could understand a bird building a nest in a situation like that. Or even a squirrel filling a vent full of acorns. But it was leaves he pulled out of there, right? He specifically said leaves?"

"A couple of fistfuls. Said they was matted in there pretty tight."

"Not pine needles?" DeMarco asked. "But actual leaves."

"My recollection is that there are some hardwoods on the kitchen end of the trailer. The leaves probably came from there."

"Right. I remember seeing those trees," DeMarco said. "So I guess it's possible that a bunch of those leaves could have blown from east to west in such a fashion that they would get sucked in past the crown and then straight down into that pipe."

"Huh," the chief said with a little laugh. "Hearing you say it like that... I mean, over the years, you know? That trailer's been setting there for what—twenty years at least, I'd say."

"So there were lots of leaves on the roof?"

"The report didn't say one way or the other."

"And old pine needles too?"

"I'm not sure what you're suggesting here."

"Just that the pine trees are significantly closer to the trailer than the hardwoods are. And the wind typically blows west to east, correct? Or north to east. So doesn't it make sense that there would be more pine needles on the roof and in the vent than oak leaves?"

The chief was silent for most of ten seconds. "Tell you what," he said. "Just to be on the safe side, I think maybe I'll get in touch with my guy and we'll run out there today and have another look at the whole thing."

"That would be great," DeMarco said. "Would you mind also keeping an eye out for any scuff marks or footprints or whatever up on the roof? Any evidence that somebody other than your inspector was up there recently?"

"It's worth checking out, isn't it? If I'm hearing you right, you're suggesting this might not have been an act of God after all."

"Just covering all the bases," DeMarco said. "Could you let us know what you find?"

"You betcha. Call you back at this number sometime this afternoon?"

DeMarco leaned back in his chair, which prompted Bowen to lean forward and say, "That would be great, Chief. We really do appreciate your help with this."

"Hey, I'm actually glad you called. Had I known there was any possibility of funny business being involved…"

"We see what we expect to see," Bowen told him. "It's human nature."

"At the time, I didn't even know about the girl's mother being deceased. Not until I heard it later that day."

"You can't put two and two together if all you have is one two,"

Bowen told him. Which caused DeMarco to lower his chin, smile and shake his head.

The moment Bowen ended the call, DeMarco stood. "Thanks, boss," he said.

"*Now* you call me boss?" said Bowen. "Twice in ten minutes? When I'm not your boss anymore?"

"Just trying to make you feel a little better about yourself. I know how insecure you are."

With that, DeMarco turned away and exited the office. To Jayme, Bowen said, "Just when I thought he was softening up a little."

"Oh, he has," Jayme answered in a half whisper. She stood and walked around the corner of the desk. Bowen stood and embraced her for a quick hug.

"Thank you," she told him, and drew away. "It's nice to know people in high places."

"Is that your idea of sarcasm?" he asked.

# FORTY-TWO

A HAND THROUGH THE CURTAIN

D eMarco opened the passenger-side door and was standing against the rear door, apparently staring over the roof of the car at the digital sign in front of the small ATM bank across the road from the state police barracks, when Jayme came out of the low brick building and into the parking lot. He didn't react to the crunch of her footsteps on the gravel, didn't respond when she stood for a few moments beside him. The sky had darkened in the past hour, was fully overcast with a low gray ceiling and a thick swath of black moving in from the north.

"So what now?" she asked, and he turned to regard her as if she had materialized out of thin air.

He said, "The last time you talked to Emma, she mentioned the memorial at the Bear Claw. Was it being held during the day or at night?"

"Night, though I don't know what time. She said 'Saturday night.'"

"And probably everybody in town would have been there."

"Probably. You think that's when the vent was tampered with?"

"The trailer would be empty. Nobody around to see a stranger up on the roof."

She laid her hand against the small of his back. "We need to talk to the judge again."

He shook his head. "I took his swab myself. So we know for a fact that he is not the father. What we don't know is who the other two men are. And how their swabs were collected."

"So we *do* need to talk to the judge."

"Let's wait till we hear from Scottville again. Keep our ducks in a row."

"And until then, babe?"

He looked away. The bank sign flashed 12:24, then 61°, then 12:24, a hypnotic sequence that held DeMarco's gaze until the time switched to 12:25. He blinked and said, "We missed yesterday."

Her forehead wrinkled. Then she remembered. "Oh my god, we did. How did we forget that?"

"Other things on our mind."

"I feel so guilty for forgetting."

"I do too."

"Can we go now?"

"I would like that," he said.

They drove back through town and to the cemetery where Baby Ryan and his never-born half sister were buried, her little wooden box resting almost five feet above his. Neither DeMarco nor Jayme knew for a fact that the child had been a girl, but it felt right, and both had accepted it.

At the grave DeMarco took the silver locket from his side pocket and they held it between their clasped hands and knelt on the grass in front of the modest gravestone. The day was dim and smelled of rain, smelled of new grass pushing up from underground, of seed sprouts straining up through husks and dense soil. A dull, steady rumble of traffic reached their ears from the interstate highway less than two miles away.

DeMarco fought to ignore the soreness blooming in his chest like a small fire rapidly spreading, though he knew that Jayme must be feeling something similar, maybe along the scar from the knife wound on her left side, their injuries acting as messengers of bad news on the horizon the way an old man's arthritic knees foretell rain. She released his hand and leaned forward on both palms, fingers spread to encompass as much of the ground as she could, and spoke softly though hoarsely to the grass. "We're sorry, my darlings, that we forgot to come yesterday. You know our hearts are always with you."

DeMarco spread his free hand atop the grass, but lightly. He brushed the grass in one direction. Then back in the other.

Jayme said, speaking to the ground, "There's a little girl who came your way sometime Saturday night or Sunday morning. Her name is Emma. She's nine years old. She's probably with her grandma, and she might be with her mommy too. If you see her anywhere…and if she looks like she needs some help…please help her, my darlings. Please help her to find peace. And tell her we're here for her too. That we're doing everything we can for her on this side."

DeMarco nodded but said nothing. The grass was underwater now. The world was underwater. Maybe it was true that everything happens for a reason, that everything is exactly as it is meant to be. But that didn't mean he had to like the state of affairs as it now existed. And he didn't. He could find no gratitude for it anywhere inside his heart.

And that was when a feathery hand grazed his cheek. It startled him for only an instant, the blink of an eye. And just as quickly he recognized the touch, knew that it wasn't his son's hand that had drawn softly across his cheek. It wasn't his daughter's, his mother's, it didn't belong to anyone who had ever touched him like that

before. He knew she was there but not there. He knew there was
no need to look.

Jayme turned to him. "Did you feel that?" she asked.

"Feel what?" he said, already knowing.

"You're smiling, babe. You felt it too, didn't you?"

He kept smiling. Brushed the grass in one direction, brushed it
back the other as if slow, deliberate movement might contain the
fire in his chest. "We are never alone," he said.

# FORTY-THREE

## You can't trust the rain

At the stoplight in front of the courthouse he sat so long after the light turned green that the driver in the car behind his beeped his horn. DeMarco tapped his accelerator but immediately snapped on the turn signal and swung the car into the Sheetz parking lot. He slipped the car into an empty slot facing the store and put the gearshift in Park.

"What's up?" Jayme asked.

"Been thinking of Flores," he told her. "Her car's in the Dollar General lot where she parks it, so she must be off today."

"Okay. And?"

"I don't know, I just…" He gazed out the side window. "Weren't we supposed to talk to Boyd about her?"

"I did, back at the barracks. He's worried that she's drinking too much."

"Drinking is just the symptom," he said.

"It's also a secondary illness to whatever is causing it."

"Okay," DeMarco said. "So who's doing anything about it?"

"Boyd's trying, I think. He says she gets angry every time he brings it up."

DeMarco nodded; he remembered those days. The bottle his only friend.

"What are *you* thinking?" she asked.

He stared out the window a few moments longer, then unsnapped his seat belt and let it retract. "I think I'll just pop in and say hello. You don't have to wait. I'll walk home."

"You want me to come too?"

"Naw. I don't want it to seem like an intervention or anything. I won't be long."

"It's going to rain soon, you know."

He smiled. Put a hand on the door latch. "I've been wet before."

"Your thinking is a bit wet already," she told him. "You can't just pop in on a woman on her day off. For all you know, somebody slept over last night."

"Okay. I'll go in the store and get a coffee and call her first."

"Maybe she worked the night shift and she's sleeping."

"So she won't answer the phone. If she doesn't answer, I'll walk home."

"Call her now and you won't have to walk home in the rain when she tells you she's busy."

"Yeah…I don't think she's with anybody."

"And how would you know that?"

"She's depressed. And she's not a whiner. People like her don't want anybody else around them. They just want to hole up somewhere like a wounded dog." He felt her eyes on the side of his face but he did not look her way.

"Isn't that a good reason to just call her, babe? Just call now and see if you can go up."

"Honey," he said, and then let the sentence trail off.

She looked at him for a moment, long enough for two blinks, then popped open her door and climbed out. Walked around the rear of the car, came to his side just as he was stepping out. "You be careful," she told him.

"What is that supposed to mean?"

"You know very well what it means."

"You think there's something going on between—"

"Oh stop it," she said. "I trust you. But she is very fragile right now, Ryan. And she's always had a crush on you, right from the start. I don't know if she sees you as a father or a lover or both. It's easy for a young woman with her past to mix those things up, and you need to be aware of that."

"You do realize that I'm only a couple of years shy of being old enough to be *your* father."

"In other words, I speak with the voice of authority."

"Okay," he said with a smile. "I'll be careful. You want me to grab some apple fritters for dessert tonight?"

She laid her hand on his belly. "Whatever you want, babe."

He looked down at her hand atop the mounded shirt. "Yeah, maybe not."

From a stool inside the store he called Flores's number. Her voice sounded surprised when she answered. "Hello?"

"Hey," DeMarco said. "I'm in town running a couple of errands. Thought maybe I would drop by for a few minutes so we could catch up."

"Really? Well… It's kind of a mess up here. I haven't cleaned in a while."

"You want to meet somewhere else?" he asked. "Can I buy you a late lunch?"

"Geez, you know, I just ate a big bowl of cereal not long ago."

"So how about the park? Can I meet you there?"

"Gee, I don't know…"

"I'll see you there in fifteen," he told her. "I'm on foot so don't look for the car."

"Sergeant, I really ought to—"

"Come spend a few minutes with me, Dani. Okay? As a favor to an old man. I'll see you in fifteen," he said, and ended the call. He waited two minutes for a text or call saying no, she wasn't coming. None arrived. So he stood and went outside and started walking.

The rain began, just a few heavy, intermittent drops at first, when he was at the bottom of the half-mile loop that circled the park. He jogged to the gazebo along the edge of the road and ducked inside just before the first curtain of rain washed through. Then stood close to the overhang and let the accompanying mist dampen his face while he inhaled the cleansing scent, a scent that promised everything would be all right, you will be all right, Jayme and Dani will be all right, Emma is all right. Everything will work out, everything always does. He smelled all this in the scent of the rain and did his best to ignore the nagging thought that said, *Yeah but you've been lied to by the rain before.*

# FORTY-FOUR

## MITOSIS, OSMOSIS, AND A HINT OF PSYCHOSIS

Several minutes passed before a red Subaru Crosstrek turned into the park and came toward him, a vehicle identical to the one Flores had totaled in the crash. She was driving slowly, the wipers slapping back and forth as she peered through the rain, looking from one side of the road to the other until she spotted DeMarco standing in the gazebo's doorway. Then she parked and got out and crossed toward him, her left leg swinging stiffly. She was dressed in baggy gray sweatpants and a black sweatshirt with the hood pulled nearly over her eyes. Five awkward, lurching strides, flip-flops slapping against the wet ground, and she was there. He had winced with every step.

Their embrace was brief. She smelled of wet clothing and mouthwash and too much time alone. She pulled away quickly and kept her eyes averted from his, stepped over to the nearest bench seat and sat down and leaned against a vertical support post, arms wrapped around her chest, her gaze going out across the wet grass and up the hill to a picnic shelter.

He sat beside her and turned so that his knee nearly touched hers. "So how have you been?" he asked.

"Good," she said. She gave him a quick, small smile and looked away again. "I'm doing okay."

"I'm sorry we haven't gotten together sooner. I don't know where the time goes."

"Are you working on anything interesting these days?"

"A little something, yeah. But right now I'm interested in you."

"Ha," she said. "Nothing interesting here."

He wanted to slip an arm around her. Wanted to hold her close the way he had when she visited him in the hospital. He cupped both hands over his knees, rubbed his hands back and forth. "I know it's a hard adjustment to make," he said. "I'm so sorry it ever happened."

"Hey," she said. "That's life, right? Life's a bitch and then you die."

He nodded, smiling. "I used to believe that too."

"It's about the only thing a person can believe."

He hesitated before speaking. Had never been a man prone to confession or lecture. Always thought it nobler to keep one's own counsel and hope that others would do the same. But what if what he knew now could help her? What if helping her was the reason he had come back? He said, "Hard times destroy the weak and strengthen the strong. Soft times weaken everyone."

"Your point being what?" she asked after a pause.

"You aren't weak, Dani. You just keep on keeping on, you know? And you'll come out of this a stronger person."

Unfortunately, though he had hoped to reassure her, his statement poked at a festering anger. "Will I come out of it with a good leg?" she asked. "And please don't tell me about the miracles of modern medicine. My mother's been driving me crazy with that bullshit. *You just have to keep your hopes up, Dani. You never know what might happen tomorrow or the day after that.* It's all crap, Sergeant, and you know it is. Please don't pretend that you don't."

What he knew was that hope is the first necessary step to progress. That hope is what drives some people to great success. But that if you hope in a vague sort of way, if all you do is hope that somebody else will come along and change your life for you, or that God or the angels will intervene, success will stand smirking at you from a distance. You have to get up on your feet and walk or run or crawl or drag yourself to it.

He knew that what weighs most people down are not the burdens they carry, but the absence of something—the absence of love, the absence of hope, the absence of confidence, the absence of belief that what one does has meaning. *And that's where Dani is now*, he told himself. *Absent everything that matters.*

"I told you a little bit about my NDE, right?" he asked.

"I thought you told me all of it."

He shrugged. "Pieces of it keep coming back. But they're like dreams. Slippery, you know? Hard to hold on to."

"So is something coming back to you now?"

He watched the rain cascading off the gazebo's roof, falling over the doorway like a beaded curtain. "You and Jayme are the only people I've ever told about it."

"Why's that?" she asked.

"Because sometimes it even sounds crazy to me. I hear myself thinking about it, and even I have to wonder if maybe I just went loony tunes for a while."

She said nothing. Glanced at the side of his face, then looked down at the wooden floor.

He followed her gaze, saw how the rain was dampening the outside edges beneath the railing, darkening the boards. Then he lifted his gaze and peered into the woods thirty yards beyond, into their muted, tangled darkness. He said, "I've been struggling ever since it happened to find a way to describe it. And even to believe it was real."

A few yards away from the gazebo a puddle had formed in a low spot in the grass, the rain pocking and pimpling the surface of the water. "I've lost so much of it already," he told her. "But there's this one piece that has always stayed with me. And it's always felt true, you know? It's about what you just said."

"What did I just say?" she asked.

"That life's a bitch and then you die."

"Well, it sure looks that way to me. If you know something different, I would love to hear it."

"I know it all seems like a mindless clusterhump sometimes," he told her. "But it's not. It's a process, and we're all a part of it. And not just for this one life either."

"You mean, like reincarnation?"

"Something like that."

"So you're saying life's a bitch and then you die and then you have to do it all again?"

He smiled. He could not blame her for her bitterness. He had been there, had lived in bitterness and recrimination for most of his life. And here he was now like a reformed drunk trying to sell her on the twelve-step program. He winced to think that he was becoming one of those people, a proselytizer. He used to cross the street when he saw one coming his way.

How to make her understand? Especially when he didn't fully understand it himself? He said, "What if you know that it's all just a game, Dani? Like one of those video games where, no matter how many times you get blown up, you'll come back to have another go at it?"

"Seriously?" she said. "That's your answer?"

He laughed because she was right, another feeble effort. "I'm sorry," he told her. "I'm no good at this kind of thing."

At this, her tone softened. "Just what is it you're trying to tell me, Sergeant? If you think you're going to cheer me up, I'm sorry but you're not."

He nodded, said nothing for a while. Then tried another tack. "So think of it like this. The beginning of everything. Nothing exists but for this huge amoeba-like something. It's not physical, just, I don't know, one great big blob of consciousness."

She chuckled. "That's the first time I ever heard God described as a blob."

"Forget the word *God*. It's misleading. And insufficient."

"Okay," she said, but cynically.

"So…mitosis," he said. "At some point, the amoeba splits in two. Or maybe into more than two. Nobody knows."

"And why would it do that?"

He turned toward her more, their knees bumped, and he smiled. "Let's say that you are that consciousness. There's just you and nothing but you. You are aware of yourself, but there is absolutely nothing else *anywhere*. How are you going to feel?"

"How would I know? I'm not a god."

"Think about it," he said. "If that were you, how would you feel?"

"Like life's a bitch, I guess. Except that I can't die."

"So what do you do about it?"

"I guess I'd split into another amoeba, since that's what amoebas do. Because misery loves company."

"Bingo," he said. Then waited. He had to allow the thoughts time to percolate and fill the pot. If she could see the process for herself, all the ramifications of it, she would be more likely to accept it. To behold the beauty in it. He watched the beaded curtain, one drop of rain after another, each falling to the ground to form the same shallow moat around the gazebo.

Then she said, frowning, "I don't mean any disrespect, sir, but… so what? I mean what does it really change anything if God's an amoeba or a cockroach or a person or whatever? You still got shot in the chest and Jayme still lost her baby and I'm still a cripple. How is anything any different?"

She was right, of course. He could talk about quantum entanglement and the consciousness of mitochondria and the interplay of the body's electromagnetic fields and all of the other things he had been teaching himself, but until she saw the truth and became the truth as he briefly had, she would remain unconvinced. Because not he or anybody else could ever say what she needed to hear and understand.

"Okay," he conceded. "I get what you're saying. But I care about you, Dani, and that's why I really, really want you to understand something."

"Understand what?" she asked.

He reached over and tapped the leg brace beneath her jogging pants. "This is temporary," he told her. "Bodies are temporary. There's only one thing about all this," he said, and moved his open palm through the air, "that isn't temporary. The essence of who we really are. Everything else is a kind of dream. Everything except for who you are right here," he said, and lightly tapped her sternum.

She stared into his eyes for a few seconds, then looked away as if embarrassed. "I guess maybe that's my problem," she told him, her voice hoarser now. "Because I don't know who I am anymore."

"Then allow me to remind you." He placed a hand under her chin and gently turned her eyes back to his. "You are fearless," he told her. "You are a warrior. You are everything good. And you are eternal."

He watched her eyes fill with tears. Felt his own throat thicken just as hers was doing. She looked at him and blinked and said, "Why does it hurt so much when you're nice to me?"

"That," he told her, "is for the big amoeba to know, and for us little ones to find out."

# FORTY-FIVE

## DOUBT, THAT CHITTERING MONKEY

Flores wanted to drive DeMarco home but he insisted on walking, even though the rain had lessened only to a fine mist. He walked in no hurry with the cool mist gathering in his hair and dripping down his back, and he felt a little better about Flores and her future but he could not help puzzling over the inherent contradiction of everything happening for a reason and everything being exactly as it should be and the mandate to be a better person. Why try to be better if everything was as it should be? If everything happened for a reason, did that not imply that everything he did, good or bad, had already been ordained?

Something in that bundle was out of whack or else he was just too dense to make sense of it. During the NDE he had known and understood everything, but awakening in the hospital to a hot radiating pain with every breath had wiped out much of that understanding. Over the months of his convalescence he had read a lot of NDE literature and had watched a lot of YouTube videos and listened to dozens of experiencers recount their out-of-body travels. Many of them had since achieved a state of serene acceptance, but his own serenity was becoming increasingly difficult to maintain.

In particular, the matter of free will troubled him. Neurological studies had demonstrated that the brain signals a decision as much as seven seconds before the conscious mind recognizes that decision. Not only before the body acts upon the decision, but *before the decision is even recognized.* The conscious mind lags *seven seconds behind*! So much for the concept of free will.

Okay, so maybe the subconscious mind was the one pulling the strings, and that was him too, an integral part of the whole DeMarco. But if he could not be conscious of what the subconscious was doing, how could he claim to be a contributing part of it?

It was all too confusing. As for the credibility of the NDE itself, there were only two schools of thought on the matter. One school held that the experience was real and truly involved the spirit's visitation to some part of the astral realm. The other held that the brain generated hallucinations whenever it was deprived of sufficient oxygen or otherwise excessively stressed. He almost wished that he could accept the latter explanation and simply move on with trying to do his best every day without worrying about the ripples his every act sent through the multiverse. Unfortunately, hallucinations did not account for the periodic flashes of insight he had been experiencing. Or for the tenacity of the images he retained, still as clear and vivid as ever, from his sojourn into the land of the disembodied. Why should those memories be brighter and sharper than the details of the houses he was now walking past? Why would real life seem drabber than hallucinated life? And why even now would he sometimes hear a voice inside his head that was not his own? Was his brain permanently short-circuited? Or was his frequency more finely tuned now to the higher vibrations?

Just asking himself these questions and taking the subject seriously made him feel foolish and embarrassed. Especially now that he had planted some of those notions in Flores's head as well.

*Let not your heart be troubled*, he heard inside his head. And he told that voice, "Just stop it already, okay? You're only making things worse."

He was nearly home, moving slowly through the damp and cloud-dimmed light, when he realized that he was not yet ready to be home. He wished he had remained in the park a while longer after Flores had driven away. He loved Jayme with all of his heart but sometimes now he felt even more alone with her than when by himself. He missed the closeness with nature he could feel only when alone or with Hero, who was a more natural part of nature than any human being could be. And the little town had long ago lost any semblance of comfort for him, had grown too noisy throughout the day and too bright at night, too many porch lights and floodlights and security lights blazing away till morning. Too many people afraid of the darkness. Afraid of silence and being alone.

How he longed for those three states of being now. Silence so that he could hear himself think. Solitude so that he could concentrate and not have to focus on somebody else's comfort or well-being. And darkness so that he could lose sight of his physical self and imagine his true self free of that prison and the inevitable sadness that accompanied it.

But it was still daylight now and his desire to be nowhere and nothing and everywhere again was a selfish one. Maybe even a delusional one. He wondered what his subconscious mind was thinking. *What a dolt!* probably. That's what he would be thinking if he were his higher self and not the feebleminded brother.

# FORTY-SIX

## IN EVERY TEAR A UNIVERSE

Jayme was sitting on the living room sofa, holding one of his books open in her hand when she heard him coming in through the back door. He stooped to remove his shoes in the kitchen, then came into the living room. Hero climbed to his feet and crossed to say hello and sniff DeMarco's damp socks.

"How'd it go?" she asked.

"Who knows?" he said.

"You're soaking wet."

He shrugged. Bent down to scratch between Hero's ears, then came into the room and nodded at the book she was holding, *The Self-Aware Universe: How Consciousness Creates the Material World.* "What do you think?"

"Heavy stuff."

He sat down beside her and lifted her feet into his lap. "You should start with one of Robert Monroe's books. They're on the shelf on my bed table."

"I saw them all. I liked the cover on this one."

He smiled. "How far did you get?"

"I'm still pretty much on the cover."

He took her left foot into his hands, pulled at her toes and kneaded her sole.

"You want to talk about dinner?" he asked.

"Anything's good, babe." She laid the book aside. "I've been stewing over the money Morrison gave us for Emma. What are we going to do with that? Sooner or later we have to give it back to him."

"Um-hmm," he said. "But if we do it now, and he doesn't know what happened to her…"

"Yeah, we'd have to tell him."

"Let's wait and see if he asks for the money back."

"Because if he does, that means he knows. And why would he? Unless…"

"Right," DeMarco said. "I'm more concerned with how much he knows about those DNA swabs. Did his buddies take them on their own or did he take them?"

"One way or the other," she said, "somebody is lying."

"So it would seem."

"I wish the Scottville chief would get back to us already."

"It's not a decision he's likely to make quickly."

"I wish we were there," she said.

"It's hard, I know."

"I really want to be there at her funeral, babe."

He nodded. Tried to think of a good reason to dissuade her. Came up with nothing.

"I just feel like crying all the time," she told him. "I've been crying ever since last summer."

"I know, baby." He laid his head back and let his eyes roll up to the ceiling. If it were true that God heard every laugh and knew the sadness of every tear…

She pulled her feet down off his lap and slid close to him, snuggled close with her head against his chest. He wrapped an arm around her. "Can you tell me anything hopeful?" she asked. "Anything at all? Something you brought back with you from, you know, wherever you went?"

He thought for a moment, and said, "I can tell you what I told Flores."

"And what was that, babe?"

"That it's temporary. Everything is temporary."

"And did that make her feel better?"

He blew out a breath. Tried to think of something hopeful to say. He waited thirty seconds for a helpful voice in his head. Heard nothing. *That's what I thought*, he told it.

# FORTY-SEVEN

A DREAM WITHIN A DREAM

In his dream that night DeMarco saw Emma standing beside the bed. She was dressed as she had been when they stopped at McDonald's, the last time he had seen her, before dropping her and her grandmother off at the hospice. Skinny jeans rolled above her ankles, a pink Old Navy long-sleeved T-shirt with a logo that read *We Are the Future*. But instead of the pink mesh sneakers she had worn that morning, her feet were bare in his dream, the toenails painted pink. The room was nearly black with darkness but he saw her clearly in every detail. He pushed himself up on his elbows and whispered, "Hi."

Hero was sitting between Emma and the bed, looking up at her, his tail swishing across the carpet with a *shhshh shhshh* sound. Her hand rested lightly atop Hero's head. DeMarco noticed that her fingernails were pink too, though they had not been painted when he saw her last. Her gaze was steady on DeMarco's face, her mouth neither smiling nor frowning. She was wearing a garland of daisies in her hair, the petals white around a sunburst heart. "I like the flowers," he whispered, and thought *Shasta daisies*, though until that moment he had never been aware of the different varieties, had thought every daisy the same. The scent of the ones in Emma's hair was light and fresh and reminded DeMarco of newly mown grass.

He smiled in his dream and wished that she would smile too, that she would tell him she was all right now, that everything was fine. But she said nothing and did not smile. And then, over the course of the next five seconds, the room's darkness closed around her and she was gone. Only dimly then could he see Hero still sitting there, now with his head turned to DeMarco, a tiny glint of eyeshine in his dark, wondering eyes. The daisy scent still lingered.

DeMarco stretched out his hand and Hero came closer and leaned against the side of the bed as DeMarco lightly scratched his snout. Then DeMarco lay back against his pillow but kept a hand against the side of Hero's face. He rolled his head to the side and saw Jayme sleeping and could hear her susurrus breath sounding like leaves stirring in a light wind. He looked back at Hero and felt the fur and the warmth of the animal's skin and knew himself then to be fully awake. He thought 4:59 but had no way of knowing the time, possessed only the certainty, and so he rolled onto his side and stood quietly and used a foot to search for his boxer shorts, and after he had pulled them on he went to the door with Hero at his heels, and all the way downstairs and outside onto the porch and in the chill of the still dark morning he smelled the vague but unmistakable scent of Shasta daisies in the air.

# FORTY-EIGHT

## A MESSAGE IN THE LEAVES

Throughout breakfast he waited to see if Jayme would mention a dream of any kind but she did not. If she too had dreamed of Emma, she would certainly have mentioned it. So he said nothing. It would hurt her to know that she had been left out. He didn't know why she had been left out, did not know what meaning it signaled, if any. Keeping his secret was not easy but he knew Jayme would ask *Was she happy?* and he could not honestly say that she was. That, too, would upset her.

He was wiping off the stove and countertops after breakfast, Jayme in the mudroom hooking Hero's leash to his collar, when DeMarco's phone beeped and vibrated. He quickly dried his hands and picked the phone off the table. *Bowen*, the screen read.

He tapped the green phone icon and said, "Morning, Captain Crunch."

"They must get up early in Michigan," Bowen said.

At the mention of *captain*, Jayme came back to the threshold and stood there listening. DeMarco put the phone on speaker.

"Did somebody wake you out of your beauty sleep?" he asked.

"The Scottville chief of police. Chief Gary."

"Like the first name Gary?"

"Last name Gary. First name Chief. He filled me in on that furnace and vent situation you're interested in."

Jayme moved closer.

"And?" DeMarco asked.

"Apparently there is cause for suspicion. A couple of small indentations near the roof on the backside of the trailer. Like from a ladder too short to prop against the roof itself. Unfortunately, there's no telling how old those indentations are."

DeMarco and Jayme shared a look. "Anything else?" he asked.

"The top of the trailer was littered with lots of pine needles and a few dead leaves. The inspector reported that the stuff he pulled out of the vent was decomposing oak leaves and dirt, right?"

"That's what he said."

"Well, that's what it was. And here's the interesting part. It appears that when Ms. Barrie would mow the yard, or whoever did, and there's an old self-propelled push mower in a little shed there, she would mow so that all of the leaves and grass blew back toward the tree line. The cuts she made nearest the trees would pile up against the trees, of course, and then lay there and decompose over the years."

"But from the bottom up," DeMarco guessed. "Anything blown on top wouldn't be completely decomposed yet."

"Precisely. They were matted up but not decomposed. And there were grass clippings mixed all through it."

"Mixed all through the stuff taken from the vent too?"

"Just like the stuff decomposing around the trees. And there is evidence in one of those piles that somebody reached in and dug out a couple of handfuls. The inspector had tossed the stuff he dug out of the vent down off the roof and onto the ground. They recovered enough of it to tell that it was consistent with the material piled up around a big oak tree on the eastern end of the trailer."

DeMarco looked at Jayme and pumped his fist.

Bowen said, "Chief Gary would like to speak with you about this paternity case you're working on. I had to tell him about it in order to get his report. I'll text you his number when we hang up here. I've filled him in on your and Jayme's former status. I might also have mentioned a couple or three of your most recent cases."

"Thanks a bunch for preserving our anonymity, Captain."

"Relax. It's all on the qt. But you should know what you're dealing with up there. It's basically a two-person force. The chief and one full-time patrol officer. They also have a handful of part-timers, but their resources are limited, to say the least. The chief hasn't called in the Michigan staties yet, but I suggest you get in touch with him ASAP if you want in on this."

"Copy that, Captain. Thanks for this. I owe you some pepperoni rolls. Text me the number." He ended the call before Bowen could protest that pepperoni rolls were insufficient payment.

To Jayme, DeMarco said, "So what do you want to do?"

She had already bent to unhook the leash from Hero's collar. Now she dropped the leash to the floor and strode across the kitchen toward the living room. "I'm going up there," she said. "I need to be there for her funeral. You don't have to come if you don't want to."

DeMarco's phone vibrated in his hand. The text icon appeared on his screen. "Don't you want to wait until I speak with Chief Gary?"

"I'm going one way or the other," she called from the living room. "It doesn't matter what he says. First flight I can get."

He looked down at Hero, who stood with his front paws in the kitchen, rear paws in the mudroom. "Sorry, pal," he said. Then he turned toward the living room and called out, "Book two seats. I'll contact the kennel."

# FORTY-NINE

## EVEN IN HEAVEN THE ANGELS CONSPIRE

The last order of business before catching the next day's dawn express to Michigan was a meeting with Judge Morrison. DeMarco phoned the judge and suggested that they meet at a small restaurant only a mile from Morrison's home, but the judge, after a few moment's hesitation, had said, "Aw, heck. Just come on over to the house. Around six, okay? I'll be out back getting my wife's flower beds ready for a new planting."

The judge had not asked about the nature of the meeting, and this got DeMarco's bullshit meter beeping a bit louder. A wholly innocent person would have been curious enough to inquire, *What's up?* Still, DeMarco wanted to give him the benefit of a doubt.

"Maybe he thinks we already sent the cashier's check," he suggested to Jayme as he drove, "and we're coming by to convey Emma's thanks. Or maybe he's just lonely since his wife died, and he's looking for a little company."

"And maybe he knows more than he's saying," she said. "Maybe he's one step ahead of us and he doesn't want to tip his hand."

The drive to the judge's home took them two miles out of town, under a railroad overpass, then onto a twisting back road past stubbly cornfields and woods beginning to bud, and eventually into a sprawling private community of approximately two hundred homes on spacious lots around the shores of a man-made lake. A deep, high wall of mixed hardwoods enclosed the entire development.

The wealth index for the community was 124, a full 25 points higher than that of the entire state, and maybe double that of the rest of the county. The diversity index nearly bottomed out at the other end of the scale. Both DeMarco and Jayme had, as troopers, responded to 911 calls from residents of the community; the disturbances usually involved alcohol and domestic abuse, though residents were also quick to report any unfamiliar vehicle cruising the streets, all of which were labeled either a Trail or Lane preceded by a real or fictitious Native American tribal name.

"There it is on the right," DeMarco said with a nod toward a two-story white contemporary backed up against a copse of paper birch trees.

"Whoa," said Jayme. "Sort of looks like an uppity Baptist church, doesn't it? From 2025 or so. It's got, like, one two three four five different levels to the roof."

The facade was of white clapboard and stone, with wide arched windows taking up most of the space above the recessed front door, the punched-out library extension, and the upstairs dormer. Six half-moon windows ran across the top of the three-stall garage doors. DeMarco eased the car onto the pebbled concrete driveway and parked along the side of the garage.

They opened their car doors and climbed out to an almost somber silence. As they crossed toward the rear of the house, Jayme whispered, "It's so quiet here! This is where we need to live."

"As soon as we triple our income," he said.

Judge Morrison was exactly where he had said he would be— wearing brown gardening gloves and gray strap-on kneepads while kneeling in a flower bed he had picked clean of last year's brown stems and roots. Piles of dead plants lay outside each of the five flower beds behind the house.

"You've been busy," DeMarco said.

Morrison turned his way. Smiled. And said, while climbing with difficulty to his feet, "I always told her, 'Perennials, Jean, perennials.' But this was her love. Winter was the only season she hated, because she couldn't work in her garden." He stripped off his dirty gardening gloves and dropped them to the ground. "I can't bear to not see these beds full of flowers each spring." He shook Jayme's hand and then DeMarco's, then led them to a set of four blue Adirondack chairs in a tight semicircle facing an empty bronze firepit.

"Can I get you good folks something to drink?" he asked. "Iced tea? A beer? I usually mix a shaker of martinis for myself this time of evening."

"Nothing for me," Jayme said as she sat on the outside chair. "But thank you."

DeMarco took the seat to her left. "I'm good too. This will only take a couple of minutes, Judge."

"So be it," Morrison said, and lowered himself into the other outside chair, leaving an empty one between himself and DeMarco.

The judge smiled at DeMarco, then at Jayme. They smiled in return, but said nothing.

"You seem to have found me all right," the judge said. "Visitors will sometimes drive around three or four times before locating the place they're looking for."

"We've both been here before," DeMarco told him. "On call."

"Really?" the judge asked. "Trouble in our peaceful little Brigadoon?"

"Even here," DeMarco said. He noticed that the judge seemed to be having some difficulty holding eye contact for more than a second or two. Unusual for a man who had stared dozens of petty

and not-so-petty criminals into submission. He seemed more interested in picking nonexistent dirt from beneath his fingernails than in
asking how Emma was doing. No *Was the money delivered yet?* No
*Who's going to be the girl's caretaker now that her mother is gone?* This
from a man who with a few well-chosen words could silence an
arrogant DA or scald a public defender for his lack of preparation.

The judge knew something, but he did not know that Emma
was dead. If he knew, he would have to assume that DeMarco and
Jayme knew too, and that to not mention it would be evidence
that he was hiding something. Until this recognition, DeMarco was
unsure of what he was going to say to the judge. Now he put his
hands on his knees and said, "Judge, the family is insisting on legal
DNA tests. Done under supervision in a certified lab."

"Really? There's, uh…" Morrison looked to the side, then back
at DeMarco. "I see no reason for that. We're all honest men. That's
beyond dispute."

"Of course," DeMarco said. "But you surely understand. You
would have ordered the same thing yourself, am I right?"

"I have. I certainly have." Morrison turned his gaze to Jayme.
"Every one of us was quite willing to accept responsibility if it
came to that."

She smiled. "Can you tell us how the initial swabs were taken?
Did you supervise them personally?"

"No," he said. "No. Each of my friends did their own swabs.
Purchased their own kits. I simply relayed them to you."

"That's what we thought," she said. "So you really don't know
if one or the other of your friends might have substituted a swab
from somebody else?"

"Young lady," he said, then pulled back a little. "I can tell you
with the utmost confidence. My friends are not liars. Nor am I."

"I understand," she said. "But the family is insisting. As is their legal right. Though they would prefer not to have to get a lawyer and a subpoena and all that. But they are prepared to do so if necessary."

"And by family you mean who—the grandmother?"

"There are also an aunt and an uncle," DeMarco told him. "At least one of each that we know of. And some cousins."

The judge sat there shaking his head, his eyes on the ground. Then he gripped the edges of the chair's arms and pushed himself upright. "I will, uh, pass the information on. And make the necessary arrangements. Assuming that my friends are…able to cooperate. They are all very busy men, you know."

"I'm sure," DeMarco said, and stood. Jayme then rose to her feet too.

"I'm not even certain that I can reach them. One might have left for a business trip already. Somewhere in Asia, I think he said."

DeMarco put out his hand. "We'll wait to hear from you, Judge." Morrison's handshake was a limp mitten.

Jayme said, "It's a beautiful place you have here, sir. Your own little piece of paradise."

The judge nodded in reply, though he could not seem to muster another smile.

# IV

How hollow and futile life can
be when it is founded on
a false belief in continuity and permanence.

# FIFTY

## Where a home is not a home

On Tuesday their first stop after leaving the car rental agency at the airport was the Gilchrist and Risher funeral home in Scottville, Michigan. They had picked up an hour on the flight, so it was still morning in Michigan. The air was cool but clear and the sky an almost startling blue. "Days like this should be full of dark clouds," Jayme remarked as they approached the front door of the funeral home. DeMarco nearly answered, *the darkness is all inside*, but stopped himself before speaking.

The door was locked. After Jayme's second set of four hard raps went unanswered, plus several jabs at the doorbell, DeMarco suggested they return to the car, look up the number, and call to request entrance. She shook her head no and knocked again, nine forceful raps in a row.

The door was opened finally by a young man in blue jeans and an untucked gray T-shirt with *Mason County Central Spartans* printed in red across the chest. He was maybe sixteen years old, of medium height, with short curly brown hair and green eyes. He looked past Jayme to DeMarco and said, "Visitation won't start until three."

Jayme leaned into his field of vision. "We're working with Chief Gary on the Barrie investigation. We need to see the bodies."

"Oh," he said, and blinked twice. "I'll get Dad. He's downstairs."

He started to close the door but Jayme stepped forward and stopped it with her hand, told him, "We'll wait inside," and pushed her way past him. DeMarco came in smiling, took the door by its edge and allowed it to close softly.

"Uh, okay," the kid said, then turned and hurried away.

The lobby was dim and smelled of incense. DeMarco whispered, "You're getting pretty good at throwing your weight around."

Her eyes were fierce when she looked up at him, the brightest objects in the room. "Nobody is going to keep me from seeing her. Nobody."

⇒————⇐

In the refrigerated preparation room in the basement, the boy's father, an older, world-weathered version of his son, led them to a pair of mortuary tables, each covered with a white sheet. "They haven't been dressed or cosmeticized yet," he explained.

"Embalmed?" DeMarco asked.

The man nodded. "Temporary preservation. The service is tomorrow afternoon."

To DeMarco the bodies looked nearly the same size beneath the sheets, but Jayme went directly to the table on the right. Without hesitating she lifted a corner of the sheet and exposed Emma to the neck. Immediately she staggered and steadied herself with a hand on the edge of the metal table. "Oh, sweet girl," she moaned.

DeMarco stood with his arm around her back, his hand holding her by the waist. Her body bucked lightly as the tears slid down her cheeks, but she made no other sounds and said nothing more. She laid a hand against Emma's cheek, did not flinch from the cold but only closed her eyes. DeMarco could hear her breath going in, going out. He could feel his own pulse in his fingers as his hand pressed against her waist.

A minute or so later Jayme opened her eyes again and gazed down at the girl's face, then she took hold of the sheet again and pulled it back into place and said "Thank you" without looking at the man, and left the room with DeMarco close behind her. Neither of them answered when the man asked, "Do you want to see the other one?"

DeMarco followed her upstairs and outside and to the car. She climbed in and leaned forward with her head against the padded dashboard. DeMarco slid in behind the wheel, switched the ignition key to his left hand and placed his right hand softly between her shoulders.

With his touch, she said, still looking down at the floor mat, her voice angry, "Why is it called a home? It's anything *but* a home, if you ask me."

"You're right," he said.

"I hate those places. I hate them!"

"I do too." He looked at her hands gripping the dashboard, knuckles white.

"I wanted her *with us*," she said, the final two words rising into the pitch of an anguished sob.

The sunlight was bright on the windshield, it stung his eyes. Out on the street the traffic passed at a steady pace, cars and trucks and a few pedestrians, unceasing life, unceasing motion, only the interior of the rental car in a still and mournful stasis.

# FIFTY-ONE

AND THE SUN BE DAMNED

In the city hall on Main Street, a two-story redbrick building that took up half a block, they introduced themselves to Chief Gary and Patrol Officer Dawn Stiple. Gary was approximately five foot six, 190 pounds, his head shaved bald, and Stiple his physical opposite, approximately five foot ten, maybe 125 pounds, her flame-red hair gathered into a tight updo.

After a shaking of hands, Gary sat on the front corner of his desk, Stiple standing near the opposite corner, nearest Jayme. In fewer than five minutes, Chief Gary and Stiple summed up everything they knew about the Barries' deaths.

"The grandmother's BAC registered .29. The thermostat in the trailer was set at sixty-six, so, given the outside temperature that night, the furnace would have kicked on around ten, no more than a half hour or so before the two of them left the Bear Claw."

"So what you're saying," DeMarco asked, "is that they came home tired, the grandmother under the influence, they probably climbed into bed and fell asleep? And never woke up?"

The chief nodded. "CO levels in the place were high enough to kill a moose by the time the bodies were discovered. It wouldn't have taken much to kill the girl. The old lady went to bed significantly impaired."

Stiple said, "Even if she woke up at some point dizzy or nauseous or with a monster headache, she probably wouldn't have attributed it to CO poisoning."

Chief Gary continued. "No signs of struggle whatsoever. No signs of forced entry. There was one CO detector in the kitchen but the battery was dead, so either the guy who stuffed the vent got lucky or he knew about the dead battery. So far we've come up with nobody who had a grudge against either one of them."

"Everybody loved Emma," Officer Stiple added. "As for the old lady, hardly anybody in town ever met her."

"Who found the bodies?" DeMarco asked.

"One of the barmaids. Named Lisa."

"Alyssa," Stiple corrected.

The chief continued. "Emma left her sketch pad at the bar the previous night, so the bar maid was returning it. Alyssa. When nobody answered the door, she got the key from underneath a stone by the steps where Jennifer kept it, let herself in and found them."

"So maybe somebody else knew about the key too," Jayme suggested.

"We already talked to three of them who did," Gary said. "All females, all Bear Claw employees."

"And all of them were at the Bear Claw the whole time during the memorial?" DeMarco asked.

"Unfortunately," said the chief.

DeMarco said, "That doesn't rule them out, though. They could have passed the information along to somebody."

The chief shrugged, *yeah, maybe.*

"Boyfriends?" Jayme asked.

"According to her friends," said Stiple, "Jen hadn't dated anybody in months. And even if somebody had it out for her, why kill the daughter and grandmother after Jen is already gone? It makes no sense whatsoever."

DeMarco asked, "Who's taking care of the funeral arrangements?"

"A couple of folks from the Bear Claw volunteered," Stiple said. "We contacted Jen's sister and she said for us to go ahead and do it."

"Which isn't our job," the chief added. "So we farmed it out to her former colleagues."

Jayme shook her head and chewed on her lip.

"So now what?" DeMarco asked.

"We called a town hall meeting for tomorrow night, after the service," Stiple said. "See if we can dredge something up. You two are welcome to join us."

Chief Gary said, "We figure it's a good idea for people to know who the strangers in town are. Otherwise everybody will be pointing the finger at you. Where are you folks staying tonight?"

"We haven't decided that yet," DeMarco said.

Stiple told them, "I recommend the Breakwater Inn, seven miles out toward Ludington on Route 10. It's nice and quiet out there this time of year."

"Thank you," DeMarco told her.

The chief asked, "You folks have any idea who would have done this? You must be looking at somebody in particular back in Pennsylvania."

"We're not," DeMarco said. "Not yet anyway."

"But you're looking at the guys who might be the father, right?" Stiple asked. "The three of them?"

With his eyes DeMarco questioned the chief, and again Gary shrugged. "We need to know what we've got here. It's just her and me so far. It'll stay that way until it needs to be otherwise."

Jayme told him, "We've mostly ruled out one of them of direct involvement. Still trying to identify the other two."

"Well, good luck to you," said the chief. "I highly doubt it was anybody hereabouts."

"And why's that?" Jayme asked.

"We don't kill little girls and old ladies up here. Two murders in the past twenty years. If you're looking for a thief or a drunk or a druggie or adulterer or sex offender, though, we've got a kit and caboodle of them for you to choose from."

"Sex offender?" Jayme asked.

Stiple shook her head. "No, no sign of anything like that. Nothing to worry about there."

Jayme nodded her thanks, her relief.

After a few beats of silence, Chief Gary stood. "If you folks want to grab yourself a room and a little rest, Officer Stiple will meet you at the church tomorrow night."

"It's the Mason County Reformed," Stiple told them. "West of here on the main drag. You can't miss it. I plan to get things rolling at seven."

Chief Gary said, "If you do any asking around between now and then, it's probably best if you're not too secretive about it. People are quick around here to spot an outsider, and I'd rather not have to field a bunch of calls about a couple of shady characters slinking around." Here he smiled at Jayme. "Not that there's anything shady about you folks. Just that, you know, it's a close-knit community. People are naturally suspicious."

Jayme asked, "Can we say that we're working with your department?"

"That ought to do it," he said.

Soon DeMarco and Jayme were on the street again. She paused just outside the building, looked up at the immaculate blue sky, squinted angrily at the blazing sun, a hand over her eyes. He waited beside her; knew what she was thinking and feeling at that moment; knew because he had been the same way a dozen years earlier, after a last look at Baby Ryan before consigning him to the ground. She was thinking, bitterly, with a murderous rage gripping her heart, *How can you be so warm and bright right now? How can you even keep shining?*

# FIFTY-TWO

## Blame it on the MSG

Their king suite at the Breakwater Inn was exactly what both of them needed, a bedroom, separate sitting room, bathroom, and kitchenette, everything clean and orderly and practical. DeMarco was restless after checking in and suggested a walk on the beach to clear their heads, but Jayme demurred, said her head was already too clear for comfort, you go, I'll be fine here by myself. He knew what that meant. *I need to be alone for a while.*

At Ludington State Park he walked the sand dunes to the Big Sable Point Lighthouse, then sat on a bench near the water and remembered the last time he had visited a lighthouse. Four years earlier he had tracked Thomas Huston to an old lighthouse on Lake Erie and had made the mistake of not taking him into custody, a mistake that resulted in Huston's death.

*That's one way of looking at it*, he told himself now. The wind coming off the water was cool and would soon turn colder with the setting of the sun. The sky was still a faultless blue, not a contrail or chemtrail in sight. Across the gray-blue water lay Wisconsin. Or maybe it was Michigan, he wasn't sure. Across each of the other Great Lakes lay Canada. Huston had stood at the rusty rail of his lighthouse and gazed hopelessly toward Canada. DeMarco had been unable to touch Huston in his grief and was unable to touch Jayme in hers. The more things changed, the more they stayed the same.

Ever since learning of Emma's death, DeMarco and Jayme seemed to be practicing a kind of crown shyness, and like trees in a forest were keeping a respectful distance from each other, so that their outermost leaves did not overlap and compete for sunlight, their branches did not entangle. Their roots, he hoped, had entwined in such a way that neither of them could be removed from the other, so that they shared nutrients and passed information back and forth, warnings and soothings, laughter and tears, each looking out for the other, always vigilant, yet each now firmly rooted in their own soil, hers of grief and anger, his of a sorrowful yet somewhat accepting curiosity. The best thing he could do for her was to leave her alone and hope that solitude would heal her as it had often healed him.

In the evening he returned to the inn with three cartons of Chinese food. Covered up to her neck in bed, Jayme declined the food but asked if he would make her a cup of hot tea from the complimentary bags in the tiny kitchen. He did, and she thanked him, and then he sat alone in the sitting room, nibbling from the lo mein noodles and the General Tso's chicken until he realized that he was tasting none of it, then placed the cartons in the refrigerator and watched a silent TV until his eyelids drooped.

They held hands in bed that night, but Jayme had gone to bed wearing pink cotton pajamas, not in the nude as she always did at home, so he did not pull her close nor did she roll up against him. After she fell asleep again he lay there trying to sleep but with no luck, an uncomfortable heaviness in his stomach and lower chest. *Must be the Chinese food*, he told himself, and, giving up on sleep, gingerly lifted a pillow off the bed and got another blanket from the closet and returned to the sofa in the sitting room.

In an attempt to smother his tumbling thoughts and the heartburn they were causing, he crept out to the bedroom and stealthily dug through his bag and found the well-worn copy of Huston's novel he had brought along. Before he met Huston it had been DeMarco's habit whenever he traveled to pack a book or two to keep him company at night, usually Hemingway's *A Moveable Feast* or Faulkner's *As I Lay Dying*, though sometimes he would substitute Márquez's *No One Writes to the Colonel* for one of them. There was something about the rhythm of the prose in those books that he found soothing and a complement to his own rhythms. Since Huston's death he had always chosen one of his friend's novels to accompany him in the darkness. His favorite companion, and the one he had with him this night, was Huston's first novel, *When All Light Fails*. DeMarco liked it best because its main character was a struggling young writer, in whose reflections he heard Thomas speaking. The title was taken from a line in Faulkner's *Light in August* in which a character refers to the quality of light at "that instant when all light has failed out of the sky and it would be night save for that faint light which day-granaried leaf and grass blade reluctant suspire, making still a little light on earth though night itself has come."

Faulkner's title, Huston had once explained, also referred to the burning house at the center of the novel, and that critics, being critics, proposed that the word *light* derived from the colloquial use of light to refer to the act of giving birth. "With Faulkner," Huston had said, "you can never really tell which explanation is the right one. The way I read it, the novel is all about misfits, and the many ways society creates them. In my opinion, we're all misfits. Some of us are just better at hiding it. Aren't we, Sergeant?"

DeMarco, smiling to himself as he remembered that conversation, carried *When All Light Fails* into the sitting room then sat in the dark with the front cover against his chest and silently asked Huston to come to him and throw a little light on the situation there in Michigan. He waited several minutes for a brilliant thought or two to illuminate the darkness. None came.

He laid the book on the coffee table and was about to turn the TV back on when he had another idea. "Tell you what," he said to Huston in a whisper. "How about if I open your book at random and you tell me something good? Can you do that for me, brother?" Again, no answer, no sense that he was not alone in the little room. Still, it was worth a shot.

He turned on the lamp beside the sofa and leaned over the book and opened it a third of the way through the pages and laid his finger on the recto page. His finger landed in the middle of a paragraph, so he traced back to the first word of the paragraph and started there:

> To succeed you must be able to face criticism and rejec-
> tion and defeat every single day, and to turn every loss
> into an even fiercer resolve to prove the censorious bas-
> tards wrong. You must be not just able but eager to climb
> into your little skiff alone every morning and paddle out
> into the deeper part of the ocean and sit there roasting
> in the sun with your flimsy line in the water. And if you are
> lucky enough to hook a prize marlin you must be ready to
> beat the sharks away with your oar even as you try to drag
> your prize back home through the tenacious currents. And
> if you succeed in finally rowing ashore only to find that
> nothing remains of your prize but for the head and tail
> and the stripped yet elegant spine of your trophy, you will
> always have the experience and satisfaction of knowing
> that you did not give up and cut the line, that you did not
> give in to the heat and the ache and the fatigue and the
> odds that were always against you, and you can claim
> your victory in the knowledge that you outlasted even the

most ravenous of the sharks and did not allow them to strip
you clean too.

DeMarco smiled. In a novel whose title paid homage to Faulkner's
*Light in August*, Huston had made use of an extended metaphor based
on Hemingway's *The Old Man and the Sea*. "You son of a gun," he
whispered. "You're always surprising me. Thank you."

What he liked about Huston's books, and what he had admired
about the man, was the wealth of suffering underlying everything
he wrote. Both he and Huston had been lonely, solitary boys who
always felt apart from others, unable to relate to their classmates'
concerns and interests. Even as family men that sense of isolation
had never fully left them, so that they always felt awkward in social
situations, out of place, like a walrus in a tutu, as Raymond Chandler
might have said.

The good thing about not fitting in, Huston had once told
him, was that it encouraged a development of one's observational
skills. As a child, DeMarco too had turned a keen eye and ear on
other people, assuming that adults like his mother and father and
teachers would be founts of information about the most effective
ways to confront the world. But both he and Huston had learned
early that little was to be learned from examining people's behavior and listening to them talk. Some things could be learned from
the written word, from books that you chose carefully by reading
only those authors whose pasts were rich with accomplishment,
but even then the knowledge was secondhand and light on practical instruction. The most useful knowledge was to be acquired
only by doing, by living, by running headlong into the burning
house of human experience and coming out singed and scorched,
lungs full of smoke. Such knowledge would arise not during but
after the experience, when you are sitting alone in the dark and

re-creating everything you did and felt and assessing the wisdom or foolishness of each moment, the penalties and rewards. That was why DeMarco had enlisted in the army despite his mother's pleas that he should not. And it was why now, after three full decades of living a life full of risk and uncertainty, he had little respect for academics and other self-appointed experts who learned only from books and lectures, and who had spent their lives moving from the safety and routine of one bubble to the next without sustaining so much as a flesh wound. While DeMarco was spending his first twenty-plus years negotiating a precipitous path through what seemed a minefield of danger and sorrow, a couple of generations of timid book-educated people were spawning children who now took offense at every pointed word, every opinion that threatened to dent their own little bubbles, that threatened to pop the illusion of safety their bubbles afforded them—a couple of generations of children and adults who were afraid of the dark, afraid of silence, afraid of nature, afraid to think for themselves. He had no respect for that kind. It was the risk-takers and rule breakers he adored. He could forgive their mistakes and errors in judgment sooner than he could forgive blind conformity and uninformed opinions and lives lived in unquestioning docility. His NDE had confirmed for him what he had come to believe by the age of fifteen—that true growth comes only from risk, that courage comes only from fear, that positive change is impossible in a bubble. Moreover, true growth comes only one person at a time, never to a group or society as a whole but to a single struggling heart fumbling its way through darkness, through grief, through hardship and despair. People who hide from that necessary journey are not worth talking to.

Thomas Huston had not hidden from that journey; he had embraced it. With gratitude for their brief friendship, DeMarco closed the book and turned off the light and curled up on the sofa again, and it wasn't long before he was asleep despite the burn of stomach acid high in his chest.

Sometime later Jayme snuggled in beside him, her back to his chest, and he spent the remainder of the dark hours curled against her, grateful for her warmth and scent. He did not need to see her sleeping face to know that it was a sunset, heartbreakingly beautiful. Or that her smile was a sunrise, an invitation to hope. She began and ended every day for him, even when they were apart. She shone like a harvest moon through every night. Without her he had no shadow, he was void of a soul. She was all the reward he needed in life. Tomorrow he would climb into his skiff again and paddle out into the deep part of the ocean and try for another bite. He could cast out his flimsy line ten thousand times and always reel the hook back empty yet still consider himself a victor. A victor with heartburn, his reminder to stay humble and uncertain and always grateful for every counterweight to the pain.

# FIFTY-THREE

## BAREFOOT THROUGH THE SANDS OF TIME

The following afternoon, they stayed for the funeral service but not the interment. The funeral director read platitudes from a well-worn pamphlet, then several of Jennifer's friends spoke tearfully of the intimate relationship between mother and daughter, two peas in a pod, twin souls, one of Jen's friends implying that the carbon monoxide poisoning had been God's way of keeping the family together. Jayme's body tightened when she heard that, and DeMarco, feeling her wince, stroked her hand. At the end of the service they left the building quickly, avoiding as many questioning eyes as possible, but they sat in the sun-heated car in the parking lot until every other car had departed, unsure of where to go next.

Jayme said, "I hope whoever did this burns in hell."

DeMarco's first thought was that, as far as he could remember, hell does not exist, but where was the good in telling her that? Hell, sometimes, is a necessary fiction, and this was one of those times.

"What now?" he asked. "Do you want to go to the beach or, I don't know, back to the inn? We have some time to kill before the town hall tonight."

She thought for a few moments. "Is the sand cold?"

"I didn't have my shoes off yesterday, but it's probably warm by now."

"For some reason, I would love to walk barefoot in the sand right now."

He slipped the key into the ignition.

"But in a black dress?" she asked. "Won't that look pretty?"

"What difference does it make what color your dress is?"

"You wouldn't mind?"

"Why would I mind?"

"People will be gawking, wondering, thinking all kinds of things."

"Let them think whatever they want."

"We're going to the meeting tonight. If anybody sees me on the beach in a black dress…it's a small town, everybody will know. They'll look at me like I'm some kind of crazy woman."

He held the key in place.

"Let's just go back to our room," she said.

"So you can change?"

She shook her head. "Let's just stay in. Watch a movie or something."

He started the engine and pulled onto the street. But her resignation bothered him. Too much loss. This was no time to surrender to public opinion or anything else. He drove only four blocks before abruptly pulling into a parking space and shutting off the engine. "What's wrong?" she asked.

"Saw something I want to check out," he said, then climbed out and sprinted back the way they had come, only to disappear into a recessed doorway. Seven minutes later he returned grinning, swinging a shopping bag at his side.

He climbed in and laid the bag on her lap and said, "I hope I got the size right."

She reached into the bag. Black yoga pants and a long-sleeved peach-colored T-shirt. "Oh, baby," she said.

"You gotta walk in the dunes," he told her.

She laid a hand on his cheek, kissed the other cheek and said, "You're all right, DeMarco. I don't care what anybody says."

"Who says I'm not all right?"

"Everybody, baby. Everybody but me."

# FIFTY-FOUR

## THE KINDNESS OF THIEVES AND OTHER STRANGERS

That evening they drove to Mason County Reformed Church a few miles west of town. Patrol Officer Dawn Stiple had somehow managed to squeeze a healthy portion of Scottville's citizens into the church's basement reception room. She took to the podium precisely at 7:00 p.m., just as DeMarco and Jayme slipped in through the doors at the rear of the room. They stood with others leaning against the back wall. They had hoped to go unnoticed but every individual nearby turned to give them the once-over. Stiple, with her thin, sharply featured face looking sternly matter-of-fact, wasted no time in bringing the room to attention.

"You all knew Jennie Barrie and her sweet little girl, Emma. And by now you all know what happened to them. What you might not know is that it's starting to look like the carbon monoxide poisoning of Emma and her grandma wasn't an accident."

A wave of murmurs and curses swept through the crowd. Everyone sat a little straighter in their seats. Stiple held up her right hand to silence the mumbles. "At this point we don't have any idea who might have done such a thing. It might have been a local, it might have been a stranger."

Jayme and DeMarco scanned the backs of the heads, alert for a slump, a slouch, an attempt at invisibility. DeMarco's eye caught two young men seated near the center aisle three rows from the last when they leaned their heads together. First one would whisper in the other's ear, then the other would reply. They were worth watching.

DeMarco had not been in favor of a town hall meeting like this one, but he had to admit that it was more private and possibly more effective than a press conference or a public call for information. Chief Gary apparently believed that he and his only full-time officer, Stiple, and maybe a couple of part-timers, all working with big shot investigators DeMarco and Matson, could wrap this thing up in a matter of days, especially if they could coax a lead or two out of the public. A high-profile victory might prompt the state treasury to lessen its death grip on law enforcement funds.

"What we need from you people," Stiple told the crowd, "is two things. We need you to keep your mouths shut about this. Don't be spewing it around to just anybody. And for God's sake don't be putting anything about it up on social media. You do, and the chief and me are not going to look very kindly on you. Everybody clear on this?"

Most of the heads nodded, accompanied by a hundred or so verbal affirmations. A man near the front said, "If you wanted us to keep mum about it, why'd you bring us here in the first place?"

"That's the second thing," Stiple said. "We need to know if you know anything. Any little thing at all. Did Jen have enemies? Somebody who hated her enough to kill her little girl? Did you know the grandmother? What's her history? Did you see anybody lurking around the Barrie trailer out on Walker Road this past week? Any unfamiliar vehicles around? We pulled the surveillance footage at every place along Route 10 that has cameras, but it's going to take us a while to work through it all. We're hoping one or more of you folks might help us zero in on an individual or two."

DeMarco sensed that somebody was staring in his direction. He looked to the right. A teenage girl standing against the side wall, her mouth grim, eyes narrowed. DeMarco smiled at her, and she raised her hand to point at him. "I seen those two at Mickey D's with Emma before she died."

Officer Stiple nodded. "Yep, you did. Those two we know. They're from out of town and working on this with us."

"Where out of town?" somebody asked.

"A long way out," she answered. "They came driving a black Jetta from Enterprise in Ludington. You might have seen them in a big RV too, Pennsylvania plates. Whatever, they're on our side. And that's all you need to know right now."

"Like hell it is."

"Listen," she told the crowd. "We're 99 percent certain there's no danger to anybody else. This thing with the Barries wasn't random. We're also pretty dang sure it has to do with whoever is Emma's biological father. So if any of you know anything about that, you need to bring that information straight to me or the chief. And I mean *now*. We know Jen used to be a party girl, like a lot of us were back in our younger days, but after Emma came along, all that changed. Jennie plowed a fairly straight and narrow row after she became a mama. We're just hoping that she might have confided in one or two of you. Any little thing at all."

A hand went up from the center of the crowd. A female voice said, "I might know something."

Stiple's hand flew up as if to stop an oncoming car. "Whoa, hold it right there, Carol. Don't say another word. You come see me as soon as we break up here, okay? Which we're about to do in just a few seconds. You and anybody else who might know something helpful. As for the rest of you, you keep your eyes and ears open and your mouths shut. I don't want a single word I said tonight to go beyond this room. Remember you're in a church. Which means you're making that promise not just to me and the walls."

A gray-haired man with a buzz cut stood and jammed on his ball cap. "Good luck with that," he said. He turned and walked toward the door.

Officer Stiple said, "I'm not counting on luck, Mr. Wooten. I'm counting on good people who want whoever did that to Emma and her grandma caught and locked up. I'm counting on common decency. Anybody here who lacks that is going to deal with me and Chief Gary."

The room was silent for five seconds. "Okay," she said. "If you got nothing to tell us, you go on home to your families. The rest of you line up in front of that table in the rear corner back there. We'll get to every one of you sooner or later, even if we have to stay here all night."

In fewer than five minutes, most of the crowd had filtered out. Jayme and DeMarco joined Officer Stiple behind the eight-foot folding table in the rear corner, one seated on each side of her. The line that queued up to speak to the officer was a mere nine persons deep.

Stiple cracked open a bottle of water, took a gulp, looked at Carol, the middle-aged woman standing with her fingers curled over the rounded back of a metal folding chair pushed against the table, ready to speak, and held up one finger. To the rest of the line, Stiple said, "I'd appreciate if all of you would back up ten, twelve feet or so. We need to keep everything each of you says to us strictly confidential. For your sake as much as ours."

The individuals behind Carol shuffled backward. When Officer Stiple was satisfied with the distance, she looked up at the waiting woman. "Have a seat, Carol," she said.

Carol pulled out the chair. Sat. Then scooted the chair closer. Looked first at DeMarco, then Jayme, then settled her gaze on Officer Stiple. She leaned forward, her breasts pushing against the edge of the table. "I've known Jen all my life," she whispered.

"I know you have."

"I don't know any names, though. She never told me a name."

"What *did* she tell you?"

"My Missy is just a year older than Emma. They went to school together. Played basketball together. I still can't believe Jen's gone, let alone Emma too."

"It is hard to stomach," Stiple said.

The woman nodded. Chewed her lower lip. "This was after a parent-teacher meeting when the girls was in third grade."

"Okay," Stiple said.

"I came out of my meeting and I seen Jen and Emma setting in the lunchroom together. There's always coffee and cookies there on parent-teacher night. Punch for the kids. So me and Missy was walking over to say hi and join them when I noticed that Jen was crying. I mean she was smiling and talking to Emma but there was tears running down her cheeks at the same time."

"So what happened?" Stiple asked.

"Well, we sat down and I asked her what was wrong, and she said nothing was wrong. She was just happy is all. So I ask, 'About what?' And she says, 'They want to put her in the gifted program. She's got an IQ of 136.'"

"That's pretty high," Stiple said.

"You're right it is. Higher than Missy's, that's for sure. Or anybody else I know."

"And then what?" Stiple asked.

"Then Jen said to Emma, 'I guess we can thank your daddy for something, anyway, can't we, sugar?' And then my Missy says, 'So who *is* your daddy? You never talk about him.' And Emma says, 'I don't know who he is.' And that's when Jen says, 'He's way too important a man to want anything to do with us.' And then she looks down and gives Emma a squeeze and says, 'But you'll show him now, won't you, baby? You're going to do great things, and he won't get to enjoy a single one of them.'"

Officer Stiple waited a few moments for more. But apparently Carol was finished.

Jayme asked, "Important how?"

"I don't know," Carol said. "Missy asked Emma about him a couple of times after that, but all she could get out of her was that he lived like a thousand miles away, she said, and had his own family and didn't want nothing to do with her. I think that's all Emma ever knew about him. Anyway, I thought you needed to know."

"Thank you, Carol," Officer Stiple said. "Thank you very much for that. If you think of anything else, you know where to find me."

"Why would he do something like that to Emma," Carol asked, "after all these years? It don't make no sense, does it?"

*Because Jennifer was dying and she reached out to him*, DeMarco thought. *And he feared exposure more than he loved his own daughter, who was nothing but a name to him. A name and an inconvenience.*

Of the remaining people waiting to speak, only two had useful information. Two high school boys. The two whom DeMarco had caught whispering to each other earlier. Long, dirty hair, hooded sweatshirts, eyes that could not meet a gaze. One sat across the table from Stiple while the other knelt on the concrete floor.

"Before we tell you anything," the one sitting told Officer Stiple, "we need to know you're not going to turn around and arrest us for something."

"Arrest you for what?" she asked.

"We didn't do nothing," the kneeling one said. "We thought about it. But we didn't do it."

Stiple said, "Then you're in luck. Cause as far as I know, we can't arrest people for what they think."

"You give us your word?" the seated one asked.

"If you didn't actually do anything criminal, then yes, I give you my word."

"What about if we attempted something?" the kneeling boy asked. "Isn't that a crime too?"

"I'll tell you what," Stiple said. "For tonight it's not. But only for tonight. As long as you tell me the truth, and I mean all of it. And don't you forget where you're sitting right now. You're sitting in a house of God. Keep that in mind."

The seated boy asked, "Does that mean you can arrest us tomorrow?"

"It means the past is past. It's forgotten. Unless you hurt somebody doing it. Did you?"

"There wasn't nobody around when we did it. I promise."

"Fair enough. I catch you doing something in the future, though, you're fair game."

The boys looked at each other. The kneeling boy whispered to the other. The seated one nodded, then spoke to the officer. "So we was out riding one night," he said.

"What night in particular?"

"The night that girl was supposed to have died in her sleep."

"Okay. Out riding where?"

"Out along Walker Road and thereabouts."

"Out past the Barrie trailer?"

The boy kneeling leaned forward over the table. "We seen a car parked, I don't know, fifty yards or so up the road from the trailer. Just setting there pulled off in the gravel."

"Around what time was this?"

"Ten or so," the seated boy said.

The kneeling one offered, "It wasn't quite ten yet. About eight minutes short. I looked at my phone."

DeMarco asked, "Can you describe that car?"

The kneeling boy answered. "I got a pretty good look at it. It was a Nissan Rogue. Dark green. The license plate holder said Enterprise, Big Rapids."

Officer Stiple nodded and said to Jayme, "Roben-Hood Airport. That's the nearest Enterprise east of Scottville. Ludington being the closest, of course." Then she turned back to the boys. "And what were you doing up so close to it that you could read the license plate holder?"

"Just looking," the kneeling boy said.

"What did you see inside of the vehicle?" DeMarco asked.

"That's just it," the seated boy answered. "Nothing worthwhile. There was a duffel bag in the front seat but we couldn't find nothing in it. Just a pair of old jeans and some underwear and shirts. The back seat had some dried dirt on it but that was it."

"In other words," Stiple said, "you jimmied the lock to get inside."

"You said we wouldn't get arrested for nothing."

"So far, so good," she told him.

"Okay then. Because we didn't take anything. Not a single thing."

"Lucky for you there wasn't anything worth stealing, right?"

The boy kneeling said, "There was a bunch of Arby's wrappers on the front passenger floor along with a empty coffee cup, a milkshake cup and a bottle that laundry detergent comes in."

"Laundry detergent?" Stiple asked.

"Yeah but that wasn't what was in it when I took off the lid and smelled it."

"What was?" she asked.

"Smelled like piss to me."

"Watch your language, junior."

"Sorry," he said.

"Maybe you should have taken a sip or two."

"Ha," the boy said. "You wish."

DeMarco barely heard the rest of the exchange. His mind was racing, assembling the pieces. The driver had flown into Roben-Hood Airport outside of Big Rapids and rented the Nissan there. Then drove north sixty miles and... No, wait; if he had flown, why not into Ludington instead? It was only a few miles from Walker Road. So maybe he hadn't flown. Maybe he drove all the way. And came in from the south, maybe the east. How far south or east was anybody's guess. He stopped at the Enterprise in Big Rapids to switch cars, didn't want to do it too close to Scottville. The credit card information would be on file but unavailable without a warrant, and they would need a lot more evidence than they currently had in order to get a warrant. The driver had then stopped at Arby's, ate in the rental car. Had used the detergent bottle to urinate in so that he did not have to use a public restroom. Probably had the bottle with him the whole way, from car to car, and had used the detergent bottle instead of rest stops. He thought he was being clever but he was dropping evidence all over the place, though only witness evidence might still be recoverable—the Arby's employee working the drive-thru window. The Arby's wrappers, potential DNA, and the Arby's time-stamped receipt, and the urine bottle—all long gone by now. As for the small ladder he'd used... It had to have been a folding ladder to fit into the car. Probably stole it, seeing as how it left dried dirt smudged on the seat. Or maybe he brought it from home too, had it with him all that time, knew what he would be getting into. In other words he knew the layout of the Barrie trailer. Had either been there himself or clued in by someone who had been there. He drove to Walker Road at a time when he knew the memorial for Jennie Barrie was taking place at the Bear Claw. But how would he know that if he wasn't a local? In any case, if he had carried the ladder through the woods on the eastern side, the darkest side, he would have been impossible to identify. He could have stopped to grab a handful of last year's leaves, then propped the ladder against the side of the trailer, climbed up and plugged the vent, never more than a shadow, if even that. Then back to the rental car and back to the airport. Maybe he dumped the ladder somewhere or maybe he took it home with him. But where was home?

Where did Morrison's friends live?

And which of them was so self-important that he was willing to sacrifice his own daughter for anonymity?

Anger rising as bitter as bile, DeMarco thought of Emma and her grandmother coming home that night. They unlock the front door, both sad, both weary and empty and heavy with sorrow after the memorial for Jennie. Grandma is also drunk, all senses impaired. They smell nothing amiss, taste nothing in the air, see not a thing out of place. And aren't looking for anything. They go to bed shortly after returning home, can feel their bodies deadening, shutting down with grief. Emma hugs her pillow, buries her face in it, convulses with an unimpeachable grief that threatens to shake her apart. And this is her last emotion. Her exit from this world of misery.

He was so angry that his fists were clenched, his body rigid. Then he saw Jayme looking past Stiple and questioning him with her eyes. Somehow she knew what he was feeling; she usually did. He flashed her a sheepish smile, opened his fists, fingers still stiff. Closed his eyes. Shook his head. *God bless you, child*, he prayed. *God bless you and keep you.*

# FIFTY-FIVE

## CAST NOT YOUR GNOSIS INTO THE URINAL

The day was April 15, a Thursday, and a lousy day thus far. DeMarco wondered, *Do other months have ides too? Or just March?*

He asked his cell phone.

The lady with great enunciation who dwelt inside his phone said, "When the Romans fixed the length of the months, they also fixed the date of the Ides. In March, May, July, and October, the ides were on the fifteenth. On other months, it was the thirteenth."

"Dang," he said aloud. "We missed the ides this month." But he did not know if it was a good or bad thing to miss the ides. The ides of March hadn't worked out very well for Julius Caesar, it's true, and so far April wasn't anything to write home about either. Maybe their luck would pick up now that the ides of April were history too.

*There is no such thing as luck,* he heard inside his head, but this time in his own voice and not in that annoying and authoritative voice from the ether. But what if the second one had taken to imitating the first? What if the first had always been a mouthpiece for the second?

He really didn't want to think about that stuff anymore. What good was any of his so-called wisdom doing? Gnosis schmosis. He still had to live, didn't he? Still had to function with all of the sturm and drang of the third dimension raging around him.

These thoughts accompanied him as he stood at the yellowed urinal in the men's room of the Shell station on State Street. In the urinal was a pink, mostly dissolved urinal cake, and atop the cake was a wad of chewing tobacco. If he were the one writing the laws of the universe, his law relevant to that situation would read: *Those who cast tobacco, gum, candy wrappers, or any item other than urine into a urinal will be subject to ten days of cleaning urinals with their teeth.*

All morning he had been drinking weak coffee and scrolling to no avail through hour after hour of surveillance footage. His breath was bad, his stomach sour, his spine sore, his mood cantankerous. His skull felt like a shoebox filled to the brim with jostling, chirping, twitching, suffocating crickets, with a couple of heavy rubber bands stretched tight around the lid.

"Surgent?" somebody called, and knocked on the restroom door. "Wigotta roke!"

At first DeMarco did not understand. The part-time officer assigned to assist him—Carson or Carlson or Carleton or Curtin or something like that—spoke with a speech impediment, the words coming out too quickly, crashing into one another, and often with emphasis on the wrong syllables. DeMarco, zipping up, called out, "Be right there!"

He turned to the sink and squirted his palms with a ball of foam and then suddenly understood what the officer had said. Turned and grabbed the doorknob but had trouble gripping it and trouble turning the lock. He spun back to his right for the paper towel dispenser but there was only the hot air dryer. "I'm coming!" he said, and smashed the back of his hand on the silver button to activate the dryer, then rubbed his soapy hands together under the stream of hot air.

When he thought his hands sufficiently dry he reached for the doorknob again, which was still soapy. But by strangling the knob he was finally able to yank open the door. And there stood Carleton or Curtin or whomever grinning. "Did you say we got the Rogue?" DeMarco asked.

The officer nodded. "Wigotta roke!"

# FIFTY-SIX

## TO DECLUTTER THE CLUTTER, LET IT FLOW, LET IT FLOW

The dark-green Nissan Rogue was clearly visible on the Shell station's surveillance footage as the vehicle passed the station, traveling west, a few minutes after 4:00 on the afternoon prior to Emma's death. Eighteen minutes later it returned east, and was not seen again until 9:21 p.m., again traveling west. It was last caught on the video speeding east past the station at 10:04 p.m. The lone occupant of the vehicle, the driver, was discernible only during the two daylight transits, but was too far from the station for any identification.

"So the airport near Big Rapids," DeMarco said to Officer Curtin. "It's southeast of here, correct? About how many miles, would you say?"

"Welsur thatidbebut sixxymows toeere morless." Well, sir, that would be about sixty miles to here, more or less.

"So he picked up the rental car in Big Rapids," DeMarco said, thinking out loud now, "got into town about four, scouted out Walker Road while he could still see it clearly, then left the area heading back east and waited till dark to go back. Somehow he knew about the memorial at the Bear Claw. But how would he?"

"Facebooknstuff?" Curtin said.

DeMarco nodded. Of course. The modern-day grapevine. Relied upon by everybody except dinosaurs like him. He pushed back his chair. "Excellent work," he said. He stood and put out his hand. "Your department will save a copy of that, correct?"

"Ofersher. Noprolemall." Oh, for sure. No problem at all.

DeMarco smiled to himself; he was getting the hang of the man's speech. All he had to do was to stop listening so hard, stop trying to suck the words in through his ears and just let them flow past. And suddenly he felt very kindly toward the officer, was surprised by the tenderness of his own feelings. How Curtin must have been teased as a child! Yet sought out a job that would help people, even the people who had misused him. The way kindness could bloom in such unlikely places, it always surprised DeMarco, always reminded him to be a better man himself. *Slow down, don't move so fast. Got to make this lifetime last.*

"Can I buy you lunch, Officer?" he asked.

"Onono thersnoneedforat." Oh, no, no. There's no need for that.

"Come on," DeMarco said, and laid a hand on the young man's shoulder. "Let me call my partner and we'll all grab a bite. What's your favorite place to eat?"

# FIFTY-SEVEN

OH THE CEASELESS GASPS AND SIGHS
AND HEAVINGS OF THE HEART!

So how do we get the credit card information for the rental?"
Jayme asked. The bison burgers at Tammy's Place were fat
and juicy and delicious, the deep-fried, beer-battered pickle chips
a tangy, salty punch in the mouth. The place was noisy with conversation, nearly every table full.

"We don't need it," DeMarco told her. "Rental car lots have
more video cameras per square foot than Taylor Swift's bedroom."

"So you've been in Taylor Swift's bedroom?"

"Well, not since you and I have been together."

She punched him in the ribs.

"Ouch! I think you cracked a rib."

"Next time I'll crack your head open."

Officer Curtin thought them hilarious. "Shedanjrous," he said.

"They're all dangerous," DeMarco told him. "That's part of
why we love them."

"Yep, yep," the officer said.

"Do you have a woman in your life?" Jayme asked.

"Ido. Certlydo."

"Children?" DeMarco asked.

"Tboys anagurl."

"You're a lucky man," DeMarco said.

"Yesur. Yesur am."

DeMarco forked the last fried pickle chip off his plate and into his mouth. Neither Jayme nor Curtin had yet finished their outsized burgers. To Curtin, he said, "Do you mind if I fill the chief in on what we found today?"

"Nosur notal. Yagorihed."

"I'll just step outside where it's a bit quieter." Along the way he caught the server's attention and ordered three slices of lemon meringue pie for his table.

Chief Gary was delighted to hear of the day's progress. He would telephone the Big Rapids chief of police and request that the car rental agency's surveillance footage be examined for the estimated times when the Nissan Rogue was picked up and returned.

"You gave me some pretty tight windows," he told DeMarco, "so it shouldn't take long. You figure to be at Tammy's awhile?"

"I just now ordered dessert for everyone."

"It better have been the lemon meringue pie."

"Yes, sir, it was. On Officer Curtin's recommendation."

"Curtin's a good man. He knows his desserts."

"He's a fine officer, Chief. I enjoyed working with him."

"He's my son-in-law, you know."

"I did not know that."

"I wish I could give him more hours. He's a cabinetmaker by trade, and a damn good one too. Unfortunately a town this size has room for only so many cabinets."

"Well, he's got a knack for our line of work too."

"You doing okay following what he has to say? Some people find it difficult till they get used to him."

"We're doing fine," DeMarco told him. "Soon as I figured out I just had to stop listening so hard."

"There you go. Patience is the key. Took me a while to get used to him too, but...he and my girl have blessed me with three beautiful grandkids, so I'm not complaining."

"That's wonderful, Chief. Right now I can't think of anything more wonderful."

"Are you a grandpap yet?"

"Not yet," DeMarco said. And with that he felt a grayness return, an ebbing of his happiness. "Would you be able to send any relevant photos from Big Rapids to my phone?" he asked. "We'll be finishing here in the next quarter hour or so."

"You're not headed home today, are you?"

"Depends on who the driver of that Nissan turns out to be. And where he's from. We'll probably head in his direction if we can identify him."

"So sit a while and enjoy your pie. You don't want to rush that pie, Sergeant. Trust me. If there's one thing we know up here, it's how to savor every bite you get."

"Copy that, Chief." DeMarco watched the traffic moving leisurely through town. Saw how many of the drivers had their windows down despite the coolness of the air. A couple of the drivers waved, as did their children in the back seat. Several others nodded and smiled. He thanked the chief for his help and ended the call, then stood there a while longer, just watching the cars and breathing the air until he felt Jayme come up beside him. Her fingertips were cool when they touched the back of his hand. "It's nice here, isn't it?" he said, and turned her way, but saw no one there.

"Hmm," he said, and then he smiled too, and, shaking his head in awe of the wonders life holds, he returned inside to enjoy his pie.

# FIFTY-EIGHT

## A BENNY FOR YOUR THOUGHTS

They had been back at their hotel for two hours—DeMarco lying on the bed with the pillows propped behind him, the television playing an episode of *Curb Your Enthusiasm* with the audio off. He had tried watching with the audio on but it was like watching a show in Japanese; the jokes generated no response in him other than confusion. And with the audio off the wild gestures seemed even more exaggerated and incomprehensible. But the screen was something to look at while he stewed and seethed. Despite his new enlightenment and understanding of the true reality, he could not keep his anger at bay. He kept seeing Emma as she had been at the McDonald's, sweet and hopeful and endearing in every way. He'd had such tender feelings for her even then, and now, her life snuffed out, his heart felt like a pulsing bruise, the wound more painful than even the bullet had been.

Jayme sat on the small gray sofa, her laptop open on the coffee table, earphones in as she attempted to read an ebook titled *Many Lives, Many Masters* while listening to Sara Bareilles's *Amidst the Chaos* CD. He could tell by the pinch in her forehead and cheeks that she was struggling too. She had felt a deep and immediate love for the girl, had probably plotted out their entire future together. And he understood why Jayme had become attached so quickly, knew that Emma had almost magically filled the deep hole left in Jayme after the miscarriage. Jayme had been deprived of a mother's happiness twice, her heart eviscerated, hope disemboweled. *Even she must be filled with rage*, he thought. Even she must be aching for revenge.

DeMarco laid his head back against the headboard and closed his eyes, an action that seemed to trigger his phone into vibrating. He grabbed the phone and opened the texts. Four photos from Chief Gary, four shots from the security cameras in the Big Rapids Enterprise lot. The man who had rented the Nissan Rogue, thin and slouching as he walked, hands held close to his body, was caught entering the office, climbing into the Nissan, climbing into his own vehicle, and driving away. Unfortunately the quality of the photos was, like most surveillance camera footage, grainy and distorted by the wide-angle lens. The man's face was uncovered but nearly feature-less in the photos. His own vehicle was a dirty black pickup truck.

DeMarco climbed off the bed, crossed to Jayme and stuck the phone in front of her face. She pulled out an earphone and looked up. "Can you get these onto your laptop?" he asked. "Do your magic. We need a face and the plate on the truck."

She worked on the photos for over thirty minutes before calling him over to the screen. He bent down, took a long look. Turned away and went to his canvas bag on the bed, fished around for his reading glasses, put them on and returned to the screen. Leaned close, his nose only four inches from the man's face. "I can't believe this," he said.

"Believe what?"

"You don't recognize this guy?"

"Obviously I don't, or I would have said something."

He leaned back and put a fingertip beside the man's head. "This," he said, "is Mercer County resident Benjamin Szabo."

"You're smudging my screen," she told him, and nudged him to the side so that she could look again. "I don't recognize him. He's from back home?"

"We put him away back in...'04, '05."

"Before my time, babe. For what?"

"Burglary, breaking and entering. He rifled the cash registers in both the Subway and Golden Dragon next door. Then, feeling lucky, I guess, he tried for the bar register at the Yellow Creek restaurant. That's where we got him and his buddy."

"Two miles from the station house?" she said. "How bright is that?"

"Benny Szabo bright. He kicked and spit at us like a camel, so we tagged him for resisting arrest and assaulting an officer too. He already had a handful of other charges on his sheet, so all told he went down for six to ten. Did five and a few months before he was released. And, as far as we knew, never came back to Mercer."

"Are you 100 percent sure that's who this is? I mean what are the odds that somebody from back home—?"

"Morrison is from back home," he said. "Maybe his friends are too. That decreases the odds significantly, don't you think?"

"So you're suggesting that one of them sent Szabo up here. Maybe Benny Szabo is Emma's father."

DeMarco gave her a look.

"Why is that not possible?" she asked.

"Because Szabo is a flea, a tick, a... What's lower and more disgusting than a tick?"

"Tick will do," she said. "I get your point."

"He's the kind of man who would go around making babies just so he could collect the government subsidy for them. But any woman who would let him would have to be just as low. Besides, didn't Emma tell her friend that her father was important somehow?"

"Maybe that's just the story Jennifer told her. To help her feel better about herself."

"Please stop raining on my party," he said.

"That's what I get paid to do, isn't it? You're sure it's Benny Szabo in those photos?"

"The brain in my gut is certain of it."

"Then we need to let Kyle know. He can put out a BOLO and maybe round Szabo up and—"

"Whoa. Slow down," DeMarco said. "They can question him but they can't charge him, so let's not get ahead of ourselves on this."

"Why, babe? What are you thinking?"

"They question him, and what's the first thing he does? He bolts. And then he alerts whoever hired him."

"You really don't believe he's capable of doing it all himself?"

"Benny Szabo? I'm surprised he was even able to drive to Michigan without screwing up six ways to Sunday. No, he didn't even know Jennie Barrie, he's the hired hand. And we don't want to tip off the boss."

"You think it's the judge?"

He pursed his lips, shook his head. "I can't see him ordering a hit on a little girl and her grandmother. But that doesn't mean he isn't involved somehow."

"You think he's covering for one of his friends."

"That's how it appears right now, yes."

"So what's our next move?"

"We jump on a plane going east. And we locate Benny before he or anybody else gets wind that we're looking for him."

"What makes you so sure he went back to Mercer County?"

"He's not the kind of guy you pay in advance. You give him his orders, some basic expense money, and wait for him to report back with proof that he completed his job."

"I guess what I'm saying is, how do we know that his boss isn't somebody up here? Maybe Emma's real father is a local guy who just coincidentally knows Benny Szabo."

"It's possible, I guess. But we have to play the odds, baby. Morrison and two of his pals get a letter from Michigan. The judge, if not the other two, is a Mercer County resident. Benny Szabo, a former Mercer County resident, is now known to have been near the Barrie home the night before Emma died. Put all that together, and what it adds up to is that the judge is likely to have known Szabo, or at least had access to his arrest records. That doesn't look like coincidence to me. It looks like dominoes lining up for you and me to knock down."

# FIFTY-NINE

A HEART THAT BURNS IS A HEART THAT YEARNS

Soon after DeMarco's and Jayme's return to Pennsylvania the following day, favors were called in, contacts reestablished. While Jayme fetched Hero from the kennel in the late afternoon and did her best to soothe his resentment with an unleashed run in the park followed by two double cheeseburgers, no condiments, from Burger King, DeMarco brought Captain Bowen into the loop in regard to Benny Szabo's apparent but still alleged presence along Scottville's Walker Road on the night preceding Emma's and her grandmother's death. Troopers Boyd and Lipinski were called into the station house meeting and also briefed by DeMarco, after which Captain Bowen tasked them with determining whether or not Szabo had returned to Mercer County, and, if he had, any link between him and Judge Morrison.

"What about bringing Flores in on this too?" DeMarco suggested.

Bowen was hesitant. "It's not in her purview anymore. Though I understand why you would suggest it."

"Then make it her purview."

"Easier said than done."

"She's struggling, Kyle. We have to do more for her. All of us do."

"And if she goes back out into the field, who is responsible if something happens to her? I am. I'm sorry, but she's just not equipped for it now."

"Isn't she the one who should decide that?"

"You know that's not the way it works."

Trooper Boyd, never one to unnecessarily inject himself into a conversation, addressed his station commander. "Sir, I think she's more capable than we give her credit for."

Bowen's head cocked, eyebrows lifted.

Boyd said, "She's started working out again at Planet Fitness. Going over and beyond what her rehab calls for. And she's been spending a lot of time on a climbing wall over in Youngstown. Plus she stopped drinking, more or less."

"Is she off the brace?"

"No, sir. That's permanent."

"Then she still runs with a stiff leg, am I right?"

"I haven't seen her run, sir, but yes, I would suppose that she does."

Bowen shook his head, then looked to DeMarco again. "I can't allow it. She poses too big a risk. For herself and her partners."

"So I'll hire her myself," DeMarco said. "As part of my team."

"Doing what?"

"What she's always done. What she longs to do. Putting the bad guys in jail."

"No way," Bowen told him. "If she wants to moonlight as a bouncer at a bar or a private party, that's fine with me. Security at a basketball game? Sure, probably. But out there in the boonies traipsing around with you and Jayme, with who knows what kind of clowns hiding behind the trees? Absolutely not. It's against policy and against common sense. Besides, have you seen her trying to climb stairs? It makes me want to cry."

DeMarco sat back in his chair. Crossed his arms. Said, "She stopped Khatri when nobody else could. Not me, not us, not the Mahoning County Sheriff's Department, not the FBI, not the Royal Canadian Mounted Police. Give the woman some credit, Captain."

Bowen held his gaze on DeMarco for a few moments, then looked down at the edge of his desk. Shook his head. Leaned forward over his desk and said in a softer, conspiratorial voice, "Look. I'm as grateful as anybody that she put Khatri down. But how did she do it? At great personal risk and permanent bodily damage to herself. You think it was easy for me to get her that commendation? She acted impulsively. And now she's living to regret it."

"She doesn't regret it," Boyd said.

"And how do you know that?" Bowen asked.

"She told me. Said she'd do it again if she had to."

"There you go," Bowen said, and held out his hands palms up. "She'd do it again. My point exactly."

And so it was decided. DeMarco and Jayme would continue their investigation on behalf of Emma Barrie, while Troopers Boyd and Lipinski would conduct their own investigation. Intel would be shared between both teams, with Bowen briefed daily at a minimum.

DeMarco returned home to a quiet house just before six that evening. He set four containers of Greek food on the kitchen counter, then walked softly from room to room. Jayme's car was parked in the backyard, so he had expected Hero to come running around the corner at any second and leap against his chest, and he was disappointed when that didn't happen. He crept upstairs and peeked into the bedroom and found both Jayme and Hero asleep on the bed. She lay curled around the dog's body, her knees tucked up to his furry butt, her chin nestled close to his head. DeMarco could hear their breathing and could distinguish between her sibilance and Hero's. The light was low outside the window, the room warm, and he was very tired. He had failed Flores and did not know what else to do for her. But he had Emma to consider too plus the continuing welfare of those two sleeping beauties on the bed. He was weary to the bone and hungry too and knew that rest was not in his immediate future.

He went downstairs and sat at the kitchen table with his laptop open, eating out of a carton of grilled lamb while searching on social media for any word or suggestion of Benjamin Szabo. The lamb was overcooked and rubbery, so he switched to the baba ghanoush but found it too bitter with excess lemon. The dolmas were a disappointment too, the grape leaves as bitter as the tahini, yet he ate his fill anyway because there is no such thing as coincidences, and apparently the universe wanted him to have heartburn again that night.

# SIXTY

## AND SOMETIMES FREE WILL SUCKS

In the morning, a bright Saturday morning scented by sunlight warming the damp greening grass, DeMarco felt good. Unnaturally good. He had slept well, no heartburn, and a couple of hours later than usual, rising at 7:23 to an empty bed and the sound of the bathroom shower blasting the tiles and glass door. The kitchen too was warm and inviting, though it did smell unpleasantly of the empty baba ghanoush container in the trash. He made coffee and, because Mrs. Nellis was surely already awake next door, checked the laundry room for a pair of pants to pull on over his boxers before he went outside. He found the chinos he had worn in Michigan, profusely wrinkled but a nice match for the Pink Floyd T-shirt in which he had slept, and escorted Hero out back to water the bushes.

Apparently Hero felt very good too. He made a running leap off the porch, then completed four high-speed laps around the yard, skidding so dangerously close to the porch each time that DeMarco, standing barefoot in the wet grass, chuckled out loud.

When Hero paused to make his first pit stop of the morning, DeMarco stood there staring off to the east, his gaze just above the rounded humps of horizon where there was nothing but light,

light as far as an eye could see. But beyond that light, he knew, there was darkness. And darkness within the light. Darkness from light and light succumbing to darkness. Always one within the other, one becoming the other. The trick was to follow the light whenever you could. Better yet, *be* the light. Because if you want to talk to a burning bush, and all light fails, you had better be carrying matches.

He laughed a little at that image. Then he stood there a while longer enjoying the warmth of the sun on his face, the way the light warmed the front of his shirt and the shirt warmed his skin.

Minutes passed before he brought his gaze back to ground level. Hero was on his next to last stop, the front driver's side tire of the RV. "Get your business done," DeMarco called to him. "I'm overdue myself."

Just as Hero headed for his last stop, a timid female voice only a few feet away startled DeMarco. "Good morning."

He turned to his left, expecting to see a neighbor. But it was Daniella Flores. "Sorry," she said. "I knocked out front but…then I heard you back here."

She looked better, healthier and happier, than he had seen her all year, her face shining, hair neatly brushed and styled, the pale-yellow shirt crisp, olive-drab cargo pants creased, her eyes as bright and eager as he had ever seen them. Only the bulge of the leg brace made him wince a little. "Dani," he said, and crossed to her. "How nice. What are you doing in this neighborhood so early?"

"Is it too early? Should I come back in an hour or so?"

"No, of course not. You want some coffee? It should be ready by now."

"I don't want to interrupt your morning. I mean I do but…"

"Let's have some coffee," he said. Then he slapped his leg twice, called "Hero! Come!" and the dog came running, though to Flores instead of his master. She petted his head and allowed him to sniff her shoes, a pair of white Fila sneakers.

In the mudroom, DeMarco dried his and Hero's feet with a towel from the laundry hamper, then in the kitchen took three mugs from the cabinet, lined them up on the counter and filled two of them. "There's half-and-half in the fridge," he told her. "Help yourself."

"Black is fine," she said.

"Finer than fine," he answered, and handed a mug to her. "Have a seat. Jayme will be coming down soon. She'll be happy to see you."

Flores held the mug in both hands but did not sit, did not sip. "Just tell me what you want me to do," she said. "I'm ready to go."

"Excuse me?" He pulled his usual chair away from the table but remained standing beside it. Hero continued to sniff Flores's legs.

"Please don't be angry with him," she said.

"Hero! Go sit!"

Hero looked at him, appeared to pout, then trotted out of the room.

"Not Hero," she said. "Mace."

"Trooper Boyd? Why would I be angry with him?"

"He told me about the meeting yesterday. With Captain Bowen."

DeMarco flashed back through the reel, found the relevant frame. DeMarco offering to hire Flores and put her on his team. "He really shouldn't have told you that."

"He didn't want to. I just sort of...coaxed it out of him."

Hmm, an interesting wrinkle. "Are you two...?"

"We're friends," she told him. Looked away momentarily. Brought her gaze back to his. "But, you know... Good friends."

He nodded. Smiled. Sipped his coffee. Then he reached for the chair nearest her, pulled it out, and motioned for her to sit. "I would like nothing better than to have us working together again," he told her. She remained standing, still squeezing the mug with both hands. "But there's a gray area, I guess, in department policy. Moonlighting is okay for some jobs but not when—"

She interrupted him with, "I'm done there."

"You're what?" The mug was burning his hands. How could she keep holding hers like that? He set his on the table. "What do you mean, you're done there?"

"I resigned."

"No, Dani, you did not."

"Yes I did. I called the captain last night. Dropped my letter of resignation off this morning."

"He accepted it?"

"He wasn't in yet, so I laid it on his desk. But he has no choice but to accept it. He can't make me stay if I don't want to, and I don't want to. I won't."

There were little pools forming in her eyelids now, and the way she was squeezing that mug… He put a hand out, took the mug from her and set it on the table. "Let's sit," he said. "Can we sit and talk about this?"

She stepped forward and sat, very rigidly, he thought, though with her left leg stretched out straight, unbendable. "We can talk," she told him, "but I'm not going back. I didn't get into law enforcement to sit and answer a phone all day. I already cleaned out my locker and my desk."

He sat beside her. Turned his chair toward hers. "Dani, this is…" He knew he had to choose his words very carefully. Where was Jayme when he needed her?

"Sir," she said, and the tear pools in her eyes were bulging now, ready to overflow at any second, "I need to feel useful again. I want this chance with you. I need it. I promise I won't let you down."

"You could never let me down," he told her. "But what about your insurance, your salary—"

"I have the reward money, thanks to you. I can pay for my own insurance. You don't even have to pay me, I'll work with you for free. What I *can't* buy is what I need. Only you can give that to me."

*Caramba*, he thought.

# SIXTY-ONE

## OF CREATURES GREAT AND SMALL AND LOATHSOME

There were times, DeMarco told himself, when he needed to put aside the NDE and the knowledge it had brought. He was back in this world and needed to look at it, if only to get the job done, as he had before being shot—as a place wholly real and solid and miles from perfection. And from that perspective, the planet was populated by six kinds of people. There were wolves, there were worms, there were sheep, there were the decents, there were soldiers, and there were angels. Hybrids did exist, but most people could be relegated to one category or another based on their dominant qualities.

Wolves were predatory, always looking to fatten themselves up on weaker specimens, typically the sheep, who were docile and compliant herd animals, happier to follow the advice and orders of others than to engage their own powers of discernment. As such, sheep were easy pickings for the wolves of this world. Worms were likely to prey on sheep too, but their strategies were more insidious and deceptive than that of wolves. Worms were opportunists who lived closer to the ground and often concealed themselves wherever sheep foraged.

The decents were just that: well-meaning individuals who did their best to live honest, caring lives. They helped out when they could, when it was convenient to do so and didn't cost too much in money or time or personal safety. They were sometimes selfish but always felt bad about it afterward, always worried a little about the ramifications of sin and karma. They won Employee of the Month awards and other minor distinctions, and when they crossed the line it was by only a step or two and they usually got off with a warning.

DeMarco was a soldier, of course, in and out of uniform. Soldiers could be herd animals too, never questioning their orders, as DeMarco had been when a young man, in which case they might be as dangerous as wolves and worms, or they could be of the opposite ilk, equipped with their own stringent codes of behavior, their own missions to complete. Some who thought of themselves as soldiers were actually wolves if their intent was not for the good of the target individual or individuals. Jayme, though she did her own kind of soldiering, was in fact an angel, armed always with compassion and empathy and an altruistic imperative to self-sacrifice. Unfortunately, even angels could sometimes turn out to be worms and wolves in disguise. DeMarco had met many false angels in his time, enough to know with certainty that Jayme was the real thing, one of the rare ones in a world so in need of the angelic.

In the end, correct categorization all came down to intent. Benny Szabo was a worm, drenched head to toe in his own slime. Whoever had hired him to assassinate a little girl and an old woman was an apex predator, a wolf-worm hybrid who lived in the damp dirt of secrecy with an avaricious hunger that knew no bounds. With luck, a few honest soldiers and one angel could flush both of them out and bring them down.

DeMarco spent over three hours that morning in the kitchen with Jayme and Flores, having breakfast and discussing their options, then searching online for some hint as to Benny Szabo's whereabouts.

Except for his early and midmorning pee breaks outside, Hero lay on the floor between DeMarco's and Jayme's chairs, occasionally looking up, occasionally swishing his tail across the linoleum.

Neither social media nor the directories and information databases available to civilians provided even a crumb. A newspaper obituary for Benny's mother, Linda Bittner Szabo, provided the only reference to her son. She had passed away "after a long illness" at the age of forty-six, while Benny, her only child, was still in prison.

Without direct access to CLEAN, the Commonwealth Law Enforcement Assistance Network, the trio of investigators could not access the Pennsylvania Justice Network, the FBI's National Crime Information Center, or NLETS, the National Law Enforcement Telecommunications System. They would have to wait for information from Lipinski and Boyd. DeMarco could remember a few of Szabo's old associates, but to shake down any of them would risk alerting Szabo. At the moment Szabo had no reason to suspect that they were on to him. And until they could definitively tie him to the Barries, DeMarco wanted it to stay that way.

In the meantime, another issue weighed heavy on his mind. To Flores, he said, "I'm going to have to call the captain, you know."

Flores winced. "I hope I didn't screw things up for you guys."

"You didn't. But I promised to keep him informed. Like it or not."

He did not tell her that his phone had been vibrating in his pocket ever since 8:00 a.m., the time when Bowen would have arrived at his office to find Flores's letter of resignation on his desk.

Flores kept wincing. "I'm sorry."

He pushed back his chair and said, "I think I'll just step outside for this call."

Jayme flashed him a wink. "That's one way to get out of helping with the dishes."

Bowen was, as DeMarco had presumed he would be, boiling over. "Did you know about this? Were you in on it from the beginning?"

DeMarco, standing on the brick path where it ended a third of the way down the backyard, tapped the thin button on the side of his phone three times, decreasing the volume. He knew Bowen well enough to know that an apologetic tone would only encourage the captain to keep venting. "Of course I did. I've been trying to make your head explode since the first day we met."

"This is bullshit, Ryan! Totally unprofessional! Whatever happened to two weeks' notice?"

"Whatever happened to Amelia Earhart? For that matter, whatever happened to the woolly mammoth? Just think how nice it would be to have a few of those still wandering around."

Bowen sputtered into his phone for a few moments, almost swearing then pulling himself back from it. After a full fifteen seconds of listening to Bowen's explosive puffs of breath gradually deteriorating into one long exhalation, DeMarco said, "Is that it, boss? You done?"

"I know you call me boss only to placate me."

"Why else would I?" DeMarco said.

"All right." Another exhalation. "Okay. Just tell me this much. Is she there now?"

"Pretty much since the break of dawn."

"I suppose you're blaming me for her resignation."

*I blame myself*, DeMarco thought. But why get into that? "We could use your help getting some intel on Szabo."

"What do you think we're doing here, sitting on our hands? You'll know something when I know something. I can't believe you actually countermanded my direct...my..."

"You weren't going to say *direct order*, were you, Kyle?"

"I specifically requested that you leave her where she was. And not to interfere."

"What choice did I have? This is her decision. Let's just make the best of it, okay?"

"Man oh man," Bowen said, and DeMarco could picture him shaking his head back and forth, staring out the window, maybe even pacing back and forth. "What a way to start a morning."

A few minutes later, back in the kitchen, DeMarco smiled at the women. Flores asked, "How mad is he?"

He winked at her. She reminded him of a little bird perched on the edge of the nest, eager to test her broken wing. "Let's hit the streets," he said. "Jayme, how about if you take Jefferson and Delaware Townships? North as far as Clark should be good. Dani, Lackawannock and East Lackawannock, and then maybe over to Shenango. I'll cover Sharon, Hermitage, Farrell, Sharpsville and north if I have the time. But keep it low-key. Circumspect, right? That's the word of the day."

Flores said, "So how do we ask about Szabo without asking about him?"

"Ask about his mother or father. Don't even mention Benny's name if you don't have to. Let the other person bring it up. I don't know anything about his father, but the obituary said his mother loved listening to local bands and attending wine festivals. You know what that means. Hit all the bars that have live music, all the wineries that give free tastings. Just don't rush it. It's probably safe to skip the pricier places, stick to the lower end. And don't appear too interested. I'll relay any intel I get from the boys at the station house."

"So what's the deal with the father?" Jayme asked.

"From what I recall, the old man was nowhere to be found back when Benny got sent away for the Golden Dragon job. His mother raised him. If you can call it that."

"What does this guy look like?" Flores asked. "Just in case I run into him."

"Five seven or eight," DeMarco said. "Caucasian. Maybe one sixty tops."

Jayme said, "From the photo I saw, I'd put him at one-fifty max."

"Age?" Flores asked.

"Midthirties," DeMarco said.

"Any identifying tattoos?" asked Flores. "Scars, facial features, anything like that?"

"I doubt you will get that close," he told her. "He's a born sneak. But let's say you get lucky and see him bent over a beer somewhere. Keep your distance, keep your eye on him, and text us immediately."

"Roger that," she said.

"Just curious," Jayme said, "but what about Morrison and his *so* considerate and cooperative friends?"

"We start at the bottom," DeMarco told her, "and work our way up."

"They're all bottom-feeders as far as I'm concerned."

*Great*, he thought. *One gung ho team member, one seriously pissed off, and one…one what, DeMarco? What are you?*

Before he could come up with an answer, Flores was on her feet. She seized his right hand in both of hers and pumped it hard. "Thank you, Sergeant! Thank you for this! I'll be in touch!" And then she was out the door, her stiff left leg swinging out wide as she went.

DeMarco looked at Jayme. She cocked her head. He cocked his in return. Then they stood, still looking at each other with eyebrows raised. He shrugged. She shrugged. DeMarco bent down to rub Hero's head.

"The house is yours, fella," he told the dog. "No parties. And don't buy anything from the shopping channel."

Jayme leaned down and pretended to whisper in Hero's ear.

"Just be sure to clean up afterward if you have anybody over. And I could use a nice pearl necklace." Then, smiling at each other, she and DeMarco followed Flores out into the light. Hero stayed alert for ten more seconds, heard the door click shut, closed his eyes and sighed.

# SIXTY-TWO

## BACK IN THE SADDLE, BUT BAREBACK

Flores was so excited that she shivered as she drove, heading southwest on Pulaski Mercer Road toward Hoagland, trying to come up with the names of all the watering holes within her assigned sector. Problem was, they were few and far between. Not much at all in the two Lackawannocks but trees and fields. There were Joseph's and the Middlesex Tavern over in Shenango Township but what else? What the fuck else?

Her foot eased off the accelerator. All of the good places were in Jayme's and DeMarco's sectors, especially his. What did he expect her to do—talk to the trees?

She pulled onto the shoulder, sat with her foot on the brake, hands on the steering wheel, and racked her brain. Surely there were some likely places in her sector. Or else why would he have assigned—

He had no faith in her, that's why. He wasn't going to risk the high-percentage places on a…on a what? A proven failure?

And for just a moment she felt like throwing open the door, puking into the dirt, crying, giving up, turning around and going home to bed with a big bottle of wine. But then she told herself, No. No, damn it! She *wasn't* a failure. And she was going to prove it.

Linda Szabo, Flores figured, would have been a lot like her own Auntie Leña, one of her mother's younger sisters, the one her mother called a lush, the one always with a bottle of beer in one hand, a cigarette in the other. "What places did Leña go?" Flores asked herself. "I know she went to Quaker Steak & Lube during the summer. She loved the bike nights there. Loved the bikers and the free beer." It was not summer yet but still, a place to start. "So anything in that general area," she told herself. "Start there and work your way outward."

She checked her side mirror, ready to pull onto the highway again, then sat more upright and blinked, as if the morning had suddenly become too bright. What would DeMarco do if she ignored him and went rogue? He would dump her, that's what. Flores the failure. Flores the washout.

She shut off the engine. Leaned her head back and closed her eyes and tried to keep from crying.

The cell phone jingle jerked her upright. She grabbed the phone from its holder, looked at the screen. Oh God, her mother again.

She thought about ignoring it, silencing the ring. But really, what else did she have to do?

"Hello, Mama," she said.

"Daniella, what's wrong? Why do you sound that way?"

"Nothing's wrong. You just caught me at a bad time. I'm a little busy right now."

"What are you doing?"

"I'm working, Mama. What would I be doing?"

"Well, it's a sad day when a child is too busy to say hello to her only mother, isn't it?"

"I said hello, Mama. Why did you call?"

"I called because I miss you. I've been lonely for you."

"I miss you too."

"Then why don't you visit more?"

"Mama," Flores said, ready to end the call. But then she had a thought. "Hey, I was just thinking about Auntie Leña a while ago. What is she up to these days?"

"What do you want with Leña?"

"I don't want anything with her. I was just thinking about her. It's been a couple of years since I even talked to her."

"You need to stay in touch with your family better. I always tell you that."

"So where is she now? Last I remember she was with some guy up around Warren."

"You see what happens when you don't stay in touch? You lose track of your own family."

"Mama, please. Is she still living in Ohio?"

"She's been right under your nose all this time and you've never even spoke to her. Not three miles from where you live in that hardware store. You should be ashamed of yourself."

"Right under my nose where? And I live *above* the hardware store, not in it, Mama, as you well know."

"I'm surprised you never run into her. You didn't know she was living there?"

"Living *where*, Mama? Can't you for God's sake just tell me where she lives?"

"She lives on Charleston Road with some woman now. I don't think there's any hanky-panky going on, though. Not that it would matter anyway. The woman's name is Margo and she seems very nice. I talk to her on the phone sometimes."

Flores had stopped listening, was thinking that Leña might have a solid tip on where a lowlife like Szabo would be hanging out. She had been a lowlife herself once upon a time. Probably still was. Flores started her engine, figured it was worth a shot. Better than interviewing the freaking trees anyway. She cut in on her mother's ramble to ask, "What's her address, Mama?"

"Why would you want to go there? She won't be there now."

Flores blew out a breath. Squeezed the steering wheel. Evenly, she said, "Where will Auntie Leña be right now if she isn't at home?"

"She has a job now."

"Wonderful. And where does she work?"

"You should visit her sometime. Catch up. She asks about you all the time."

"I intend to go visit her, Mama, if you will tell me where she works."

"I thought you were busy working today."

"I'm on a little break."

"How nice of them to give you a break! Do you get one every morning? You should call your mama more."

"I will, I promise. Where is Auntie Leña working *right now*, Mama?"

"Do you know where the VFW is?"

The Hickory VFW was a few minutes behind her. "The Hickory one or the one near Daffin's Candies?"

"It's right across the road from the Historical Society. She keeps asking me to go there, but I say what for? I don't drink spirits and I am not going to start now just so I can say hello to my own sister."

Flores told herself, *Okay, the Hickory one.* "Are you saying she tends bar there?"

"I told you that, didn't I?"

"Yes, Mama. Thank you. I have to say goodbye now. I will call you again in a day or so."

"How is your leg, my darling? Is it doing okay?"

"It's doing fine, Mama."

"Do you still have to wear the brace?"

"Always, Mama. I always will. I have to go now. I love you. Bye."

"What if—" was the last thing she heard her mother say before she tapped the little red phone icon to end the call, then rammed the gearshift into Drive.

# SIXTY-THREE

## Of old acquaintances seldom thought

While Jayme and DeMarco were panning for information in other parts of the county, and coming up with only the tiniest of flakes, Flores found a promising vein in her Auntie Leña. After their initial reunion in the VFW bar—when Leña had loudly introduced her to the entire room with "Hey, everybody! This here is my beautiful niece, Daniella! I haven't seen her in years! She's a state po-po now so all of you lowlifes better watch your step!"—Flores sipped the glass of iced tea her aunt kept refilling.

Leña looked like a different woman from the one she remembered: at least forty pounds heavier, but happier, more energetic, no longer morose and complaining. She had given up cigarettes and all alcohol but for an occasional wine cooler. Wore no makeup now except for "a bit of foundation," and spoke with such fondness and enthusiasm of her housemate Margo and their "womb to womb" women's circle that Flores had to wonder. "You have to join us," Leña told her. "You *have* to. There are some real healers in our group. You'll be amazed. I know I was."

It was an interesting idea but not the reason why Flores was pumping herself full of iced tea she did not want or need. She hadn't expected to find the VFW barroom so busy in the middle of the morning and was waiting for the right moment to deflect the subject, which, for the past fifteen minutes, had been Dani herself. Leña didn't mind continuing their conversation as she moved up and down behind the bar, drawing beers from the taps and serving platters of eggs and burgers and other meals passed to her from the kitchen, but Flores kept reminding herself of DeMarco's word for the day, *circumspect*, so she did her best to be patient.

"You know I wanted to come see you in the hospital," Leña said.

"Then why didn't you?" Her delivery, she noticed, was flat, as if to balance out all of her aunt's exclamations.

"Your mother told me you didn't want any visitors! Said all you did was to snarl and curse at her and tell her to go home."

Flores sipped her tea. Was in no mood to revisit those days.

"Said she never heard so many f-bombs in her life. And from the mouth of her own little girl!"

"So how long have you been working here? Last I knew you were living in Ohio."

Leña nodded, her mouth in a pucker. Stepped back from the bar, found the bar rag and started polishing the counter and the beer taps. "The last of a long line of mistakes," she said, and shook her head and grinned. "Our family."

"What about it?"

"The women."

"What about the women?"

"We're slow learners. But we *do* learn. Eventually we learn."

Flores wasn't exactly sure what Leña meant by that. Something about getting rid of the men, probably. Or about always picking the wrong kind. But that was a conversation for another day. She said, "Hey. You knew Linda Szabo, didn't you?"

"Sure I knew her. We went to high school together. She was a Bittner then."

"I just found out the other day that she died a while back."

Again Leña nodded. Stepped over to the taps again to serve an elderly man waiting at the bar for a beer. While he waited he inched closer to Flores, and eventually allowed his shoulder to rub against hers. She jerked away and told him, "Hey! You're in my space, old man. Get your skin off my skin."

He took his beer, mumbled something, and shuffled back to his table.

Leña chuckled. "He's harmless."

"Nobody touches me without my permission."

"Geez, baby girl. You *have* changed, haven't you?"

Flores looked away. Shook her shoulders. Sipped her tea.

"How did you know Linda?" Leña asked.

"I'm not sure how we met." Flores pretended to think about it. "I seem to remember it was at some event at the school. She came up and introduced herself to me. Said she knew you and Mama."

"Huh. More like she knew your daddy."

"What?" Flores asked.

"Don't pretend you didn't know what he was like."

"Oh, I know what he was like."

"You ever hear from him these days?"

"He knows better."

"I guess so. My baby girl the po-po. Who would ever have thought?"

"Anyway," Flores said. "Did Linda have any kids? Do I have any half siblings I don't know about?"

"Doubtful," Leña told her. "She just had that one boy, Benny."

"He could still be my half brother. If she and the asshole had a thing."

"I wouldn't bet on it," Leña said. "Linda had a thing with every dick in the county. Never met a penis she didn't like."

"Which only means that this Benny guy *could* be my half brother."

"I'm talking odds here. Powerball jackpot odds. Plus Benny is all white bread."

Flores chuckled. "So what ever happened to him? Is he still around?"

Leña shrugged. "He never comes in here, that's all I know. He was up in Albion for a while."

"No kidding? What was he in for?"

"Drugs, I'm sure. Him and some other dildo got high one night and ripped off three places in a row. Tried to, anyway."

"Ha," Flores said. "Who was the other dildo?"

"Mmm...I'm thinking his name was something odd. Something like Milo or Millich or something like that."

"And they both went down for it?"

"I think so. Honestly, honey, I quit trying a long time ago to keep track of all the people I used to know who went to jail or died. There's just too many of them."

"I hear that," Flores said, and took another sip of tea.

Leña reached for the pitcher under the bar and brought it up to refill the glass, but Flores covered the brim with her hand. "I can't, Tía. My bladder's floating already."

"So go empty it and I'll get you a burger and some fries."

"I wish I could," Flores said, and slid off the stool. "I have stuff I need to get to. Just wanted to see my Auntie Leña again. I've missed you."

"Oh, baby girl," Leña said, and leaned over the bar. "Gimme a kiss."

They embraced, kissed cheeks, and drew apart. Flores whispered, "I'm about ready to pee my pants."

"Right back there," Leña said, and pointed to the rear.

In the restroom, Flores entered a stall, wrestled her pants down over the leg brace, and sat on the toilet. When she was finished she worked the cell phone out of a pocket and called Boyd at the station house. "Can you pull the sheet on the guy who was with Benny Szabo the night he got arrested? Guy's name is Milo, Millich, something that sounds like that. Sorry, that's the best I can do."

She then said goodbye to Leña once more and returned to her vehicle, left the VFW parking lot and drove into Hermitage, where she parked in the big lot in front of the little strip mall behind Lowe's. Six minutes later she received Boyd's text: **Eugene Miklos. A.k.a. Poindexter, Dexter, Dex. Released eleven months before Szabo. Current address 1873 Fredonia Road. Want me to relay to D?**

**I got it,** she texted. **Thanks.**

**Welcome. Get together tonite?**

**Yes please.**

He ended the conversation with a smiley face wearing sunglasses.

Flores laid the phone on the passenger seat, popped open her glove box, took out her Glock, checked the clip, slammed it back in, started the engine, and peeled out.

# SIXTY-FOUR

THE DAY THE LIGHTS WENT OUT IN FREDONIA

The black metal numbers on the mailbox post, nailed in place vertically, said 1873. She turned onto the gravel driveway, drove fifteen yards and parked facing the front door of the small saltbox house. A face at the window, then only curtain. She shut off the engine and climbed out, lingering behind the open door only long enough to toss the keys onto the floor, stuff the Glock into a pocket holster, attach the holster to her side and pull the hem of her shirt down over it. She walked quickly to the door, knocked three sharp raps. Waited five seconds, knocked in triplicate again. Finally the door squeaked open twelve inches.

One look at Eugene Miklos and she knew exactly why he was called Poindexter. A small, balding, scrawny man with a round, boyish face, startled eyes behind thick black-framed glasses. A cartoon of a man.

"Hi," she said. "You must be Dex. Is Benny around?"

Poindexter blinked. "He is not. I do not know where he might be. I haven't seen him in a very long time."

"Come on," she said. "He told me he was staying here."

Another blink. "When did he tell you that?"

"When I saw him yesterday," she said, and pushed past him into the house. She barely had time to take a quick look around the living room, to glimpse the battered blue sofa and green easy chair and the coffee table with five empty beer bottles clustered in front of the chair, before something blew hard against the back of her head and knocked her forward, something like a blast of scorching wind hard and heavy carrying a fireworks finale that exploded inside her skull then almost instantly went black.

# SIXTY-FIVE

## THE WINDOW TO THE CONSCIENCE

Conrail tracks ran past the Marigold only a few steps from the front door, the Shenango River a short jog across North Water Avenue. The backstreet bar, sometimes now called Marigold I ever since a second Marigold had opened in nearby Sharpsville, had added the word *restaurant* to its Facebook page, but to DeMarco the place was the same old Marigold Bar & Grille in which, as a younger man, he had searched on maybe two or three occasions for a deadbeat dad or dope dealer. He had never been a bar drinker himself, had been an exception to the rule that misery loves company, so he was not certain that he had ever been inside this particular bar before or not; most small-town taverns, this one included, considered a place to sit and a well-stocked bar all the ambiance required. The lottery ticket machine, pool table, video slots, dart board and beer signs and TVs were mere distractions to keep the drinks flowing and the cash register ringing.

There were still a few minutes of morning left when DeMarco stepped inside and took a quick look around. One gray-haired pensioner in a booth by himself, just him and his boilermaker. Another one at a corner of the three-sided bar, sipping from a mug of draft beer. An aging Scott and Zelda seated in front of the beer

taps, both drinking what appeared to be gin and tonics, both looking excessively happy to be who and where they were. And, like
a past reflection of the old guy on the corner, a man maybe thirty
staring into his whiskey neat, oblivious to everything but the ripples
of whatever new misfortune had set him there, his ball cap brim
pulled low over his forehead.

DeMarco knew that he could probably walk into any roadhouse
in the county, maybe even in the country, and see these same types.
Happier people would fill the bar by six that evening, but happy
people don't drink in the morning, though Scott and Zelda were
loudly trying to convince themselves that life was their cherry.

The woman behind the bar wasn't exactly effervescing either.
Seventyish, with short but neatly styled white hair, a round face
and rounded shoulders, tired gray eyes that had seen too much, she
regarded DeMarco with neither a smile nor a frown. He gave her
a nod and crossed to the bar, where he stood midway between the
laughing couple and the younger man.

He said, "Any chance you have a fresh pot of coffee on? I can't
seem to keep my eyes open this morning."

She turned and went into the kitchen, came back with a thick
enameled white mug filled nearly to the brim and a quart carton of
2 percent milk. "This is the best I can do," she told him.

"Perfect," he said, and took a long sip.

She nodded toward the milk. "You don't need that?"

"And ruin a good cup of coffee?"

The smile she offered was tentative. She set the carton into the
nearest well. Then, without sliding farther down the bar, she turned
sideways to him and looked up at the small TV, its audio off. A dog
show of some kind. Dogs of every breed racing off a ramp over a
swimming pool in pursuit of a rubber rod tossed into the air.

"You must like dogs," DeMarco said.

"Not necessarily," she answered.

The pseudohappy man to DeMarco's left said, "I was a breeder for a while."

The bartender gave him a look, then turned back to the screen before saying, "Most women wouldn't put up with that kind of thing."

It took the man a moment to get the joke. Then he laughed, too loud, and explained the joke to his companion, who then chuckled and said, "Oh, that's awful."

DeMarco sipped his coffee. Lowered his eyes and looked to his right. The young man would be more or less Benny Szabo's age. Might know a little something. However, the two old guys might know Szabo's old man. It was worth a shot.

DeMarco leaned back a bit on his stool. "So I've been sitting over there in the empty lot across from Warehouse Sales for most of two hours. Waiting for a guy named Sabo or Szabo, I'm not sure how it's pronounced. Anybody seen him around recently? Older guy? Late sixties I'd guess, maybe more?"

Every customer but the young man shook his or her head. The bartender asked, "What did you want with him?"

"I ran into him up at Lowe's. He heard me asking what they charge for house painting, came up and offered to give me an estimate. I was going to drive him to my place for a quick look."

She nodded, then turned to the dogs again.

DeMarco asked, "Do you know him?"

"I've heard the name," she said.

"But you don't know him?"

"Not to see him," she said. "There's a handful of Szabos in the area."

"Well, this one said he's painted a lot of houses in his time. Said he has his own ladders. Which would save me from having to rent them."

Now she shook her head. Turned and looked him in the eye. "Like I said, I've heard the name. Wouldn't know him if I passed him on the street, though."

DeMarco didn't believe her. She knew a Szabo or two, though maybe not the old man. But she wasn't going to tell him that in front of anybody. He said, "Any chance I could leave my number with you in case he shows up here later?"

She turned to the cash register, picked up a small white pad and short pencil, and laid them before him. He wrote down his number and pushed the pad back to her. "Just tell him the guy who needs his house painted. From Lowe's."

She laid the pad beside the cash register again, then returned her attention to the TV.

DeMarco took another sip of coffee, stood, laid a five on the bar. "Good coffee," he told her. "Thanks."

She gave him another look and a curt nod before turning away again.

*Those tired gray eyes*, he told himself as he headed for the door. *Those eyes know something.*

# SIXTY-SIX

## QUID PRO CROW

DeMarco was standing in the trees on a hill overlooking the Oak Tree Lake dam when he got the call. He had had no luck in any of the bars he'd visited, looked too out of place to be trusted by the local barflies and those whose businesses depended on them. Most of the morning drinkers were low-income graybeards, guys needing some hair of the dog, guys with a broken heart, or else petty punks with a chip on the shoulder. He suspected that he had been made fairly early in his rounds because every bar he entered immediately went hushed and few eyes would meet his gaze. Maybe the Marigold's bartender had set the grapevine to singing. So now he was standing in the trees and waiting for an idea. The air was gray and cool and the water in the lake was the color of a chocolate milkshake, swollen with runoff and littered with natural and unnatural debris. He was alone with the parking lot and restroom and trees except for a crow perched on a high branch not far to his left. Its caws were sharp, one coming every fifteen seconds or so and sharpened by the intervening silences.

"Screw you," he told it, because he knew that the crow was shrieking at him, trying to scare him out of its territory, away from its lunch, which DeMarco could not see but could certainly smell, a familiar odor of rotting flesh. Probably a dead fish or two down there on the rocks, suffocated by the thick water. A boom made of bright orange foam barrels roped together lay stretched across the water twenty or so yards ahead of the dam, and trapped behind the boom were branches and plastic bottles and a half-deflated beach ball and what looked like a lampshade, all of them bouncing up and down because of the water rushing under the boom and over the dam.

DeMarco had never been a devotee of spring. Too wet, too sloppy, too fickle. As far as he was concerned, E. E. Cummings could keep all of spring's mud-lusciousness to himself. Early fall was the best season. Colorful and comfortable, fewer gnats and mosquitoes, clear blue skies and sunsets to knock your socks off. In the fall the riot of colors from the trees would be reflected in a body of water, and if the water was quiet the double image would take your breath away. He wished he could find a place where it was always late October. But then he remembered that he had been shot in late October. And that his friend Thomas Huston had been killed in late October. And that he and Jayme had lost their unborn baby girl in late October. Maybe April wasn't so bad after all.

Life was but a temporary bivouac anyway, this he knew. Yet how strange and dark and ugly it could be. *The avidity with which we thieve and kill and ruin one another!* The flesh is undeserving of the souls with which it has been entrusted. *We might be the highest of beasts*, he told himself, *but beasts we truly are in these bodies*. It was a wonder to him that the soul is not made rancid by the poison of the blood, the bile of human beings' rancorous nature. *The ego rots everything it touches*, he thought. Everything it breathes its toxic breath upon. He recognized that this life might be nothing more than a coed Kabuki, nothing more real than a video game, yet it was now and then disgusting to him all the same, its more sinister characters worthy of a hundred floods and a thousand Armageddons.

He shook his head. Worked up a gob of saliva and spit it into the matted leaves. Then gazed up through the branches and said, "You should have saved the dinosaurs instead."

*Caw!* the crow told him.

"Okay, okay," he answered, and turned away from the water, headed back toward his car. "Go eat your stinking fish."

And then the phone vibrated in his pocket. He pulled it out. Didn't recognize the number, though it was a local one. "Hello?" he said.

"Is this Sergeant Ryan DeMarco?" a woman's voice asked.

"It is. And to whom am I speaking?"

"I'm a nurse at UPMC Horizon Urgent Care in Greenville. We have a patient here who asked me to call and make you aware of her situation. A Ms. Daniella Flores?"

"Oh god," he said. "What happened?"

"She was brought in with a head trauma about an hour ago. She's doing okay but she does have a concussion, so we're sending her over to our imaging facility for a CT scan."

"How did it happen?"

"I don't really know about that, sir, but there is—"

"Thank you," he said, and ended the call, and jogged heavily toward his car. The crow dropped down with a final shriek and descended to the shore.

# SIXTY-SEVEN

## THE MEEK SHALL INHERIT THE BOLD WHO GET INJURED

Every second seemed a minute long. *Too many hospitals,* DeMarco complained to himself as he waited for the elevator. *Ever since Kentucky.* He'd returned from his and Jayme's first road trip in the RV because his estranged wife, Laraine, was in the hospital following a suicide attempt. Then Jayme landed in one. Then Amber Sullivan, the poetry girl. Then himself and Flores and now Flores again.

He gave up waiting for the elevator and looked around, spotted the stairwell sign, strode to it and took the stairs two at a time. Didn't know if he was winded because of the stress or the bad lung and didn't much care which, just didn't want to be in a hospital again. Didn't like the way they smelled, didn't like the fluorescent lighting, didn't like the concrete walls or the tiled floors and what the hell had Flores done to get herself hurt again? He pushed through the double metal doors at the top of the second-floor landing and thought, *if this is what it's like being a father, I don't like it much.*

When Jayme received DeMarco's call alerting her to Flores's hospitalization, she had been canvassing the shops around Mercer's courthouse square, pretending to be a long-lost cousin of Linda Szabo researching the family tree. She had jumped into her car and sped onto Route 58 north, a quiet two-lane country road, and arrived at the imaging facility a full ten minutes before DeMarco, who seemed to hit every red light between Farrell and Greenville. He spotted Jayme standing on the threshold of the waiting room, looking his way.

Immediately she hurried up to him and laid a hand on his chest. "Don't be angry," she told him. "She's terrified that you're going to rip her head off. And it already has sixteen staples in it."

"What the hell happened?"

"She got a tip that Szabo was staying in a little place out on Fredonia Road."

"And she went there on her own?" His voice was louder than he wanted it to be, but that too seemed out of his control for now.

"Baby, calm down. She's going to be okay."

"Jesus fu—" he started, then turned and, muttering and walking away from her, spoke to the empty hallway. "Jesus on a crutch!"

She followed. Laid a hand on his arm. "I know," she said. "I know."

He turned. "Tell me exactly what happened."

"So she found the place and went up and knocked on the door. And the guy you arrested with Szabo back in the day? He's the one who came to the door."

He thought back. Hard to see into the past through a fog of anger and worry. But okay, yep, there it was. "Miklos?" he said. He had forgotten all about him. Meek and invisible. Not cut from the same cloth as Szabo. "Eugene Miklos?"

Jayme nodded. "And Dani stepped inside, and bam. Somebody whacked her from behind."

"Miklos did that?" he asked.

"No, somebody else. She never caught a glimpse of him. But yeah, it was Szabo."

"And you know that how?"

"It was Miklos who called the ambulance for her. He didn't run. Szabo did. In Dani's car apparently."

"Great," DeMarco said.

"The Greenville police turned the house upside down looking for some clue as to where he might be. They took some hairs and fibers but there was no scrapbook of his favorite places, unfortunately. They have an ATL out on him."

"And Miklos?"

"They're just holding him for now. I told them you'll be there ASAP."

"Okay," he said, nodding. "That's good. Good."

"Maybe you should go there straightaway."

"And not see Dani? What do you think I'm going to say to her?"

"She's really torn up, baby. She thinks she failed you again. She thinks you're going to think she's nothing but a screwup."

He frowned, shook his head. "Where is she?"

"How about if I go back first and let her know you're not angry?"

"How about you tell me where she is."

She held her gaze steady on his eyes, her hand on his chest now, atop his racing heart.

He said, "Give me a little credit, okay?"

She nodded. Smiled. "She's in recovery room 3. They're basically just keeping her until her BP and heart rate come down a little more. Plus she's thrown up a couple of times from the concussion. I told her I'll drive her home when she's ready."

"The scan came out okay?"

"Thank God. No intracranial bleeding."

He nodded. Said, "I won't be long," and headed down the hallway to the recovery rooms.

Flores, fully dressed and seated in a chair against the wall, her feet pressed together, jerked when he eased open the door and peeked inside. "Hey," he said.

Tears welled up in her eyes. "I'm sorry."

He went to her and stood beside the chair and pulled her head to his chest. He stroked her hair and kissed the top of her head, careful to avoid the gauze and the injury underneath, and told her, "I'm going to catch him and bring him to you, Dani. I'll give you fifteen minutes alone with him to do whatever you want. Nobody hurts one of my people and gets away with it."

She pulled away a little and looked up at him and said, "I'm going to need at least an hour with him."

"Done," he said, and pulled her close again.

# SIXTY-EIGHT

## THE POETRY OF THE PROSAIC

Sergeant Moore of the Greenville police had placed Eugene "Poindexter" Miklos in a small interview room, gave him a mug of hot tea and a PayDay candy bar and left him alone with his thoughts and an empty chair. He was in the process of folding the candy bar wrapper into a tight little square with its corners tucked into each other when the door swung open and DeMarco came in smiling.

"Well, well, well," DeMarco said, and eased himself down onto the chair facing Miklos. "Aren't you a blast from the past?"

"Yes, sir," Miklos answered, and tucked the square of crinkly paper into his shirt pocket. He had dressed for the occasion in a red-and-black-checkered short-sleeve shirt, a pair of neatly pressed tan chinos and a pair of clean white sneakers from Walmart.

"Do you remember me?" DeMarco asked.

"Yes, sir," Miklos said. The empty tea mug—cream-colored ceramic, not paper, with the Greenville Police emblem printed on one side—sat on the floor, wedged into the corner behind Miklos's chair. *The boy is neat*, DeMarco remembered. *Excessively so. Asperger's.*

"It's nice to see you again, Eugene. You're looking well."

"Thank you."

"And how has life been treating you?"

"Good. Quiet. Until recently."

DeMarco nodded. "We'll get to that in a minute. So what have you been doing with yourself these past months since you've been out?"

"I build computers," Miklos said.

"You mean, like, from kits?"

"No, sir. From scratch. I purchase all of the necessary components online and build them to the customer's specifications. I specialize in see-through."

"See-through computers?"

"Yes, sir. The walls of the tower are made of shatterproof glass. Tinted, if requested. I prefer them clear myself."

"And that keeps you busy?"

"Yes, sir. I currently have a five-month waiting list."

"Good for you," DeMarco said. "And how about Benny? Does he build computers too?"

"Ha!" Miklos said, an awkward, involuntary laugh.

"No?" said DeMarco. "Then why was he at your house today?"

"He was…uninvited," Miklos said. "A temporary guest."

"For how long?"

"He arrived on the evening of April 12. 7:12 p.m."

And DeMarco thought, *The day after Emma's murder.* "7:12 p.m. That's fairly specific."

"I had a dozen Pillsbury peanut butter cookies in the oven. I was watching the clock. Even if you line the cookie sheet with parchment paper, as is suggested in the instructions, and I use a double layer, the cookies can burn. Because my oven is electric. Dry heat. I would prefer a gas range but the house is all electric."

"Gotcha," DeMarco said. "So you didn't invite him, yet there he was."

"Yes, sir."

"Did you want him staying in your house?"

"I would have preferred not. I prefer to be alone."

"Just as you didn't want to participate in those robberies several years back?"

"Yes, sir."

"And that's why you stayed in the house today when he took off with Ms. Flores's car?"

"Yes, sir. I ran outside first and hid behind the house."

"You mean after you saw him strike Ms. Flores and knock her unconscious?"

"Yes, sir. I went back inside when he drove off."

"And called the ambulance for Ms. Flores."

"Yes, sir. Her head was bleeding. I applied a folded towel to the wound to diminish the blood loss."

"Right," said DeMarco, nodding. "I got all that from Sergeant Moore. But here's what I'm wondering, Eugene. I'm wondering about your conversations with Benny. Did you know about his trip to Michigan before he came to stay with you?"

"To Michigan? Why would he go to Michigan?"

"That's what I'm asking you."

"I do not know very much about Michigan. I know where it is. I know that Lansing is the state capital. I know the volume of Lake Michigan in cubic kilometers. Four thousand, nine hundred, and... twenty! And I know that only Lake Superior's volume is greater. Although Lake Huron has a larger surface area than Lake Michigan."

"Okay," DeMarco said. There was a kind of sad poetry to the way Miklos thought. Just as there was to Flores's limp. And the knife scar along Jayme's breast. He wished he had Huston's gift for words so that he could express that sadness better, if only to himself.

He said, "What do you know about where Benny has been

living since he was released, Eugene? And who he's been associating with since then."

"Nothing, sir. I do not know anything about any of that."

"You and Benny didn't converse during the past few days?"

"He watches TV in the living room. I build computers in my workroom."

"That's it?"

"I make the meals. He eats them. I clean up. He doesn't."

"Interesting. So tell me this, Eugene. Did you get the feeling, while he was staying with you, that he might have been hiding from something or somebody?"

"I did not think about it, sir."

"You mean you tried not to think about it."

"Yes, sir."

"Is that even possible? To not think about something that is staring you right in the face?"

"I learned to do it in prison. The trick is to build picture stories in the head. I build picture stories of a superhero I call Equilibrium. He can balance on a one-centimeter pebble, if need be. His supernatural equilibrium is his only superpower, yet it allows him to do wondrous things."

"Right," DeMarco said. "Okay."

"Would you like to hear of some of his adventures? The one I like best takes place on a distant planet I call Little Tenninger. There is also a Greater Tenninger but the gravity there is too oppressive for humans."

"Maybe some other time, Eugene."

"Yes, sir."

"I can see how a facility for building picture stories could come in handy in prison."

"I would have died otherwise."

"Figuratively, of course."

"Yes, sir. And also literally. My death was imminent on numerous occasions."

"In what way?"

"Every way possible."

"I understand." He had forgotten how pathetic Miklos had been at his earlier trial. His lawyer had pleaded for no jail time, had painted Eugene as a young man incapable of protecting himself. "If you send him to prison," the lawyer had told the jury, "you are sending him to his death. He won't survive." The jury hadn't bought it. And, despite how hellish those years must have been for Miklos, there he was, visibly well. *But at what cost?* DeMarco wondered.

Miklos said, "May I ask you a question, sir?"

"She's okay," DeMarco answered. "She needed staples and she has a concussion, but she'll be okay. You did a very good thing, Eugene, when you chose to stay there with her and call the ambulance."

"I was afraid."

"I understand."

"Not for her. For me."

"It's all right. I've never served time and I never want to. Sometimes fear can be a great motivator. You took care of her nonetheless, whatever your reasons."

"I try to feel empathy sometimes but usually I can't. Only for myself."

"We are what we are, right? We try to improve what we can, we accept what can't be improved."

"Yes, sir."

"I have just one more question for you, Eugene. And then I will ask one of the officers to drive you home. Okay? You ready for one more?"

"Yes, sir."

"Do you have any idea where Benny might be now?"

"I haven't thought about it. I will if you want me to."

"I would appreciate it very much. But in the meantime, you have no idea at all about where he might have gone?"

"I do not. I don't know where other people go to hide. I go inside myself."

DeMarco nodded. Smiled. "Probably the safest place there is," he said. He took a business card from his credit card case and handed it to Miklos. "You call me if you think of anything."

"Yes, sir," Miklos said, but he kept staring at the card. Then he looked at DeMarco again, and extended the card to him. "It says Private Investigations, not Pennsylvania State Police."

"I retired from the state police. I'm self-employed now, like you."

"There is no health insurance," Miklos said.

"Well, yeah, there is. But I hear what you're saying."

"I worry that I might get sick."

"We all do. It's a very common fear among the living."

Miklos cocked his head, then smiled. He had caught the joke. "The dead don't have to worry about getting sick."

"That's right. All they have to worry about is getting sent back to this...this you-know-what."

"This *trou à merde*," Miklos said, and blushed. "I learned that in prison."

DeMarco nodded. "A useful phrase."

"My cellmate sang it to the tune of 'Frère Jacques.' First thing every morning."

"Well," DeMarco said, and stood, "at least you had that, Eugene."

"Yes, sir. But it wasn't enough. Songs are never enough."

*So true*, DeMarco thought, and nodded again, then turned to the door. There he remembered something else, and looked back.

"When you get back home, Eugene," he said, "you're going to find your place in a bit of a mess. The police had to search it. Things won't be the way you left them. Are you going to be able to handle that?"

"How bad is it?" Miklos asked.

"For you, it's going to look bad. But just remember that you can put everything back in place again. And when you finish, nobody will even know how messy it was."

"I will, though."

"Yes, I know you will. Just try not to think about it."

"I will build a picture story."

"Excellent idea, Eugene. You might want to start building one now."

# SIXTY-NINE

## SOMETIMES AN INSPIRATION

O n the drive home the tension of failure tightened like a steel
band around DeMarco's skull. It was late afternoon now, or
maybe early evening, he wasn't sure of the demarcation, only that
the sun was low and the shadows long. He had failed Emma, had
failed Flores, had maybe lost Szabo for good now, and with him
any chance of nailing whomever had paid Szabo to silence Emma
and her grandmother. He knew that he shouldn't hold himself
responsible for Miklos's misery either, but he did.

*You're reverting to old habits*, he told himself. *Start practicing what
you preach or you will drive yourself off the deep end again.*

So he tried. Instead of focusing on Flores and Emma he paid
attention to his surroundings, let his gaze move about as freely as
possible along the winding country roads. He looked at the houses,
the farms, the woods and passing fields, and he isolated certain details
that he found attractive or interesting, the yellow glow on window
glass, a gray cat poised to pounce on a field mouse. He glanced up
at the sky, the thick white clouds layered like trifle. There was a
softness to all that he saw, a trick of the golden light and the stillness and the openness of the land and sky. Soon he found himself
slowing and enjoying the slowness, taking note of all the sights

that pleased him. He lowered the window so that he could smell the clean country air, the scents of leaves and fertile soil and grass. Then he thought about Jayme and how she, if beside him in the car, would be watching out her side window and softly smiling at the beauty of this ordinary moment. He remembered too that she had asked him a while back, during one of those ordinary moments, to write another poem for her. He had written only one so far, almost a year ago. He was not a good poet by even his unschooled standards, too literal for the literati, too self-conscious, and he had an outdated tendency to rhyme that would make real poets sneer. But maybe he could put something simple together for Jayme now, something spontaneous and raw that would make her happy when she heard it, and she would know that he had been thinking of her at this very moment, and that he always thought of her whenever they were apart.

When he came to a pull off along the side of the road, adjacent to a cornfield covered with stubble, he parked and got out and walked out into the stubble while holding his cell phone to his mouth, the voice recorder on as he talked softly into the phone, glad nobody was listening.

"For a poem about ordinary things," he said, a note to himself, "things I like. In fact that should be the title of the poem. 'I Like.' And then it will go something like, I don't know, 'little white churches with music playing inside.' Then maybe, what? 'Puffy white clouds in a blue summer sky.'" He walked slowly and let the images come to him freely, some he could see and some that arose in his memory...

"Cows in the pasture and horses on the run...a big dog sleeping in a small patch of sun." Soon the poem itself seemed to take over, pulling distant images and sensations from his subconsciousness: "a violin crying and a saxophone wailing...a pretty girl laughing and a big ship sailing…a long gravel driveway with grass growing between the rocks…a wooden swing on the porch and a lakeshore without docks."

He paused. Lifted his eyes to the far blue horizon. "The wind in my face and rain on the roof…kindness and tenderness, affection and truth…an early morning mist and an early morning dew and the early morning sunshine when I'm waking up with you. You in my arms and me slipping inside…and your happy sleepy murmurs on our slow sleepy ride."

His thoughts stopped coming then and he stopped talking and stood there in the middle of the field with the phone to his lips. The poem was over. The mood and the inspiration had slipped away, no more phrases sliding through his mind like something playful and warm, something like happiness as a syrup spreading through him. And then it was all gone and there was only him and the field and the stubble and the sun, and his car a good fifty yards away. How had he walked that far without even noticing it?

He looked around. Good, nobody watching. Nobody wondering what he was doing out there. He shut off the voice recorder and pocketed his phone and walked back to the car with long, purposeful strides. But he kept a small secret smile to himself. That a poem, even a mediocre one, had come so effortlessly from inside that thick skull of his…it was a wonderment. Or had it come from outside of his brain, outside of his being? It seemed to have written itself. Had used him as its instrument. *We wrote a poem*, he told himself, still marveling. *Right out of the blue. How weird is that?*

# SEVENTY

## LAYING ANOTHER LOG ON THE FIRE OF FAILURE

There is a significant difference between feeling like a failure and admitting failure. The first can be a driving force; the second is the relinquishment of all effort, and therefore all hope. DeMarco understood this in his bones but had never articulated it to himself or anybody else. It had taken Thomas Huston to put it into words for him.

They had been sitting on lawn chairs in Huston's backyard, the summer before Huston's death, and only a few weeks after first meeting each other. The congested baby, David Ryan Huston—not named after DeMarco but a coincidence DeMarco had enjoyed—finally asleep on his father's chest, his cherubic face turned toward DeMarco. The men had been talking sotto voce so as not to awaken the cherub from its stertorous breathing, discussing Tom's writing and how difficult it was to carry a novel around in one's head for a year or more.

"I never think I'm going to pull it off," Huston had said. "Every morning when I sit down to write, I think, you can't do this, it isn't working. It's not until the final third or so, after a couple hundred pages or more, that I realize I am going to do it. I know where I'm going now. Is that how it is with you too, Sergeant? When you're working on a case, I mean?"

"We don't get many big cases around here," DeMarco had replied. "Certainly not ones that take a year or more to solve."

"But in a condensed version? Days instead of months?"

"Sure," DeMarco said. "I'm always afraid that I'm going to drop the ball."

Huston smiled. Kissed his baby's head. "I think it's a good thing, don't you? The fear of failure? It's what keeps you going, doesn't it? It feeds the fire."

"That's probably so."

"Because you *know*, don't you? That you're never going to give up until you succeed. You are never going to admit defeat."

Their friendship had been too brief. Yet even in its brevity it had left an indelible impression on DeMarco. Things Huston had said were always coming back to him, and he sometimes dreamed of him, sometimes felt his presence near. And now, the morning after Flores's encounter with Benny Szabo, he thought he could feel Tom watching him from a corner of the living room, smiling that small knowing smile he seemed to wear so easily and naturally.

Or maybe DeMarco felt that way only because it was Sunday again, and soon he and Jayme would make their weekly trip to the cemetery. Sundays always felt different to DeMarco. He had buried a lot of people. Or had caused them to be buried. Sundays used to fill him with a heaviness, a dark foreboding. But since the NDE he had not felt that way, but lighter, still a bit melancholy but absent the sense of dread.

Then, too, this morning had brought a surprise from FedEx, and one that further lightened his mood even as it deepened the bittersweet undertone, adding both a dash of the sweet and a pinch of the sad. An advanced reading copy of the collection of Tom's thoughts and observations that DeMarco and Jayme had helped to curate. He was pleased with the cover, a deep royal blue, no images, only the words in white cursive, all small caps except in Tom's name, a nontitular title, *from the notebooks of Thomas Huston*. The words looked like clouds across an evening sky, like very carefully crafted sky writing.

*Tom would like this*, DeMarco thought. He sat holding the book and looking at it and at Tom's photo on the back cover for a long time. But he would not open the book until Jayme came downstairs. And maybe that night they would read the book together, the same way they had read the loose pages months earlier. Reading each other into sleep.

He wondered if the poem he had written yesterday had been from Tom. That would explain the ease with which it had come to him. As if Tom had looked into DeMarco's heart and saw all the things he enjoyed. All the simple things he loved.

The previous night, in bed, DeMarco had played his phone recording for Jayme. Tears had come to her eyes. She said, "I love it, baby. I really do. But it took you long enough to get to me, didn't it? Not until the last two lines."

"Everything else is prelude to you," he told her. "The one thing I love most."

"Nice save." She kissed his cheek. His nose. His lips. "Will you type it up and print it out for me? Or better yet write it out by hand?"

"Of course. Whenever I have time I'll sit and polish it up some first."

"Don't you dare change a word of it," she'd said.

And now, another day. Another in the long procession of days. *And how are you going to make use of this day?* he asked himself. He could dig around for the name of the bartender at the Marigold, maybe catch her off guard with a visit at home. But she hadn't seemed the type to be caught off guard. She was the type to clam up when pressed. Maybe she had recognized him. Maybe sniffed the cop on him. In any case she wasn't about to ruin her business by getting known as a blabbermouth. His best bet was to leave her on the back burner for a while.

He laid the book on the coffee table. "Fact one," he said out loud, because speaking his thoughts was nearly as helpful as writing them down, an aid to his memory, "we know that Benny Szabo was in Michigan the day and evening prior to Emma's death. Fact two, we know that he attacked Dani and made off with her car. We know that the car hasn't been located and Szabo hasn't been caught, but there's a warrant out for him, and Troop D and all neighboring counties have been alerted. We know he won't go back to Eugene's place. We know that his mother's dead and there's no sign of his father, no info on him since long before Benny's mother died. Carmichael and the guys are working on that, better than Jayme and I can. So fact three…what the heck is fact three?"

"Fact three," Jayme said as she came down the stairs with Hero trotting behind her, "even though you left a lot of facts unnumbered, is Morrison and his pals."

DeMarco picked up the book and held it up for her to see as she approached.

She took it from him and read the cover. "Already?" she asked.

"It's called an ARC. An advance reader's copy. They send them out to reviewers a few months before publication." He pointed to the brown padded envelope that still lay on the foyer floor. "It came with a letter from the editor."

She opened the book's cover. Turned two pages. Read for a moment. "He mentioned us in the foreword!"

"That was nice of him," DeMarco said.

She flipped another page. "'Introduction by Sergeant Ryan DeMarco'!"

"Really?" he said. "He actually used it? I hope he fixed my grammar."

"You didn't read it yet?"

"I thought we might read it together tonight. We have other fish to fry today."

She closed the book. "And how I do want to see them fried," she said. "Incinerated, in fact."

"Any ideas?"

She laid the book on the coffee table again. "We need to see if we can tie Szabo to Morrison somehow."

"Yep," he said. "And I repeat: any ideas?"

"Did Morrison officiate at his trial?"

"Nope. Anyway not the one in which I was involved. But Benny was arrested more than once."

She crossed her arms. Stared out the window at his back. "What about the rental car? The Nissan Rogue? Did the boys have any luck identifying who paid for it?"

"The credit card was stolen."

"When did you find *that* out?"

"This morning. While you were in the shower."

"Why wasn't it reported stolen?"

"The owner is ninety-two years old. Lives in New Philadelphia, Ohio. According to Carmichael, the old guy said he hadn't used the card in a couple of years. Didn't even know it was missing until the police questioned him."

"Does *he* have some relationship to Benny Szabo? Or to Morrison?"

"Not that he can recall."

"Who talked to him?" she asked.

"Bowen contacted the New Philly police. The old guy goes to the park every day it doesn't rain. Noonish. It didn't rain the day before or the day of Emma's death."

"So Benny Szabo did what? Just drove around until he found an easy mark?"

"That's a bit of a stretch, isn't it?"

"In other words, *somebody* knew the old guy's routine. And passed that information on to Benny Szabo."

"According to the officer who talked to the old guy, he's very friendly. Always picks up a half dozen doughnuts on his way to the park and shares them with anybody who comes along."

"Does he recall talking to anybody who fits Szabo's description?"

"He does not. But admits that he might have and just can't remember."

"It had to have been either Szabo or Morrison or one of his pals. We need to find out who those guys are."

"Let us not forget," DeMarco said, "that no record exists of Benny Szabo's physical whereabouts from the day of his release from prison until he showed up on the surveillance camera in Big Rapids. He provided an address but it's a small apartment with hardly any furniture in it. He might have been living there for a while or he might not have."

"What about checking in with his parole agent?"

"He never missed an appointment. But most of them were by phone. He wasn't supposed to be traveling out of state without permission, but he wasn't considered violent, not a danger to himself or others, so he just wasn't monitored all that closely."

"Son of a *bitch*!" she said.

DeMarco chuckled a little. Stood and stretched his back. The arrival of Huston's posthumous book had put him in a sanguine mood. He and Jayme were not yet at the point in their case where they could see an ending, they still had many pages to turn, but they were moving forward, if only a page at a time.

"My suggestion," he told her, "is that we find a pressure point and see if we can make it squeal."

"The only pressure point we have access to is on Morrison."

"Then what do you say we pay another friendly visit to His Honor?"

"Oh, goody!" she said, and clapped her hands together so loudly that Hero started barking.

# SEVENTY-ONE

## With the dead in their merriment

First they went to the cemetery. For DeMarco the routine was no longer what it appeared to be on the surface, not what it had originally been for him and later for Jayme. Not a shared communion of grief. For him, at least, it had become something far less heavy. A recharge of his energies. A remembrance and silent expression of gratitude for the time he and his son had shared. And would always share. The alchemical love that would always remain alive inside his heart.

The day was overcast, the sky low but with a muted silvery glow above the trees. The air smelled of mowed grass. He noticed on their walk from the car that there were many more people out this morning, fixing up their loved ones' graves, clearing away the litter of winter, planting daffodil and crocus bulbs, bunches of pansies and mums and geraniums. Bits of conversation floated across the grounds from other grave sites but he did his best to ignore them. And also ignored the sense of amusement that made his mouth want to turn up at the corner. *This maudlin little play*, he thought. *If only everybody knew.* A part of him still longed to be with the dead, as lively and full and unfettered as he now knew the dead to be. *It's the living who should be mourned*, he thought.

As usual, he and Jayme picked at a few weeds, brushed away brown leaves and bits of dirt clinging to the granite. They talked very little and kept their thoughts to themselves. He knew that she was still grieving and would probably not understand or appreciate that all but a small shadow of his grief was gone now. It had been replaced with gratitude. He hoped that Jayme would eventually come to that change as well, but he had had several months with his son whereas she had only the sensation of their daughter, the knowledge of her presence.

He hoped that maybe Emma would join them too, but he did not feel her presence that day. No caress of his cheek. *That's okay,* he told her. *You have better things to do.*

Only on their way back to the car a half hour later did he realize that he had not once fingered the silver locket he always carried in his pocket, the shiny container with a snip of his son's fine hair inside. Had not cupped it tight while chanting his tiresome mantra of *I'm sorry, I'm sorry.* Now he slipped a hand into his pocket, found the trinket and held it for a moment between finger and thumb, its surface cool against his skin. And told his son, with a smile, *Love you, my boy.*

In the car, Jayme did not speak during the fifteen-minute ride to Morrison's house. DeMarco made no attempt to engage her in conversation. He guessed that the grief she had carried to and from the graves would, in Morrison's presence, blossom into anger. He could only hope that it would not get the better of her. For her sake as well as Morrison's.

# SEVENTY-TWO

THE FOLLOWING STATEMENT IS TRUE
THE PREVIOUS STATEMENT IS FALSE

J ayme could smell barbecue the moment they entered the little
community where Morrison lived. At nearly every house they
passed, a resident or two was visible outside. Yards were being
mowed, beds of charcoal briquettes burning, mulch beds being
raked, miniature dachshunds and borzois and cockapoos and a
teacup pomsky being walked. "The rich are out in numbers," she
said, and immediately regretted the sneer in her voice. She could
have been one of those residents, had been raised in affluence. But
since then she had learned something about money. In both dearth
and abundance, it could bring out the worst in people. Because
the worst is always there, always waiting for an excuse to send out
its tendrils.

Outside Morrison's house she smelled meat sizzling on a
grill. Music drifted from somewhere behind the house. She and
DeMarco stood at the corner of the house and listened. "'Don't
Stop Believin'?" she said. "I don't see Morrison as a Journey kind
of guy."

DeMarco shook his head. "There's a woman singing along.
Badly. He has company."

"Great!" Jayme said, and started briskly toward the sound. "I love a good party."

The woman was turned sideways to them when they came around the corner of the house. Of average height, blond and pretty, dressed in a blue denim jacket over a V-neck white T-shirt, black yoga pants and leather flip-flops. A necklace with a large turquoise pendant around her neck, a tennis bracelet weighty with colorful balls and bangles around one wrist. *Late thirties*, Jayme guessed. Everything but the flip-flops and jewelry seemed to have been applied with a spray gun. With a Corona in her left hand, she sang along with the music while using a long fork to turn brats and burgers and rings of kielbasa atop the grill. Three patio tables atop the brick patio were already laid with red disposable plates and clear plastic tableware and colorful plastic glasses.

Jayme stood there smiling, DeMarco half a step behind off her right shoulder, until the song ended. Then she said, "Hey there."

"Hi!" the woman sang before she was even turned their way. Then her brilliant smile dimmed. "Oh. Hi. I don't think I've met you folks yet."

Jayme moved forward, and DeMarco with her. "We're not here for the party," Jayme said. "Is the judge around?"

"Oh!" the woman said, and flashed her expensive smile again. "I thought you were with the Spring Crawl."

"Spring is crawling?" Jayme asked happily, and DeMarco suppressed a wince.

"It's an annual thing around here. The whole community just goes from house to house, eating and drinking and, you know, welcoming spring. It can get pretty crazy by the time the fireworks go off."

"I bet it can," Jayme said.

"You guys want a beer or something? Just help yourself to the cooler there. I'll go see what Big Daddy is up to."

She hung the fork from the side of the grill and sashayed into the house.

Jayme turned to DeMarco. "Big Daddy?" she said. "She's his daughter?"

"I suspect not," he said.

"Care to join me in a beer?"

He gave her a look.

She nudged him with an elbow. "Whatever you say, Big Daddy."

Morrison came out carrying a large bowl of guacamole covered with plastic wrap, followed closely by the woman and her jangling jewelry. She danced to the new song, "Any Way You Want It," as she crossed back to the grill and took up the fork again.

"Greetings," Morrison said with a crooked smile. "I didn't expect to see you folks today." He set the guac on a table and approached DeMarco and Jayme. "Today is our annual Spring—"

"Crawl," Jayme interrupted. "For all of the Crawlers. We heard."

He was taken aback; looked to DeMarco.

"Maybe we should walk around front for a minute," DeMarco said.

"Of course," Morrison said. Then, to the woman, "Back in a minute, honey."

"Okay, pooches!"

They allowed Morrison to take the lead and followed at his pace, which was slow but not faltering. He was dressed in blue Nike sneakers, pressed tan chinos and a Hawaiian shirt. Near the front porch he turned and asked, "This okay?"

"It's fine," DeMarco said.

Jayme smiled and asked, "How's the myocardial infarction thing these days? You're looking a lot more chipper than the last time we met."

"I'm on a new medication," he answered, though his smile seemed, to Jayme, tentative.

"How nice for you," she told him. "Emma is dead."

He blinked. Leaned forward a little. "Say again, please."

"Emma Barrie?" Jayme said. "Your almost daughter? She and her grandmother died of carbon monoxide poisoning seven days ago. You didn't hear?"

He stared at her, motionless for a few seconds. Then one leg buckled. DeMarco reached out quickly to grab him by the arm and steady him.

"Over here," DeMarco said. "Come sit on the steps, Judge. Let you catch your breath."

He sat bent over, breathing hard. Jayme stood on one side, DeMarco the other. Neither spoke. A full minute passed before Morrison lifted his head, looked at DeMarco and said, "How could this happen?"

DeMarco said, "Intentionally, we think."

"By whom?"

Jayme said, "We need the names of your friends, Judge. The ones who submitted the DNA swabs."

"Why?" he asked. "You don't think one of them could—"

Again she interrupted. "Of course we think one of them could. Could and did. Who else would have done it?"

He looked to DeMarco, was shaking his head back and forth. "It simply isn't conceivable."

DeMarco told him, "We think we know who made it happen. And I've got to tell you, Judge, he isn't the kind of person to protect his employer. So if you know anything…hell, you know the drill. Better we hear it from you now than in front of a jury."

"I don't," Morrison stammered, still shaking his head. "I swear to God I don't. And I trust my friends. I swore an oath not to reveal their identities to anybody until the results were in. And even then…"

"The results are already in," Jayme told him. "And one of your friends provided a fake sample. One of your friends lied to you. Or else you are lying to us. Which is it?"

His head kept moving back and forth, eyes on the concrete pad at his feet now, hands squeezing his knees. His voice was halting and weak, with no trace of the authoritative courtroom persona. "I just can't process this. I can't…get my head around any of it."

Jayme said, "Which part don't you understand? That a little girl and her grandmother are dead, or that one of your trusty pals is probably involved?"

Morrison looked up at DeMarco with pleading eyes. Jayme stepped in front of DeMarco. She said, "What are we looking at here, Your Honor? Aiding and abetting, conspiracy to commit murder? Obstructing justice? Concealing evidence? You're the expert. How's that going to look on your legacy?"

The judge's eyes were clouding over, his shoulders slumping. DeMarco laid a gentle hand on Jayme's arm; when she turned to look at him, eyes full of fire, he whispered, "You're going to give him a stroke."

She glanced at Morrison, then blew out a little breath.

Some of the rigidity went out of her then, and DeMarco stepped to the side a little to address the judge. "Okay," he said. "We'll talk again soon. The state boys are likely to call in the FBI on this, so be prepared for an interview. Until then, sir, you need to keep this conversation to yourself."

Morrison said nothing for a moment, then looked up at Jayme. She saw desperation in his eyes. "The little girl?" he asked. "What kind of man…?"

Jayme left the question unanswered. "Enjoy your Crawl," she told him, then turned and crossed to DeMarco's car.

# SEVENTY-THREE

## AND THE OSCAR GOES TO...

I still smell barbecue," DeMarco said as he drove.

Jayme pointed through the windshield at a bright orange food truck parked in the library's lot. "Where did that come from?"

"It's a Christmas miracle!" he said, and put on the turn signal.

"An illegal one maybe. Not to mention a few months late."

"So let's grab something before the law sends them packing." He parked within a few yards of the truck. Six people were already queued up at the open window. As he was hurrying to unbuckle his seat belt and climb out, his cell phone buzzed. He snatched it out of the cup holder and, standing up outside his door, looked at the screen. Bowen. He punched the Answer icon and said, "Hold just a second, Cappie."

He spoke to Jayme over the hood of the car. "Get me the brisket and a kielbasa if they have it. Plus some mac and cheese?"

"Really?" she said. "Mac and cheese too?"

"I won't eat the bun."

She shook her head and crossed to get in line.

"Top of the day to you," DeMarco said into the phone.

"You're calling me Cappie now?"

"That's how I always picture you. A little boy in his police pajamas. What's happening?"

"Are you sitting down?"

"I will be soon."

"Guess whose body was just pulled out of the Shenango River."

DeMarco's left knee went weak. "Do not say Benny Szabo. Please, Captain. Do not say Benny Szabo."

"Okay, I won't. Oscar Szabo."

"Oscar? Is that his old man?"

"It's his old man's brother. Benny's uncle."

DeMarco let out a long breath. "Okay. That's interesting, but…"

"But how is it relevant?" Bowen said. "Maybe it's not. The coroner is calling it an accident. They figure he took a header off either the Route 18 bridge or the old railroad bridge just off the Trout Island trail."

"And why would he do that?"

"Because he's a drunk. Hasn't been sober, I'm told, since the Bicentennial."

DeMarco watched Jayme moving up in the line. He hoped she remembered to ask for extra sauce. "Okay," he told Bowen. "Does seem something of a coincidence, doesn't it?"

"Which, as I recall, you don't believe in anymore."

"I'll contact the coroner."

"I thought you might."

"Thanks for the heads-up."

"And don't call me Cappie anymore."

"It's an endearment. Because I'm so fond of you."

"I still don't like it," Bowen said, and ended the call.

# SEVENTY-FOUR

## THE CONTENTS OF A DEAD MAN'S POCKETS

The Mercer County coroner's office was in Greenville, fifteen miles north. DeMarco would have preferred to speak with the coroner in person, but there was the brisket to consider, charred black and shiny with sauce and piled high inside a bun soggy with grease. Plus it was a Sunday—all day long, as DeMarco's mother would have said—so he and Jayme left the car at the library and walked toward the courthouse square a three-minute walk away.

"Turns out that the food truck was headed to a gig in New Castle when some kind of transmission problem popped up," she told him as they walked. "Can't get out of second gear. So now they have a hundred pounds of barbecue to sell at half price before it goes bad."

DeMarco stopped in midstride, turned and looked back. "Half price? Let's go buy up the rest of it."

"Keep moving," she told him with a nudge. "We haven't even tasted it yet."

"It's barbecue. Even bad barbecue is good."

"After we eat maybe. But only one more serving each. For tomorrow. Not a freezer full. You know what too much meat does to you."

He conceded with a huff. "You are a hard taskmaster, Mistress Matson."

"Bet you can't say that three times fast."

"I'd rather eat," he said. "Let's grab this bench."

The courthouse was quiet that afternoon, its only day of full rest, both parking lots empty but for a few cars. The grayness of morning had broken up a little but the patches of blue overhead were sparse. They settled onto the nearest bench and set the foam boxes between them.

DeMarco allowed himself two forkfuls of the shredded brisket, then pulled the coroner's number on his cell phone. The call went to voicemail, so DeMarco tried the home number. It was answered on the third ring.

"Mazzoni residence," the coroner said. He had a fairly high voice for such a tall man, at least six foot three when he stood plumb line straight, which he didn't often do these days. Thin, red-haired, and brittle-looking, but always cheerful, a quality DeMarco found fascinating in light of the man's line of work.

"Hey, Connie," DeMarco said. The full name was Conrad but he had always been Connie to those who knew him. Connie the coroner. "Ryan DeMarco here. Sorry to bother you on a Sunday."

"Been expecting your call," Connie said. "Oscar Carl Szabo."

"You mind if I put you on speaker? Jayme is here with me."

"The Dynamic Duo. Good afternoon, young lady."

"Hey, Connie," she said, her mouth full of pulled pork.

"The late Mr. Szabo," Connie said, getting right down to business. "You know him?"

"We do not," DeMarco said.

"Five seven, 163 pounds, a good portion of that weight in the breadbasket. Seventy-two years old but with the organs of a man twice that age. Nice thick beard and head of hair, though— bountiful, in fact. Both as white as snow after a dust storm, the hair held together in a ponytail with a red rubber band. Reminded me of Jerry Garcia. I kept hoping he would break into a few bars of 'Tangled Up in Blue.'"

DeMarco smiled; he always enjoyed the coroner's descriptions. "I prefer the Dylan version," he said. "But please continue."

"Lifelong smoker of Pall Malls and his lungs showed it. Cirrhosis, atherosclerosis, early signs of congestive heart failure. Triglycerides off the chart. Blood alcohol content at time of death is approximate, 178, sample taken from the vitreous humor. What put him out of his misery, though, was a blow to the head, frontal calvarium. Consistent with a fall from an elevated position."

"He didn't drown?" DeMarco asked.

"Negative. Took a dive into the shallows is the way I see it. Should have worn his water wings. A helmet wouldn't have hurt either."

"The captain said either the Route 18 bridge or the railroad bridge. Based on what?"

"Educated guess. He didn't fall from a kneeling or standing position, that's for sure. Opened his skull up like Gallagher with a watermelon."

"There are fairly high walls on both of the bridges, Connie."

"Not so high that anybody with sufficient intent can't climb up over them."

"My money is on the old railroad bridge. Route 18 is too well-trafficked. Somebody would have seen him."

"That supposition is favored all around. But, since covering our asses is always SOP, I'm including both possibilities on the report."

"And you're calling it suicide?"

"Yeah, probably not. Forty-sixty, I'd say, in favor of accidental death. Anybody who knows those bridges knows they aren't high enough to do anything but cripple and maim. Remember that drunken kid last August? Thought he was doing a cannonball but forgot to check the water level first and stretched out too soon.

Ruined his ankles and knees instead of his noggin. Our Mr. Szabo, as it turned out, was no Greg Louganis either. Went headfirst into six feet of water."

"That doesn't necessarily mean it was an accident."

"Like I said, forty-sixty. Seeing as how his zipper was down and his wingwang was hanging out."

"Huh," said DeMarco. "So you figure he climbed up on the wall to take a leak in the river."

"Either that or to show the world what he had. Which, in my honest opinion, wasn't worth the price of a ticket."

Again DeMarco smiled. "No indication of foul play?"

"Zippo. No signs of struggle, no defensive wounds, torn clothing, zilch. Sharpsville police went over both venues, didn't find diddly-squat."

"How long do you think he was in the water?"

"Half a day or so. Hard to tell, though, thanks to the water temp. As cold as brass titties. Whoops, sorry there, Jayme."

"No problem. I imagine brass ones are fairly cold."

DeMarco asked, "Where exactly did he end up?"

"Across the river at the campground. A bunch of Boy Scouts were having a powwow or something. I wonder how many corpses you have to drag out of the drink to get a merit badge?"

"The campground, that's what—maybe a quarter of a mile from the bridge?"

"Give or take. The currents are tricky, though. Not to mention all the snags this time of year. He could have drifted right over, could've gotten hung up a while on the bottom and spent some time counting fishies."

"I suppose it's too much to ask that you found anything interesting in his pockets," DeMarco said.

"Actually, I did. Forty-two cents in change, a St. Christopher metal, one of the small Altoids tins filled with what turned out to be baby aspirins, half a pack of soggy Pall Malls, and a book of matches from the Marigold."

"Whoa," DeMarco said. "A matchbook from the Marigold?"

"Do you find a matchbook illuminating, young man?"

"I visited the Marigold yesterday, trying to drum up some intel. Dropped the Szabo name and everybody looked at me like I was speaking Sumerian."

"Well now. That paints an interesting scenario, doesn't it?"

"You bet it does."

Jayme leaned toward the phone and asked, "Have you talked to the relatives?"

"Relatively speaking," the coroner said, "no. He and that boy you're after appear to be the end of the Szabo line."

"Interesting," DeMarco said. "How did you know we're looking for Benny?"

"Trade secret. Sorry."

"Somebody from the Greenville hospital, I assume."

"When you assume you make an ass out of u and me. Even when you're right."

Jayme asked, "Do you have Oscar Szabo's address? It might be interesting to talk with the neighbors."

"I do, and it is a very simple address to remember. Address unknown."

"He was homeless?" DeMarco asked.

"So saith the thin blue line."

DeMarco blew out a breath. "I appreciate this, Connie. Good stuff."

"That's why they pay me the big bucks. Anything else I can do for you two?"

"No, sir. We're all set. You have a good evening."

"*Vaya con dios, amigos.*"

# SEVENTY-FIVE

Can 1+1 ever = 1?

A fter Jayme had unbuckled her seat belt, then popped open the door to climb out in DeMarco's backyard, he said, still behind the wheel, the engine still running, "I think I'll drive over to Trout Island and sniff around that railroad bridge a little."

She turned in her seat. "The police already went over it, right?"

"Yep," he said, his right hand still fingering the key, left hand at ten o'clock on the steering wheel.

"You have a feeling?" she asked.

"I guess I do. It will give me a chance to work off some of that mac and cheese."

"Okay. I'll grab Hero and be right back."

"You know…" he said, which was enough to signal what he was thinking.

"No problem," she told him, and swung her feet and legs outside the car.

"It's just that I can—"

"Baby," she interrupted, "it's okay. I could use some downtime with my hairy little boy."

DeMarco had always gotten hunches, gut feelings, a sixth sense, whatever you wanted to call it. So did she. So did all investigators.

But since his NDE he had been more reluctant to ignore them, to talk himself out of them. She appreciated his efforts to not revert fully to the lone wolf he had been when they first met, but by now she had spent enough time around him to know that he still preferred to be alone sometimes. Not always, but especially when some thought or notion was gnawing at him. He had a way of talking to himself when he worked alone. "Hearing myself think," he called it. "Getting the ducks in a row." A second person made him too self-conscious to do it.

Yes, the NDE had changed him, and he was still wrestling with that change, still holding on to maybe, she guessed, 30 percent of his old cynicism, and she was okay with the other 70 percent. More than okay. It made him kinder, gentler, a happier man. What she was not okay with but had no way to change was the NDE itself. Whatever he had experienced was beyond her understanding, no matter how many books she read or YouTube videos she watched, and it would always keep them, so to speak, a room apart. Yes, that's what it was like for her, as if they were always a room apart now, him in the dining room, for example, her a few feet away in the kitchen.

She leaned backward and puckered up for a kiss, which he was happy to give. Then she climbed out and closed the door. But as she started around the front of the car, his door popped open.

He stood outside the door and handed her the foam box heavy with two more servings of barbecued brisket and pork. "Tonight?" he asked.

"*And* a salad," she said as she took the box.

"Aye, Captain." A wink before he closed the door and started the engine.

She walked toward the house and told herself not to turn and wave as he drove away. Such a trivial thing really, him going off alone for an hour or two. But it was more than that and she knew it. She had hunches too, and she could feel this one in her bones.

# SEVENTY-SIX

## A BRIDGE OVER RUBBLED WATER

He drove as far as he could on the road that ran alongside the Trout Island trail, a 2.4-mile asphalt walking and biking path that paralleled the old Erie and Pennsylvania railroad tracks and ended not far from where the tracks crossed the Shenango River. At mile 1.9, about a half mile from the trestle bridge, he parked in the little lot off Thomason Road, locked his car and strode onto the path.

The afternoon was growing cooler, and with the heavy canopy on his left shading that side of the path, he wished he'd worn a light jacket. Through the sparser brush on his right he could glimpse swamp and field and an occasional house. But the path was flat and even and made for easier walking, and the movement loosed his joints and soon became pleasant.

As far as he could tell, he had the path to himself. Summer would bring heavier traffic, walkers and runners and bikers and parents pushing babies in their strollers. It had been a couple of years since he'd been there, and he wondered why he'd never suggested the place for him and Jayme and Hero to walk. Probably because his previous outings there had been in troubled times, fall and winter Sunday mornings after brooding alone beside Baby

Ryan's grave, times when his mood was as unrelentingly dark as the swamp water. He made a mental note to bring Jayme and Hero here next Sunday, and with their company to change the quality of the light.

He walked for fifteen minutes before the path ended. There a narrow footpath led through high weeds a while longer, then veered sharply left up a small bank to the Norfolk Southern railroad tracks. From there to the trestle the rails were elevated several feet above the natural ground level, the bed and banks packed for stability with chunks of limestone the size of a woman's fist. Trains still made infrequent trips along those tracks, though he had no idea what the boxcars held or where they were headed.

The trestle seemed unchanged from the last time he'd seen it but for the graffiti. Nearly every section of the bridge's walls sported a chalk or spray-painted declamation of love for a person or drug or the venue itself, a curse aimed at the scrawler's school, girlfriend, or life in general, or an amateurish sketch of some kind. Why, DeMarco wondered with a smile, do kids so love to draw an erect penis and balls? Had it become the modern Kilroy?

His favorite piece of graffiti was a triptych spray-painted in white on three contiguous metal panels, each rusty panel separated by a vertical beam, which gave each of the periods more emphasis, a chance to sigh and gather one's strength: *It's fine. I'm fine. Everything is fine.* To DeMarco it seemed an echo of Beckett's famous existential cry at the end of *The Unnamable*, which he now quoted aloud, just as he had many times throughout his life: "'You must go on, I can't go on, I'll go on.'"

But he didn't linger long with the graffiti. He walked out over the water, looked down at the little cove full of driftwood and snags. Though the water was brown he could see the rocky bottom. Farther out along the bridge, the river deepened. "If he jumped or was pushed," he mused, "it was here. Near the shallows." But the shallows showed no evidence. "Nor would they," he said.

Now he lifted his head and gazed downstream toward the concrete Route 18 bridge. Then turned to his left to look down the long parallax view of the tracks to the campground on the other side of the river. A few seconds later, he peered down at the ties and tracks again, then took another long look along the top of the bridge wall.

"Nothing," he said out loud. "No blood. No recent scuff or drag marks. No evidence, no smoking gun. No X marks the spot."

He came back across the bridge and crawled down on the right side, moving carefully over the bed of loose limestone chunks. "Wouldn't want to twist an ankle here," he warned himself. The limestone soon gave way to hard-packed earth and tufts of scraggly grass and weeds.

He ducked under the rails. Here there was a relatively level area directly under the bridge, maybe thirty square yards of well-trampled dirt before it sloped steeply down to the river. This slope, except for a very narrow footpath, was thick with larger rocks, basketball-sized and smaller, and congested with thorny vines and other weeds. The bank was littered with dented beer cans and broken bottles. Here in this dim little alcove teenagers huddled, he imagined, to pass a joint around, or to spread a blanket for some quick, furtive sex. He remembered the time a younger, miserable DeMarco had once sat out the rain in this place, hoping in vain for a leavening of his sorrow and guilt.

Here, now, he searched for something of interest, something the police might have missed. Something that was responsible for the insistent urge that had brought him there. He went up and down the slope three times, from water to bridge and back again. Then, convinced he had missed nothing, he stood a few feet from the water's edge and peered up the slope.

"Nothing," he conceded. Nothing in the dim space directly under the bridge, nothing on the sloping bank, nothing along the uneven shore. Only dirt and rocks and litter and weeds and water. Nothing to tell the tale, nor even to suggest the presence of a tale to be told. "Son of a gun," he said aloud.

He was three-quarters of the way up the slope, a few steps from the level area, when a rumbling sound caught his attention. It was faint at first, but quickly grew louder. He turned and peered up through the ties and rails. Something moving in the distance. A train. And coming on fast.

Long strides up the remainder of the slope. He had almost reached the level area as the train rumbled overhead. Bits of rock rained down from the nooks and niches where they had lain, chips of rust falling from the bridge walls. The ties shook, the bridge rattled, the train raced by with a deafening roar. He hurried to the side, moving too quickly in a low hunch, and lost his footing when he moved from the dirt and vines to the looser chunks of limestone. Tumbled and rolled.

Long after the train was gone, he lay motionless. "Dumb shit," he told himself. Bruised but not broken. And when he got his breath back, he chuckled. Life always found a way to humble him.

Okay, so he had been wrong. There was nothing here. "So pick yourself up, DeMarco, and get your sorry ass back home."

He rolled over onto his hands and knees, intending to crawl away from the limestone before standing. He wasn't about to chance those slippery chunks again. He started slowly, then, wincing when a sharp edge bit into his kneecap, decided that standing might be less painful. This, too, he executed an inch at a time, not convinced that every joint and rib and vertebra was going to cooperate. "No more mac and cheese for you," he groaned. Then stood for a moment, caught his breath, and looked down to pick out his next step. And saw, or thought he saw, something red. Maybe an inch long, half as wide. Something red smeared on the rough edge of rock half-buried beneath a larger rock. Was that blood? *His* blood?

He patted his head, looked at his hands. Nothing. Felt around his neck. Checked his bare arms and hands. No blood there. Knees, legs, thighs, small of his back. No torn clothing anywhere. A couple of scratches but no blood. Anyway not enough to be dabbed on that rock.

He put the toe of his shoe against the rock, pried it up and flipped it over. More red. Lots of it. "Is that hair on it too?" he asked, squinting. Something wispy and white. "Probably just a cobweb." He hunkered down for a closer look.

A moment later he stood upright again, fumbled in his pocket, felt for the cell phone. "Don't be broken," he muttered as his hand closed around it, a kind of prayer. "Please don't be broken."

# SEVENTY-SEVEN

## IT'S IN THE BAG

The Sharpsville Police Department sent two officers to bag and tag the bloody rock. He walked a few steps behind them as they strode, youthful and confident, back to their SUV in the little lot off Thomason Road. His right shoulder ached from where it had impacted the limestone when he fell. A twinge of pain stabbed at his pelvis with each forward swing of his right leg.

"Well, at least this will solve one mystery," the officer carrying the evidence bag said.

"If it's the old guy's blood it will."

"Who else's would it be?"

"I'm just saying if it is. We won't know until we know," the second officer said. "It won't tell us who put it there, though."

"Did I say it would?"

"In fact, when it turns out it *is* his, it will solve three mysteries, not one."

"How's that?"

"First, whose blood is it? Second, was it a suicide or an accident or a homicide that killed him?"

"And third, where it actually happened."

"Like I said, three mysteries solved. But not the big one. Not the one that really matters."

In the lot, DeMarco thanked both officers, then climbed into his own vehicle and started the engine and powered down the front windows to let the imprisoned heat flow out. As the police SUV pulled away, he shut off the engine and phoned the coroner.

"Yel-low," the coroner answered.

"You have your Wite-Out ready?" DeMarco asked.

"New development?"

"Murder weapon. That's my guess anyway. About an eight-pound rock. The flat side has been painted red."

"Ho ho!" Mazzoni said.

"It's headed for the lab now. With instructions to notify you with the results ASAP."

"And just where did this Rosetta Stone reveal itself?"

"Half-buried in the limestone bed off to the side of the railroad bridge."

"Found by you?"

"I was on my way home empty-handed," DeMarco told him. "Just happened to look down and see a little sliver of red."

"You old dog, you. Always digging, aren't you?"

"Just wanted to give you a heads-up, Connie. You mind calling me back when you get the results?"

"Can do," the coroner said. "Could be as early as tomorrow if the lab's not busy."

"Let's hope so."

"I guess maybe dead men do tell lies."

"They keep secrets, that's for sure," DeMarco said. "Have a good night, Connie."

"We don't use Wite-Out anymore, by the way. We use the Delete button."

"That just doesn't have the same ring to it, though, does it?" DeMarco said.

After he hung up, DeMarco sat there a while longer with the windows down and everything quiet. The air was fragrant and cool, the walls of living green blending their scents, leaves and grasses and weeds and vines. "I wish I could bottle that," he said. He would dab a little of it under his nose every morning, keep a vial in his pocket for emergencies. "Nature's perfume." It wasn't as dizzying and stomach-fluttering as Jayme's scent when she climbed into bed freshly showered and scantily clothed, nor as saliva-generating as a plate full of heavily sauced barbecued meat, but it was a terrific scent all the same, subtle, soothing, and satisfying. Very satisfying indeed.

But too much satisfaction is a kind of stagnancy, and the night was not yet over for him. Even as the light softened and the sky deepened its gray, even as the second helping of brisket waited, a bit of work remained to be done.

# SEVENTY-EIGHT

OH, FOR A DAB OF NATURE'S PERFUME!

Inside the Marigold, a couple of servers were setting up equipment for the Sunday night karaoke. DeMarco counted eight customers already seated facing the little stage, nursing beers and other drinks. Five of the bar stools were occupied too. A low hum of conversation ran through the room, with one voice or another rising now and then above the others.

DeMarco went to an empty end of the bar and waited. Besides the older woman he had spoken with earlier, another bartender, a tall, broad-shouldered young man with a loose mop of long black hair, was working the bar that night, filling the wells and checking the ice.

DeMarco caught the woman's eye, but she ignored him. He waited.

Eventually the young man pulled his hands out of the ice bin, dried them on a bar rag, crossed to DeMarco and asked, "What can I get you?"

"Her," DeMarco said with a nod to the woman.

"Rose?" the bartender asked after a look her way.

"If you wouldn't mind," DeMarco said.

Rose didn't even glance his way when the young bartender

passed on the information. She nodded but made no reply. Did a little shuffling of the bottles lined up beneath the bar. Turned and went to the cash register, moved the order pad closer to the register. Popped open the drawer, checked the cash inside, closed the drawer again. Then, otherwise motionless, she lifted her eyes to the mirror behind the bar. DeMarco met her gaze in the glass and raised his eyebrows in question.

She looked away. Moved the order pad a half inch from the cash register. Then turned sharply. Came down behind the bar to pass in front of DeMarco without looking his way and crossed under the open archway into the kitchen. He watched her through the doorway as she walked to the back of the kitchen and out a door.

Whether it was a door to a bathroom or a pantry or a door to the outside, he did not know. But he had a feeling. "Door number 3," he whispered to himself. Turned away from the bar and headed for the entrance just as a noisy group of five twentysomethings came barreling in.

Behind the Marigold, there wasn't much of interest to see. To his right, the backside of the Hot Dog Shop. Straight ahead, the back of Laskey's Furniture. Beyond that, Water Street, more buildings, and the Shenango River. But to his left, close up against the side of the adjacent building, a dumpster. With a wisp of smoke drifting over it. And the figure producing that smoke standing in the shadows between the dumpster and the building.

He crossed to her and stood with his left shoulder toward her, as if he were appraising something out near Water Street. The stench coming from inside the dumpster was strong. Soiled meat and rotting vegetables, dirty diapers and other putrescence.

Rose took another drag on her cigarette, released the smoke and said, "You know what happens to my business if it gets out I'm talking to you."

"I understand," he said.

"It's not like you're just anybody. Your picture's been in the paper how many times now?"

"So you own the Marigold?"

"Some of it. Used to be all of it."

He nodded. "Looks like business will be good tonight."

She tossed down her cigarette. Watched its tip glowing in the dirt. When she looked up at him there were tears in her eyes. "I've known OC all my life," she said.

"OC being Oscar Szabo?"

"You could never meet a kinder man than him. He'd give you the shirt off his back."

"You heard what happened to him?"

"Why do you think I'm standing here now?"

"I'm guessing you wouldn't be surprised to hear that it's looking less and less like either suicide or an accident."

Her mouth went into a scowling pout; her nostrils flared as she inhaled.

"Do you know where Benny is?"

She looked at the cigarette a few moments longer, then ground it out beneath a foot. "No," she said.

He waited for more, but it wasn't forthcoming. "What *do* you know?"

She had seemed so authoritative behind the bar, a woman not to be crossed. But now she appeared to shrink before his very eyes, perhaps not physically but in terms of resolve. She leaned forward a bit to peek around him. Then straightened again.

She said, "A few days back, I think it was Wednesday or Thursday, I'd have to check my receipts to be sure. OC's up at the bar as usual. But this time he's buying for the house, and that *never* happens. Usually he just sits there waiting for somebody else to buy him one, or for me to fill his glass again. And I never begrudged doing so. There was a time…" She blinked. Sniffed. Looked away from DeMarco.

"You said you've known him a long time."

She nodded. "He wasn't always like that. Vietnam did that to him. He came back and, I don't know. All his gumption was gone. He worked construction before he got drafted, and he could do it all. Carpentry, plumbing, wiring, whatever needed done, he could do it. It was that fucking war."

"War has ruined a lot of good people."

"He lent me some of the money for the down payment on that place," she said with a nod toward the Marigold's back door. "And I paid him back, every penny of it. Not that he ever once asked for it. Or ever would."

"So where did he get the money he had last week? Did he have some savings?"

"Savings? OC? He had the clothes he wore and that's about all he had."

"And that's why it was so surprising that he was buying for the house."

"I asked him, but he was…I guess you'd call it being coy. Said he wasn't allowed to tell. And then he'd wink at me and laugh. I just figured it had something to do with where he'd disappeared to earlier."

"Earlier when?" DeMarco asked.

"He missed coming in three whole days. Nobody knew where he was. That wasn't like him either. He spent most of every day here. Sometimes I'd let him sleep here."

"So he was gone for a while," DeMarco said, "three days. And then he showed up again with a little money on him?"

"A little?" she said. "He had this fat roll of paper he kept pulling out of his pants. Held it together with a red rubber band."

"Like the one he used for his ponytail."

She nodded. "I saw him peel off three fifties before that nephew of his came in and dragged him out again."

"You're talking Benny Szabo, right?"

"That's the only nephew of his I know."

"And why do you think Benny did that?"

She shook her head. Patted her pockets. Finally she said, "I guess I left them inside."

"Your cigarettes?"

"I keep trying to quit."

"That's better than not trying."

A brief blast of music came from the Marigold, then was quickly extinguished. She looked to the door. "I got to be getting back." She moved to step past him, but he moved too.

He said, "Do you have any idea where Benny is now?"

"No and I hope I never lay eyes on him again. That piece of shit and his uncle... Two more different men you will never meet. OC was the very sweetest man I have ever known. Benny is garbage. If I knew where he was, I'd tell you."

"You think he's responsible, don't you? For what happened to OC."

"I think garbage stinks. Always has and always will." She pushed past him then and strode away.

"I'm sorry for your loss," DeMarco said.

# SEVENTY-NINE

IT'S THE LITTLE PRICKS THAT TICKLE

F rom his car in the lot across from Warehouse Sales, DeMarco phoned Bowen at home. Bowen answered with a "What's up?"

"Lots," DeMarco said, and recounted for him the trip to the railroad bridge, the bloody rock, his back alley convo with Rose from the Marigold.

"You've been a busy boy today."

"And we're not done yet," DeMarco said. "Can you call Chief Gary up in Scottville and ask him to have Officer Curtin take another look at the security camera footage of Benny? Specifically to see if there might be another person in the car or truck with him."

"Don't you think you would have noticed that already?" Bowen asked.

"It's crappy footage. And we weren't looking for a passenger. We were focused on identifying the driver."

"Yeah, okay. I wouldn't expect any information tonight, though."

"I don't. Just want to get the wheels turning."

"I bet those Sharpsville boys are a little red in the face now, huh?"

"The blood was easy to miss. I just happened to look down at the right time and right place." He hadn't mentioned scurrying out from beneath the bridge and stumbling on the rocks, rolling through the weeds. Nor did he plan to. His relationship with Bowen had always been one of friendly jousting, of seeing who could prick the other with the sharpest lance. It made no sense to rearm a defenseless opponent.

"Well, whatever," Bowen said. "Did you give Mazzoni a heads-up?"

"I did. You never need to do that, though, do you?"

"What do you mean?"

"He's already a head taller than you."

"Bite me, DeMarco."

"I would, Captain, but I need more of a meal than that. Sleep tight."

"I hope Jayme suffocates you with her pillow."

DeMarco laughed, stopped what he was about to say, and hung up. He had almost said "Love you, bud" before hanging up. That would have been disastrous. Like handing your opponent a nuclear bomb.

# EIGHTY

## Going nowhere as fast as you can

DeMarco fell asleep that night just minutes after Jayme had started to read aloud from Huston's book. And when he awoke the next morning to find the book closed between them, Jayme still asleep, he could not remember a word of what he'd heard. So he carried the book downstairs with him and left it on the kitchen table, thinking they might read from it at breakfast. For some reason he didn't want to read it alone, wanted the experience to be just as it had been when they read through Huston's notebooks to pick out the best passages for the book. They had made a kind of child together through those conspiratorial readings, and he wanted her to feel as much a parent of the finished book as he did.

Unfortunately Jayme slept late and did not come downstairs until DeMarco had gone ahead and fixed himself and Hero some scrambled eggs, then cleaned up after both of them. He offered to make eggs Benedict for her, though with strip bacon instead of Canadian, but she shook her head no, poured a cup of coffee, and went back upstairs with Hero on her heels. Her eyes, DeMarco had noticed, were bloodshot, her energy low, and he knew that she had spent the morning grieving Emma, and wanted to continue to do so alone.

And the day passed, one little chore after another. No call came in from Mazzoni announcing a match between the blood on the rock and the ponytailed corpse chilling in the coroner's basement room. Bowen called in the afternoon to say that Chief Gary's man had gone cross-eyed going over and over the video footage, but could report only that "it looks like there *might* be somebody else in the Rogue when it goes west past the gas station the first time. But it's just a shadow. Might even be Benny's reflection. Impossible to identify. Sorry."

Now that Morrison had been rattled with the news of Emma's death, Captain Bowen agreed to set up surveillance on the judge's house, just in case he went running to one of his pals.

Said that as soon as DeMarco had a game plan for continuing the search for Benny Szabo, he would assign Boyd and anybody else he could spare, and would, if warranted, ask the municipalities to volunteer personnel to round out the team.

And DeMarco had said, "I want to bring Flores aboard too."

"No way!" Bowen exclaimed.

"Yes, sir," DeMarco said. "I consider it an imperative. Otherwise she's going to go under."

"How do you know that?"

"How do you know she won't?"

Bowen was adamant until DeMarco reminded him that Flores was no longer under his authority. "She's part of *my* team. So it's my decision to make."

"You and your team—" Bowen started, only to be cut off.

DeMarco kept his voice even and emotionless. "My team and I are not working for you, Captain. Our employer is Emma Barrie. We are happy to cooperate with you, but let's not forget that my team is in no way obliged to be dictated to by you. You can be a hard-ass about it if you want, threaten us with obstruction or some other charge, but I have never known you to be that kind of cop, Kyle."

Bowen took a couple of breaths before responding. "I know you care about her," he said. "I care about her too. But, Ryan, come on, man, be reasonable. She put herself in harm's way twice already. Sooner or later she's going to get herself killed, and probably somebody else with her."

"If she were your daughter," DeMarco said, "would you give her another chance?"

"She isn't my daughter. And she isn't yours either."

"Not on paper she isn't. But in every other way, you know that she is. Both yours and mine."

Another silence from Bowen. Then the captain had said, "You're giving me more headaches now than you did when you were in uniform."

"I consider it one of my principal duties in life, Captain. And certainly the most fun."

With nothing else of significance for DeMarco to do, the day crept by slow and long and empty, and felt twice as drawn out as his busy yesterday had been.

That evening, standing at his bedroom window, DeMarco looked out on the fading light gradually retreating from the street below, easing away as if embarrassed somehow, or guilty of something, or just too tired anymore to give a damn. He and Jayme had set all but one of the investigation's wheels in motion, yet they were at a standstill. And until Benny Szabo was found, nobody was going anywhere.

And now, as the sun burned low in the west, DeMarco had nothing much to do but to enjoy the sunset from his south-facing window while Jayme read downstairs. A line of clouds with flat black bottoms lay across the horizon like a long train of flatcars loaded with mounds of fluffy white meringue.

All day long Jayme had moved from bedroom to living room to the back porch and then inside again, reading and dozing and reading a little more from Eben Alexander's *Proof of Heaven*. DeMarco knew well the healing power of solitude and didn't begrudge her a moment of it. He hoped they would go to bed early and read from Huston's book together. It would be good to spend some time with his friend again, to hear his comforting voice, and to watch Jayme being comforted as well.

Across the street, a splash of red caught his eye. A cardinal in his neighbor's dogwood. How long do cardinals live? He wished he knew. What are their mating habits? What do they eat? He had been seeing the occasional cardinal for as long as he could remember yet he knew nothing about them. Could identify only a small number of bird species. He needed to be more attentive. More knowledgeable. All around him plants and animals were coming into and passing out of his world with barely a thought on his part. And the same would be true of him. He could have died on that dirty asphalt and ten years later be but a dim memory to only a few people. Thirty years down the road, who but Jayme would think of him? Feathers and flesh and hair and organs decompose and disappear every moment of every day. Bones and eventually teeth too turning into powder. The original owner not just irrelevant or merely insignificant but as if he never existed. The dust you brush from your cuff. The dirt you scrape from your shoe.

It would be sad if that were the way of things, the culmination of every life. He felt sorry for those who went through life believing it. Wondered if any one of them did not in their darkest hours secretly hope and maybe pray that they were wrong. He, who knew in his heart that such a belief was wrong, did not pray. He hadn't seen a brilliant white light, hadn't passed through a dark tunnel into a place of all-enveloping love. He hadn't met God. Nor even

Jesus. Who else might be listening to a prayer? He still had no idea to whom that occasional authoritative voice in his head belonged. Maybe it was his own subconscious mind speaking. Or what the New Agers called his higher self. He had given up on trying to ascertain the source. As long as the voice continued to make sense, why not go with it?

His thoughts were interrupted then by a noisy pickup truck stopping in front of DeMarco's house, a vehicle black and battered, its running boards all but rusted away, the rusty muffler rattling and roaring with every cough of the engine. The truck did not pull to the curb but simply stopped on the street adjacent to that point where the sidewalk junctioned with the walk leading up to DeMarco's front door. An old man climbed out, late seventies at least, wearing faded jeans and work boots and an untucked blue flannel shirt with the sleeves rolled to the elbow. He looked like a grizzled Marlboro Man with stage 4 lung cancer. Except for the newsboy hat, red-and-gray herringbone, the short brim pulled down low on his forehead. *You don't see many of those these days*, DeMarco thought.

He watched for a few more moments as the old man shuffled stiffly toward the house, his head lowered and his eyes on the concrete, now with the black pickup truck roaring away, not quickly but loud, the gears grinding. Then DeMarco turned from the window and went downstairs and past Jayme sitting on the sofa reading with Hero at her feet.

She looked up from her book and raised her eyebrows, and he said, "I just now got this really strong premonition. I think somebody's going to knock on the door." He waited in the foyer, his head cocked. Then it happened, four strong, hard-knuckled raps. His eyes widened. "I think I must be psychic."

She said, smiling, "I think you must be psycho," and returned to her book.

He crossed to pull open the door.

The old man raised his eyes but not his chin and said, in a deep but muted rasp, "You DeMarco?" His face was as wrinkled as a bloodhound's but without the flaps and folds of skin, a gaunt, sun-hardened, age-eroded face with deep-set, hooded gray eyes, his close-cut sideburns white, his scruff of whiskers like tiny splinters of glass.

"Who's asking?" DeMarco said.

The man came forward then to squeeze past DeMarco and into the foyer. He smelled of tobacco and Old Spice. "Name's Szabo," he whispered as he slid past.

# EIGHTY-ONE

FROM THE MOUTH OF A BAD VENTRILOQUIST

D eMarco stepped aside and allowed the man to enter. "That's some hat you have there."

Szabo turned and pushed the door out of DeMarco's loose grasp until the latch clicked. "My disguise," he said.

"Who are you hiding from? Your son?"

"I ain't hiding. Just don't like people knowing my business. Never have." His lips barely moved when he spoke, and the words came out like polysyllabic grunts emanating deep in his throat.

"I can appreciate that," DeMarco told him. "You want to come in and sit down? Can I get you a cup of coffee?"

"You could give me a ride back home if you want."

"You came here just for that?"

Szabo leaned into the foyer a little farther, enough to peek around the open archway and into the living room, where both Jayme and Hero had alerted to his presence. He whispered, "You looking for my son, ain't you?"

"Where did you hear that?"

"I might have an idea where he is," Szabo said. "We can talk about it on the ride home."

DeMarco turned to the living room. "I'm going to give Mr. Szabo a ride home," he told Jayme.

"Have fun," she answered, but she wasn't smiling when she said it, was looking at him with her forehead furrowed, eyes worried.

To Szabo, DeMarco said, "We'll go out through the kitchen. The car is out back."

"I figured," Szabo said. He shot a sideways glance Jayme's way as he followed DeMarco, and at the last moment added a tip of the tiny brim of his hat.

# EIGHTY-TWO

NEVER UNDERESTIMATE THE POWER OF INTENTION

D eMarco led Benny Szabo's father out the back door and
down off the porch and into the yard. Szabo cast a disdainful
look at the unfinished brick path. "How long you been working
on that?" he asked.

"Too long," DeMarco said.

"Pretty obvious from the grass growing up between the bricks.
You one of those start stuff but never finish it kind of guys?"

"I seem to be when it comes to that path."

"What's the problem?"

"Memories," DeMarco said.

"Huh," the old man said. "A fucking burden is what they are."

DeMarco said nothing. Was matching his gait to the old man's,
knew better than to hurry him. A quiet nervousness had raised goose
bumps on DeMarco's arm; he had been standing at the upstairs
window hoping for a break in the case, and now here was Benny
Szabo's long-lost father. In the past when such things happened he
would have thought *we got lucky*, but the truth was that they happened frequently, and he no longer believed in luck as an accidental
agent of change.

For every step Szabo took, the old man's gaze covered another fifty square feet of ground. Now he fixed his eyes on the two sedans and one RV parked at the end of the yard. "You running a used car lot here?" he asked.

"Just getting started," DeMarco told him. "Which one do you want to test ride?"

"How about that big one?"

"It's just for show," DeMarco said. "We'll take the Accord."

But the old man wasn't finished with the RV yet. He looked it up and down as they approached DeMarco's car. "Where you all been in it?" he asked. "You and your lady friend."

"Been to Kentucky and back." DeMarco used the remote to unlock his vehicle's doors. "And we spent a couple of days up in Michigan recently."

This got the old man's attention. "You been to Michigan, huh?"

At the front of his car, DeMarco split off to cross to the driver's side. "You like Michigan?"

"Don't know nothing about it."

"That seems to be a common affliction these days." DeMarco popped open his car door, climbed in and buckled up. It took another full minute before the old man was seated beside him. DeMarco started the car, and immediately the passenger side seat belt warning beeped.

"You'll need to buckle up, Mr. Szabo."

"I don't use those things." He sat motionless, leaning slightly forward in his seat. "They ain't good for my back."

DeMarco thought for a moment, then decided *what the hell*, and slipped the gearshift into Reverse.

At the end of the alley, the seat belt warning still beeping, he asked, "Which way to home?"

"Don't that bother you?" the old man asked. "That damn thing beeping all the time?"

"It will stop as soon as you buckle up."

Szabo stared straight ahead. "Up in French Creek Township," he said. "Ten-Right Road."

DeMarco knew that road. Had investigated a homicide there some nine or ten years earlier. A young woman had had her throat slit while in bed. He turned north and said, "As I recall, Mr. Szabo, there are only three, maybe four houses on that road."

"Mine's the end one."

DeMarco reeled up the memory. "So that would be the Fletcher house?" The home in which the young woman had died.

"Across the road from it. The teacher's."

"Name of Hickman, I believe."

"You believe right. Supposed to've been one of them child molesters."

"So I heard. He sold you the house?"

"Bought it for taxes."

"Really? And what happened to Mr. Hickman?"

"For all I know he might be living in the attic. Never been up there myself. Can't climb ladders no more."

"No sense climbing them if you don't have to," DeMarco told him.

"My feelings exactly. Long as whoever's up there behaves hisself."

"How long have you been living there?" DeMarco asked. He and others had tried to locate Benny's father back when Benny was busted for the Golden Dragon robbery, and more recently in trying to track down Benny, all to no avail.

"A while," Szabo said.

"I bet you got a sweet deal on the house, didn't you?"

"I didn't get nothin'."

DeMarco kept silent as he tried to puzzle out that reply.

Soon Szabo completed his statement. "Don't belong to me."

*Aha*, DeMarco thought. Szabo's name wasn't on the deed. He probably had some old sins shadowing him, crimes the law had forgotten but he hadn't. Old retributions he still feared. Men like that learn how to hide in plain sight, no credit cards, no cell phones, men grown meek and embarrassed by their younger selves' transgressions.

DeMarco drove in silence for another five minutes. Szabo had apparently come out of hiding to share information that was weighing heavy on him. Plus he was a naturally taciturn man, and taciturn men do not like to be pushed.

Three miles out of town, DeMarco said, "Would you mind sitting back in the seat a bit, Mr. Szabo? If I have to stop all of a sudden, you're likely to bang your head on the windshield."

"Then don't stop all of a sudden," Szabo said, and budged not an inch.

"What if some fool pulls out in front of me?"

"I like to see where I'm going."

DeMarco smiled. Tried to relax. Every passing minute seemed like ten.

And finally Szabo came to his subject. "What are you looking at my son for?"

"We'd just like to talk to him."

"Unh-huh," the old man said. Then, a few seconds later, "Whatever it is, he probly done it."

"Is that right?"

"The boy never was no good. Sad to say but it's the truth. And in all likelihood he ain't about to start changing now."

DeMarco said nothing. Now it was coming. *Don't get in the way*.

"Me being so old when we had him was one thing. Other thing was his mother being how she was."

The old man's posture seldom moved a millimeter, forearms on his knees, eyes on the road. "I finally got myself a decent life," he said. "And then he comes back into the picture."

"I heard he was back in town."

"You heard more'n that or you wouldn't of gone looking for him. How come you sent a woman cop after him and didn't go yourself?"

"Because I'm not a trooper anymore. I'm a civilian. How did you hear about that incident?"

"Carrier pigeon."

DeMarco couldn't tell how much of what the old man said was truth and how much a cranky deflection. So he played along. "You keep pigeons?" he asked.

Now, for the first time since they had climbed into the car, Szabo turned his head a little and showed DeMarco a small, unfathomable smirk. "I read about you a while back. You're still a cop far as I'm concerned."

"And yet you came to see me."

"Like I said, I don't want nothin' to do with him no more. All he ever brung me was worry. Plus he and Loretta don't get along."

"And Loretta is his mother?"

"Ha," Szabo said. "His mother put herself in the grave a long time ago. Whoring and heroin. Never a healthy combination. Course, you already know that, don't ya?"

DeMarco chose to keep silent. Soon they would be entering French Creek Township. And a few minutes later, Ten-Right Road.

Then Szabo said. "OC didn't deserve to go out the way he did."

"So I've heard." DeMarco was walking a fine line now; say too much and Szabo might spook. Say too little and he might suspect that he holds better cards than the law does, more information, and clam up. The point was to keep him talking.

"I know that the O is for Oscar," DeMarco told him, "but what does the C stand for?"

"Carl. After a great-uncle. Lifelong drunkard. And look at what my brother turned out to be."

"Interesting," DeMarco said. "And what's your middle name?"

"Trumbull. 'Cause I was born in Trumbull County. So what am I supposed to turn into—a piece of real estate?"

"Huh," DeMarco said, and laughed a little.

"I was overly fond of drink myself," the old man continued. "Hell, I used to swim in it."

That confession was followed by another long pause. DeMarco did nothing to interrupt it. Silence, he knew, is its own conversation. It can speak of contentment, fear, uncertainty, ignorance... It is spoken in a language everybody knows but few attempt to understand. DeMarco, however, was fluent in silence. He waited.

"For a while there," the old man eventually said, "I blamed myself for the way the boy was. Like there was something wrong with my sperm from all that weed and bad whiskey and stuff. But I been off it all now for most of twenty years. And he's old enough to know what he's doing, ain't he? He just don't want to help hisself. It's almost like he enjoys stepping in the shit all the time."

Again, DeMarco asked no questions. He let the miles roll past. Wondered if his own father would have straightened up if he had lived long enough.

"You need to turn here," Szabo said.

DeMarco looked up, hit his turn signal and pumped the brake. Szabo put a hand out to the dashboard and caught himself just in time. "I thought you said you knew where you was going."

"It's been a long time. Sorry."

"You'd a been a helluva lot sorrier with my head bleeding all over your seats. The way you drive, that's a lawsuit just waiting to happen."

DeMarco did not respond. He breathed evenly, heart racing just a bit. At the former Hickman home he eased into the driveway. The house had been painted recently, a too-bright yellow but neatly done. Two flower beds that had not been there in Hickman's day now ran along the front of the house, both cleaned out and showing a deep brown of new mulch, tulips and gladiolas and hosta pushing up through the ground. *A woman's touch*, he told himself.

He brought the car to a stop and slipped the gearshift into Park. Szabo was still sitting forward, staring straight ahead. DeMarco asked, "Has Benny been living here, Mr. Szabo?"

"Not hardly," the old man said. "You want to come in and look around, be my guest. You won't find nothing."

Both men sat silent for a few moments. Then Szabo continued. "He's been coming and going since they let him out of that prison, helping himself to whatever he wants. Rifling Loretta's purse even. Did my own pockets one time when I was sleeping, my pants laying right there on the floor. The boy thinks because we're old he can do us that way. And I guess he's right. Ain't a damn thing we can do to stop him without risking a beating or two."

There it was, a sliver of opportunity. "Do you think that's what happened to your brother? Benny beat him to death?"

"What I think don't really matter here. Hasn't for a long time now."

"It matters to me, sir. How long since you've seen him last?"

Once again, Szabo looked his way. "What day is this?"

"This is Monday, April 19."

Szabo turned his gaze forward again. "Been quite a few days then. He come by to grab a old duffel bag I had. First time he didn't try to hit me up for everything I had on me."

"What was the duffel bag for?"

"Said he had a job up in Michigan. Seems like you might already know about that."

DeMarco waited.

"I said to him, how you plan on getting there? And he says, I'm driving. I says, whose car, and he says that's none of your goddamn business. And I ask him how he's paying for it and he says, if you know what's good for you, you'd better just keep your mouth shut for a change. You think you can pull that off?" Something glimmered in the old man's eye. Grizzled cheeks flushed with either embarrassment or anger.

"Mr. Szabo, do you know where your son is now?"

"It's a helluva thing to have to turn against your own family. It's an awful thing to do, and I ain't doing it with a clean conscience, I can tell you that. Thing is, what happened to OC was the last straw. Just has to be that way."

Again DeMarco kept silent.

Szabo put a gnarled hand on the door handle, pushed the lever and popped open the door. He turned as if to slide out but went no further, and held firm to the handle. "Back before he went off to prison he always used to hide out when need be at that Westinghouse place over in Sharon. He called it his cooling-down place. That's the only place I can think he might be after what all he done. First to that woman cop of yours, and now this."

"Sir, who told you about what happened to her?"

"I told you once already. I get all my news by carrier pigeon." He shoved the door open. Held to the doorframe to pull himself out and erect. Then he turned and, standing sideways to DeMarco, bent forward a little and spoke out of the corner of his mouth. "Any chance you'd want to tell me what he done up there? That job he had in Michigan?"

DeMarco blew out a breath. "It's bad, Mr. Szabo. Very bad."

Old man Szabo nodded. "Figures he'd come to that sooner or later." He held himself motionless for several seconds. Then gripped the top edge of the door and pulled himself as straight as he could stand. "Said he was taking OC up there with him," he said without looking back.

DeMarco dove across the console for a better view of the old man. "Benny took his uncle to Michigan with him?"

"Whatever it was they got into up there, you can bet your last dollar my brother didn't have nothin' to do with it."

"Sir," DeMarco said, "if we could talk for just another minute or so—"

"I thank you for the ride," Szabo said. He shut the door and shuffled away.

# V

WHAT IS BORN WILL DIE,
WHAT HAS BEEN GATHERED WILL BE DISPERSED,
WHAT HAS BEEN ACCUMULATED WILL BE EXHAUSTED,
WHAT HAS BEEN BUILT UP WILL COLLAPSE,
AND WHAT HAS BEEN HIGH WILL BE BROUGHT LOW.

# EIGHTY-THREE

## INTO THE DEPTHS WHERE THE NIGHT CRAWLERS GO

From 1922 through 1984, the Westinghouse Electric Corporation employed the majority of Sharon, Pennsylvania's working adults, as many as ten thousand at a time. Covering fifty-eight acres and nearly 1.5 million square feet of space, the plant produced, at various times, gun barrels, Vulcan trucks, Ritz and Twombly cars, torpedoes, machine guns, and huge transformers. At a half mile in length, it was the longest single building in the country. It was also the source of the PCBs that still polluted the groundwater that found its way into the Shenango River and into the drinking water of seventy-five thousand Shenango Valley residents.

Attempts in the past few years to revitalize the city's economy and curb the exodus of its population brought a few private businesses in as small-space tenants of the vast building—a dance studio for children, a metal sculptor's studio, a music recording studio, and a gemstone store with a Reiki massage room. For the most part the plant remained as it was the day it was cleaned out and shut down—gargantuan in its hollow height and breadth and length and scope, awesome in its silent uselessness.

When in full operation, the plant was comprised of several

sections, squarish two-story buildings used principally as offices, and massive interconnected manufacturing sections, long and narrow and high, lined with windows and topped with a translucent dome roof. The offices were all bare now, the paint flaking off like leprous skin, windows filmed with decades of grime, dusty floors where men and women had sat at their desks and phones and enjoyed the fruits of prosperity. In 1984 those workers had been unceremoniously informed of a temporary suspension of operations; they left their desks immediately and went home without cleaning out their drawers or lockers, expecting to return to work soon. They never did.

The former manufacturing sections on the ground floor were great concrete tunnels long and wide enough to hold three football games at the same time, the goalposts lined up end to end. In most of them the heavy equipment had been cleared out and sold for scrap, but the heavy steel support beams remained, and in some of the sections enormous yellow hooks weighing over a thousand pounds each, used to lift and move multiton transformers along the production lines, still hung from beams beneath the forty-feet-high dome ceilings. Puddles of water formed on the concrete floor after every rainstorm, having dripped from cracks in that ceiling or blown through broken windows.

The below-ground floor was a warren of dark, dirty rooms, wire cages, and abandoned boilers. Below this floor were the "tunnels," which were not tunnels at all but silent, dark, decaying corridors with rooms of various sizes opening on each side, including one cavernous one-hundred-by-one-hundred-foot room, approximately eighty feet high. Here, with the walls and ceiling honeycombed with huge blocks of soundproofing material, enormous transformers were moved into place on railroad tracks, then tested before being shipped out to buyers.

The existence of the plant and some of its history were known to DeMarco and his team, though vaguely. No one on his team had ever entered the building before that sunny morning. Flores, who on doctor's orders was permitted no strenuous activity, was allowed only a quick peek inside the front lobby before being stationed outside in Jayme's car. She and two other officers, one from the township force and another from the city police, were positioned at different external points to provide surveillance should Benny Szabo or anyone else attempt to enter or exit the building. The dozen or so tenants and maintenance employees had all been alerted the previous night upon receipt of the search warrant. The building that morning was supposed to be empty.

A representative of the corporation that now owned the building and was refurbishing it bit by bit in an attempt to persuade more tenants of the building's potential unlocked the heavy metal door at a side entrance, directed DeMarco and his team to the main lobby, gave them a quick, unsolicited sketch of the plant's history, then drove away to enjoy a Grand Slam breakfast in town. The interior search team consisted of DeMarco, Jayme, and Boyd, an additional state police trooper and an officer from the city's police department.

Initially the corridor leading away from the attractive refurbished lobby was well lit, the floor smooth and clean and polished as an example to prospective tenants of how elegant their own spaces could look. At the first stairwell, DeMarco cautioned his team, "If you hear or see anybody besides the five of us, assume that it's Szabo. And assume that he's armed. Text me immediately, maintain a safe position, and wait for backup."

He waited for a question, but none came. "Anybody have any questions or concerns?" he asked.

Only the trooper and patrol officer spoke, both whispering, "No, sir."

"Check your flashlights."

Five flashlights blinked on. Blinked off.

DeMarco nodded. Smiled at Jayme. Then went through the double doors and down toward the unlighted tunnels, with Jayme two stairs behind him, and Boyd behind her. Jayme and Boyd peeled off at the first underground level, one turning right, the other left, leaving DeMarco descending alone. Above them, the city's patrol officer proceeded along the first floor hallway, working his way from room to room in decent lighting. The trooper ascended to the top floor, where morning light through the grimy windows rendered his flashlight necessary only to illuminate the corners.

DeMarco had not intended to check the tunnels alone. But neither had he expected there to be so many points of potential egress from the building. He had been told that all but two of the entrances were securely locked. But a cursory check of the outside of just the main building revealed a couple of places on the ground floor where a man could squeeze into or out of the building through a broken or loose window. An agile individual could also scale the wall to the roof using sills and lintels and pipes as handholds, so DeMarco had had to sacrifice team members for exterior surveillance, with each of the three outside responsible for keeping an eye on a thousand square yards of linear and vertical surface—which still left acres of walls unguarded.

What he really needed was a team of thirty people to sweep the building from end to end to end. But to reassign that many personnel based on a suspicion was something no department was willing to do. Cars could be dispatched if necessary, but first there had to be some evidence to justify a full-fledged operation. For now all they had was the guess of an old, bitter, frightened man.

Off the main floor, all was dust and debris. And where there was dust there were footprints. But no way to tell which were Szabo's, if any of them were. A two-person security team spent every night in the building, wandering the halls from floor to floor, and probably, DeMarco knew, making so much noise that anyone hiding inside could easily evade them. Chances were they were either moonlighting cops or retired cops or otherwise unemployable misanthropes. In any case, if they had been at the job very long, they had likely grown lackadaisical in their nightly inspections. Maybe walked around with earbuds blasting music to keep them awake. Probably ignored the darkest and creepiest parts of the building. Fifty-eight acres multiplied by four floors equaled way too much acreage to cover in a night, too many dark rooms, nooks, crevices, crannies and crawl spaces.

Surprisingly, DeMarco encountered no graffiti, which suggested that the building was at least visually imposing against casual or impulsive penetration. But that did not exclude the possibility that somebody who had been familiar with the place for over a decade hadn't found a number of ways to sneak in and out, places DeMarco in his initial inspection had not noticed.

And Benny Szabo was nothing if not a sneak. A sneak and a weasel. A slimy night crawler who time and again had proved that he would do anything for a few bucks. And now he was afraid. Even if he hadn't done what DeMarco was certain he did in Michigan, Szabo had definitely committed assault. He had hidden behind Eugene Miklos's front door, beer bottle in hand as he listened to Flores ask about him. He would not have known her identity but he would have recognized the tone of her voice. He recognized authority when he heard it.

If he had any brains at all he had been watching from a higher point in the building when the team's vehicles arrived that morning. Then had quickly scurried away to a hiding place he had picked out earlier. Either that or, like the weasel he was, he had raced straight to his favored exit and ran for the weeds where the law dogs couldn't sniff him out. But if he had chosen to remain in the building, he would be tense and alert now. There were lots of things lying around that could be used to knock somebody out, lots of broken two-by-fours and pipes and heavy chunks of metal. He had a nest somewhere inside the building, of that DeMarco was certain. Might even have an arsenal tucked into his little hidey-hole. If discovered, he would run if he could, but if he could not run, he would fight back, just as he had when DeMarco had arrested him many years earlier. All weasels will fight when cornered. Viciously.

DeMarco moved slowly and deliberately through what seemed to him a labyrinth, a long, heavy flashlight burning in his left hand, a 9mm pistol in his right. Every closed door, every open doorway, every black unfilled space could be hiding a murderer. And DeMarco was not going to approach Szabo as he had approached his last murderer, not rashly or without due consideration. He was in no mood to get shot again, nor conked on the hood or slammed in the grill with a board. Szabo was indeed a weasel but even small, solitary animals should not be underestimated. DeMarco was not going to make that mistake again. If he did, and failed again, it was doubtful that the handsome Mr. Death would come a second time to gather him up. Not in this place. DeMarco felt no angel's presence here, only darkness and dirt and danger.

# EIGHTY-FOUR

## The light toward which the darkness creeps

A long, tedious forty minutes had passed and all Flores had seen was nothing. Nothing but uninterrupted and motionless wall. Her eyes stung from staring into the sun rising above the far end of the building, and from raising and lowering the field glasses to her unprotected eyes. And her leg ached. The console in Jayme's car did not allow her to slide to the right so that she could stretch out her braced leg. So she popped open the door and turned in the seat and put her leg outside. There, that was better. But this assignment was still bullshit. Sitting in a car and staring at a wall? Everything was bullshit.

Okay, all right, she had screwed up again. She should not have approached Szabo on her own. Okay, she recognized that mistake. She owned it. So now she was benched. A freaking spectator. Was it ever going to change? Was she ever going to get another chance to prove what she could do?

What a roller coaster her emotions were! Sometimes she loved DeMarco like a father and sometimes she resented him. Sometimes she was jealous of Jayme and sometimes she felt nothing but love and admiration for her. She liked Boyd, maybe more than she should, but he was inside and she wasn't and that made her resent him as well. What a stew of emotions she had become!

Some stew would be good right now. Her mother's stew. The black beans and corn, the albondigas and chipotle salsa, the chunks of potato and squash. Damn, she should have brought something to eat. Maybe she could flag down some little kid off the sidewalk and send him over to the GetGo for a couple of spicy beef sticks and a—

Hey, what was that?

There it was again! A shadow at the ground floor window. There and then gone.

No, wait, it was still there. Was that somebody's head? Somebody at the corner of the window peeking out?

She raised the field glasses, focused in on the window. No, nothing there now.

But she had seen something, damn it. She was sure of it. And who could it be but Szabo? Had to be. Why would anybody else be so furtive?

She turned a bit more on her seat, slid out and stood beside the car. There it was again—she hadn't imagined it! Was he looking her way now?

And in the next instant the shadow grew, rose higher on the window. *He's standing…* Then it flicked across the glass and was gone. *He's running!*

And then she was running too, swinging her left leg out in an arc, right leg thrusting ahead. As she ran she gripped her cell phone in her left hand, glanced from it to the building as she tried to thumb type a text. Then gave up until she was standing at the building, scanning the windows, seeing nothing amiss.

She texted DeMarco: South wall ground floor face at window. One of you? And waited.

Nothing. No response.

She waited another minute, which felt like ten. Still no response.

Maybe the phones didn't work inside. Too much steel and

concrete. If that were true, nobody would know that she had seen him. She had seen that slimy little worm at the window. And nobody inside was going to know about it.

She scanned the exterior wall. Hurried along it in one direction, searching for a point of entry. Nothing. Then returned to her original position, the window where she had seen the shadow of his head and shoulders. She put her face to the dirty window, cupped hands around her eyes. Was that a flicker of movement on the other side of the room? Maybe. Maybe not.

She looked at her phone's screen. Nothing. No response to her text.

"Son of a bitch!" she muttered.

She pulled the flashlight from her belt and smashed out a pane in the window, the glass tinkling as it fell to the floor, the noise quickly swallowed by the emptiness inside. She peered through the opening, was surprised to see how much illumination could enter through filmy windows, the open doorway across the room a rectangle of muted light. She reached through the broken pane, felt around for and finally found the small locking lever centered atop the frame, pushed it with a thumb until she felt her thumb would break. Then the lock gave way with a rusty creak. She eased her arm out past the jagged glass, placed the heels of both palms against the exterior side of the frame, heaved and grunted and shoved till the layers of paint and grime split open.

She raised the window as far as it would go, made a space maybe fifteen inches high and twenty wide. Stuck the flashlight and half of her arm inside and waved the light from wall to wall and across the floor. A floor stripped of its tiles, leaving only the wavy pattern of old tile cement. Three buckets lined up against the far wall. Four still-wrapped bundles of new tile. The walls looked newly painted. The ceiling newly plastered. Dusty footprints all over the floor, leading in and out of the doorway.

She shut off the flashlight and slipped it into her belt, stretched to get hold of the inside of the sill with both hands. Then shifted her weight to the good leg and leapt up, diving head and shoulders through the opening so that her belly caught on the bottom frame, legs dangling off the ground. She paused for a moment to squint again through the now dimmer light, then took a deep breath and crawled and wriggled and dragged herself inside, a fiery tracer of pain shooting up her leg as she did so.

# EIGHTY-FIVE

LIKE A GASTROPOD IN SEARCH OF SLIME

For forty minutes DeMarco crept along through the tunnels at a snail's pace and assumed that those above him were doing more or less the same, though perhaps in less filthy and better illuminated surroundings. The sluggish pace, though necessary in such dimness, made him wish he had a snail's shell for protection, plus tentacles that could turn his eyeballs from side to side and to the rear, and another set that could sniff the floor for Szabo's scent. Unfortunately he had none of that equipment, only a flashlight whose beam seemed intimidated by the darkness, leaving him forced to shuffle along like a blind and naked snail with a sticky foot.

His neck and shoulders ached from the tension of having his spine and skull exposed, but to relax was to invite an ambush. He worried less about what lay ahead in the flashlight's beam than in what might be approaching in the pitch-darkness behind him or off to the side. The air was cooler there twenty feet below ground, but it lay heavy in his lungs. Went in thick and dark and came out darker. He paused frequently to listen. Had something rustled behind him? Was that a footstep's squeak?

The so-called tunnels, he soon realized, bore no resemblance to actual tunnels. Just neglected corridors branching off in every direction and opening frequently into disemboweled rooms large and small, all right angles and corners. Chips of paint dangling from ceilings and walls like tiny tattered prayer flags in the mountains of Tibet. Chunks of ceiling plaster littering the floors. Splotches and streaks of rust bleeding through once-white paint. Here and there a puddle of stagnant water on the floor. All that was missing, he told himself, was the scurry of rodents and cockroaches. But there were none, not even spiders. Only paint chips and dust to eat.

DeMarco could not imagine what had gone on in these rooms. Whatever the captains of industry had ordained. He had been told that some ten thousand torpedoes had been designed and built and tested in the facility during World War II, torpedoes that had eventually sunk ships and blasted souls out of their flesh. He could not remember ever being in a place so thick with darkness.

At one point he thought he might have gotten turned around. Had entered a room, worked his way around the walls, looking for hidden alcoves and niches. Found a space that had worried him until he painted every inch of it with light, a hole in the floor stuffed with rags, pipes emanating a few inches above the floor, more sticking out from a wall. A bathroom. Empty. But upon coming out into the larger room and into the corridor, had he turned the wrong way? Was he following the dusty tracings of his own footsteps now?

The vibration in his pocket startled him as much as a shout would have, so that his whole body jerked and tightened. Quickly he fished the phone from his pocket. Read *Text from Dani*. Opened it and read: South wall ground floor face at window. One of you? It took him a couple of seconds to make sense of it. Then he shoved the phone back into his pocket and, whipping the flashlight beam back and forth, up and down, plunged in what he could only hope was the right direction. *Stairs!* he told himself, his heart racing now, pulse beginning to drum. *Where are the damn stairs!*

# EIGHTY-SIX

IN PURSUIT OF THE SHADOW OF SELF-RESPECT

She moved as quickly as she could through the empty room, then peeked out into the hallway. Nobody. Nothing. Some kind of rumbling noise in the distance. Traffic? The blood and adrenaline roaring in her head? Or just the building itself grumbling?

She could see clearly now, no need for the flashlight. She laid a hand on her holstered weapon, let her thumb slip down to the safety. Stepped out into the hallway and froze in a half crouch, right knee bent, left leg stretched out to her side so that her legs formed an isosceles triangle atop the shiny floor. Cocked her head and listened. Cocked her head the other way. Only the dull, muted rumbling.

She straightened her back. Two options, right or left. Well, three options really, but going back to Jayme's car was out of the question. She knew what some of the guys at the barracks had called her behind her back, just because she had been so exacting and, okay, maybe a little too brusque at times. *Bitchpatcher.* Yeah, well, this bitchpatcher had the long eye on the subject, and she wasn't about to let a chance to go habeas grabus on him slip out of her hands.

Her motto at the academy, whether on the obstacle course or while dealing with the mutters of other cadets, had been *never retreat.* There had been no end to having to prove herself. She was always being sold short. Besides, she had already committed herself by abandoning her surveillance position. So she said it again now, a steely whisper. "Never retreat."

Question was, which way to go? The light seemed brighter to her right. So go left, into the darkness. That was where someone like Benny Szabo would go. Rats always run for the darkness. Cockroaches too. Szabo was the embodiment of both. If given the chance, she would shoot one and step on the other. The staples in her scalp throbbed.

Within five minutes she had lost all sense of direction. Too many rooms, too many sets of double swinging doors. And after the last set the surroundings changed significantly, no more new tile, no more finished walls. The light had diminished by half. *Okay, good.* That was the way Szabo would run. She kept moving, each forward lurch making her left shoulder dip. And eventually she came to a T. Peeked around one corner and then the other. Which way?

Maybe she should try texting again. She eased her left hand into a pocket but kept her head turning, eyes focused down the long hallway. And there, yes…something anomalous. What was that? She leaned forward and squinted. Yes, there was somebody or something there, down at the end of the long hallway, a darkness against the wall. It was just a silhouette but…it looked smaller than Szabo. *But that's at least fifty feet away*, she told herself. *Of course he looks smaller.* But no, it couldn't be him, it was just a wisp of a thing. And for a moment she had the strangest feeling that it was looking at her.

Then the shadow moved across the wall and disappeared to the right. Flores jerked her left hand off the cell phone in her pocket and slapped her right hand over the holster, gripped the butt of the pistol and, with her scalp throbbing with the urgency of Morse code, hobbled in pursuit of that shadow as fast as her broken body would allow.

# EIGHTY-SEVEN

TRIAL AND ERROR

t took DeMarco a lot longer than he would have liked to find the
stairs and race up to the ground floor. Longer still to catch his breath
and orient himself and determine direction by glancing up at the light
through the high windows. He had emerged onto the ground floor
far from the attractive front entrance and its fancy lobby. The walls
were of white-painted concrete here, the floors of gray concrete, a
high-peaked metal ceiling held aloft by fat metal beams and a series of
thinner metal spiderwebs. A row of high windows, catwalks running
along both sides of the room. The place was enormous. Down at the
far end to his left, at least fifty or sixty yards away, several RVs were
parked against a wall. Also a few vintage cars, boats covered in tarps.
They looked tiny from where he stood. *Storage*, he told himself.

No sign of Szabo. In the other direction, corridors branched off
from each side of the room. DeMarco started in that direction but
took only three steps before thinking, *The RVs! He could be hiding
in one of them.*

He crossed toward the RVs quickly but alert, eyes fixed forward.
Took out his cell phone and stole glances at the keyboard while typ-
ing a group text to his team: Dani saw something in south window
ground floor. I'm near there now. Might flush him your way. Stay sharp.

# EIGHTY-EIGHT

## SOMETHING IN HER EYE

The size of the room stunned her, swallowed her, was too vast to be believed. The space was huge and everything in it was huge. The standing and overhead beams, the giant yellow hook so thick and ominous hanging from its yellow bar, everything was huge but for tiny her. Flores felt like an ant in the Astrodome, a speck of dirt on the threshold of infinity. And where was Szabo? The enormous concrete floor was empty, not a person or thing or—

An echoing clang. It seemed to emanate from above. She lifted her gaze and swept it side to side and saw him then, saw a man who must be Benny Szabo fifteen feet up on the far wall, crawling quickly up a steel ladder inside a circular metal cage.

"Hey!" she yelled. Her voice echoed once and was swallowed. But he turned, looked at her, then climbed faster. She lurched across the floor, felt blood rushing to her face, tightening the skin, and yelled, "Freeze, asshole! Don't move or I will shoot you down!"

He kept climbing. A full story and a half above her, he crawled out onto the metal catwalk and raced off to her left. Where was he going? Moving quickly but awkwardly in his direction, Flores whipped her gaze ahead of him down the catwalk, her eyes stinging again, watering. The distance between them was increasing. She was going to lose him.

The catwalk ran behind a large yellow box of some kind, a crane operator's control station, to emerge on the other side onto a balcony. Set in the center of that balcony was a black rectangle. An open doorway. If he reached that he would disappear into the bowels of the building again. Another failure for her. And he *would* reach it if she didn't do something *now*.

Ahead of him, descending a few feet from the crane operator's station, was another caged ladder, but she could never get to it in time. Even if she could, climbing that ladder would be nearly impossible with an unbendable leg.

She stopped in the middle of the floor. Took aim at his skinny chest. Slid the barrel an inch ahead to the left. And fired.

The bullet pinged off the metal rail in front of him, though she heard only the blast of the gunshot itself and saw the spark of contact. Szabo stopped abruptly but only long enough to shoot a glance at her, then started running again. Again she took aim.

But then the strangest thing happened. The strangest thing she had ever seen. For just a moment, between the space of one rapid blink to clear her eyes and the next, she thought she saw something appear on the catwalk ahead of Szabo. Something both shadowy and quivering and impossible at the corner of the control station.

Szabo slid, stopped, went down onto his knees. Had he seen it too? He stared straight ahead, momentarily frozen. Then turned to shoot a quick glance down at Flores hobbling toward him as fast as she could. He stood again and started forward, gingerly this time, his back to the wall, eyes on that spot where the apparition had appeared.

Flores pushed herself harder, still thinking, *What the hell? What the hell?*

Szabo reached the caged ladder and swung himself down into it, descending but with his eyes looking up, then back down at Flores angling toward the center of the floor, then upward again.

Flores could see nothing on the catwalk now, only the shimmer of liquid in her watery eyes, and she did not look in that direction again. Szabo would hit the floor a good ten seconds before she could reach him, and there was another open doorway directly below the one on the balcony. But if she could get herself in the right position, he would be running *into* the path of her bullets and not away from them, and she still had one stopper in the chamber and six in the clip.

# EIGHTY-NINE

A muted voice screaming *Freeze asshole don't move!* Was that Flores? *For Christ's sake, what was she doing in here?* His answer was a single gunshot, muffled but unmistakable. DeMarco had been in the business too long not to recognize that sound, had logged too many hours on firing ranges outside and inside of buildings. The sound stopped him for an instant, the double doors of the landing only six steps ahead, only three long strides. But in that instant he recognized that he was breathing too hard, his heart thrashing as if a bird were trapped inside, his mouth suddenly sour and dry as if he had bitten into a lime, and he recognized too that another gunshot would happen any second now, before he could reach the double doors, would happen inevitably and was beginning to happen even now, its possibility being born in the dull echo of its predecessor.

And it came, but amplified beyond all possibility, not the muted thump of a gunshot but a thunderous crashing sound that shoved the double doors open so that a heavy blast of hot air raced through and nearly knocked him over. It shook the stairs and vibrated throughout his body and pelted his face with particles of dust, knocked paint flakes and plaster from the walls and ceiling. No, that was not a gunshot. Not even close. It was followed by another crash and another tremor, though both smaller than the first.

Breathless, left hand to his mouth and nose as he moved through the cloud of suffocating dust, DeMarco entered the room from the very doorway Szabo had been running toward. The first thing he saw was the giant yellow hook lying on its side on the floor forty feet away, the slack in the thick chain still weaving back and forth, the links still clinking. "What the hell?" he muttered, then immediately thought, *Where's Dani?*

He stepped sideways and crept closer with gun drawn as he moved to see around the hook. And then he spotted her, and she was down, maybe ten yards beyond the hook. Lying on her right hip, raised up on an elbow, left leg stretched out straight. She raised her left hand to him and waved. The crash had knocked her off her feet. *She's okay. Thank God she's okay.* He looked around for Szabo, but only for a few moments, because somehow in those syrupy and unreal moments, in that slowing *clink clink clink* of the chain, he knew exactly where to find him.

# NINETY

*E PUR SI MUOVE,* MOFO

Accoring to the safety inspector, there was no way the hook could have fallen of its own accord. Too many precautions in place. It hadn't moved in over thirty-five years.

*And yet it moves,* Galileo had allegedly mumbled to himself. *E pur si muove.* DeMarco had no Inquisition to consider, no torture looming. Whether one claimed that the Earth did or did not revolve around the sun, and whether one claimed that the hook could or could not have fallen, to him the obvious was incontrovertible: the Earth does, the hook had.

The inspector also concluded that Flores's warning shot had not ricocheted off the rail to strike one of the cables or to carom into the crane operator's box to somehow release the tension holding the giant hook aloft. Nothing was amiss. All locks were still locked, all levers in place. "Equipment failure somewhere," was his conclusion. "I don't know where, can't find any evidence of it anywhere, but there's no other explanation possible. Time and gravity, that's all I can figure."

DeMarco's entire team, and every other individual summoned to the scene that day, was stunned by the obvious. DeMarco suggested that his team leave the building before the crane operator arrived and power was restored to the control station to lift the hook out of its concrete crater and above what was left of Benny Szabo's body. In the parking lot outside, with the sun nearly at zenith and too bright in their eyes, the mica in the sidewalk glinting, DeMarco kept only Flores and Boyd behind with him and Jayme, and only long enough to tell them, "So here's the problem. The only person who might have told us who hired Szabo was Szabo. So the real killer is still out there."

"Morrison might crack," Jayme said.

"I don't know," DeMarco answered. "I have a feeling it's personal with him. He sees himself as an avatar of integrity. But it's a personal brand of integrity. And he's going to hold on to it for as long as he can, especially when he finds out that Szabo is out of the picture."

"In that case," she said, "we need to find out the identity of at least one of his other friends. We just need to find that one weak link."

DeMarco nodded, they all nodded. "It's not the what, it's the how," he said.

Boyd said, "What about that bar up in Michigan? Maybe there's still somebody around who would remember his group."

"Possibly," DeMarco said.

"Or that woman from Jensen's grocery store," Jayme added. "Or the owner of whichever cabin they rented. Maybe they hired a fishing guide. There could be a lot of information up there that we can tap into."

DeMarco turned his gaze to Boyd. And Boyd said, "I'll start making the calls as soon as I get back."

"Tell Bowen you can't do it all on your own."

"He'll understand."

DeMarco shrugged, then nodded. "Okay. That's it then."

Boyd nodded in return, then headed for his vehicle.

Not until Boyd was out of earshot did DeMarco look in Flores's direction. Throughout the conversation she had said nothing, had leaned against the fender of Jayme's car and stared at her feet, her trembles barely perceptible, her exhalations little hisses of air.

One quick glance at Flores, then DeMarco turned to Jayme. She was already looking at him, already waiting. She said, "You mind running Dani back to her place? I have a couple of things I need to do in town first."

He smiled. She was so smart, so quick. Sometimes he thought she must be able to read his thoughts. It was scary. "No problema," he said.

# NINETY-ONE

BESIDE A COLONY OF THE DAMMED

He waited until they had left both Sharon and Hermitage behind before he said anything. He chose to take what he called "the scenic route" back to Mercer, nine miles of winding country road past woods and a small pond that had formed where a colony of beavers had dammed a stream. The route would take a few minutes longer than the direct route into town; would give him a few minutes longer with her. He hoped the relative solitude would calm her as it did him.

She was the first to speak. She sat buckled in but with her chin on her chest, shoulders hunched. She kept her eyes on the dashboard. "I know I blew it again. I'm sorry. You told me to stay in the car and I didn't."

He looked at her. Looked back to the road. If necessary he would pull over beside the beaver pond. Would put the windows down so they could hear the birds. "What if you had?" he asked.

She cocked her head his way.

"There's a very good chance we never would have found him," he told her. "That place is immense."

Her smile was small and crooked and uncertain. She turned to look out the side window.

"Can you tell me what happened?" he asked. "You're going to get questioned anyway. You might as well start with me."

She was silent for a few moments. Could see her own reflection in the glass, and through it the passing trees. "Can I ask you a question first?"

"Fire away," he said.

Again she paused before speaking. "That stuff you told me about your NDE. Does that mean that you believe in ghosts?"

"Ghosts?" he said. "I've never seen a ghost. What I saw were spirits. Ghosts are spirits here in this world, right?"

"I guess," she said.

"I only see them in dreams or when I was in a coma. So it wasn't really in this world, if you know what I mean."

She lapsed into silence again. He said, "There's a beaver dam coming up not far from here. It just popped up one day. Have you seen it yet?"

She nodded.

"I can stop if you'd like to see it again."

She turned at the waist. "The last time you saw Emma Barrie," she said, "what was she wearing?"

His eyebrows lifted, a suspicion forming in his brain. "How about you tell me," he said.

She thought for a moment before speaking. "Blue jeans, rolled up above the ankle. Bright pink socks. And a long-sleeve yellow T-shirt."

He nodded. Smiled. "The words *We Are the Future* were stenciled across the front of the T-shirt. In white glitter."

"How can that be?" she asked.

The plaintive tone of her question told him that she wasn't asking about the T-shirt. "Where did you see her?"

"It was just for a second. Just a blink. She was there and then gone. Up on the catwalk. I'm pretty sure Szabo saw her too."

*Carefully,* he told himself. "Why do you think that?"

"He stopped running across the catwalk all of a sudden. Then started climbing down instead of continuing toward the exit just a couple of yards away."

Now it was DeMarco's turn to let a few moments pass. "He started climbing *toward* you?"

"That's what I'm saying. Why would he do that?"

"What do you think?"

"I think he saw her too. And figured he'd rather take his chances with me."

DeMarco nodded. "And then what happened?"

"After he climbed down? He started toward the exit, but then for some reason he stopped and looked up at her again."

"What reason?"

"I don't know. But it was like… It was the way you might stop and turn around if somebody called out to you. That's what it felt like to me."

"You didn't hear anything?"

She shook her head. "I couldn't see her then either. It was only for that one second. But why else would he have stopped like that?"

"And he was right under the hook?"

She nodded. "But he was looking up at her. At where I had seen her. I don't think he had any idea where he was standing at that moment."

DeMarco pursed his lips. There was the beaver pond coming up. He drove slightly past it, slowing, checked his rearview mirror, then eased across the road onto a grassy pullout. Held his foot on the brake. "Do you want to get out?" he asked.

"Not really," she said.

He shut off the engine. "I saw a bald eagle here just last week. Right up there in that big tree."

She didn't even look. Kept staring out the side window.

"Did you see the hook fall?" he asked.

She nodded. Then turned to meet his gaze. "Do you think Emma could have done it? Made it fall?"

He took his time. Asked, "What do you want to believe, Dani?"

"I don't know."

He waited.

"It's scary to think that a ghost could do something like that."

"Then don't believe it."

Her forehead wrinkled, her mouth pinched into a frown.

He smiled. "'Veil after veil will fall,'" he told her, "'yet veil after veil will remain.' That's from the Buddha. He was a pretty smart guy."

"What does it mean?"

He shrugged. "It means we will never understand everything there is to understand. No matter how much we know or think we know, there is always more to learn."

"That's depressing," she said.

"Is it? I find it kind of, I don't know, energizing."

She studied him a moment longer before shifting in her seat again, and again she turned her gaze forward. "So what's going to happen now?" she asked.

"Captain Bowen will be calling or texting you soon. He'll need a detailed statement from you, since you're the only person who saw what happened."

"Should I tell him about seeing Emma? He's going to think I'm loony."

"My advice is that you tell him everything. You will need to justify why you discharged your weapon in there."

"He was running and I wanted to slow him down. I wasn't aiming to kill. I could have shot him if I'd wanted to."

"The captain will need to hear that."

"Okay," she said. "What about the rest?"

"The rest of what?"

"About me and, you know…working with you."

"Are you thinking about getting your old job back?"

"No way," she said.

"Then you might as well stick around with Jayme and me a while. Until something better comes along. This case isn't finished yet. After that… We've put the house on the market, so…"

She nodded. "Will you ever trust me again?"

"What is there not to trust, Dani?"

He looked away when the tears welled in her eyes. Turned the key and started the engine.

She said, "Which tree was it you saw that eagle in?"

# NINETY-TWO

## NESTING IN EVIL

More searching of the facility by the municipal and state police eventually uncovered Benny Szabo's nest. He had built it out of several old blankets, probably stolen off wash lines or out of the laundromat or the Goodwill box, plus fast-food wrappers, cardboard cups and greasy foam containers. These were all tagged and bagged and forwarded to the lab in Erie in hopes of finding prints and DNA from people other than Szabo himself—from individuals who might have been providing for him until he could find a secure way out of the county and points beyond. DeMarco and his civilian team did not participate in the search but were kept apprised of the discoveries by phone.

The nest had been laid at one of the highest points in the mammoth building, on a ledge of old wooden planks laid across two beams that met in a tight corner. Szabo had punched a hole in the sheet metal soffit so that he could lie on his blankets and look out across the city. Or maybe just for the light, though thin strings of it came in through the vents and other slender openings between roof and wall. The duffel bag he had taken from his father was there, likely used for a pillow, and in that bag was a long-handled screwdriver with a set of interchangeable heads, a fifteen-inch black enameled steel pry bar, a Sheetz gift card with $67 remaining from the original $400, a Walmart gift card with $140 remaining from the original $300, a pair of size 9 black sneakers—he was found to be wearing, at the time of his death, a pair of new Ozark Trail rubber boots—plus three pairs of sunglasses, two of them broken, a pair of inexpensive binoculars, a nineteen-inch nightstick with a flashlight and glass breaker and concealed stun gun, and a tight roll of bills totaling $3,420, held together with a blue rubber band. And a second roll of bills totaling $820. Held together with a red rubber band.

All told, it seemed a paltry sum to DeMarco. But then, any sum was paltry in exchange for a life, or, in this case, three lives. Plus Szabo had lost his own in the bargain. It struck DeMarco as odd that Judge Morrison would hand over $20,000 in a cashier's check for the girl, yet Szabo would be paid far less to kill her and her grandmother.

As for Oscar Szabo, he had been killed, DeMarco felt certain, for a few hours of playing the big shot in the Marigold bar. In all likelihood, Oscar died without ever knowing that he had helped to murder a little girl and her grandmother. Probably stood as watchout while Benny secretly stuffed the vent pipe. A second set of eyes, that's all he had been. And when, later, OC got fed up with hiding out, maybe living under the bridge until he found an opportunity to sneak away to his favorite bar, Benny knew just where to find him. Dragged him out of the bar and back to the bridge. But could no longer trust him to keep his mouth shut. And so, a rock to the head. Oscar never saw it coming. Never expected it. His own nephew. His own blood.

That scenario could never be proved now, but it was a damn good bet. On the other hand, Morrison's DNA sample was the only one of three they could verify. DeMarco had swabbed the man's cheek. So maybe Morrison was not directly complicit in the Michigan murders either. But he must surely know by now which of his friends was, or at least have his suspicions. That person would be whoever had lowballed Benny Szabo. Whoever had the most to lose in terms of fortune or reputation or marriage.

Jayme got started in the library that very afternoon, wading through newsprint and microfiche from ten years of stories that mentioned Judge Morrison. DeMarco spent that same time at his laptop, searching online while intermittently taking calls from the Scottville, Michigan, police, who were busy canvasing local residents for any recollections about Morrison and his friends' fishing trip a decade earlier. Flores spent the afternoon providing and repeating her statement to local law enforcement personnel, including two FBI agents from Erie working on behalf of the Marquette, Michigan, office.

The day was bright and clear, a balmy April afternoon with a high of sixty-two degrees. After school let out, the parks filled with noisy kids playing basketball and tennis and Frisbee, and with smaller children and their young parents enjoying the community's playgrounds. Citizens jogged for the first time all year, while others walked their dogs or simply found a sunny bench from which to enjoy the day. Homeowners spent some time tidying up their yards and flower beds, washing their cars, hosing the dust and debris from their porches and decks and driveways. Spring was in full bloom. Sap was flowing, blood was warming, a whole new crop of lusty teenagers were flexing their new muscles and flaunting their new curves.

For DeMarco, it could not have been a more somber day. Even after a long shower he could smell the dusty air of the Westinghouse facility in his nostrils. If he closed his eyes for a moment he could feel again the thunderous vibrations of the giant hook striking the floor, and the second tremor when the hook fell over. At one point he became short of breath and fished a baby aspirin from the bottle in the medicine cabinet, swallowed it and then returned to his laptop at the kitchen table, where he sat very still, working to modulate his breathing. Hero, stretched out underneath the table, must have felt his owner's discomfort, for he climbed to his feet and shoved his snout between DeMarco's knees.

DeMarco laid a few fingers between Hero's ears. "It's crazy, isn't it, boy?" he said. "We talk about how sacred life is, but when push comes to shove there are few who won't do whatever it takes to save their own skins. Because of course their lives are more sacred than other people's."

He knew full well that many individuals needed even less incentive to do harm. And that some people, mostly of the good variety, or at least preferring to think of themselves as good, will claim there exists a balance of good and evil in this world but that good will eventually triumph. DeMarco in his new enlightened state believed otherwise—that this Earth is not a place where good will triumph, except in the individual soul. On this beautiful planet he loved, with its breathtaking natural beauty shrinking daily, bloody struggle and ordeal and the machinations of darkness would always maintain the upper hand, or else where was the incentive to strive for something better? He understood now why stasis of any kind would not be tolerated, not on this planet or any other or in any dimension or plane of existence. The prohibition included the stasis of goodness. Even in heaven, the angels rebel.

"Evil exists, boy," he told patient Hero, "and it will always exist in abundance, if only to give the good an opportunity to shine." He scratched Hero's skull. "Truth #4."

# NINETY-THREE

## Low friends in high places

In the morning, work began anew on attempts to identify Morrison's friends. DeMarco believed, or wanted to believe, that Morrison, when confronted with a set of confirmed names, would tell what he knew. He would not rat out his friends but neither was he going to take the fall for one of them. He had made a serious error by giving one of them his full trust, but his reputation and ego would survive that error if, in the end, he confessed to it and had had no part in the larger conspiracy. He had been loyal to his friends, that's all. Had promised not to reveal their identities, and had kept that promise. Who could fault him for that? The fact that he could easily survive such a revelation, and even be admired for his loyalty, soured DeMarco's stomach.

For him, it all came down to the girl. To Emma. Her grandmother's death was in no way inconsequential, though the extinguishment of a life just beginning to flower would surely and to his mind fairly elicit more sympathy than a life already withering away. He felt a little guilty about feeling that way, and knew how the thought police would admonish him for it, but he really did not care. His thoughts were his own and always would be. The thought police could rail against the sins of fat shaming or race shaming or lifestyle shaming all they wanted, but never would they admit or recognize their own vituperous thought shaming. That's just the way it was and always would be. C'est la vie. If he wanted to mourn the death of a little girl more than that of a cranky old woman or a cowardly weasel, nobody was going to shame him into not doing it.

Chances were, only one of Morrison's friends had hired Benny Szabo and sent him to Michigan. The other one, and Morrison, might truly be in the dark in regard to who killed Emma Barrie. But which one was not in the dark? With two of the remaining suspects unknown, DeMarco and everyone else trying to identify them were chasing ghosts.

The break came at 4:19 in the afternoon, when Jayme came in through the back door, removed her shoes and light jacket, strode up to the kitchen table and slapped an eight-by-twelve-inch sheet of printer paper on the table. DeMarco leaned away from the laptop to look at the paper. A photocopy of a faded photograph from the *Philadelphia Inquirer.* Two men in tuxes standing side by side and grinning for the camera, their wives in gowns at their sides, each of them holding a flute of champagne. One of the men was Morrison, in his sixties then. The other one looked several years younger or just better preserved. The caption read: "Deputy Commissioner Jeff Thompkins and his beautiful wife, Laura, née Bader, enjoy this year's Black Tie Tailgate festivities with the commissioner's college pal District Court Judge James Morrison and his lovely wife, Linda."

Jayme jabbed a finger down on Laura's face. "Her family is worth zillions."

DeMarco looked up at her. "And him?"

"Before he married her? He was doing okay, divorce lawyer, had his own practice. But her family? She stands to inherit something like four hundred million."

"Interesting," he said. "It's a good place to start. Find anything on any other friends?"

"Tons of people Morrison schmoozed with over the years, but I had to go a lot farther back to find any 'pals.' Maybe the other two guys were the commissioner's friends and not Morrison's."

"Maybe," DeMarco said.

She pulled out a chair and sat down. "And how about you? Learn anything useful?"

"I made some calls to Michigan. A former bartender at the Bear Claw claims to remember serving two guys who came in with Emma's mother one night. Said she remembers them all standing at the bar laughing and drinking, even dancing in a threesome together, but that's it. Memories are vague. She remembers that one of them, though, was very tall."

"I can't really picture Morrison dancing with another man, can you?"

DeMarco shrugged. "Alcohol, like love, makes fools of us all."

"Like lust, you mean."

He smiled and thought, *Love too sometimes*.

"And that's it?" she asked. "I leave you here alone all day, and that's the best you came up with? Morrison and one of his buddies at the bar?"

"Preprandial stupidity. I haven't eaten since breakfast."

"Tell you what," she said. "I'll open up a can of wedding soup and make us a couple of grilled cheese sandwiches."

"Sounds perfect."

"*If*," she said, "you think about our next step. How do we proceed with Mr. Deputy Commissioner?"

"I'm already thinking about it."

She pushed back her chair and stood. "As soon as you stop thinking about it," she told him, and gave his forehead a gentle bump with the heel of her palm, "start talking."

# NINETY-FOUR

## THE BIRTH OF LITTLE CHIEF LONGVIEW

After the wedding soup and grilled cheese sandwiches, things were clearer for DeMarco. Their job was done. For all intents and purposes, he and Jayme and Flores had but one job to complete, if indeed they could: to identify Emma Barrie's biological father. DeMarco was forced to concede that perhaps this job could never be completed, and even if it were, the outcome would produce no positive results. Still, he wanted to try.

By phone he informed Captain Bowen about the Philadelphia connection. Bowen would call the FBI and turn the case over to them. As he should. Unemployment for Jayme and DeMarco would provide the exact same pay and benefits as the employment had, but their expenses would be lower and they would have more free time to sweep up dog hair.

When he told Jayme this, they were seated on the edge of the back porch, watching Hero sniffing at the wheels of the RV. The sun was an orange smear across the horizon, a fat juicy orange still spilling its juice behind the trees. Jayme nodded, and showed no signs of being surprised or disappointed. She asked, "What about Dani?"

"She'll be okay financially for a while."

"You know that's not what I'm talking about."

"I know," he said. Dani had some things to work out. And she would need their help in doing it. Who else did she have but him and Jayme and Boyd and Captain Bowen? They were her tribe. They were responsible for her now.

It was the first time in his life DeMarco had ever thought of himself as a member of a tribe. No, that wasn't true. With Ryan Jr. he had felt like the father of a small tribe coming into being. And how satisfying that had been! And then, after all those years of self-imposed solitary confinement, he'd met Huston, and felt unexpectedly in the company of a brother. Then that relationship too dissolved. Although neither had really dissolved. Ryan Jr. and Huston were still with him. Had never really left. Nobody he had known and loved had ever really left him.

"Okay," Jayme said, and interrupted his reverie. "We'll leave Dani for further discussion. What about Morrison?"

What a beautiful shade of orange the northern sky was assuming! He wished they had a more panoramic view, at least twenty miles or so to heighten the natural magnificence of a sunset. He said, "I wish we lived on the top of a hill somewhere. In a house with a wraparound porch. I would walk around that porch all day long, moving from chair to chair, sunrise to sunset."

"Won't be long now," she told him. "In fact if we don't find a house before closing, we'll be living in the RV."

He smiled. Loved the way she could reduce something difficult to its simplest form. And why not? He had been overthinking things for too long. Time to start dumping the ballast.

"Then we're done with Morrison?" she asked. "Write our report and smack the dirt from our hands and that's the end of it?"

"Well," he said, and let the sentence dangle.

"Don't leave me hanging, DeMarco."

He was already getting bored with doing nothing. It occurred

to him then that the key to happiness is to stay curious, stay interested. Happy people are never apathetic. To think that you already
know everything is not only foolish but deadening. There is always
something new that can be learned. And knowledge, if only for its
own sake, is a wonderful thing.

"I think we need one last meeting with the good judge," he
said. "For old time's sake."

"Oh, I was *so* hoping you would say that!"

# NINETY-FIVE

A JUDGMENT DEFERRED

Here's the deal," DeMarco told him. He had placed the call to Morrison while still seated on the porch, Jayme's hand resting atop his thigh, and gave the judge only time to say hello. "We know about your buddy Thompkins. And within the hour, so will the FBI. Unless you agree to meet with us *right now*."

His ultimatum was met with a long silence. Then Morrison said, "Allow me to finish my meal first. All right?"

"How long?" DeMarco asked.

"My beautiful dinner companion and I have only now sat down to eat. She made a lovely chicken marsala for us. With spice-rubbed potatoes. Brussel sprouts seared with mushrooms and bacon. The scent in the room is dizzying. I wish you could smell it."

DeMarco heard the resignation in Morrison's voice. And the quiet plea to keep his companion uninformed. "Eight tonight," DeMarco told him. "On the steps of the courthouse."

"Touché," Morrison answered, then ended the call.

The next couple of hours passed lugubriously, moving for DeMarco like a bear coming out of hibernation. But evening finally arrived, vibrating with expectation. 7:58 p.m. The air was cool, the traffic sparse out on Main Street, nonexistent on the side street running past the courthouse's main entrance. The town was quiet, the big lighted clock in the courthouse's tower silently ticking off the minutes, the hours, the years. DeMarco and Jayme and Flores stood in the darkness against the massive wooden door at the top of the sandstone steps. He had invited Flores to join them because, as he put it, she had "provided the opportunity." Plus he thought it would be good for her. Closure, of a kind.

She kept stepping forward to peek around the white columns. The street curved around the courthouse in a one-way U, with Main Street closing the bottom edge. After a wait of another six minutes, she said, "Here he comes," and stepped back alongside DeMarco again.

He moved forward to the edge of the top step to show himself. The judge was on foot, had probably parked on the lower side of the courthouse, on a dark alley where his vehicle might not be seen. He approached slowly, head down, his limp noticeable again, and did his best to stay out of the light, walking in the grass close to the building and as far off the street as he could get. He was wearing a long overcoat that hung to midshins, the collar high around his neck, and a kind of Australian bush hat with a broad brim. He reminded DeMarco of a character from an old movie, a British spy in his Burberry topcoat. And at first DeMarco had to smile, pleased with the work they had done, their own culmination no matter how anticlimactic. But then the satisfaction changed to sympathy, and he almost regretted this meeting and the necessity for it. Regretted what it was doing and would continue to do for a man who, at least publicly, had conducted himself with unimpeachable integrity throughout the duration of his career. Morrison had put a lot of bad guys behind bars. And had held hundreds of others responsible for the evil they had done. And now he had to do so again, if only to save himself by throwing a friend under the bus.

DeMarco watched Morrison coming toward them and suspected that Flores must be exulting at the man's fall from grace. Jayme too probably. Both of them seeing in the judge's laborious gait a kind of recompense for their own losses. A year ago, DeMarco would have been gleeful too. But he felt the opposite of glee now. No man can control the things that happen to him and all around him. The only thing he can control is how he responds to those things. This is the essence of free will, and the right choice is always the same: to act with courage, fairness, and temperance.

The judge came up the steps wearily, holding tight to the wrought iron rail. Only when he reached the next to top step did he raise his eyes. Out of breath, he said, "I never took you for the melodramatic type, Sergeant."

"Life is melodrama," DeMarco answered. He moved back beside the others, nodded toward Flores. "This is Daniella Flores," he told Morrison. "Formerly with the State Police. She's responsible for apprehending Benny Szabo."

Morrison looked to her and nodded, but only briefly. Her smirk was evident even in the darkness. To DeMarco, he said, "That name is familiar, but…"

There was no way of telling if he was lying or not. "Szabo? He's the hired hand who killed Emma and her grandmother."

"Really?" Morrison said. "You know that for sure?"

"We know a lot of things for sure, Judge." DeMarco had already decided to keep his cards not just close to the vest but beneath it. "Let's talk about Deputy Commissioner Thompkins."

Morrison put a hand to his forehead, then dragged the fingertips over his right eye, then his left. Then finished by drawing his palm down across his mouth and chin. He said, "He promised me that he would do right by the girl. I had no reason whatsoever to disbelieve him."

"So you knew all along that he was the father?"

"Not until my own test results came back. It was fifty–fifty either way."

*Huh?* DeMarco thought. *Fifty-fifty?* He said, "Whose idea was it to turn in three swabs?"

"Jeff thought it would, I don't know, look better. If there were three or four of us with Jennifer that week. If there were just the two of us…"

*People might think there was something sexual between you and him too.* Whether there was or wasn't, DeMarco didn't care. But apparently the judge and the deputy commissioner did.

"And you went for that?" DeMarco asked. "After all those years on the bench listening to lies?"

Morrison shook his head. "He's my oldest and most trusted friend."

"And he supplied both swabs? His and the fake friend's?"

"Correct. But I wasn't there when he collected them, so I have no idea whom it, or they, came from. I honestly don't."

"And when the results all came in negative? What did you think then?"

"What life has taught me to think."

"I assume that you confronted him on it?"

Morrison nodded. "He admitted that he had run a separate test on himself, and that it was a match. But he swore to me, he literally swore to me, that he would own up to it. He asked for a week. So that he could find a way to tell his wife. We both knew that she would not take it well."

"And when I informed you that the family was insisting on taking the tests again, in a certified lab setting?"

"He held to his story. He promised that he would cooperate. I had no choice but to trust him."

"Do you still feel that way?" Jayme asked.

He stood motionless, his face old, tired, his expression wooden. "All I feel is shame and embarrassment and remorse."

DeMarco did not want to give either Jayme or Flores time to say more. Their own grief, though justified, was red hot. It could only inflame the situation. And he could not risk having Morrison go silent on them. The man had his hands on too many strings, could start pulling them anytime he wished.

"So here's how it's going to play out, Judge," he said. "I will go home and call Captain Bowen. I will inform him that you asked me to let him know that you have information pertinent to the deaths of Emma and Lois Barrie. He will pass that information on to the FBI, and they will be contacting you soon. And you, sir, will cooperate 110 percent."

Wearily, Morrison nodded. The relief in his eyes was obvious. "I will, yes. Thank you."

DeMarco felt no need to remind the judge that three former law enforcement personnel had heard him confess to a deceit that had led to a double homicide. Or to inform him that both Jayme and Flores were holding their cell phones against their legs, recorders running. But now that Morrison had pledged his cooperation, one question remained.

"Who put Thompkins on to Benny Szabo in the first place?"

Morrison sniffed. Blinked. Looked out into the darkness.

DeMarco watched his face, the jowly profile, and thought he knew a little something about what was racing through the man's mind, the desperate hope even yet for an out, a way to avoid all the nastiness ahead. To shut down Morrison's mental search for a painless exit from his dilemma, DeMarco said, his voice almost a whisper, "It's the whole truth or nothing, Judge. That's the deal. Who put Thompkins on to Benny Szabo?"

Morrison did not look at him again. Did not look at any of them. He finally said, "I am sure that question will come up in due time. When that transpires, I will answer it." Then he turned away and went down the steps, his quivering hand riding the rail all the way to the bottom.

# VI

Be at ease, be as natural and
spacious as possible...

Your confusion evaporating slowly like mist
into the vast and stainless sky
of your absolute nature.

# NINETY-SIX

### THE HEAVINESS OF A DOUGHNUT HOLE,
### THE LIGHTNESS OF A SOUL

B oyd learned the good news through Flores, and later felt that his praise and congratulations to her weren't enough, that he should say something to Jayme and DeMarco too. When they had worked together, brothers and sisters in uniform, there was never a need for further recognition because the shared experience was recognition enough. But things were different now. He missed being a part of their daily lives. The barracks weren't the same without them there. He wasn't the same. The only way to explain it was that there was a hole in his life. DeMarco and Jayme had filled that hole. Especially DeMarco. He'd been a kind of stern big brother to Boyd, the kind who doesn't have to say anything, doesn't have to coach or mentor in any verbal way, but is just there, you know? When just being there is enough.

Why couldn't he just drop by DeMarco's house sometime? Hadn't he earned that privilege? *Hey, I heard the news. Good job. Congratulations.* Such gestures were easy for some people but not for him. But why should it be so difficult?

He thought about it for the next two days, kept urging himself to do it, chastised himself when he did not. On the third day he and a sheriff's deputy were scheduled to pick up a prisoner on furlough at 8:00 a.m. and return him to the county jail, but as Boyd was squaring up his desk that morning, preparing to leave, he received a call from the deputy: the jail van needed some quick servicing, the pickup was being pushed back an hour.

Boyd hung up the phone, sat back and studied his desk. He kept a neat desk, everything in its place. If he jumped into something new now, pulled out a file and dove into the paperwork, he would only have to drop it before completion so as to drive to the jail. And it always unsettled him to leave something half-done. Something like checking in with DeMarco and Jayme.

He drove first to Sheetz and picked up a box of mixed pastries, muffins and fritters and doughnut holes, three large cups of black coffee, French roast, the darkest blend. Then to DeMarco's house. The *For Sale* sign now had a smaller sign dangling beneath it: *Sold!* He saw that word and felt the hole in his life yawn open even wider. They would be moving soon. To where? Maybe he would never see them again.

He carried the box of pastries in one hand, the coffee carrier in the other. Had to set the pastries down to knock on the door. Rapped four times, bent down to pick up the box again, and the door swung open.

"Hey, Mace," DeMarco said. "What's happening?"

DeMarco was barefoot in a pair of baggy blue scrub pants and a gray T-shirt, and Boyd was unable to suppress a smile. He pushed the coffee carrier toward him and said, "I just dropped by to congratulate you guys on the Michigan case. Another job well done." The words sounded phony to his ears, though he meant every one of them.

"Thanks, pardner," DeMarco said. "You're welcome to come in if you can stop laughing at my feet."

"It's just that I've never seen them before."

"What did you think I have—hooves?"

"Sometimes, yeah." He followed DeMarco into the house. "You get those pants in the hospital?"

"Those gowns they try to make you wear are undignified. Not to mention drafty."

"Yeah, I'm glad I'm not looking at you in one of those right now."

DeMarco laughed and kept walking through the living room and into the kitchen.

"Jayme went to Home Depot to get some more totes and stuff," he said.

The house was warm and full of light, all the curtains open, a lingering scent of fried bacon in the air. Yet the place felt sad to Boyd, cardboard boxes and plastic totes lined up against bare walls. DeMarco did not seem sad, however. He looked downright happy. The moment Boyd set the box of pastries on the kitchen table and opened the lid, DeMarco's face glowed. "If we start now," he told Boyd, "we can polish off the entire box before Jayme gets back. She'll be none the wiser."

*Okay*, Boyd thought, and smiled as he reached for one of the coffees. *Maybe the house isn't sad at all. Maybe it's just me.*

"Have a seat," DeMarco told him. "I'll get us a couple of plates. You don't take cream or milk, do you?"

"I can drink it black," Boyd said, and pulled out a chair.

"Drink it the way you like it. A little half-and-half?"

"Perfect," Boyd said.

DeMarco fetched the creamer and plates, sat across from Boyd and took an apple fritter and three chocolate cake doughnut holes from the box. "Dani told you about the meeting with Morrison?" he asked.

"Yes, sir, she did. That must have felt good."

"Very good," DeMarco told him, "in a bittersweet kind of way."

Boyd nodded.

"So what are you working on now? Anything interesting?"

"Same old same old," Boyd told him. "Picking up a prisoner on furlough this morning."

"Back to the slammer," DeMarco said with a grin.

The coffee was hot and pleasantly strong, Boyd's cranberry muffin sweet, the berries tart. Feeling awkward, unsure of what to say next, he broke off the bottom of the muffin and concentrated on eating it first, one small bite at a time. He and DeMarco sat there smiling at each other, looking away, looking back, smiling again.

"That place down in Avella is pretty interesting, isn't it?" Boyd said.

DeMarco looked up again. "Are you talking about Meadowcroft?"

"Yeah, I, uh, I stopped by there one day a while back. Saw a sign and just thought I'd have a look."

"Jayme and I have been there a couple of times."

"Yeah, I remember you talking about that once. It kind of piqued my interest when I saw the sign for it."

"What were you doing down that way?" DeMarco asked.

"Just out driving one day is all. Nothing else to do."

"I remember those days," DeMarco said. "Just get in the car and drive."

Boyd looked around. "Where's Hero?"

"With Jayme. They'll do a couple of laps around the park before they come back."

"She's taken up running?"

"Trot-walking, she calls it. She gained seven ounces over the winter. Can barely fit through the door now," he said, and shoved the last piece of fritter into his mouth.

Boyd nodded, grinning. Took a sip of coffee. "I heard once that's how much the soul weighs. Just over seven ounces."

"Seems a little high to me," DeMarco said with another smile.

Boyd nodded and smiled in return. Felt himself still nodding and told himself to stop.

"That reminds me of an old quote," DeMarco said. "By a guy named Chesterton. 'Angels can fly because they can take themselves lightly.'"

Boyd couldn't help nodding again. "That's pretty good. Who was that guy?"

"Chesterton? British writer, very prolific. He even wrote mysteries about a priest-detective."

"No kidding? I should read one of those."

Unfortunately, that thread of the conversation came to an end too soon. Boyd grew uncomfortable again. "So how's everything else going these days?" he asked.

"Which everything?"

"You know, Jayme and the miscarriage. You and the coma and all."

"Tickety-boo, Mace. We're both just tickety-boo. How have you been doing?"

His inclination was to say what he always said, *Doing well, thanks for asking*, and then the conversation would wither as it always did. But he didn't want it to wither and fade into silence. He didn't want the silence anymore, he wanted to find a way out of it. He wanted more of whatever it was DeMarco could provide. "What's it like to almost die?" he asked.

DeMarco's eyebrows went up a little, then came back down. "It's very interesting," he said. He paused for a moment, then asked, "Are you sure you want to hear about it?"

"Yeah," Boyd said, and slid his chair closer to the table. "I really do."

# NINETY-SEVEN

## LET GO MY EGO

A n hour later, after walking Boyd outside to his car parked at the curb, and watching Boyd drive away, DeMarco stood for a while with his bare feet atop cold concrete. The air was rich with competing scents, the sound of light traffic down the block, a snatch of conversation. And for just a few moments it all brought him to a halt.

He stood on the sidewalk with his toes touching the curb. Down at the corner somebody was crossing the street. A woman, he decided. No longer young. He watched her until she passed out of sight behind a house, then told himself, *It's funny the way people walk.* He could tell the young ones from the middle-aged and the middle-aged from the elderly even from a distance. The ones under twenty-five, for example, moved differently from those already shouldering life's burdens. The young strolled along with a buoyancy, their posture upright, heads full of helium, while a majority of the older ones, those from whom most of the helium had already leaked out, they had centers of gravity that had downshifted from the chest to the lower body, the thickened hips and thighs. Even those older ones who tried to hold on to their youthful swagger were betrayed by the heavy pendulum of time below their waists.

As for how DeMarco appeared walking, he felt lighter in the hips now than he had a year ago. And then he chuckled, remembering Chesterton's observation that angels can fly because they can take themselves lightly. DeMarco was no angel but that's what he was doing now, taking himself more lightly. This self anyway, not the true self. The true self was already in the ether, as weightless as laughter, as untethered as a kiss blown across the room. With luck, his heavier self might lose enough weight someday to meet his true self. DeMarco hoped they would recognize each other.

He turned then to face his house again. His home for more than fifteen years. He had loved and suffered and worked and lived there. The cemetery a mile away held two precious pieces of him. Yet at that moment, he felt no resentment, no regret.

And as he looked around, considering the whole neighborhood and the town beyond, he told himself, *You can never really know a place until you have spent some time there.* And not only where the visitors go, not at the historical sites and trendy restaurants and the places listed in the guidebooks, but where the locals lived. You have to sleep and walk and eat and play and work where the locals do. You have to break bread with them and listen to their stories and the timbre of their voices and you have to see the shine of joy and the clouds of despair in their eyes. Only then can you know the true essence of a place, what Lawrence Durrell called the genius loci, the soul and protective spirit of a place.

The same held true, DeMarco realized, for any profession. Unless you worked it for a while you could never really know it or understand its demands and rewards. You had nothing to go by but theory, and theory is useless without a solid and robust foundation of real experience. Theory alone is a half-built house upon a hill of sand.

The same applied to every lifestyle, every wise or foolish choice. You could not know marriage unless you had lived it and done so wholeheartedly. Or solitude or hunger or parenting or depression or anything. The problem with the world today was that there were too many people with unyielding opinions about things they had never experienced, things they had only heard about or observed from a distance. And when those people became teachers they did irreparable harm to the growth of young people looking to them for wisdom. Theory was the very opposite of wisdom. Theory was a guess and nothing more, a nada. Science was nada and most religions were nada and a lot of lives were being wasted in blind adherence to nada y nada.

DeMarco gazed across the yards for a while, saw a car speed through the intersection, watched another one approach and go by. Then he lifted his eyes to the sky. A field of blue. *But new every time you look at it.*

It used to be that he could not look at the sky without getting angry, because the sky made him think of God. For a long time, starting as a boy of four or five and continuing for the next several decades, DeMarco had been angry at God. Angry that God would create such a world full of cruelty and suffering and ignorance and those who perpetrated or allowed it. A world where fathers and mothers got drunk and violent or depressed and neglectful, where children were abused, teased, ridiculed, bullied, made to starve, made to feel worthless, made to lie awake at night in fear of what evil might enter their rooms. And as DeMarco had grown older, his anger grew too—in Panama, in Iraq, in bucolic Mercer County. But his anger had been uninformed. He had known only one face of a multifaceted issue. He had viewed God and his works only from a very limited three-dimensional perspective, a binary perspective in which something was either good or evil, dark or light. And that was unfair.

Things were clearer now. DeMarco's time on the other side had been brief, at most the four days of his coma. It had felt longer, but there was no way to gauge time in a place where there is no time, or rather where there are all times. Either way, his time there had been limited, and so too his increase in knowledge and understanding. But he had learned a little something. And what he had learned was that this world, this three-dimensional reality, was exactly what it was supposed to be.

Not a single day on this world would pass when people weren't killing each other. They killed under orders and without orders, they killed for food, for drugs, for sex, for money, for liberty, or just for the thrill of killing. They killed over a horse, over a dog, over a woman, over a child, over a look, over a laugh, over a word. They killed for any and every reason. And now DeMarco had no expectations that this scenario would ever change.

Yes, it had been too easy to believe that God was an empty promise. It is the natural thing to think when someone you love or have begun to love has been taken from you abruptly with no explanation or apology. It is easy then to think of God as a fraud or a malicious psychopath or as anything but a loving and kind and merciful creator. DeMarco had thought the same thing not too long ago. How many times as a younger man had he railed at God, cursed and shaken his fist at the sky?

It amused him now to remember how angry he had been. What a waste of energy! But now, finally, he knew a different truth. It had been shown to him, downloaded into him, had been blasted into his chest and out the other side. God is not malicious, nor perfect. Perfection is that state of being at which no higher state is possible. And not a thing in the universe, no matter how large or small, how visible or invisible, is perfect. All is change. Including God. God is engaged in an endless struggle to understand itself, and we are all participants in that struggle. What we experience, God experiences through us. And God is insatiable for these experiences and for the self-knowledge they bring. And if the source of all knowledge is ever curious, ever eager to learn, how could DeMarco not be too?

In the end, all he could know with the slightest degree of certainty was what his own body and mind told him based on his own experiences. The body told him that everything deteriorates, everything falls apart. The mind told him that he had only just begun to glimpse the vastness of life beyond the body. The body said that he would die, and the mind scoffed at that statement as a childish fear. The body spoke of limitations; the mind assured him that everything was possible. His body groaned and hurt and strained. His mind dreamed and sang and soared. The body had sex; the mind made love.

This tiny bit of knowledge was all he possessed, but it comforted and even thrilled him. After this life he might take up temporary residence in a different physical body, maybe a thousand times more, and each time he would be forced to subscribe to the limitations of the flesh, just as all of his neighbors were doing right now. He might be a cop, a pilot, a teacher, a junkie, an exotic dancer, a quadriplegic. Maybe a Black professor, an Asian orphan, a Martian, a fruit bat, a jackal loping through the moonlight. But with luck and diligence he might also add a grain or two of knowledge each time. It is through the vicissitudes of flesh that the spirit grows. And in turn the spirit infuses its energy and vibrancy into the flesh, transforming it, each increasing the health and aptitude of the other.

Still, no matter how much DeMarco learned, the mystery would always hold. And now, as he smiled to himself and walked up the sidewalk to his door, each step with its own new chill on the bottom of his feet, he was okay with that. Each life would bring a new discovery, another fold of mystery. That was the way of things, and he was a part of it. And it was all so infinitely and hilariously beautiful. It deserved another fritter.

# NINETY-EIGHT

OH, HOW SWEET THE SONG THE CANARY SINGS!

Judge Morrison had been true to his word, which he had never really given to DeMarco except obliquely, by an implication more assumed by DeMarco than suggested by Morrison. Not that it mattered to DeMarco. Just so long as the judge spilled the beans to the feds, which he did, but only after the proffer of immunity from the charge of conspiracy to commit murder. According to the FBI agent who briefed Captain Bowen and DeMarco, Morrison had admitted how he and his college pal Jeff Thompkins, both married at the time, had spent a week in Michigan without their spouses, fishing and drinking and sharing the favors of a young and financially strapped barmaid by the name of Jennifer Barrie. They had then returned home to their wives and public lives without much of a thought. Morrison described the young Barrie as "a free spirit," and professed no surprise that she had wanted to raise her daughter alone, without the aid of a man more than twice her age.

"I wouldn't go as far as to say that she was a man-hater," Morrison had said, "considering how much she enjoyed sex. But she was adamantly opposed to monogamy and considered it a masculine ploy to harness a woman's independence. Jeff and I, I am ashamed to admit, were all too eager to encourage her rebellion."

"I suppose," he also said, "that when she instructed the girl to write to us, she felt she had no other choice. I can't fault her for reaching out. Nor can I fault her for using the girl to entice and, yes, in a sense, to manipulate us. Not that I am attempting to shift the blame to her. I hold myself and Jeff culpable for the decisions we made."

At Thompkins's insistence, they had invented two phantom friends who accompanied them on the fishing trip, one long dead. Morrison claimed a faulty memory when asked about the rationale for such an invention, just as he claimed no knowledge that Thompkins would turn in two fraudulent DNA samples to be tested. The cashier's check for $20,000, however, had been Morrison's idea, he claimed. Thompkins was reluctant at first to participate, felt he had no obligation to provide for another man's child. Felt certain, or at least pretended to be certain, that his and the judge's "romp" with Jennifer Barrie was only one of many in which she had regularly indulged. Only when pressured by the judge did Thompkins admit that his own secret DNA test had shown Emma Barrie to be his closest genetic match.

As for how the deputy commissioner came to know Benny Szabo, "Yes," Morrison admitted, "I did pass his name on to Jeff. But I had no idea—of course I had no idea!—of what Jeff had planned. If, indeed, Szabo was used as you assume. That is yet to be proven.

"Jeff was in need of an individual," Morrison claimed, "with the facility to recover a piece of his wife's jewelry. Stolen, he'd said, during a dinner party at his home. By the wife of a man he did not wish to insult. The woman, he said, was well known for her tendencies. She was widely rumored to be a kleptomaniac."

Did Morrison actually believe this story? "I had my doubts," he said. "To be honest, I didn't really want to know. Jeff asked for my help and I felt duty bound by our friendship to trust that he would not abuse our friendship. I provided him with Mr. Szabo's contact information, and that is all I did. I had no idea whatsoever that Szabo would be sent to Michigan."

The agent, when he recounted this conversation, had been unable to suppress a chuckle. "It was all bull and we knew it. We'll see how it plays out after Thompkins gets a good taste of prison life. If Morrison is dirty once, he's been dirty before, and my money is on Thompkins to start looking for a little revenge down the road. Rich guys doing hard time like to spread the misery around."

# NINETY-NINE

## WHEN THE SILENCE SPEAKS, SHUT UP AND LISTEN

B y evening, Morrison's and Thompkins's troubles were all yesterday's news to DeMarco. He would remember Emma forever and would always hold a warm and tender love for her in his heart. As for this picture-perfect gloaming in May, the forsythia in brilliant bloom in his neighbor's yard, the air clear and warm and fresh with spring, he had other fish to fry. Eight beautiful halibut steaks, to be specific. He seared them in a cast iron skillet atop his barbecue that evening, then served them in the dining room with roasted asparagus and a beurre blanc sauce. Boyd and Flores were there, plus Bowen and his wife. Ben Brinker and Vee drove over from Youngstown.

It had been Jayme's idea that they all get together for what she called an Amateur Talent Night, though all present understood that the RV in the backyard would soon take to the highway. Where it might find a permanent parking spot, nobody knew. Dani had written a song on her keyboard for the occasion, called it "Half-Past Midnight on a Monday Afternoon," and performed it after dinner, all gathered in the living room with coffee and Baileys Irish Cream, with Boyd accompanying on acoustic guitar, a talent DeMarco had hitherto been unaware of. Boyd a guitarist! And a pretty darned good one at that. Who would ever have thought?

Ben and Vee Brinker sang a medley of songs made famous by Peaches and Herb, including "Reunited," "Love Is Strange," and "Shake Your Groove Thing." Jayme and DeMarco, both of whom claimed to be "artistically challenged," planned to read excerpts from Thomas Huston's forthcoming collection of reflections. DeMarco went first. "It's a little poem called 'Si la jeunesse savait!'" he announced as he stood in front of his chair.

"See June what?" Ben Brinker asked.

"It's French," DeMarco told him. "It means 'If youth knew.'"

"Knew what?" Brinker asked, teasing now.

"Shut up and listen, Ben," DeMarco said, already blushing a little. He did not like being the center of attention in a situation like this, but he had spent a couple of hours going through the advance copy of Huston's work and was determined to pay homage to his friend. There was so much good stuff in Huston's book; DeMarco wished he could read it all aloud, but he had settled finally on a single poem that, to his mind, captured what he loved about his friend, his insatiable curiosity, his pain, his all-embracing love. He hoped it came through in his reading, and, judging by the silence and attention paid to his brief performance, it did.

> If youth knew, I would not
> have broken your heart.
> I would have said I love you,
> I do, but we are young,
> so young, let us not cling
> with desperation to only one.
> Let us enfold the world
> inside our love, let us ride
> that fever into a deeper understanding
> of what love is and means.

If youth knew, I would have paused
for a while and asked my parents
how did you meet? What were you
like as a child? Are you happy now?
And what has life been that you
never expected it to be? What
can I learn from you? Tell me
everything you know as true!
If youth knew, I would not have doubted

God. I would not have asked
how could you make us this way,
so frail, so flawed, so weak?
If youth knew, I would have said Aha!

I see! How intricate and complex
and beautiful it is! Oh thank you
for this chance, this pain, this fear, the love,
the rare transports of joy.
Oh thank you for this me!

He sat down awkwardly as his guests applauded, grinning at his own unease but pleased that he had made it through the poem without butchering it too badly. "Looks like you can still carry the ball without fumbling, 27," Brinker said.

"Twenty-seven?" Flores asked. "What does that mean?"

"That was his jersey's number back in high school. All-City fullback."

"Really?" Flores said. "Geez. The things we don't know."

"Oh, I could tell you some stories," Brinker said.

"No you can't," DeMarco told him, and put his hand on Jayme's arm. "Your turn, beauty. We saved the best for last."

As far as DeMarco knew, she too was about to read a Huston poem. But she surprised him and everyone else there. "This is a poem Ryan wrote for me," she announced.

"Uh-oh," Brinker said in a stage whisper. "This should be good."

"Shut up and listen, Ben," she responded. And then she read the poem that had come to DeMarco in the field of corn stubble only a month earlier, when he had felt the need to focus not on anger but on happiness. "It's called 'I Like,'" she said.

"Wow, great title," Brinker said. "How long did it take you to come up with that one?"

"Ben, darling," his wife Vee told him, and squeezed his knee, "shut up and listen."

Jayme read the poem then, and as she read it DeMarco held his head low, his body bent forward so that he could scratch Hero's ears and hide the blush burning in his cheeks.

When she finished, and while the applause continued, she crossed to DeMarco and pulled his head to her stomach. "Encore!" Brinker called out, and then Boyd and Flores joined him. "Encore! Encore!"

"How about this for an encore?" Jayme asked, and threw everyone into a startled silence, DeMarco included. "Ryan and I are nine weeks pregnant!"

He rose to embrace her, surrounded then by cheers and congratulations, his friends' embraces, his and Jayme's and Vee Brinker's tears, a furry tail whipping back and forth, a few happy barks, a cold nose squeezing between his legs.

Later in the evening, saying goodbye to Ben and Vee at the door, Jayme and DeMarco were again congratulated on their happy news. "I'm going to be needing some advice along the way," Jayme told them. "You guys will help me out, right?"

Vee said, "Oh, there's really nothing to it, sweetie. You just have to love your child with all of your heart."

Ben nodded in agreement. "There are some nuances involved. Some tweaks to your behavior you might have to make. Especially yours, 27," he said with a teasing nudge.

"Roger that," DeMarco said.

"Vee's right, though. It's a pretty simple formula once you get the hang of it. Just love them for who they are. Don't make their lives all about you; make your life all about them."

"That we can do," Jayme said, and took DeMarco's arm. "Can't we, baby?"

"That we can do," he promised.

# ONE HUNDRED

E PLURIBUS YUM-YUM

They made a different kind of love that night, slow and gentle and thoughtful, as if each was discovering the other's body for the first time and wanted to memorize and preserve every turn of it against any kind of loss, against age and illness and disease and forgetfulness and death, so that it would last and live forever exactly as it was that night. And afterward neither spoke for a long time but remained keenly awake, continuing the slow strokes and light touches of their gratitude even after Hero, ever watchful during their lovemaking, fell asleep, his breath filled with the tiniest of whimpers.

They were no longer young and felt no need to speak of love as the young often do, as if they had happened upon a shiny coin from some foreign land, had found it in the grass and now felt compelled to turn it over and over in their hands, handing it back and forth, wondering aloud about its value, who might have dropped it there, what they could buy with it, where they could sell it. No, they were not young and had no need for such dissection. All they wanted was to hold that coin, to share its warmth and shine, not to worry it with unnecessary movement and analysis that could only tarnish and decrease its value.

DeMarco was the first to speak, his voice low and soft, his mouth against her hair as she lay there looking up at the ceiling. "What are you thinking about, angel?"

She rolled her head to meet his gaze. "Just dreaming, I guess."

"Aren't you supposed to do that with your eyes closed?"

She smiled but offered no response.

"What are you dreaming about?" he asked.

"Trying to come up with some other kind of work we could get into."

So, she had been fretting after all and not simply basking in the afterglow of their lovemaking. "We're okay for a while," he told her. "We have your pension and mine, plus my savings and the money I'll get from the house at closing."

"I'm not talking about the money necessarily, even though as parents we do have to think about that."

"What then?"

"We've had a lot of misery the past couple of years."

"Yes we have," he said. "Are you sorry you hooked up with me?"

"Never," she said. "I'm just wondering what it might be like if we had another profession. Something less dangerous, to begin with. But also something that, you know, brings happiness, not misery."

"What do you have in mind?"

"That's just it. I can't think of any. None we're qualified for anyway."

"You could teach," he told her. "Tom loved teaching. Teaching and writing brought him a lot of joy, I think."

"But writing got him killed," she said. "His entire family."

He was forced to concede the truth of that. If Tom hadn't been researching another novel, hadn't crossed paths with Bonnie and Inman... "Children's books," he said. "You could do that, I bet."

She smiled at the possibility, but remained quiet a while longer.

Then said, "There's a theory, you know, that our thoughts create parallel worlds. Which would mean that every time your friend wrote a new novel, he created a world in which all of those characters existed and lived those lives, and had no idea that they were somebody else's thought projections."

"I hear what you're saying. Tom didn't write humor or light romance." His novels had been dark, filled with deeply troubled people struggling with the consequences of their actions. Would he have written those books if he'd believed that his characters actually suffered through the tragedies he fabricated?

"If you could do anything you wanted for a living," she asked, "what would you do?"

He didn't have to think long about that one. "I would make music. I can't imagine a happier profession than that. I would write it and play it, like Van Morrison, for example."

"Didn't you tell me once that he's kind of nasty toward others?"

"That's his rep, anyway. Thanks for shattering my illusion. What would you do?"

"Something with children. I wish I had some talents to share with them. Writing, painting, dancing—I would love to be that kind of teacher for little children."

"You will be," he told her. "For one, at least."

She smiled. "Wouldn't it be nice if parenting were a paid profession?"

"It should be. Should require an advanced degree. That's one degree that might actually do the world a lot of good."

She nodded. "We should write a book and create a world where that is the reality. Where every child is cherished and showered with love."

"I like that world."

"We can make one for ourselves."

"I'm all in," he said.

Again they were silent for a while. Then she told him, "Wasn't it wonderful to hear everybody laughing tonight? And I loved how your face lit up when I told you my secret. You didn't mind that I hit you with it in front of everybody, did you?"

"Only for a second. Then I was happy you did."

"I'm going to be so very careful this time. I want you to be too. Promise me you will."

"I promise."

"You have a family now. And we all need you very, very much."

"And I need all of you," he said. "You most of all." His fingertips glided from her wrist to elbow crease and back to the wrist with the slowness of a recurring sigh.

"I've also been thinking about Emma," she told him. "Poor sweet darling innocent Emma. I fell so deeply in love with her that day we took them to breakfast. You did too, I know. I could see it when you looked at her."

He nodded. "She touched my soul."

"I've been lying here wondering about all of them. Emma and our little girl and your baby boy. I wish I could just gather them up in my arms and hold them close to me forever."

He kissed her hair and wrapped his fingers around her forearm, could feel the pulse of her blood with his thumb pressed into the crease of her elbow, the fragility of flesh, the tenuous complexity and miracle of the body.

"I can't decide whether I believe it all or not," she told him. "I really want to, though. Don't you?"

"Believe what, baby?"

"About Dani seeing Emma just before Szabo was killed. About Emma causing it. I want to believe it happened that way, I really do."

"Then believe it," he told her.

When she nodded, her hair brushed across his face and made him smile. Her breath was sibilant in the stillness. He could feel the beat and warmth and depth of her heart through his thumb. Felt her longing and her love.

She said, "But sometimes I tell myself that it's too much to believe. Too much to hope for. It just all seems too impossible sometimes. Doesn't it to you?"

He kissed her hair again. Smelled peaches and sunshine and the fierce tenacity of life. "There is no such thing as impossible," he told her.

And yes, sometimes he did feel as if the whole near-death experience thing had been a dream. Just an extraordinarily vivid, nonlinear, recalcitrant dream. And sometimes he felt as if his real life were the dream, a thought projection, fleeting and vague, evanescing smoke even as it rushed past him. And sometimes he felt as if it were an old black-and-white movie, him as a stand-in for a slightly paunchy, out-of-breath Robert Mitchum, for example, chasing the bad guy through an old warehouse, a lot of mediocre acting and shades of gray. But sometimes, thank God, he felt precisely as he did right then at 12:42 a.m. in his moon-illuminated bedroom, wholly solid and three-dimensional, with every sense receptor turned to maximum. The air in the room was cool to breathe, pleasantly cool going in through his nostrils but warming quickly in his lungs, the comforter soft and almost weightless atop him. He felt its weight only against his naked toes, a couple of them pressed to Jayme's foot, the back of his right hand against her thigh, her skin warmer than his and smoother, silkier, her face on the pillow only a few inches from his, one hand with fingers spread rising up and down atop his chest as he breathed. Her skin smelled of soap, her breath smelled of mouthwash. His own mouth tasted vaguely of the briny green olives he had gobbled down after bringing Hero in from his final pee before bed. His stomach gurgled softly but that was pleasant too, the innards still working, that unimaginably complex mechanism of his body still doing its stuff, forty trillion cells going about their business absent of any collusion or approval on his part. Heart still thumping, pulse still drumming, digestive juices stewing, white blood cells charging up and down his veins like miniature kamikaze pilots in a relentless but silent war. It was all in working order, maybe not as efficient as it once had been but still getting the job done. He was alive and glad to be so. Jayme was alive and a tiny wonder inside of her was alive and Hero asleep on the other side of the bed was alive and the night was alive and the darkness and the muted moonlight outside the window were alive. The house was alive with an occasional creak and an occasional hum when the furnace blower kicked on, and sometimes alive with its silence. It was all alive and vibrantly so, and damn if he wasn't glad to be a part of it all, a creature in unceasing motion and awareness even when lying perfectly still. He was a miracle, there were no two ways about it. It was all a miracle and he was a part of it. A mystery. An unsolvable, frustrating, aggravating, maddening, exhilarating and eternal mystery.

And with this thought a feeling of grace descended on him, a soft sifting as of warm snow, though there was not a flake to be seen. "Thank you," he whispered to no one in particular, to Jayme, to Hero, to all and to everything. He had forgotten it for a while but now he remembered. He would die someday as everybody must but the story would not end, not for him or anybody else. He knew this not only in his bones but in every cell and in an invisible place even deeper than that. The story would not end. Only the individual chapters would end. And there would always be another chapter. And in this way the story would go on and on forever.

Change is all.

He thought back on the full sweep of the day then, from leaving his bed to returning to it. He could not have planned a finer day, a finer second chance at life. There was no denying the haunting sadness that always clung to life like a mist on the edge of the woods, there even on the sunniest of days, the knowledge that nothing gold can stay, but it was all of a piece, each moment giving currency to the others.

It wasn't going to be easy to leave this house and all of its history behind. And harder still to leave the dead. His and Jayme's little girl and Baby Ryan were buried not far away, DeMarco's parents' graves a thirty-minute drive. All in the ground, though not really. Still, who would clean away the dead leaves and debris from the tombstones? Somebody or nobody. A part of him knew that it wouldn't matter one way or the other, but the other part still clung to those attachments and obligations. It would be hard to let them go.

He was going to miss Bowen, Boyd and Flores, Ben and Vee too. But they would never be more than a phone call away, just as Baby Ryan and Huston and Emma were only a thought away. He was learning so much about people he had believed he knew as well as he needed to know them. Now he understood that he could never know enough, would never get his fill of friendship and felicity, of shared joys and responsibilities and memories and hopes—no matter how many opportunities he might be given. No matter how many times he lived and died and lived again.

Nothing is real until you make it so. Truth #1.

LOVE RYAN DEMARCO?
DON'T MISS HIS FIRST ADVENTURE
IN *TWO DAYS GONE*

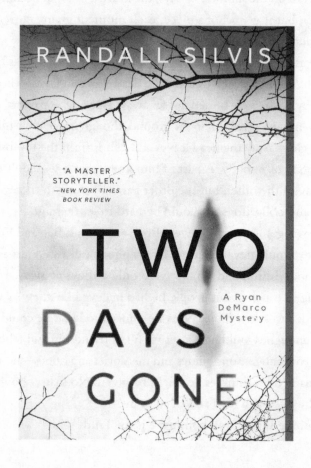

RANDALL SILVIS

"A MASTER
STORYTELLER."
—*NEW YORK TIMES
BOOK REVIEW*

TWO
DAYS
GONE

A Ryan
DeMarco
Mystery

# ONE

DeMarco took the call at home just a few minutes after kickoff on Sunday afternoon. He was halfway through his first bottle of Corona. The Browns, after only four plays, had already driven inside the red zone. Pittsburgh's Steel Curtain appeared made of aluminum foil. DeMarco was settling in for an afternoon of mumbling and cursing when the call came in from Trooper Lipinski, who was working the desk at the State Police barracks.

The bodies of the Huston family had been discovered approximately twenty minutes earlier. Claire's mother and father had driven up from nearby Oniontown, just as they did every Sunday through the fall and early winter, "to watch the Steelers beat themselves," as Ed O'Patchen liked to say that season. The O'Patchens went up the walk and onto the covered porch as they always had, Ed lugging two six-packs of Pabst Blue Ribbon, Rosemary cradling her Crock-Pot of cheese and sausage dip. As always, they walked inside without knocking. Rosemary went searching for the silent family upstairs while Ed tried to figure out how to work the remote on the new wide-screen Sony.

The Browns scored while DeMarco was taking the call. He saw no more of the game.

Later that day, DeMarco and three other troopers began interviewing the Hustons' neighbors up and down Mayfield Road. Not a single resident along the tree-lined street had anything negative to say about the family, and none were aware of any financial or other marital problems between Thomas and Claire. All were stunned, most were grief-stricken.

Two residents, however, a homemaker and an elderly man, reported that they had seen a man who might or might not have been Thomas Huston walking through the neighborhood in the weak light of false dawn. "Kind of shuffling along," the homemaker said. "Looking confused," said the elderly man.

Both witnesses had been standing close to their own homes while keeping an eye on their dogs as they sniffed through dewy yards and saw the man from the rear as he was walking away from them. The woman hadn't yet put in her contact lenses and saw the man as "Just a shape, you know? Just the shape of a man." The elderly gentleman, who saw the man at a nearer distance, reported that the man who might have been Huston stopped twice, paused with his head down, and once turned fully around to look back down the street. The elderly gentleman asked from two houses away, "You lost?" But the man in question did not respond, and eventually he continued moving away again.

Four women traveling north on Interstate 79 at around eight thirty Sunday morning, on their way to breakfast at Bob Evans and then a day of shopping at the Millcreek Mall, telephoned 911 at around ten that morning to report passing a man as he leaned over the low concrete bridge abutment where the highway spans a spindly extension of Lake Wilhelm. He was staring into the dark water, they said. They agreed with the other witnesses as to what Huston was wearing: khaki trousers, a dark blue knit shirt, brown belt, and brown loafers or moccasins. They could not agree as to whether the man looked as if he were about to jump into the water or if perhaps he were watching something as it fell and disappeared beneath the surface. Only one woman claimed to have seen the object in his hand before it disappeared into the lake. "It was shiny," she said. "Like a knife. But a big knife." They would have called sooner but had come up from New Castle and weren't aware of the tragedy until a salesclerk mentioned it to one of them.

In the chill of the following morning, just two days before Halloween, a gray mist hung over the lake, clinging to the water like a spirit reluctant to tear itself free from the memory of flesh. DeMarco stood next to the same bridge abutment where Huston had paused the day before. Two dozen men and women from the criminal investigation units of Troops D and E huddled close on either side—primarily troopers from the two county stations affected by the apparent homicide in Mercer County and consequent search for the primary suspect in Crawford County. All wore blaze-orange plastic vests over black jackets. Four of the troopers knelt beside their search dogs, keeping the leashes snug for now. The dogs, all of mixed breed, were certified in tracking, search and rescue, and cadaver identification.

DeMarco's eyes stung from the morning's cold. A thin pool of dampness lay in his left lower lid, blurring his vision. The left eye was DeMarco's weak eye, the one he had injured long ago. It watered up at the slightest provocation these days—from a gust of wind, a blast of air-conditioning, an invisible speck of dust—and no matter how often he blinked, he could not whisk away that tiny pool of dampness that warped a corner of the world behind a rain-streaked window. Sometimes the eye would water for no reason at all, most frequently in the stillness of a new morning when he sat in his dark house with the television on, a glass of tepid Jack in his hand. Now, there on the low bridge, his eyes felt heavy from a lack of sleep. But that was nothing new either; his eyes always felt heavy.

Along the entire length of the bridge, and for some distance on either side—a total of two hundred yards or so—the right lane of the two northbound lanes of Interstate 79 had been blocked off to traffic with orange cones and yellow flashing lights. The passing lane, however, was still open, so DeMarco's voice as he spoke to the troopers frequently rose to a shout to carry above the rumbling approach and passage of a vehicle.

"If he managed to get ahold of a tarp or a blanket of some kind," DeMarco said, "he can last out there for two weeks or so. He might still be carrying the murder weapon with him. You should assume that he is. And according to the lab, it's no piddling little switchblade. Think machete, Bowie knife, maybe even a decorative sword of some kind. Where he might be headed or what might be going through that brain of his is anybody's guess, so *do not attempt to apprehend*. You are here to assist in the tracking of a suspect in a multiple homicide. Tracking is the full extent of your job. Any other action you engage in had best be warranted."

An eighteen-wheeler roared over the bridge now; the vibration rattled up through DeMarco's boots and into his knees. "Under no circumstances should you lose visual contact with the trooper nearest you. You see anything, and I mean anything, you radio it in to me. You see tracks, you call me. You find a recent campfire, you call me. You see Huston, you back off immediately and call me. Do not approach. The order to close in and apprehend will come from me and me alone. Also, be aware that there are field officers from the Game Commission stationed all around the perimeter of these woods to keep the public out, but that doesn't mean one or two of them won't slip past and come sneaking up on us. Therefore, you *will* exercise all due restraint."

Now DeMarco gazed out across the tannic water, squinted into the wisps of rising fog, and wondered what else he needed to say. Should he mention the uneasiness he had felt in his gut all morning, the sense of being slightly off balance, as if the floor were canted, ever since the moment the day before when he had walked into the Huston home? Should he attempt to describe the peculiar ache of grief that buffeted him like a bruising wind each time he considered Huston's smallest victim, the toddler with whom DeMarco shared a name? Should he tell them he had read all of Huston's novels, that autographed first editions stood side by side in the armoire his wife had left behind, one of them personally inscribed to DeMarco, all sharing the top shelf with his other prized first editions, nearly all of them gifts from Laraine, including the jewels of his collection, Umberto Eco's *The Name of the Rose* and J. M. Synge's *Riders to the Sea*?

Should he tell them of the three lunches he had shared with Thomas Huston, the fondness and admiration he felt for the man— the growing sense, and hope, for the first time in far too many years, that here, perhaps, was a friend?

Would any of that information do anybody any good, least of all himself?

"If all he's got are the clothes on his back," DeMarco told them, "he's not going to last long out there. He's probably cold and wet and hungry by now. So let's just get in there and do our job, all right?"

A red-winged blackbird flitted past DeMarco, so close that, had he been quick enough, he could have reached out and grabbed it, could have caught it in his hand. The bird stiffened its wings and glided low over the water. It rested on the tip of a reed at the water's edge. The reed swayed back and forth under the bird's weight—so gracefully, DeMarco thought, *like water.*

He became aware then, as if it had materialized out of nowhere, of the roar of a panel truck as it crossed the bridge. The rumble sent a chill through him, a frisson of fear. Strangely, his wife came to mind, and he hoped she was all right, hoped that whatever stranger she had taken to her bed the night before had been kind to her, tender, and had not given her what she craved. He turned his back to the vehicle, but its wake of cold air blasted over him. He wiped the dampness from the corner of his eye.

The troopers were watching him, waiting. Their stillness angered him. But he bit down hard on his anger. It was an old anger, he knew, and misdirected. "All right, let's get to it!" he shouted. "I want Thomas Huston sitting in the back of my vehicle, alive and well and cuffed, by the time the sun goes down on this fine October day."

# READING GROUP GUIDE

1. *No Woods So Dark as These* ended on a serious cliffhanger. How did the results in *When All Light Fails* compare to your ideas of what happened next?

2. What did you think of DeMarco's NDE? In what ways, big and small, did it change his outlook on life? Have you ever had an experience that altered your perspective that dramatically?

3. Compare the injuries that DeMarco and Flores received during the Khatri exchange, physical and otherwise. How do they support each other through the healing process?

4. What was your first impression of Judge Morrison? Did you think his intention was really to do right by Emma? Would you have taken the job if you were in DeMarco and Jayme's place?

5. Describe Jayme's relationship to Emma. What roles did they fill for each other? All told, they didn't know each other that well. Why does Jayme take Emma's death so hard?

6. Discuss Trooper Boyd. What is he looking for?

7. After her injury, Flores works hard to assert her independence. Do you think she does so in a healthy way? How does her reaction reflect larger societal attitudes toward disability?

8. What did you think of Benny Szabo? He went from unsuccessful robber to killer for hire. How do you think he ended up in a life of crime? Who holds responsibility for Emma's death—Szabo or the man who ordered him to kill her?

9. What really happened in the old Westinghouse Electric Plant? Do you think Benny Szabo deserved his fate?

10. One of DeMarco's universal truths is "Evil exists." Do you agree? How do you define evil?

11. Do you think Judge Morrison and Deputy Commissioner Thompkins are good examples of the types of people in power? Do you think they will face consequences for their involvement in Emma's death?

12. Did DeMarco do enough in his final confrontation with Judge Morrison? Would you have handled things differently in his position?

13. Do you think the characters got the endings they deserved? What do you think Jayme and DeMarco will end up trying for work? What do you think will become of Flores and Boyd?

# ACKNOWLEDGMENTS

As always, I am grateful to my wonderful agent, Sandy Lu, and to my ever-insightful editor, Anna Michels, and to the entire Sourcebooks team. And—it goes without saying, yet I am delighted to say it—to my readers.

# ABOUT THE AUTHOR

Randall Silvis is the critically acclaimed author of nineteen novels, one book of narrative nonfiction, and two collections of short fiction. His literary awards include the Drue Heinz Literature Prize, two National Endowment for the Arts Literature Fellowship awards, a Fulbright Senior Scholar Research award, six fellowship grants from the Pennsylvania Council on the Arts for his fiction, drama, and screenwriting, and an honorary Doctor of Letters degree for "a sustained record of distinguished literary achievement."

# PRAISE FOR THE RYAN
# DEMARCO MYSTERIES

"[A] chilly suspense novel."
—*New York Times Sunday Book Review* for *Two Days Gone*

"A suspenseful, literary thriller that will resonate with readers long after the book is finished."
—*Library Journal*, Starred Review, for *Two Days Gone*

"An absolute gem of literary suspense, pitting ordinary people in extraordinary circumstances and told in a smooth, assured, and often haunting voice, *Two Days Gone* is a terrific read."
—Michael Koryta, *New York Times* bestselling author of *Those Who Wish Me Dead*, for *Two Days Gone*

"A smart, twisting, vividly written thriller anchored by two deeply flawed yet fascinating protagonists. Yes, the novel provides cat-and-mouse suspense as a horrific murder in a college town is investigated, but it's also a deeply rewarding story about friendship, family, fame, and the complicated relationship between readers and writers. Anyone who wants to dismiss thrillers as mere genre fluff should read *Two Days Gone*."
—David Bell, author of *Since She Went Away*, for *Two Days Gone*

"Deeply satisfying... This solid procedural offers heart-pounding moments of suspense. Silvis smoothly blends moments of exquisite beauty into a sea of darker emotion to create a moving story heavy with the theme of the 'past is never past.'"
—*Publishers Weekly* for *Walking the Bones*

"This is a stellar work. Silvis provides an intimate look at a relationship in jeopardy, one that readers will root for as they delve into DeMarco's and Matson's painful pasts… The author's insightful portrayal of small-town secrets and loyalties plunges readers deep into a Southern mystery that will keep them wondering right up to the end."

—*IndiePicks Magazine* for *Walking the Bones*

"Silvis is at it again, striving for a blend of crime story and literature, mutilated bodies and lapidary prose."

—*Booklist* for *A Long Way Down*

"A poignant and gritty thriller that reveals humanity's best and worst."

—Kate Kessler, bestselling author, for *No Woods So Dark as These*

"The rare crime novel infused with both darkness and light. The characters are so real I expected to meet them for a drink at the end of the day."

—Kelly Simmons, international bestselling author of *Where She Went* and *One More Day*, for *No Woods So Dark as These*

"Well-crafted prose, smart dialogue, and complex characters create a chilling thriller."

—Mary Burton, *New York Times* and *USA Today* bestselling author, for *No Woods So Dark as These*